THE MISSING FACTOR

THE MISSING FACTOR

A Jim Factor Novel

DANIEL C. LORTI

OPEN ROAD

INTEGRATED MEDIA

NEW YORK

ISBN: 978-1-5040-7940-2

This edition published in 2022 by Open Road Integrated Media, Inc.
180 Maiden Lane
New York, NY 10038
www.openroadmedia.com

For my agent, Jeanie Loiacono of the Loiacono Literary Agency—
your support and advice serve as my inspiration.

THE MISSING FACTOR

PART ONE

Chapter One

THE WARNING

Tuesday, May 7
Newport Beach, California

Jim Factor leaned his tall frame back in the leather desk chair, arms behind his head, absentmindedly running his fingers through his thick brown hair. He was in his favorite attire when home; brown cotton slacks, a short-sleeve faded blue shirt with a buttondown collar and brown loafers. He straightened up, glanced down at his stomach and winced at the sight of the paunch. The outside dinners during his travels were taking their toll. He made a mental note to set up a golf date for the next day. The fashionable neighborhood in Newport Beach, California was quiet at this time in the morning. Diane had left early with a friend to go to Los Angeles for the day but out of habit he kept the door to the study closed. He stifled a yawn, a reminder he arrived home the prior evening from business meetings in Kuwait. The advantage of flying west was the time zones were in your favor. He enjoyed the exotic and var ied cultures he encountered and formed an integral part of his profession.

He smiled as he recalled the previous evening. As usual after a long absence, he and Diane enjoy a romantic interlude starting with a cocktail followed by a candlelight dinner complete with a bottle of fine wine. He sighed contently and reached into his briefcase. He placed his notebook computer, passport and Motorola satellite phone on the desk. It was a perfect time to write trip reports, go through the pile of mail and check the messages which had accumulated. He took another drink of coffee and set the cup down. His steel-blue eyes took in the comfortable warm feeling of the beam ceiling, paneled walls, the built-in floor-to-ceiling bookcase and cabinets, the padded high-back armchairs and walnut plank floor with the forest-green throw rug. The large flat screen PC monitor and the accompanying keyboard were to the right of the desk. The cabinets housed locked filing cabinets, television, fax machine and printer on slide-away drawers to maintain the traditional atmosphere of the room. A framed oil painting of an old English foxhunting scene complete with riders on horses, groundskeeper and barking dogs hung on the wall behind his desk. The double French doors on the side of the study each contained a leaded glass panel with clear English Flemish glass panes and opened to the backyard. They filled the study with distorted rays of the early May sun. A slight breeze disturbed the trees in the rear yard. As was typical, the weather was cool to start the morning with a promise of being pleasantly warm by noontime.

The ring of the satellite phone interrupted his reverie. Jim checked the display out of habit. He answered with a cautious hello.

"Factor, is that you?" questioned a familiar voice with a sense of urgency.

A frown appeared on his face as he recognized the voice. "Carlos? Why are you calling?"

"Just listen," was the clipped response. "There's a real serious problem. Borichov and I have been made. I just managed to get away. I'm on my way south if you read me. Borichov thinks you did it and has made arrangements on you. They're already on the way, you understand? Get the hell out of there right now and get lost."

The phone went dead before Factor could reply. He stared at the phone and slowly placed it down. He swallowed and fought an impulse to react. A sense of dread coupled with the sudden chill in his bones took his breath away. He sat erect in his chair and willed himself to relax. It was if a block of ice had been placed against his bare back. He stretched his legs and took deep breaths. He was keenly aware survival in his business demanded paranoia and deliberateness in reading between the lines. Procrastination was never an option.

To take his mind off the danger Carlos Sengretti's call represented, Jim reviewed the past. He was a first-generation American of Italian and French parents born and raised in New York City. He learned to survive and thrive on the streets. After graduating from high school at seventeen his father, recognizing Jim needed both discipline and direction, encouraged him to enlist in the Air Force over the objections of his mother. His aptitude and intelligence, with a modest command of language skills, found him assigned to Air Force bases on foreign soils. More often than not, his assignments were prefaced by tough survival training curriculums. After four years in the Air Force, he enrolled at Arizona State University. He received bachelor and master degrees in electrical engineering. It was during his final year he met Diane who was getting her degree in communications. Her beauty, resourcefulness and independence attracted him. She went to work for a large corporation and advanced in a public relations position. They were married three years after they graduated.

Eager to get back in the defense area after college Jim went to work for a major aerospace and defense contractor which, in turn, led to work under subcontract to the Pentagon and intelligence agencies analyzing U.S., Soviet and Warsaw Pact radar and weapon systems. After the Cold War ended, his efforts included analyses of NATO systems. Aerospace employers sent him internationally to gather information and market their sophisticated defense products in Europe and the Middle East, most often to third world countries and their militaries. He acquired useful and powerful contacts resulting in a transition to an independent consultant. Thereafter, he became registered with the State Department as an arms dealer. He preferred to work alone and, as time progressed, became acutely aware of illicit arms dealing. He rejected the temptation to participate in the trafficking of illegal goods. That is, until he met Carlos Sengretti.

Last December should have been the end of his involvement. Jim suspected Carlos had been careless or greedy, probably both and the arms deal had been uncovered by the U.S. Customs Service. Apparently Mikhail Borichov surmised Jim was responsible for the leak and, seeking vengeance, placed a contract with a Russian hit team to kill him. Sengretti must have managed to elude U.S. authorities and was on his way to South America. Jim realized if he was to save his family and himself, he had to disappear immediately without a trace. He harbored no illusions it was an empty threat. He had witnessed too much about Borichov's methods of business and temperament to believe he could reason with him.

His concern was Diane and how he could soften the blow. He couldn't reveal any of the information he possessed and place her in danger. Nor could he tell her where he was going. He had to make a clean break with his present life. Further, he had to make unpredictable decisions to protect them both, buy time to assess his predicament, and determine a future course of action against the threat. Jim glanced at his watch and saw barely a half-hour had passed since Sengretti's call. He calmly rose from his chair and left the study. He climbed the stairs to the master bedroom where he gathered jeans, shirts, underwear, toiletries, sneakers and a windbreaker into a small travel bag. He returned to the study and opened the wall safe. He extracted $10,000 in cash and placed it in the bag. Diane would have access to ample finances to start again. He placed his watch and wedding band in the safe. He pulled out his wallet and pocketed some of the money leaving the credit cards. It also went into the safe. He glanced at his sat phone. He doubted the police would go through the trouble of checking the calls. It wouldn't matter, there was nothing incriminating. As far as the computers were concerned, the data was protected by password and encryption. If anyone happened to gain access, without a roadmap they would just be saturated with clients, customers and products information.

He exited at the rear of the house. In his intense anxiety, the sounds of the door closing and latching, birds singing and occasional passing traffic were amplified to distraction. He shook off his apprehension and looked back at the house one final time. "I'll be back, Diane. I promise." Carefully he made his way down the rear hillside slope, thankful the foliage masked his departure.

Jim walked away and reached the end of the block. He turned his head and slowly looked both ways to check for any strange vehicles. He saw an older model car with Florida license plates and two occupants driving away from him. The hairs in back of his neck stood. At once he chided himself, don't appear suspicious or you'll attract attention. He waited until the car turned before making his way along the brush to the back entrance of the tract. Take a deep breath and walk casually, he thought.

He had no doubt Sengretti told the truth. What did surprise him was Carlos took the time to warn him. Everything he learned about the man indicated a selfish and uncaring attitude. Enough of that; concentrate on what's going on. How much time do I have, two or three days? I've got to lose myself. Think. I need a disguise. Anything changing my appearance will help no matter how simple or mundane it is. How about transportation? Taxis, trains and buses don't require ID and cash is routinely accepted.

He made his way to a local gas station, bought a baseball cap and sunglasses, and stashed them in the bag. After walking another block, he hailed a passing taxi and directed it to the downtown area within a few blocks of the Santa Ana Greyhound Bus Terminal. On the way, they passed a novelty store. He stopped the cab, got out and walked back to the shop. He entered and searched the aisles and found a small theatrical makeup kit. Okay, assume someone is searching and checks taxi records. Let's put a little confusion into the process. In a nearby alley, he put on the cap and sun glasses along with a beard from the kit.

At the bus terminal he separately bought tickets to three destinations; San Diego, Tucson and San Francisco. He went into the men's room where the beard was discarded and replaced with a moustache. The cap and sunglasses went into the bag. He acknowledged it wasn't a great disguise. Hell, it's not even a good one but uncertainty and confusion was what he wanted to accomplish. It should throw anybody off at first glance. He boarded the bus heading for San Francisco. The long bus trip would give him time to think about his next move. He was mindful Diane, used to his job's idiosyncrasies, would only notify the police of his disappearance after a number of days when she didn't hear from him. He planned to avoid the resultant missing person search.

He couldn't quell the jackhammer thumping of his heart as he unwillingly thought of the June the year before, when he attended the Paris Air Show and the ensuing events.

Chapter Two

THE PROPOSITION

The Previous Year, Friday, June 15
Paris, France

Jim Factor had flown to Paris a few days before the opening of the Paris Air Show at the Le Bourget Airport just north of the city. The elite international aerospace trade fair was held every other year. It displayed the latest high technology hardware by global defense contractors and was ritually attended by military representatives from countries around the world who comprised the customer base. The temperature was not yet uncomfortably warm and rain was not in the immediate forecast. Crowds of Parisians, students, tourists and expatriates roamed the streets of the city while half again their number flooded the outdoor cafés. They waved glasses of wine and cigarettes animatedly as they conversed, oblivious to background music, the neighboring tables or the street sounds about them. Waiters wearing their traditional black vests over white shirts with white aprons around their waists deftly maneuvered their way around tables taking and delivering orders, miraculously without incident.

Jim preferred the Queen Elizabeth Hotel on the Av. Pierre 1er de Serbie, right around the corner from the prestigious Georges V Hotel and the popular promenade for the ostentatious aristocrats of old, the Avenue des Champs-Élysées. The Queen Elizabeth was far less pretentious than Georges V but picturesque and more comfortable in its own right with deep piled sofas and 18th century wall-coverings. The small ground floor restaurant served a cuisine as good as anywhere in Paris. His third-floor suite contained 18th and 19th century furniture, a four-poster bed and a marble bathroom.

A terrace overlooked the narrow, cobblestone street where activity went on to well after midnight, and street cleaners and delivery trucks started the day at sunrise. An early summer wind blew the scent of opened blossoms and bakery smells in through the opened window. He could have requested an inside room facing the quiet rear grounds but fancied the day-long echoing sounds of people on foot or scooters and traffic horns. Noise never disturbed his sleep.

Jim began his obligatory appearance at the Paris Air Show. It afforded him an excellent opportunity to visit with contractor clients and visiting customers in the week before and during the exhibition.

When he arrived back at the Queen Elizabeth Hotel lobby in the late afternoon of the opening day, he was given a phone message. Monsieur Carlos Sengretti desired to have a business meeting with him in the evening. He struggled to recall that Sengretti was a Florida-based small arms broker and puzzled there could be anything in common between them. He took the small lift up to his room where he took off his jacket and loosened his tie. He sat down at the desk, called the number on the message and was put through by a hotel switchboard operator.

When it was answered, he said hesitantly, "Mr. Sengretti? This is Jim Factor. I'm returning your call."

An amiable voice with a South American accent responded, "Mr. Factor. Thank you for contacting me so quickly. I would like to meet with you regarding a business matter tonight if it's not terribly inconvenient. Have you eaten yet?"

Jim wrinkled his brow. "No, I haven't. Could you tell me what you would like to discuss?"

"In due time, Mr. Factor. I will pick you up in front of your hotel at eight. I will explain over dinner and I assure you it will be most interesting and profitable."

Jim hung up the phone and shrugged. He hadn't any plans for the evening so he might as well see what Sengretti had on his mind. Unbuttoning his shirt he decided he had time to clean up. He was curious about the call. Perhaps Sengretti had run into a possible customer demand for a big ticket item and wanted to pass it on for a finder's fee. In this business, it rarely happened but who knows. Well, no harm in checking.

Sengretti arrived in a taxi promptly on the hour. Jim noticed the onset of dusk was accompanied by a drop in temperature. He climbed in the cab and they shook hands and exchanged pleasantries. He started to speak but

Sengretti shook his head. Jim looked closely at the man by his side. Sengretti was short and slender with a square chin on a narrow face, long dark hair combed straight back, thick sideburns, a thin mustache under a thin nose and a dark complexion. He wore a diamond stud earring and had a gold bracelet on his right wrist. He was dressed in a dark green, long sleeve silk shirt, brown slacks and hand-tooled leather loafers. The man definitely was South American.

The cab took them to the La Taverne du Sergent Recruteur on a narrow side street within the proximity of the Notre Dame Cathedral. The restaurant, he knew from past experience, offered country French cuisine served on wooden tables and chairs. They entered and were seated at the back of the restaurant according to the wishes of Monsieur Sengretti. The room was not yet filled at this relatively early hour. Jim waited until the waiter departed after depositing a wooden bowl containing various types of sausages with a cutting knife and a bowl of vegetables along with the house bottle of red wine.

He impatiently demanded, "Okay Mr. Sengretti. What is it you want to talk about that couldn't wait until tomorrow?"

Sengretti poured each of them a glass of wine. He raised the glass and appraised the color and viscosity. Satisfied, he began. "May I call you Jim? And I am Carlos. I am in a position with a client, who shall remain nameless, to make a very handsome commission on an arms sale but I require your assistance as a consultant." Before Jim could protest, he continued as if anticipating the response. "Oh yes, I am aware you function only with major clients and are only concerned with legitimate arms deals but I beg you to listen to my proposition before you answer. This is for your ears only."

Jim sipped his wine, curious as to where this was going. "Go on," he said.

Sengretti took a drink of wine, paused to look about the restaurant at the scattered diners, and explained in a lowered voice. "Within the past two months, I have been contacted by a man who introduced himself as having interests in South America and I suspect is affiliated with a drug cartel. He's in the market for sophisticated weaponry and gave me his requirements." He hesitated for effect and took a drink of wine. "I went through the list; the content isn't important for now. I told him the cost would easily exceed $10 million. I felt then, as you do now, my time was being wasted. I observed no change in his expression upon hearing my estimate. Rather, he surprised me by indicating it was acceptable." Seeing Factor's skeptical expression, Sengretti added, "To test his credibility I informed him I required a $500,000 retainer and sixty days to make confidential inquiries on the availability of his requirements and explore logistical arrangements."

Jim raised his eyebrows at the substantial sum requested and nodded his approval at the precaution taken. "I gather that was the end of it or did he make a counter-offer?"

"No to both counts. I received the total amount within fortyeight hours in an offshore bank account I provided. I also received future contact instructions."

He shrugged. "Impressive. How does that concern me?"

"I am interested in hiring an experienced arms broker such as you who would guide my best interests while I conduct the necessary transactions. I am willing to pay cash for your counsel. Shall we say $75,000 as a retainer every three months, in advance, plus a fee when we meet and expenses?" Seeing he had Jim's attention, Sengretti continued. "In the meantime I have made quiet inquiries and been referred to a Russian national, Mikhail Borichov. Do you know him?"

"Not personally. I've heard the name."

"He has been presented as a broker of weapons with contacts in the governments of Russia, Bulgaria and Lithuania and reported ties to the Russian mafia. He claims to associate with a wellknown Bulgarian military electronics company, KAS Engineering. He states he's in a position to sell a whole range of weaponry from Kalashnikov assault rifles to rocket-propelled grenade launchers at low prices through Cortex International, his company in Bulgaria which is licensed to manufacture Russian weapons." Sengretti paused for effect. "Now, for the major requirement of my customer; he is interested in acquiring a respectable number of Russian Igla SA-18 shoulder-fired, surface-to-air missiles or SAMs with infrared or IR heat seekers designed, as you know, to destroy lowflying airplanes and helicopters. The customer would prefer the U.S. Stinger SAM but he realizes the weapon is inaccessible and, anyway, wants to maintain a low profile."

Jim picked up his wine glass and took a moment to reflect on the proposition. Hell. Sengretti could get much of the information off the Internet and other sources. All he would be doing is pointing out the pitfalls and suggesting alternative avenues. He couldn't deny the fee was good. The money could be routed to his Swiss account to further isolate his involvement. His interest thus peaked, Jim stated. "You mentioned cash. I take it we're talking U.S. dollars. If I agree to assist you, I would want the money wired to a bank account in Europe. Is that a problem?"

"Not at all."

"Okay, here's my second condition. I want no part of the actual implementation of any transaction. My only role will be to strategize, identify potential problems and issues, and suggest ways of circumventing them. The execution of any scheme developed is between you and Borichov. My exposure is to be limited to just the two of you. If these conditions are acceptable, I'm your consultant."

"Excellent."

They shook hands and settled back.

"Jim, I have a question relating to your business if you don't mind."

"Go ahead."

"Is it true your services are paid exclusively by commission?" Jim nodded. "It is for the most part. I front the expenses which can be significant since a sale, if it occurs, can take up to eighteen months. It's the reason I maintain a number of clients and products. Occasionally, I'll ask for a retainer or fee when information gathering is requested. How about you?"

"My business is different. I insist on a large up-front payment with the final due before delivery. Obviously, in many cases I cannot rely on my customer's integrity. My suppliers demand full payment before the products leave their possession. My fee comes off the top."

As Jim prepared for bed, he thought back to the meeting. He knew the arms transaction being considered would be illegal. On the other hand, he consoled himself again with the knowledge Sengretti could get the advice from others. He had made it clear he could back out anytime. Anyway, he'd soon find out if it was a serious proposition. He looked out the open window onto the street and took a big breath. To say he enjoyed his living as an arms dealer brokering, arranging and facilitating arms deals was an understatement. He liked the independence which suited him fine. Interfacing with people was relegated to clients and customers. Business-wise he preferred European defense companies to their U.S. counterparts principally because he didn't need to obtain prior written approval for proposed transactions from the State Department. In addition, the commissions were greater since his international clients didn't concern themselves with the U.S. 1977 Foreign Corrupt Practices Act. He didn't have any problem that the law unilaterally prohibited American companies from bribing foreign or domestic government officials or employees but it indirectly capped commissions under the inference large amounts were an indication of under the table payments. This led U.S. arms dealers like him to seek international clients and directly contributed to an increase in foreign arms sales at the expense of American companies. Jim observed the increasing number of businessmen, with military and security backgrounds who went into arms brokering. In some cases, they obtained small arms as cheaply as possible and shipped them by circuitous international routes to conflict-torn countries and regions of human rights abuse. Mikhail Borichov was no exception. Jim chose to stay away from arms dealing destined for individuals and organizations. Instead, he focused on technology driven weapon systems whose end user was a legitimate third world country's military. A major reason for his success was the technical expertise he possessed to understand the theory and operational complexities of the systems he sold, and detailed knowledge of the competition's systems from his years as an intelligence analyst.

He admonished himself. Come on, Jim. Let's not continue with this holier than thou bullshit. Not to say he hadn't bent the laws. Years in the arms trade and exposure to large money deals had subdued his moral unrest. Some of his commissions were siphoned to his numbered account at the Union Bancaire Privée in Geneva, Switzerland. His family's vacations in Europe were financed by wire transfers to local European banks from that account. His wife Diane knew nothing about the existence of the account or of his customers or the arms transactions consummated over the years. It had nothing to do with trust; it was that the business was not one which lent itself to sharing with family and friends in these days of political correctness, not to mention the requirement to divulge overseas bank accounts to the IRS.

He sat before his notebook computer and instituted an Internet search on Mikhail Borichov. Although it was established he would be just a third party consultant to the planned arms deal, he felt the extra precaution was necessary. He saw Borichov was no stranger to the Internet. He was listed as a prominent small arms weapons supplier whose multitude of wares included assault rifles, machine guns, hand-held under-barrel and mounted grenade launchers, portable anti-tank and anti-aircraft guns, and mortars. He profited from systematic proliferation of small wars and local strife in mainly smaller nations. Africa, in 1998 alone, lay claim to eleven major armed conflicts and was the most war-torn region in the world. It was alleged Borichov supplied weapons to the perpetrators of the 1994 genocide in and to governments directly or indirectly involved in the war in the Democratic Republic of Congo (DRC). Angola, Burundi, Chad Namibia, Rwanda, Sudan, Uganda and Zimbabwe were mentioned. There were cryptic references to the ruthlessness of Borichov in his suppression of competitors and unscrupulous dealings with opposing sides of conflicts accepting cash, diamonds and other valuable commodities from warring factions.

He closed the computer and leaned back. He resolved to tread carefully in his dealings with Sengretti and Borichov, and terminate the association prior to their arms deals implementation.

Borichov was clearly a dangerous adversary.

Before the Paris Air Show had run its course that week, Jim received a confirmed deposit to his Swiss bank account of $75,000.

Chapter Three

ARMS DEAL MEETINGS

The Previous Year, Tuesday, July 10
Düsseldorf, Germany

The first meeting between the parties was scheduled less than a month after the Paris Air Show. Sengretti contacted Jim from Florida and confirmed the involvement of Mikhail Borichov. Sengretti and Borichov had concurred the meetings would take place randomly in large European cities. The first was to be held in Düsseldorf, Germany.

As the capital of the Federal State of Nordrhein-Westfalen since 1946, Düsseldorf had developed into an important political and economic metropolis in the course of the twentieth century. Jim was familiar with the city as a result of trips to several German firms. He had flown into the Rhein-Ruhr Airport several times. He gathered his luggage and went outside to stand in line at the curb for a taxi. The weather was agreeable although the blue sky held patches of gray clouds. He welcomed visiting these old cities. Europe for him was a comfortable business and vacation ground. For prudence and efficiency, he had arranged his travel schedule to attend the meeting at the back half of a visit to Blohm+Voss AG Naval Shipbuilding in Hamburg. It was a simple matter to take a Lufthansa Air shuttle down in the late afternoon.

Jim was aware the traditional luxury hotels were situated in the center of the city. He favored the Steigenberger Parkhotel, situated on the König-

sallee, a world-famous boulevard with exquisite jewelry shops and pricey fashion outlets like Chanel and Prada. Only a few yards away from the
Königsallee laid the heart of Düsseldorf: the historic Old Town. Sometimes
known as 'the longest bar in the world,' Düsseldorf's Altstadt contained some
two hundred bars, cafés and restaurants. Despite its relatively small size of
just a few blocks, large crowds flocked here on the weekends filling most of
the bars to bursting point. When closing time loomed, the revelers continued partying until the wee hours in one of the nearby clubs. The Altstadt
wasn't just for night owls. Row upon row of atmospheric old town houses
had been converted into shops and boutiques. The main railway station was
centrally situated and endowed with a striking clock tower. Five times a day,
locals and tourists gathered in front of the carillon to marvel at the *glock-
enspiel*, a chiming clock with mechanical figures that reenact the story of
Schneider Wibbel. Wibbel was a dressmaker who insulted Napoleon and
was sent to prison. Instead of going to prison himself, Wibbel sent his ap-
prentice who died in jail, leading everyone to believe Wibbel was dead while
in reality he was alive and kicking. Over the centuries, Wibbel has come to
represent the typical, clever Rhinelander. Schneider-Wibbel-Gasse, a small
street in the center of Old Town, was named after the cunning dressmaker.

Borichov had selected the ultra-exclusive Schloss Hugenpoet housed for
over fifty years in the historical Wasserburg or Castle on the Water. The hotel
had a total of twenty-five rooms and offered small private conference rooms.
It was actually located in Kettwig, a suburb of Essen, but easily reached quickly
by car from Düsseldorf. On arrival, Jim found the hotel lobby to his taste as he
checked in. The eventful history of the Wasserburg was displayed through various precious features such as the marble staircase and collection of art works.
His reserved luxury room contained 17th century furniture and provided all
the necessary comforts. An antique desk in the corner of the room held a dinner invitation and the name of the next day conference room.

Jim harbored a little trepidation about the evening and the uncertainty of what
he was getting into. He comforted himself with the thought he could get out
anytime he wanted, no questions asked. On the other hand, he'd been advanced
$75,000 just to listen and comment. What could be the harm in it? Still, he
couldn't shake off the uneasy feeling. He took the elevator down to the ground
floor and made his way to the restaurant. He gave the Matre d' the name of the
reservation and was guided between tables to a private booth at the corner of
the dining room. His two dinner companions were already seated. They rose
and Sengretti made the introductions. Carlos wore a brown double-breasted

black suit, light blue shirt, and black and red striped tie. Jim noticed his choice of jewelry was more subdued. Borichov was dress in a dark blue, pinstriped Sevile Row suit expertly tailored to minimize his upper-body bulk. A breast pocket handkerchief matched his royal blue tie. Bushy eyebrows, a close hair-cut, large jowls, thick neck and high forehead made up most of his face. His recessed brown eyes reflected intelligence and hardness.

Mikhail Borichov smiled and extended his hand. "Mr. Factor. I know of your work and am not a little jealous of your elite clientele. It's a sincere pleasure to meet you. Shall we dispense with the formalities? Please call me Mikhail."

Jim relaxed at the warm greeting. "Nice to meet you as well, Mikhail."

They sat down. Borichov set the tone of the dinner conversation. "Perhaps we can learn about each other without discussing the reason for our meeting until tomorrow. There are several dishes I can recommend for your pleasure. We will start with a drink." He motioned to a waiter who stood on the outskirts of the booth and orders were given. When the drinks arrived, they toasted to a successful business transaction and to each other. True to his earlier sugges-tion, they ate and talked in social and general business terms.

Wednesday, July 11

The following morning they met at nine in one of the hotel's comfortable conference rooms. Borichov opened a large briefcase and placed an elec-tronic unit on the table. He explained. "Before we begin, I want to cover some security issues. This is a KAS Engineering state-of-the-art microwave scanner and white noise frequency generator. It transmits across frequency bands to search for any listening or recording devices using a principle of retroreflection. It then cloaks discussions with an appropriate jamming signal. It is strictly precautionary. In addition, it is absolutely essential you purchase and use phone cards at all times from public telephones when it is necessary to discuss details with one another. Cell phones used in pub-lic are safe as a rule but I strongly recommend you keep the conversations vague just in case. Lastly, keep note taking to a minimum employing vague or shorthand references." Satisfied he had their attention and agreement, he turned towards Jim. "You have the floor."

Jim lectured them on the issues confronting an arms sale comprised of weapons banned by U.S., European Union or EU, NATO treaty and international law. He pointed to a rareness of agreement in all of the entities and the lack of international arms transfer controls; weaknesses that were open to exploitation. "The unilateral action of the U.S. in attempting to enforce an embargo of illicit arms into Central and South America has to be taken seriously. Keep in mind that the EU will indirectly cooperate through their inspections of international cargo egressing from the Mediterranean."

He pointed to the wall screen. "There are five main avenues used to circumvent the regulatory process and the degree of complexity is related to the breadth of the arms sale. The first is the use of loopholes and enclaves of weak regulation between national legal systems to conduct legal but unethical business via third party countries. Second, one places a reliance on personal contacts and networks more than corporate identities. The third consists of arranging complex international banking transactions and company formations in cooperative countries. The fourth involves the use of agents and techniques employed in the modern transport industry for covert deliveries to sensitive destinations. The fifth avenue relies on corruptible officials and weak law enforcement."

Borichov observed as he inclined his head towards the screen, "My business with the African continent and Middle East were mostly straightforward arms deals. I have utilized some of these measures you have described though not all at one time. However, I acknowledge the scope and the large financial gain of our proposed venture. Do you have any recommendations to propose at this time?"

Jim nodded. "I propose drop shipping be considered in conjunction with creating a documentation trail and money laundering. It will require an experienced transporter. The sheer physical size of the arms dictates a sea shipment. I don't have to caution you against an approach requiring accurate records especially about paymasters, payments and cash depositories."

Sengretti chimed in, "The transportation I've used in the past are aircraft, trucks and boats. It seems to me transportation is the least of the problems we have to worry about."

Jim countered, "On the surface it seems so but it's not as simple as it sounds. There'll be Customs officials at every border, seaport and airport who'll want to inspect the paperwork. Some may even expect bribes. Remember, any suspicion or misstep may result in a wholesale inspection of the cargo."

Borichov smiled knowingly and added his agreement to the retort. "Quite so. Generating unimpeachable documentation will be extremely important if this deal is to succeed."

The discussion between the three men on the virtues and application of each of the possible avenues went on for a second day. At the end of the last session, Borichov recommended he and Factor develop a preliminary scheme that could be expanded upon at the next meeting. This time it would take place in Amsterdam. Once again he would make the arrangements.

Wednesday, August 8
Amsterdam, The Netherlands

Jim arrived at the Amsterdam Airport from London on a wind-swept rainy day. The airport was only ten miles southwest of the city center but the traffic and the extreme shortage of parking places in Amsterdam proper made a taxi convenient for transportation. From previous visits he considered Amsterdam, The Netherlands' capital, one of the world's best hangouts. The city was a canny blend of old and new; scattered art installations hung off 17th-century eaves. Autos give way to bicycles and triple-strength monk-made beer was served in steel and glass *grand cafés*. Many of Amsterdam's canals were filled in around the start of the twentieth century, mainly for sanitary reasons. The remaining waterways were still fairly dirty but he knew first-hand there was nothing like seeing Amsterdam by boat. The houses looked impossibly balanced, leaning, looming and jostling on both sides of the canal. Small colorful cars lined the canals like a row of metallic flowers. Bridges arched over the water, some of them opening for tall water traffic; and all those magnificent houseboats, ranging from restored barges overflowing with plants and pets peering from the portholes to sleek purpose-built 'arks' with feature windows and sundecks.

The last time here he had come with Diane. She read in a tourist brochure Amsterdam had over half a million bicycles, an ideal way to get around although you needed to get used to the idea of having your bike stolen. The brochure also stated that Amsterdam, as a cosmopolitan cauldron, had been enticing migrants and non-conformists for decades. It was a thriving city and one of the hardest for travelers to leave, judging by the number of expatriates that hung around the bars and coffee houses. This made it an ideal meeting place where nationalities blended into the cultural atmosphere. Jim considered Borichov's preoccupation with caution on the extreme side but agreed with the carefulness expended. Actually, he enjoyed the meetings and appreciated the deliberateness and thoughtfulness of the planning process.

* * *

The taxi took forty-five minutes to reach the Krasnapolsky, a renowned hotel on Dam Square facing the Royal Palace. An executive room had been reserved for Mr. Factor. The room had enormous walls, red satin wallpaper, ornate period furniture, old embroidered throw rugs on polished wooden floors, a ten-foot sofa with heavily padded arms and gold tinged pattern, a large wall tapestry, and two large windows. A bottle of champagne with a white linen cloth about its neck nestled in a bucket by the table along with a basket of fruit. A small, white desk with thin ornate legs held a dinner invitation and the following day's private conference room information. In the evening they gathered in the dining room and kept to the format of exchanging pleasantries.

Thursday, August 9

The mood of the meeting convened in one of the private conference rooms of the hotel was upbeat. Borichov once again went through the electronic cleansing ritual and when satisfied started the presentation by declaring; "The conceived scheme we are to discuss was designed to make the arms transaction appear legitimate from the very beginning. Jim has been extremely instrumental in identifying weaknesses and hazards, and suggesting possible workaround solutions. It relies on a combination of elements such as front companies on both sides of the Atlantic, money laundering, bribing government officials, and drop shipping. Accordingly, our first step requires Carlos to set up a front company in both Florida and New York while I will be responsible for setting up bank accounts on the European side to conduct money transfers without questions or major documentation."

Sengretti spoke up. "My client wants assurances the product is exactly what he has ordered. He won't put up any money without proof."

Borichov nodded and replied. "I expected his demand for verification. Your customer will need to put up another sum of goodwill money to cover our time and expenses, shall we say $1 million. When it is received, we shall start executing the scheme and provide the necessary evidence. Does he wish to directly see the product?"

"I can't speak for him there. When this meeting ends, I'll change my flight plans and meet with him. I'll bring up both subjects."

"Carlos, one more thing; the less people who know the details associated with getting the weapons to your customer, the safer we all will be. Be prudent on offering explanations. I wait to hear from you before the next meeting is planned. At that time we shall go into the details so Jim can critique the arrangements."

They broke up shortly after the presentation. Borichov left immediately for the airport and his private plane. Jim and Carlos were staying overnight before taking their airline flights. They met for dinner in the hotel restaurant where they discussed the events in lowered voices careful not to divulge details.

Carlos sipped on the wine. "You know Jim, when we first started out two months ago I wondered if I was overly cautious by bringing you on as a consultant. I'd have to say it was one of the best decisions I ever made. You know the intricacies of arms dealing and you're doing a fine job of keeping us from tripping over our feet."

Jim lifted his wine glass. "Thanks, Carlos. It's been interesting to say the least. I am curious to hear if your client will step up to the next phase of the venture. After that, you and Borichov will have your hands full developing the details of the transactions. I am anxious to see where it'll be headed."

Monday, August 13
Miami, Florida

Carlos Sengretti arrived in Miami, went through Customs, and took an airport limousine to his home. He dumped his suitcase on the bed and went into the living room to make a drink. He had just spent three days in Medellin, Columbia with the Cali cartel's leaders discussing the type of weapons sought and their estimated costs. This time he was treated with deference. He did not reveal details of his business associates and offered to take a representative of the cartel with him to Russia to witness the shoulder-fired SAM in an actual test. They declined the invitation fearing that the potential for exposure from any overseas trip would jeopardize their security. Instead, they insisted on proof in the form of a videotape which shows Sengretti witnessing the firing. The $1 million installment would be wired to his Cayman Islands bank account within the month. He chose to wait until the transfer went through before notifying Borichov and Factor. After that, he had things to do. He made up his mind Factor should accompany them on the Russian trip.

Thursday, September 6
Moscow, Russia

Borichov set up the meeting with KB Mashinostroeniya, the Design Bureau in Reutov, Russia, located in Central Russia not far from Moscow. The huge complex with test ranges and a landing strip occupied over ten square miles. Borichov served as the Russian translator for Factor and Sengretti when they met with senior officials. He explained the purpose of the visit was to obtain technical information and a videotape of a missile firing for an un-named customer who was interested in purchasing a quantity of Igla SA-18 Grouse SAMs.

Factor was particularly interested in the proceedings since in the past he had been privy to Stinger SAM live firings in U.S. Army exercises. He knew the Russians had obtained black market Stingers left over from their war in Afghanistan and performed reverse engineering to bring their earlier versions of the missile to a more advanced state. They were told earlier in the year the Kolomna Machine-Building Design Bureau, also located in the area, earned about $40 million in a deal for the delivery of over two-hundred Igla portable SAMs. They were prepared to give them a good price of $4 million for twenty-five of the missiles.

Jim closely observed the canister, sight setup and even the firing protocol was similar to the U.S. missile. Preparing for firing at a target flare mounted on a distant tower, a technician placed the missile tube on his right shoulder and aimed the missile. Jim noted he carefully made sure it was balanced on his shoulder. The Igla system obviously was heavier than Stinger's thirty-five pounds. Satisfied, the technician activated a bottle of nitrogen to cool the missile's IR sensor. An emitted high-pitched sound signaled the missile seeker had detected and locked onto the target. The operator pulled the trigger launching the missile.

At one side, a cameraman filmed the sequence and the subsequent impact of the missile with the tower. He had been directed to make sure only Sengretti was present in the video for the entire test since Borichov and Factor had previously made it clear they were to be excluded. Borichov informed Jim he already had a license to manufacture the older SA-16 Gimlet model. Accordingly, it had earlier been decided Cortex would purchase the updated missiles and receive shipment. Satisfied with the visit and the weapon's performance, they needed to await the outcome of Sengretti's next customer meeting.

Wednesday, September 19
Milan, Italy

Jim was ecstatic when he heard Milan was to be the location for the next meeting. In keeping with his previous practice of scheduling prior visits to clients, he flew into Marseille, France the day before to meet with Dassault Electronique in St. Cloud, France, an aircraft avionics manufacturer. Northern Italy loomed in his heritage and he always enjoyed the trips made there whether for business or vacation. One of his clients, Alenia Aeronautica, an Italian aerospace company, had a large division near Milan. Although other visitors normally shunned rental cars in favor of taxis, he was comfortable driving in the city. Milan's layout is best understood as a historic nucleus around the Cathedral, from which a star-shaped axis of arteries spread through modern suburbs to the ring road. One had to cope with street signs which were largely unreadable at night because they were generally situated on the upper unlit sides of building corners.

He had taken a short flight into Malpensa, Milan's largest airport thirty miles northwest of the city, handling transcontinental and other international flights. Situated on the flat plains of the Po Valley, Milan is the capital of Lombardy and Italy's richest and second largest city. Wealthy and cosmopolitan, the Milanese had a reputation as successful business people, equally at home and overseas. Embracing tradition, sophistication and ambition in equal measure, they were just as likely to follow opera at La Scala as their shares on the city's stock market or their chosen football team AC or Inter Milan, at the San Siro Stadium. Jim was aware visitors were generally not drawn to the city for its culture which he considered a pity since the city center had many museums and a particularly good selection of world-class art exhibitions and individual pieces. The center possessed an attractive number of quarters where a cocktail of architectural styles—the grandeur of Imperial Austria, the grace of Renaissance Italy and the optimistic bravado of the Belle Epoque stood shoulder-to-shoulder with a very modern and stylish effect. Milan remained the capital of Italy's automobile industry and financial markets, however, its fashion houses stole the limelight. The sunny and mild climate always brought out the genuine warmth of the region's inhabitants.

Jim drove to the Grand Hotel et De Milan. Once home to composer Giuseppe Verdi for twenty years, it was located on one edge of Milan's Quadrilateral now regarded as the home of Milanese fashion, only steps away from the La Scala Theater. He had to hand it to Borichov; the man knew his way around Europe. As before, a suite was reserved in his name. The gracious guest suite was individually designed and decorated with Italian fine fabrics, parquet floors, *objets d'art*, period furniture, marble bathrooms, and state-of-the-art amenities. In a separate area in the second room, he found up-to-date technology for Internet access, directdial telephones with voicemail, fax, additional phone lines, and video and stereo equipment. A message on the desk gave the instructions for reaching the ground floor's elegant lounge reserved for his business meetings. The Restaurante Don Carlos held his reservation for eight in the evening.

He unpacked and changed. Promptly on the hour, he stood in front of the restaurant. The dining room had terra-cotta floors, clean white walls hung with dramatic contemporary paintings, large windows overlooking the outside street, and discreet round tables topped with white linen, crystal glassware and candles. He was shown to the table where Borichov and Sengretti were already seated. They greeted each other warmly and sat down to the initial offering of wine and bread. Business would wait as usual until the next morning.

Thursday, September 20

Borichov took the floor, opened his briefcase and performed his routine electronic sweep. Signaling all was well, he deferred to Sengretti who stood to one side with papers and a videotape cartridge in his hand.

Sengretti began. "As you know, my last meeting with the customer was in August. As per the customer's instructions, a videotape was made of the Igla missile system and the test firing." Carlos proceeded to insert the cartridge in a VCR and played the tape complete with a Spanish narrative and audio of the firing. When it ended he resumed. "Along with a copy of the videotape and technical data, I reported the findings to the customer. Within days, he agreed to a purchase price of $16 million and is prepared to release an additional $10 million when the logistics are in place."

Borichov responded by applauding and Jim joined him.

Jim noted. "Your customer gets more than the amount of missiles he requested and the deal could clear $10 million in profit. I'd say that was a good payoff for the work you're going through." Borichov corrected him. "Don't forget we have extraordinary expenses in the logistics and transportation of the weapons. However, I won't deny we will have an excellent share left." He asked Sengretti, "Are you ready to start the details at your end?"

Sengretti was pleased with their reaction and nodded. "I'm prepared to set up two companies in Tampa, Florida. It will take sixty days to complete the paperwork. The first one shall operate as an import/export company. The second shall be listed as a securities company with an office in New York. This company will act as the escrow agent for the transaction."

"Excellent." Borichov rose and stood in front of them. "I am poised to open two accounts at an offshore bank which will receive the money wire transferred from the U.S. Within days, this money will be transferred to another bank where the buyer of the weapon systems or, should I say the paper recipient, will be expecting delivery. From there I shall make transportation arrangements. In the interest of security for our venture, I propose each principal complete his part of the scheme by, say, early December. We shall meet once more to review the exacting details and have on again as devil's advocate to critique the final plans and preparations."

Thursday, December 6
Paris, France

When Jim learned Paris was to be the site for the meeting, he was both surprised and amused. It was as if Borichov decided to take them back to where the venture originated. Jim arranged a meeting with the Eurocopter Group, the former French Aerospatiale helicopter company, near Marseille, France. From there he took an Air France shuttle flight into the Paris Orly Airport. The weather took a turn for the worse. France was caught in a cold wave which extended from the U.K. into Germany and as far south as Rome. Gloves and scarves accompanying a top coat were necessary accessories if one was to brave the icy wind-driven temperatures.

Borichov had made reservations at the Hotel Trocadero Dokhan's. Jim was impressed by the elegance and charm of this Parisian townhouse between the Place du Trocadero and the Arc de Triomphe. His room was an elegant blending of sophisticated period décor and leading edge comfort. As always, a corner desk held a dinner invitation and the name of the functional conference room for the next day's meeting.

Friday, December 7

The significance of the date did not escape Jim as he put on his suit jacket and stepped outside of the room. Over three score years had passed since Japan attacked Pearl Harbor. Talk about an unsettling coincidence. He shrugged it off. He was looking forward to hearing the final details of the complex scheme which had evolved over the past six months.

Borichov excised the electronic demons and settled back in his chair. He deferred to Sengretti who referred to written notes. Jim saw a flash of anger in Borichov's expression at this break of protocol.

"I began with setting up a company called Saturn International LLC in Tampa, Florida whose business is the import and export of construction machinery. Next, I created TransStar Corporation, a securities brokerage firm in Tampa and established an office in New York. This company will act as the escrow agent. Each of these companies opened bank accounts with two separate banks in Florida. TransStar will receive a $7 million wire transfer from my Cayman Island account. In turn it will notify Saturn International and issue a Line of Credit for the money."

Borichov interjected. "About the same time, another company and two bank accounts on the Isle of Man were opened in order to facilitate the European financial end."

"When I receive the payment," Sengretti continued, "as an officer of Saturn International, I'll instruct the TransStar securities company office in Florida to transfer the money to its New York office and account at the Central Bank of Seychelles in the Federal Reserve Bank. A few days after that, $6 million will be transferred from New York to the Isle of Man."

Borichov added. "From there, it will be wired to a Cortex International account at the Skoras Bank in Vilnius, Lithuania." Borichov turned to Jim. "Cortex will in turn wire $4 million to KB Mashinostroeniya who, on receipt, will ship the missiles to Cortex. Because Cortex can sell these kinds of weapons only to governments, on Jim's advice we have arranged to acquire an end-user certificate from the Republic of Lithuania. Money will exchange hands and we will have the documentation signed by and bearing the seal of the Lithuanian Minister of Defence."

Sengretti resumed. "I've assured my client when the missile systems are used, they could not be traced back to any source and the Lithuanian Ministry of Defence would issue a false letter of receipt upon delivery of the weapons."

Jim reviewed the intricate steps of the scheme noting the objective of the legal arms transaction accompanied by bona fide documentation was accomplished. It would take the weapons as far as Lithuania where the transportation was to originate. Timing had to be keyed to the $10 million payment, which meant Sengretti had to go back to his client and assure him of their readiness. "I want to remind you again to be careful of activities in the U.S." Jim cautioned. "The enforcement of the international arms brokering controls is being aggressively pursued by the U.S. Customs Service. It would be a serious mistake to underestimate them. Their extensive powers of investigation include wiretaps, search and bank account seizure warrants, and undercover sting operations. Once they become aware of large sums of money moving via wire transfers, flags will come up. If you adhere to the agreed upon plan of action and take the necessary precautions, it'll appear as a legitimate transaction and avoid their attention."

An installment payment of $10 million was wire transferred to the Cayman Islands in early February. Following verification Borichov ordered the SAM systems. By April, Cortex had received the shipment and reshipped them from Bulgaria to Lithuania without incident. Borichov had arranged for the transport of the Igla missiles through the services of Aristotle Zuni, the Greek owner of merchant ships who, for a price, had offered one of his vessels to smuggle the Russian missile systems to a Puerto Rican port. Zuni would send the ship into the Black Sea to Varna, Bulgaria to pick up the weapons systems from Cortex. He would use the bogus paperwork provided by the Lithuanians stating the cargo ship would be transporting forty twenty-foot containers of machinery and general cargo to Puerto Rico. Four cargo containers with the missile systems would be commingled with the others in order to pass inspection at the Straits of Gibraltar. Once in Puerto Rico, they would be transferred to a South American-bound ship.

It was at this meeting Jim decided he had gone as far as was prudent and chose to extricate himself from further involvement in the impending illegal arms transactions. He informed Sengretti and Borichov he was terminating his services. By then he had collected $250,000 in cash channeled into his Swiss account.

Chapter Four

MIKHAIL
BORICHOV

Sunday, May 5
Varna, Bulgaria

Mikhail Borichov walked out of the spacious master bedroom suite smoking a cigarette. He savored a passion for fine living and favored foreign cigarettes and Russian vodka. Underneath the long red velvet robe monogrammed with his initials on the sleeve he wore black silk pajamas with black slippers. Borichov was well aware of his keen business acumen, violent temper and his feared reputation. His mind wandered back to his youth growing up in the corrupt atmosphere of Moscow where one either succumbed to the squalor or took chances with crime until old enough to join the military. He learned the streets and the inherent brutality associated with asserting power. Once in the military, his intelligence and initiative led to the Moscow Military Institute where they discovered his aptitude for languages. He trained as a translator and was sent to embassies and consulates in Central Africa where he developed relationships in the under-developed countries. The collapse of the Soviet Union gave him and fellow comrades the opportunity to assemble a fortune by exploiting their international contacts stealing, buying and selling new and used Russian weapons.

He acquired a high-level contact in the Russian mafia when his sister married Dimitri Federov. With a major loan from Federov's organization, he started Cortex International, a Bulgarian arms manufacturing company.

It functioned as a merchant buying and selling quantities of arms and supplying ammunition and weapons to Somalia, the Congo, Sudan, Yemen and Afghanistan. His strategy was to employ long-distance flights from Eastern Europe to Central African airfields. For large shipments with various distribution sites, he favored his Ilyushin Il-76 for arms delivery from Bulgaria to Andulo. Such flights would normally require refueling stops in the sub-region. For this purpose, local air-cargo companies with East European owners were in place to handle aircraft operations. He frequented the sub-Saharan region due to the lack of sufficiently skilled air traffic controllers, radar equipment and motivated personnel to monitor the vast air space between the southern border of Egypt and the northern borders of South Africa.

Borichov entered his library where books lined one wall from floor to ceiling. The sunlight streaming in the heavy glass panels of the library windows was filtered by the branches of a large tree in front of the villa nestled at a moderate elevation in the wooded foothills west of Varna. The busy Black Sea port of Varna stretched out to the distant haze in the front of the house punctuated by the lighthouse at Sveti Georgi Point off Varna Bay. He grunted with a slight sneer as he recalled it was once a resort for the Russian politburo elite. He observed his armed guards with automatic weapons patrolling his property on the perimeter of the surrounding stone wall. Turning from the window, he crossed the room to a large desk, settled his large body into the chair and turned on the computer. His face clouded in rage as he thought about the Bulgarian arms transfer which was supposed to go smoothly with the Lithuanian documentation. Somehow, U.S. authorities had been alerted to the scheme. Since he and Sengretti had the most to lose, it could only have been Factor who revealed it. He swiveled in his chair, picked up the phone and dialed a number.

"Dimitri? This is Mikhail. I have a favor to ask. I have a disposal problem in the U.S. and you have assets there." He winced when he heard the superior tone of the voice at the other end.

"Borichov, those sensitive assets are for my business interests, not for your pleasure and personal use. Any compromise of them could place us all in a dangerous position."

"I would use them for a very simple clean-up job related to our company which would not involve any exposure. Please, Dimitri."

God, he hated begging to this Politburo member who besides being a Russian mafia head with a large organization was his brother-in-law. What had his sister Erika seen in him?

"Borichov, you shit, just this once I will do it. Don't ask me ever again. If anything goes wrong, remember I'll find you. It better not affect my investment. I'll fax you the necessary contact information and inform them you will be in touch. Keep in mind the expenses are yours."

Borichov hung up the phone with a cold smile. "Now, Mr. James Factor, you shall pay dearly for your treachery." He opened a desk drawer and extracted a file folder assembled on Factor with multiple photographs. He prepared a fax header sheet with the information and transmitted it to the U.S. number given to him by Federov. Next, he arranged a money transfer to the bank specified in the instructions and sat back. Now, for the other pressing business, a search in his personal organizer since he needed to find a customer for Igla SAMs intended for Columbia. There still might be an opportunity to make a profit.

Chapter Five

RUSSIAN HIT TEAM

Sunday, May 5
Miami, Florida

Two brawny men lounged a rundown Miami suburb house with the curtains closed. Sergey Kasakov and Petra Shovinstky similarly dressed in worn slacks and colorful beach shirts read the newly arrived fax from Dimitri Federov cryptically describing their next assignment for Mikhail Borichov. As a seasoned hit team, they knew a file on the target would soon be received.

Sergey frowned and turned to Petra, "I don't much like the idea of doing a job for someone other than Mr. Federov. It's one more person who knows about us. And of all people, it's Borichov. The bastard nearly got us killed selling weapons to both sides in the Congo."

Petra shrugged. "I don't see we have any choice. The faster we do it, the sooner we're rid of him."

Both men had been together since their early years in the Soviet Army. They had an easy familiarity going back to combat action against the rebels in Afghanistan and Angola. Sergey handled firearms and explosives while Petra provided electronics skills and backup. After they left the army they hired out as mercenaries in the Congo teaching tactics and small arms skills until Dimitri Federov recruited them as a hit team and based them in the Miami Beach area with its proximity to the Central and South American area. They interfaced with other criminal organizations and conducted hits in Europe and the Americas. Both men were of average height and tanned with muscular physiques from lifting weights in the fenced backyard of the rented house. They routinely kept in shape by practicing a version of Russian karate on a mat in the garage. A padlocked, heavy-duty garage locker held the tools of their trade; armor vests, pistols and knives, assault rifles, sniper scopes, ammunition, night finders and electronic surveillance equipment. In addition, false IDs, counterfeit passports and currencies from various countries were stored in the locker.

They spent the next few hours packing clothes, cleaning guns and loading the nondescript used car before turning in to get some sleep. The last thing they did was to install another license plate on the car. They expected to pick up the wired expense money in the morning at the bank on the way out of Miami and drive non-stop to Newport Beach, California. There would be little opportunity to rest once the information on the target arrived from Borichov during the night.

Tuesday, May 7
Newport Beach, California

It was early morning when they entered Factor's neighborhood. They had taken turns driving from Miami and other than for hygiene were fresh. They were both looking at street names and house numbers. Sergey caught a glimpse in the rear view mirror of a figure behind a bush looking at them before he turned the corner.

Petra exclaimed, "There's the house. Slow down."

They drove past examining the front entrance and garage door.

Petra observed. "There's no alley behind the house so everything we do has to be from the front."

Sergey agreed. "In this neighborhood, we stick out in this his car. We'll need something else." They turned and left.

Chapter Six

FLIGHT

Tuesday, May 7
Bus to San Francisco, California

Jim had to come up with a strategy during the time the bus made its way to Northern California. He closed his eyes and reflected on his personal characteristics and habits which could undermine his attempt to escape detection. It would be wise to limit the use of his engineering background. He had to assume a cold determination if he was to achieve the objective of getting out of this mess. It meant storing away the memories of his former life while he ruthlessly pursued essential survival skills. Suddenly, he felt the travel bag leaving his grasp and opened his eyes to a bearded, ill-kempt passenger trying to take it from him.

Jim grabbed the man's wrist hard and growled, "What the hell do you think you're doing?"

The man drew back his other arm to strike him but Jim bent his wrist down. At once the rage kindled by his situation fueled his reflexes. He jerked the wrist until the man's head came near. He launched his fist from the depths of his anger and caught the man flush in the face. The passenger dropped unconscious to the bus floor. Several nearby riders turned at the sound but quickly looked away. The bus driver yelled and pulled the bus over to the side of the highway. Jim explained the man had tried to rob him. "I'll put him off at the next stop. If he has any complaints, he can put a claim in to the company. In the meantime, he'll sit in the front where I can keep an eye on him."

* * *

Jim sat back in his seat in order to catch his breath. That was close. It doesn't appear anyone paid any attention. He relaxed and resumed his thoughts. "An older appearance may be better suited. I'll cut my hair short and grow a beard for the first time in my life. I wish I hadn't shaved this morning." His first priority was to find a room for the night before it got too late. Hotels were out of the question and he certainly couldn't take a chance on sleeping in the streets. Maybe he could locate a room and board. Then what? How about work? He'd have to consider some type of manual or unskilled labor. Jim inwardly grimaced. Shit. This telltale New York accent of mine was a detail I hope the driver hadn't noticed. Speaking slowly should mitigate it somewhat. San Francisco has a variety of ethnic cultures; which one should he choose? He would have to leave the U.S. and its obsession for bureau-cratic paperwork. Europe would be a logical final destination with its many cultures and territorial privacy. He knew the Continent and spoke a little French, Italian and Spanish. His Swiss bank account would give him finan-cial freedom. If they surmised he would head for Europe, he would also be assumed to go to countries frequently visited over the years. How about Spain? France and Italy with ties to his heritage, business and vacations were out. So it was Spain but where? He had a fondness for coasts. The Costal del Blanca region on the eastern part of Spain was moderately populated and within reasonable distance to neighboring countries by rail and air.

He looked around the bus out of the corner of his eyes. There weren't many passengers and a few had dozed off. With a start he realized he hadn't given a single thought to his clients, customers or his Kuwaiti partner. That part of his past now had to be shoved aside. He had to think quickly. "What trade could he learn in San Francisco which could be usable and untraceable?" For the first time in hours, he allowed himself a smile as a notion found its way in his thoughts. He would seek any employment in a marina to get a basic knowledge of boats, not just any boats but reasonably sized boats with a bridge and quarters. In this way, he would be apt to be exposed to the nuances and his technical training would provide him with more options. He would allow at most six months before he made the next big move assuming he was successful at losing himself. The key to survival was to change his lifetime of habits, take on a new identity, and patiently bide his time. He had to remember paper trails can be followed and use it to his advantage. He needed to get fake ID. Interestingly enough, he felt it might not be difficult in a state harboring so many illegal immigrants. He realized he should take a nap during the bus trip but his mind kept him too occupied.

Newport Beach, California

Late that afternoon, Diane Factor pulled into her driveway. As the garage door rose, she saw Jim's car was in its regular space. Entering the house, she called out to him and received no answer. He was probably in the study with the door closed so he would not be disturbed. She would leave him alone until supper was ready.

In the evening, Diane paused at the study door, turned the knob and entered. With a surprised expression, she saw that the room was dark and empty. He must have had to leave for business on short notice and taken a taxi to the John Wayne Airport. He even left his phone. She futilely searched the house for a note. He must have really been in a hurry. Never mind, he'd contact her as always when he had a chance.

It was early afternoon when Sergey drove the old model Chevrolet Caprice north along Pacific Coast Highway into Newport Beach. Lights in the Factor house indicated it was occupied. The problem was maintaining surveillance on a street where the houses were set back and spaced apart. A parked car would draw attention.

They searched afterwards for a low-end motel where the ground floor rooms had doors facing the parking lot. Headed towards Huntington Beach, Sergey selected the first one he came to and rented a room with two beds for a few days. They noted their lightweight and colorful Miami Beach clothes fit the coastal scene. Their large, muscular appearances and European accent were accepted as normal tourist traits and aroused no undue attention.

When they had settled in their room, Sergey addressed Petra. "We have two choices; barge right in at night and hope to get the job done or plant a phone tap at the house and pick our time. Factor won't be expecting us so it would be simple enough except for the neighborhood. Let's be careful and plant the tap first. All it'll cost is a few extra days."

Petra nodded. "Suits me. We'll need a truck which would be normal in the area. I'll check the classifieds for a carpet cleaning we could hit for one. I'm going out to change the license plates on the car."

Chapter Seven

DESTINATION

Same Day
San Francisco, California

Hours the bus pulled into the San Francisco bus terminal. Jim decided to gamble and try to find a room in the Mexican area of the city. It would provide an opportunity to get quickly lost without a trail, look for a job and at the same time acquire Spanish for his eventual flight to Spain. It would be necessary to find a way to obtain false ID but working part time or for cash would forestall the eventuality. He didn't want for money but it was important to have a visible source to avoid questions. He went to the phone booth in the bus station and opened the telephone directory. He searched the restaurant pages for a geographical trend in Mexican restaurants. There seemed to be more of them in the Mission area south of the city. Satisfied he had identified the section, he took a cab to one of the restaurants on Dolores Street. He paid the fare and looked up and down the block. He walked down the street towards a nearby residential area. Darkness was rapidly falling and he realized he had to find a place to stay before too long. A stranger at night in the neighborhood was going to raise suspicion or run into trouble. He stayed close to the shadows making their way in his direction.

Suddenly, two Mexican youths came out of an alley and confronted him. One of them with his hand in his jacket pocket asked him what he was carrying. The other moved around to block his path. Jim grasped the handle of his bag tightly. He looked up and down the street but they seemed to be alone. He didn't see anything within reach that could be used as a weapon. He was again told to hand the bag over. He had no choice but to make a stand.

He pressed his back against a building's wall and waited. The closer youth pulled a knife and waved it back and forth. Jim forced himself to stand still and let him get closer. He planted his left foot against the wall and moved his right foot slowly out. When thevknife holder was within reach, Jim thrust out from the wall and kicked out making solid contact with the man's groin. He quickly turned to face the other thug, bag in hand defensively. The man looked down at his groaning companion, turned and fled. Jim stepped over the fallen assailant and walked rapidly away. After a while, he checked behind him and saw with relief things were quiet.

Once he was on a residential street, he slowed his pace and paid attention to the homes. He paused at a house where a sign on the front porch advertised room-to-let. He didn't think twice. This beggar can't be choosy. Taking a deep breath, he climbed the steps to the front door and with apprehension pressed the doorbell. He had just started the beginning of a new life.

The porch light went on and the front door cautiously opened. A woman with an apron peered at him through the closed screen door. Accompanying her were cooking smells while a Spanish radio station played from within; both were unrecognizable. The woman was five foot three in her mid-fifties with a roundish figure and a wisp of graying hair across her forehead. With an easy and friendly manner, she asked his business in Spanish. Jim pointed to the sign resulting in her closer scrutiny. Satisfied, she opened the screen door and motioned him in. As he reminded himself to speak slowly, it dawned on him he had not given any thought to a new name and background. He stammered out a name of an acquaintance he was friendly with in France. "Hello, my name is Nicolas Germain. I'm interested in your room."

The woman introduced herself in accented English as Marie Queterras and led him upstairs to an end bedroom. The room was clean and efficiently furnished. It contained a double bed with night table, dresser with a mirror, a wooden chair with a seat cushion, an adequate closet, a wood floor with a large throw rug, and an aging print of a boat on the sea over the bed. There was an overhead light, and a clock radio and lamp on the night table. To the side was a window whose view was obscured by evening shadows and curtains. She pointed to the hallway bathroom and, with eyebrows framing a question, informed him. "The room is $80 per week with breakfast and supper promptly at seven in the evening. It has a lock for your privacy. I clean the room and change the linen once a week."

Jim nodded his approval, reached in his pocket and paid for a week. When the door closed, he locked the door, placed his bag in the closet, took off his shoes and lay fully clothed on the bed. He tried to review his steps leading to the present but within moments the hectic events of the day and the security of the room like the overhead light were shut out by a deep slumber.

Chapter Eight

CARLOS SENGRETTI

Wednesday, May 8
Atlantic Ocean off Central America

Carlos Sengretti stood at the railing of the aged, heaving freighter smoking a cigarette. He pulled up the collar of his suit jacket to cover his neck against the biting wind. Occasionally, random drops of sea spray fell across his face. He scrutinized his soiled white linen pants and jacket. His fine silk shirt was dull and wrinkled from the humidity. Two weeks ago he was on his way to making more money than he ever had with an arms deal which would have positioned him at the top with the big players. He would have never had to worry again about scratching out an existence brokering small arms. In frustration he threw the cigarette over the side and tightly grasped the rail with both hands ignoring the flakes of rust and dirt that permeated the metal surface.

Black smoke billowed out of the two stacks into the wind stream. The deck was unevenly discolored from grease, oil and salt. The ancient freighter was one of hundreds that plied the eastern Central and South American coasts picking up and discharging cargo. It was on its way to Caracas, Venezuela after leaving Miami. Afterwards, its east-southeasterly direction would take it to Brazil where he had obscure relations and would get lost until the heat died down. He didn't dare go back to Columbia where his customer would undoubtedly take his revenge on losing over ten million dollars. He still had good money on him even after paying the captain an exorbitant amount for the passage, no questions asked. At least the stateroom was clean if furnished with a sagging bed, worn desk and tarnished fixtures. The captain stocked the cabinet with liquor and the food was passable. He bemoaned the events which led him to skulk out of the country hunted by the U.S. Customs Service for illegal arms transactions activities. The sheer stupidity of his action weighed on him. He pounded the railing with his hands until the pain and blood forced him to stop.

Carlos thought back to his poor childhood in Bogotá, Columbia here he was born and raised. The heat and the rain were always with them. The rain gave the people their identity. At certain times in the afternoon, Bogotá was a river of umbrellas. It seemed that the city was full of contradicting contrasts; gray by day and colorful by night, surrounded by green mountains protecting the vast valley, sunshine intermingle with rain, professional beggars, and abject poverty next to modern shopping centers. It was a city where energy and chaos, insecurity and emotion, violence and creativity came together. His father labored as a shoemaker and his mother cleaned the houses of those who had wealth. It was she who insisted on and enrolled him in a catholic school to get the education which had eluded them. He learned to read and write in Spanish and English. Later, his mother managed to get him a job doing odd jobs for the people who owned those houses. One of the men, Henry Mendoza, had seen the intelligence behind the brown eyes and the eagerness with which he attacked the jobs given to him. Soon, the boy was running errands involving packages not to be compromised. His reading and writing capability allowed him to rise in statue above the other boys and even the older ones soon reported to him. In time he was making good money and wearing stylish clothes. In his late teens, he was sent on business to different areas of Columbia but the city he took a fancy to was Medellin. Although Venezuela's chief manufacturing center, it gained notoriety as the headquarters of the cocaine cartel that became the world's leading distributor of the illegal drug. Violent turf battles and reprisals became commonplace. Additionally, the cartel was forced into open confrontation with the Columbia military aided by U.S. military advisors. Assault rifles and numbers were no match for the armed helicopter gunships with infrared sensors employed to track and destroy their cocaine factories and trafficking carriers. With his command of English and his inside knowledge of the cartel, Carlos was often sent out of the country to purchase arms and explosives. He conspired to have the arms shipped to the port of Puerto Barrios, Guatemala and transported by truck through Honduras and Nicaragua to Costa Rica. There he arranged sea transportation into one of the north coastal cities of Columbia. He skimmed weapons off the shipments and sold them independently to mercenaries in Honduras and El Salvador. Later, he added his money to the cartel's to get lower prices and resold the weapons for a good profit.

During his early twenties, he decided to relocate to Tampa, Florida and set up an office to broker small arms. It gave him a presence to U.S., and Central and South American markets. Accumulated contacts enabled him to thrive for several years but he came to realize Europe could give him access to more sophisticated weapons. It was at military aviation and arms shows in the U.S., Farnborough International in England, and the Paris Air Show where he met large-scale arms dealers. He began to formulate a plan whereby he would approach members of the cartel about acquiring specialized weapons to counter the military threat to their business interests. He flew to Bogotá, met with his benefactors and laid out a scheme for acquiring equalizing weaponry. Upon their approval, he took the short flight to Medellin and met with the cartel. He explained the U.S. barriers to anti-helicopter missiles were formidable but he could get a similar weapon from Eastern European sources. If they provided him with $100,000 expense money, he would look into the prospect and report back to them. He estimated it would take ninety days. During the trip in Europe, he learned numerous Russian arms available on the arms market included the sought-after shoulder-held, surface-to-air missile or SAM. Inquiries brought him face-to-face with Mikhail Borichov of Varna, Bulgaria. He collected vital information on missile capability, availability and prices.

Carlos returned and briefed all of the interested parties in Medellin. He stated the weapons would cost around $15 to $20 million U.S. dollars. The price took into account the expense necessary to covertly transport the weapons from Europe to Columbia. In May, he was authorized to pursue the purchase and a commitment was made to provide him with an initial $500,000 to transact the business. Carlos's first priority was to acquire insurance protection from any potential Borichov treachery. He remembered James Factor, an American arms dealer he had briefly encountered during an arms show. He was certain Factor would be attending the upcoming Paris Air Show and decided to enlist his help with an enticing proposition.

He lit up another cigarette oblivious to the cold wind, salty mist and throbbing hands. God, what a fool he'd been. Jim Factor was brought in and within months of the Paris Air Show, the three of them had developed a bold scheme. He had kept the secret of his customer's identity from them but they had seen evidence of the money behind him. Borichov orchestrated the events in Europe with Factor identifying risks and recommending ways of circumventing discovery. Then, in December, Jim decided he had gone far enough and bowed out. As far as Carlos was concerned, Jim had earned the money he was paid. Between Borichov and himself, they implemented the details of the plan over the next four months. The money from the cartel had been successfully routed through a front company to an overseas, offshore bank in the Isle of Man where it had been rewired to Borichov's bank account in Lithuania.

He had continued to operate out of his Tampa, Florida office. Cell phones and phone cards handled overseas calls. One day in March, he received a visitor who inquired about getting electroshock weapons and stun guns prohibited from export by U.S. regulations into an unspecified country. Against Jim's admonition about the potential pitfalls of illegitimate activities in the U.S., he accepted a retainer and promised an answer in a week. It never occurred to him to check out the authenticity of the request. He should have thrown the guy out of his office. What's the expression? When you're out hunting bear, you don't stop to chase rabbits. He had been repeatedly warned about the devious U.S. Customs Service. His office had been bugged, then searched and his financial transactions with Borichov uncovered. If it hadn't been for a drunken binge with one of the local girls in Orlando, he would be languishing in jail right now. He had barely spotted the stakeout at his home and kept going. When he contacted Borichov to warn him their scheme had been compromised. Borichov instantly assumed Factor had talked and turned them in. In an outburst laced with profanities, he vowed he would get a hit squad to kill him. Sengretti hung up with a cold sweat. If Borichov ever found out it was his fault, he'd be the dead man. He had to protect himself but Jim had been an okay guy. In a rare moment of guilt and conscience, he called his satellite phone number and warned him.

He kept a locker in a Tampa storage area especially for such an emergency. After a taxi dropped him off, he went to the locker and removed clothes, money and a counterfeit passport. He took a cab to the train station and left for Miami. Upon his arrival, he took a taxi to the waterfront. He perused the Shipping News for a freighter leaving within twenty-four hours for South America. It was a simple matter after that to locate the captain and strike a bargain. He had considered notifying the cartel of the loss of their money and cargo. You could bet they were going to ask, more likely insist, he meet with them. He knew they'd assume he lined his pockets with their money. Their methods of extracting information and dealing with disappointment and failure were a matter of record. He had witnessed the horrific brutality growing up. He was not going to take a chance on being found, not by the cartel and not by Borichov.

Chapter Nine

NEW DAY, NEW PLACE

Wednesday, May 8
San Francisco, California

Daylight and sounds emanating into the room from the slightly opened window awakened Jim. He glanced, without moving, at the bedside clock. He had slept for over twelve hours. The door was still locked and his bag was where he left it. He undressed and put his few clothes away before he went to the bathroom for a shower. He decided against shaving and used the contents of the makeup kit to plant some gray in his hair. A short haircut would help. He put on a pair of jeans, shirt and sneakers. The casual clothes he wore from home were stored in the closet and the dresser.

There was the problem of where to hide the money. Renting a safe deposit box at a bank without proper documentation was out of the question. The room would be cleaned on a regular basis and besides there didn't seem to be any places large enough to conceal the cash. When Jim had turned off the light, he noticed it was an older oversized fixture. He pulled the chair up underneath, stood carefully on it and unscrewed the glass dome over two light bulbs. He then unscrewed the light bulb assembly and let it hang by the wires. There was a gap inside the ceiling surrounding the assembly. After confirming the area did not get overheated from the burning light, he arranged the cash inside the ceiling but away from the opening. He reassembled the light and sat on the edge of the bed. He needed to come up with a plausible background and reason for his appearance in San Francisco. After considering several explanations, he decided he would admit reluctantly having been released from prison for a minor offense and a preference not to dwell on it. This would also account for his reluctance to get personal, lack of trade skills, and choice of part time and low paying jobs. He put on his windbreaker and went downstairs to explore the house. A lack of curiosity on his part about the home and its inhabitants might raise unwanted attention and draw suspicion.

Marie Queterras heard the footsteps on the stairs and walked over to greet him. "Good morning, Mr. Germain. Everyone has already gone to work but they're usually home by six." She continued as if anticipating his question. "My husband Joe works for a contractor and my son Jimmy is an engine mechanic. He even has his own garage." She paused, waiting for him to volunteer his situation.

"Please call me Nick. I've recently been released from prison for a stupid mistake and I'd rather put it behind me." He added politely and in a sincere tone. "If it creates a problem for you and your family, I'll leave and seek a room elsewhere."

She shook her head and sized him up. Finally, she responded. "Don't worry about it. I'll make sure my family knows it's a sensitive subject so they don't pester you."

Thanking her, Jim turned and went out the door to the street. In the daylight, he could see it was a working class neighborhood with sounds of traffic and scattered barking dogs. There was a concrete driveway alongside of the house that led to the rear garage. He sensed rather than saw the alley behind the house. He noted the wooden fence on two sides along with the garage and the house framed the backyard. The lawn was freshly mown and trimmed. The centerpiece in the backyard was a large leafy tree. An outdoor table with four chairs rested on a concrete slab underneath a patio overhang alongside a barbecue. The house was old but well maintained. A stroll down the block revealed the condition of the rest of the homes similarly reflected a pride of ownership. He continued walking and passed by several retail stores. He went into a gas station with a local map on the wall for lost motorists. Jim determined he was about five miles southwest of a marina next to Fisherman's Wharf. The map showed it was accessible by a nearby bus line. He decided tomorrow he would spend the day there. Tonight though, at the dinner table, he'd inquire about the marina from the men.

He stopped at a small neighborhood department store. He went in and slowly perused the aisles. He purchased a plain waterproof watch, an inexpensive wallet and a pullover sweatshirt. Outside, Jim remembered a laundromat on his walk and on an impulse returned to it. He entered and looked for the traditional bulletin board, a staple for small business and sales advertisements. He thought, It's time to prepare for my future course of action. He harbored no doubts his running would be temporary. However he had to acquire the skills to survive and more, to strike back. He quickly found something of interest, Spanish and English tutoring. His gaze wandered to a circular on self-defense courses taught in small groups at a local martial arts studio. He made a judgement; I'm going to need six months.

He exited and continued to explore the neighborhood around the Queterras house for the rest of the day. Two blocks away, he found another place of interest, a barbershop. He sat down on an empty chair and motioned short with his hand. Afterward, when he looked in the mirror, he saw an unfamiliar sight and forced a smile. He hadn't worn a crew cut since the Air Force. Toward late afternoon, he started thinking about dinner and his first encounter that evening with the entire Queterras family.

As Jim approached the dining table, Marie took his arm and brought him to her husband and son. She introduced him as Mr. Nicolas Germain. He requested they call him Nick. Joe Queterras was a large man with brown weathered skin and broad shoulders, black curly hair, large callused hands and a ready grin. Jimmy appeared to be in his early thirties and as tall as his father but leaner and more wiry with strong hands and evidence of grease under his fingernails. Both men had washed and changed into clean jeans and short sleeve shirts. Jim was treated friendly as they passed the dinner dishes.

As they ate, Joe turned to Jim and volunteered, "I'm foreman of a commercial construction crew for one of the largest development companies in the city. There are usually five or six projects going on at a time. Mine is a five-story apartment house about ten miles from here."

Jimmy put his fork down and added, "I have a garage a few miles from here with two employees. We specialize in piston and diesel engine overhauls and repairs."

Thankfully, or more than likely because of a word from Marie, no one asked him any personal questions. As the dinner was completed, Jim informed them, "I'm new in town and looking for a job. I've been told marinas are a good source of part-time work."

"Well, Nick," Jimmy replied, "You're in luck. My garage has done a few marine engine overhauls and repairs for the Pier 39 Marina dry dock company. If you like, I'll be happy to run you over tomorrow to meet the manager on my way to the garage."

That night as he lay in bed, Jim thought about Diane and her reaction to his disappearance. He had deliberately left his things out in the study so she wouldn't think anything was amiss except he had to hastily go out of town. It had happened before. She was a head-strong woman and he needed to buy time before she became suspicious or took any action. To take his mind off Diane he recalled his business meeting two days before Sengretti's phone call.

Chapter Ten

THE RECENT PAST

Monday, May 6
Kuwait

The small elevated windows on one side of the room resonated in their frames from the vibration caused by the unmuffled roar from a Kuwaiti Hornet F/A-18C fighter as it accelerated down the runway adjacent to the headquarter building. It drowned out the sounds of the viewgraph presentation on the airborne electrooptical pod offered by Jim Factor's client, Northrop Grumman. The briefing was being held in the Royal Kuwaiti Air Force Commander's conference room at the Ali Al Salem Air Force Base co-located with the Kuwait International Airport but on the opposite side in a large secured area. The headquarters was in one of the large single-story buildings with cinder block construction and plain white walls. The military buildings contrasted sharply from the modern multi-storied civilian airport terminal across the runway. The interior of those walls were punctuated with pictures of Kuwait's royal family and Air Force fighter aircraft from a number of other nations. In one corner of the room, the Kuwaiti flag stood upright in its stand. Although it was mid-spring the outside temperature was well over one hundred-ten degrees even this late in the evening but the efficient air conditioning kept the room at a comfortable level.

Jim absentmindedly fingered his Kuwait Air Force Base visitor's picture badge hanging on his suit breast pocket while listening to the assembled uniformed Air Force representatives discuss the pod in Arabic. He was the only one in the room wearing a suit. They all spoke excellent English but preferred to revert to Arabic for the deliberations. He was on personal terms with Brig.

Saber M. Al Suwaiden, the Air Force Commander, BG Faleh Abdullah Al Shatti, Assistant Chief of Staff for Operations and Col. Farid Al Anzi, Aircraft Maintenance. He observed his Kuwaiti partner and friend, Ahmad Al Matawa, wearing the native white dishdasha, listening attentively to the discussions and interjecting an occasional comment. Ahmad, in keeping with the upper-level Middle East custom of sending their youth abroad, obtained his primary and college education at Oxford in England and spoke with an acquired British accent. Jim was marketing airborne navigation and reconnaissance pods for forty Boeing F/A-18C/D's in the Royal Kuwait Air Force inventory. He was aware that English and French contractors were also vying for the lucrative contract.

Ahmad turned and held up his hand to get Jim's attention. "Mr. Factor. A question has come up about using the pod for ground targeting in conjunction with airborne laser-guided weapons."

God damn it, here we go again. Both he and Ahmad had gone over this issue and its ramifications many times over the past two days. The U.S. State Department had repeatedly rejected offering this advanced technical capability of the pod. It had less to do with trusting Kuwait than their concern the technology would be compromised to neighboring Iran through porous security. It was a bullshit excuse. The real reason for the denial was the U.S. Air Force, under pressure from Northrop Grumman, wanted to keep it out of the hands of the competition as long as possible. It was a misguided strategy since both the English and French offered the additional capability to some degree. Anticipating the inquiry, they had agreed on a tactic to skirt the problem.

Jim replied softly as if reluctant to divulge a potential workaround solution to the U.S. embargo. "The laser targeting feature, as you are aware, is an option not available for export at this time." He saw them shift in their seats with frustration and annoyance. He paused for effect then added. "However, it could be retro-fitted later on. The pod has the potential to be modified for the function providing unmatched performance with any on the market." He continued in a low voice. "We would have to talk further about this possibility off-line from this meeting."

Ahmad turned to the Air Force officials and expanded on this explanation in Arabic. Jim knew they understood his English reply but Ahmad was giving them some extra material relating to their question. They nodded in agreement and looked up. The Air Force group's spokesman addressed him. "Mr. Factor. We have the information we need and will evaluate the pod during the coming week. We shall include Mr. Ahmad Al Matawa for his insights. Thank you for your exacting presentation. The fact Northrop Grumman is a major contractor of the F/A-18 Hornet aircraft weighs heavily in your client's favor. We will await the clarification on the obtainability of the advanced capability."

Jim quickly interpreted the response. Damn. It's their way of telling me the English and French would include targeting in their versions. He nodded his head to show he understood the unspoken message. "Thank you for your time today and I look forward to answering any questions you may have through Mr. Al Matawa."

As the meeting broke up, Jim gathered the viewgraphs and notebook computer and placed them in his briefcase. On the way out of the room, he gave an imperceptible nod to Ahmad that implied they would talk in the car. They walked under the glare of brightly lit lights. He could see the unfilled bullet holes in the walls, a poignant reminder of the Iraqi invasion in August 1991. As they walked towards the visitor's carport to get Ahmad's car, he glanced at his watch. It was almost eleven at night. By Middle East standards, this time was part of the business acumen due to the afternoon hiatus because of the intense heat of the day.

They exited the Air Force base in silence. Once on the highway, he frowned as he asked. "Ahmed, are they really serious about wanting the laser targeting option for the pod? Even if they got it, what in the hell would they use it for?"

Ahmad cleared his throat and lit a cigarette before replying. Jim, used to this pattern of deliberateness, patiently waited. Ahmad shrugged and replied after a moment. "I would say it was a clear statement they want the feature. The Europeans have offered it to them. It's like the Jones' next door has it and they want it too. It doesn't matter they may not need it. And my friend, they know they can arm twist because the English and French are chomping at the bit to sell them a complete pod system."

He paused with a sly smile. "Jim, they know you have the technical knowledge to direct the development and installation of a modification. We could tell them we would provide the upgrade if they purchased the pod. I dare say they'd pay extra for the retrofit just to have it."

Jim shook his head and answered with a touch of irritation. "Our arguments on cost-effectiveness, size, and operational simplicity should have gone a long way. We could promote a condensed delivery schedule but we know goddamn well their budget approval cycle will eat up the time anyway." He looked outside and reflected. "Shit. If we could lick this obstacle I figure they'd acquire twenty of them for half their F/A-18 fleet. The training, spares and upgrades could bring the total amount to over $50 million."

Ahmad thought a moment. "Out of curiosity my friend, how much and how long do you estimate it would take to develop this modification for the pod?"

Jim considered the question. "To start with, it would have to be done in another country to avoid a conflict with U.S. export laws. There is certainly precedent for things like this being done by foreign powers. The Japanese helped Iran get the appropriate parts and maintenance for the Grumman F-14 Tomcats left there when the Shah was overthrown. The expertise can also be found in Germany, Italy and Sweden. The Pacific Rim may not be such a bad location for shielding the project and keeping the cost down. It would isolate and protect our involvement. My guess is the development and testing could be within a year and would cost around $500,000; producing twenty kits at $50,000 each would add another million."

Ahmad rapidly made a calculation. "I would say it amounts to an extra $100,000 per pod."

"I make it at $75,000." Jim suddenly grinned. "Oh I see; our commission. It's not a bad return considering it would be around $2,000,000. Of course, they'd have to award a modification kit contract as soon as possible with at least one-half down. They'd be committed with the advance payment." He shrugged. "Anyway, it's a moot point. I doubt they would do it."

Ahmad turned towards him with an ironic smile. "If they want the targeting, nothing would stop them. You know how they favor U.S. military products. Besides we have an edge because of our good friends on the Air Force committee. Let me get their feeling on it this week."

The large silver Lincoln Town Car with Ahmad at the wheel came to a stop in front of a barricade framed by police cars and Humvees with flashing red lights. Soldiers stood in the shadows with weapons trained on the two occupants. Ahmad lowered his window and spoke in Arabic to the Royal Kuwaiti Army sergeant who had approached the car. He switched to English and pointed at his passenger. Jim handed over his American passport and Ahmad showed his driver's license. He explained. "We're heading for the airport." The army man returned the ID and motioned them on. The barricade swung open and the Lincoln went through.

Jim noted. "These stops used to be rare."

Ahmad agreed. "Sadly, everything has changed since your 9/11."

The car's air conditioning quietly blew at full strength and managed to keep the car at a comfortable temperature even though the outside temperature was still above one hundred degrees at one o'clock in the morning. Powdery white sand swirled across the straight modern concrete highway illuminated by the evenly spaced overhead halogen streetlights. There was a minimum amount of traffic bound for the Kuwait International Airport. Ahmad Al Matawa had been his contact, representative and friend since they met at the end of the seven-year Iran-Iraq conflict in 1987. Ahmad's appearance belied his keen intelligence and the immense wealth of his family. Outside of the window Jim could see the intermittent contemporary-shaped water towers that were part of the landscape. He appreciated the Kuwaiti nights when there was hardly any traffic. The prohibition on liquor sales kept the populace home at night instead of in restaurants in order to drink their illicit alcohol. He had adjusted easily to the region's late dinner hour custom of anytime between ten and midnight.

Jim leaned back in his seat. "Ahmad. We'll need to follow up with Colonel Farid. You can bet our competition will hear about tonight's meeting and its outcome. I assume we'll be played off against them as usual?"

Ahmad nodded his agreement. "I'll host a small dinner for the appropriate senior officers within the week. What should I tell them our position is on the targeting request?"

Jim hesitated. "Feel them out on the possibility of purchasing modification kits with the pods to accomplish their objectives. Meanwhile I'll give some thought how it could get done. I'm scheduled to meet with a couple of our European clients next week to review some of their new military products." As an afterthought he asked, "Just out of curiosity Ahmed, what do you think the chances are they'd go for a separate funding line for the kits if they ordered the pods?"

Ahmad pondered the posssibility. He looked carefully at Jim before answering. "It could be as high as forty percent."

Jim gasped in surprise tinged with a sense of apprehensiveness. "You've got to be kidding." He checked the dash clock as if to put the possibility behind him. The British Airways flight to London was scheduled to leave in slightly more than two hours. All European bound flights from Kuwait left around two in the morning resulting in arrival times in major European cities from early to mid-morning. Within ninety minutes of landing at Heathrow, he would be in the air to Los Angeles. He closed his eyes and relaxed. Once on the plane, he would reset his watch to London time and take a nap. He was looking forward to getting home to Diane.

Ahmad pulled the car over to the terminal's departure curb and motioned to a porter to collect Jim's suitcase from the trunk. They walked into the terminal. Ahmad took him around the customs line directly to the passport control office where he was quickly waved through. They shook hands.

"Let me know if anything else comes up, especially on the option."

Ahmad smiled and bowed. "You can be sure I will call right away."

The business class lounge was in the main terminal. Jim entered and gave his ticket to the reception hostess. She verified his seat and gave him a boarding pass. He went to the bar, got a bottle of water and sat in one of the oversized chairs. He'd have to wait until his flight left Kuwait when he would be served a drink on the aircraft. Businessmen from all nationalities started to filter into the lounge to await their flights. He pulled a paperback novel from his briefcase to avoid being drawn into a conversation. As he turned the pages he thought about the consequences of his offer to provide a way around the U.S. export control restrictions of the pod's functions. God, he almost wished the Kuwaiti Air Force would reject the proposal even though it would also doom any chance of selling them the electro-optical pod. What in the hell had got into him? Come on, who was he kidding? The money would be more than ample. Eighteen months ago he would have expressed a take it or leave it attitude. With trepidation, he knew it stemmed from his past dealings with Sengretti and Borichov. He told himself to forget it. After all, he had made a nice tax-free amount from legitimate consulting on the perils of illicit arms transactions. Well, maybe not that legitimate because he had been involved in the preliminary planning for an illegal arms sale and subsequent smuggling. He congratulated himself for quitting while he was ahead. Anyhow, it was behind him and buried in the past. These thoughts vanished when his flight was called and he left for the boarding gate.

It was early evening the same day and many hours later when Jim gathered his suitcase and computer bag from the taxi and took in his house with a fond and eager expression. The front slope of the hillside on the other side of the street afforded his cherished privacy. The tri-level home with its enclosed courtyard gave the entrance a Mediterranean atmosphere. He walked to the front gate and rang the doorbell. He gave a chortle when his wife's voice came through the intercom.

"Who is it?"

He replied with a grin. "A man with a package."

"Go away," came the reply, "before I release the dogs."

He laughed as the gate was buzzed unlocked. The front door opened and his wife looked out. An apron covered a tall slender woman with reddish hair wearing a red chiffon dress and heels. They clung to each other for a time and went inside.

Wednesday Night, May 8
San Francisco, California

Jim wiped the tears from his eyes at the recollection. He wondered how long it would take Borichov to send someone after him; probably very soon. He was always quick on action and short on patience. Jim had to keep himself busy both mentally and physically to maintain his isolation, sanity and safety. It was a matter of being patient and systematically working at all aspects of his new persona. He never took anything lying down and he wasn't about to start. Preparation was the key element of his future actions. He found himself looking forward to the next day's trip to the marina. He felt it might provide Nick Germain with the direction which could affect his future. Still thinking about his near term plans, he closed his eyes and peacefully went to sleep.

Chapter Eleven

A START FOR EVERYONE

Thursday, May 9

As Nick Germain, Jim was up early and went downstairs to the kitchen for coffee where he found Jimmy sitting at the table. Joe had left an hour earlier for his construction site. The cloudy day contained an early morning chill as Jimmy drove down Market Street towards the Embarcadero for about thirty minutes before they arrived at the Pier 39 Marina. He went into a parking garage across the street.

They walked crossed the trolley tracks to the sidewalk which ran along the dark green water. Jim looked out at the frigid waters of San Francisco Bay. As they approached the marina, he spied white sails unfurling against the backdrop of the gray mist. Seagulls rode the light breeze and called to each other as they neared the opened entrance of the marina. An aquarium with its colorful displays beckoned to the passing visitors. Clustered throughout the complex were restaurants, fishermen's cafes, specialty stores, food shops and bars. There were two and three levels of businesses in the large central complex. On the eastside of the marina were boat docks. Jim noticed the docks were designated by letter in increasing order in direction from the shore out to the open water.

The Pier 39 Marina was geographically situated on the San Francisco waterfront between the San Francisco to Oakland Bay Bridge and the Golden Gate Bridge and faced north into San Francisco Bay. In a north-westerly direction slightly more than a mile into the bay, Jim could barely see the outline of the infamous Alcatraz Island through the fog. He involuntarily shuddered as he thought it would be anything but a casual swim with the treacherous currents and the fifty-five degree water temperature. Three miles west of the marina, he could see the two majestic towers of the Golden Gate Bridge seemingly floating on top of a cushion of fog extending into the bay. He heard an intermittent foghorn. Mixed in with the sounds, was the incessant honking of sea lions as they lounged on the jetty rocks to the west of the marina. The marina enjoyed a favorable location with its proximity to the nearby scenic Fisherman's Wharf, Telegraph Hill and Embarcadero.

Jimmy led the way to the Halyard Boat Company where he introduced Jim to Mike Sweeney, the manager. Sweeney was a stocky man in his late forties with windblown hair, swarthy skin and casually dressed in a pair of blue cotton slacks with a light yellow shirt with rolled up sleeves. They shook hands and Jimmy explained the reason for the visit.

"Sorry Nick, right now there's nothing available here but the boat owners are always looking for help with odd jobs at the spur of the moment. They may call me or Charlie Ford at the Dockside Marine Hardware store right on the pier. Check with him too. Leave your phone number with me in case anything comes up."

Jim thanked him and they walked outside. "Jimmy. Thanks for taking the time and for the introduction. I think I'll stay and look around." He assured him, "I'll take the bus back and see you tonight."

Jim walked down the pier to Dockside Marine Hardware. The front windows displayed all types of brass nautical accessories for boats and yachts. He entered and asked for Charlie Ford. A young salesman pointed to an older man talking to a customer. Jim wandered into the electronics area and inspected the various navigation systems. As he was reading the application sheets, he heard a voice behind him.

"Can I help you?"

The owner of the question had white hair, a large white mustache, dark rim reading glasses at the bridge of his nose, a pair of jeans and a white shirt with pencil and pen in the breast pocket.

Jim asked. "Charlie Ford?"

"Yep, that's me. How can I help you?"

"I'm Nick Germain. I was at Halyard's earlier asking about odd jobs in the marina and Mike Sweeney suggested I stop by your store and talk to you too."

Ford replied. "We frequently get boat owners asking about assistance with their boat. Leave your phone number and I'll call if something comes up."

Jim gave him the Queterras' phone number and thanked him.

The sun broke through the overcast as Jim went to take a closer look at the boat dock area. He noted the cardkey-locked gates at every lettered dock designed to keep out unauthorized visitors. While staring at the boats, a man carrying a large carton walked up to the gate. He stumbled and dropped his cardkey. Jim was close enough to put out a hand to steady him and picked up the cardkey. He slipped it in the slot and the gate opened. He held out the card. The man took it and smiled appreciably. "Glad you happened by when you did. Thanks." He held the gate open for Jim who slipped in.

Jim slowly shuffled along the F dock on planked walkways that hosted the slips, moorings and utilities to the boat owners. He was instantly caught up in the variety of shapes and sizes of the boats. He had never really paid attention to boats and was enthralled by the contours and streamlining generated with fiberglass and plastics. Absorbed, he almost didn't hear the shout from the bridge of an impressive fifty-seven-foot Viking cruiser. Glancing up he saw a distinguished looking man with pepper gray wavy hair wearing a pullover, Bermuda shorts, and cap beckon to him.

"Hey friend, can you give me a hand?"

Jim climbed the short boarding ladder to the large aft deck. He observed the poser of the question was in his early fifties, trim and bronzed from the sun. He had a confident manner about him and stuck out his hand.

"I'm Wayne Collier and you are?"

"Nick, Nick Germain, How can I help you?"

Collier asked if he knew anything about marine electronics to which Jim answered hesitantly. "Not much."

Collier laughed. "I'm still learning myself." He turned serious. "Here's my problem, Nick. I want to take the boat out for a few days but the new radar and navigation system is throwing me." He pointed to the wood paneled console containing an impressive array of illuminated instruments on the right side of the bridge. Dual chrome throttle controls were positioned to the right of a stylish steering wheel. A ten-inch CRT display was mounted on the left side. "Think you can figure it out from the manual?"

Jim instinctively replied. "I'll take a crack at it. If I can't, you don't owe me a fee."

Collier laughed easily again. "That's rich. I get a no-charge guarantee from a maintenance man. Okay, Nick, you're on. Here's the manual."

Jim sat down in the captain's seat and positioned the manual in front of the radar and navigational color display and controls. He silently reflected that, compared to complicated weapon systems operational manuals, this one was relatively simple. He had to be careful not to let on he was as much interested in the technical aspects of the system as its operation. He followed the steps outlined for setting up and calibrating the system, then went out of the bridge to the antenna installation on the roof. The manual recommended more height separation to avoid multipath interference with the boat's structure. He could see the GPS antenna to the right and slightly above the radar antenna. He followed the microwave line from the antenna housing and the GPS antenna down to the inside of the bridge and the rear of the console. Satisfied the cables were connected properly, he turned on the system. The display had a color LCD.

The operational manual was straightforward and graphically illustrated. The X-band radar had a thirty-six nautical mile maximum range limited by the line-of-sight or LOS. The system permitted a navigational map overlay called a chart plotter on the display. A short search produced a box of chart cards labeled with the corresponding index. Jim pulled out the Northern California coast chart and inserted it into the bottom right slot built into the display. The GPS receiver downloaded the marina coordinates and in moments the coastal area was superimposed on the radar display. The radar return for the coast neatly superimposed the map overlay. The movement of the boat and the map coincided to present a clear picture to the pilot.

Jim called Wayne Collier over to the radar/chart plotter display and went through the capability and the operational procedure. He mentioned the radar antenna height recommendation.

"That's a nice job of figuring it out and explaining it. How much do you want for the time you spent?" Collier asked.

Jim shook his head. "I spent less than an hour and besides, it was interesting."

Collier inspected him closely. "You're a terrible businessman but I like you. Tell you what. I have a law firm in the city and generally take clients for a cruise. Join my party on the boat Saturday morning as my guest and let's check out the system together when we're in the bay. I'll pay you $200 for the day but I also expect you to mingle and have a good time."

Jim agreed and left the boat.

After supper, Jim went to his room and turned on the radio. He was interested in the news even though he knew his disappearance would hardly create a stir. The Queterras' house was as safe a haven as he could have hoped for. He decided to buy a small TV with an earphone attachment so his interests in programs would go unnoticed. He thought about his interaction with Wayne Collier during the day. The interface with the marine electronics interested him more than he would have imagined. He was already looking forward to the cruise on Saturday. Tomorrow, he'd drop by a department store and purchase appropriate clothing. The casual ones he fled with were too expensive looking.

Newport Beach, California

In a neighboring city, Sergey and Petra located a carpet cleaning service with a number of trucks and vans in an opened rear parking area. They figured a truck wouldn't be noticed missing right away and time was what they needed. Petra hotwired the van and drove it away noting coveralls inside the interior. Sergey followed closely in their car. Petra parked the van in the lot of an allnight market and climbed into the car. Sergey told him. "Tomorrow morning I'll call Factor's house and try to catch them out. We'll transfer the equipment to the van and go if no one answers."

Friday, May 10

When Sergey called, an answering machine responded on the third ring. He hung up the phone and pointed to the door. "Let's go."

He parked the carpet cleaning van in the Factor driveway and watched Petra with his satchel go around the side of the house. The wiretap was best placed on the line entering the house rather than the old way of placing bugs on the phone receivers.

In less than three minutes Petra walked back to the van and placed his satchel on the seat. He put on a set of headphones and dialed the Factor telephone number. "Okay, it's working."

Surgery pulled out and went back to the market's parking lot where they abandoned the van and drove to the motel.

Chapter Twelve

MARINA. BUSINESS

Saturday, May11
San Francisco, California

Jim managed to time his entrance at the gate with the other guests. When he arrived at the dock slip, Wayne Collier greeted him and introduced his wife Jeanne and their guests. Jeanne Collier was a striking blonde who wore a nautical blouse and white shorts revealing a trim athletic figure and deep tan. Her energized conversation held sway over the guests who were a combination of businessmen and friends. The interior of the yacht held three wellappointed staterooms and a galley. It featured wood-grain cabinetry in genuine teak and holly flooring. An LCD flat screen TV, DVD player and surround-sound system provided entertainment. A cook worked in the galley staffed with a two-burner electric cooktop, a convection oven and microwave. The salon lounge focus was a wrap-around sofa with color-coordinated throw pillows which encircled an adjustable marble top coffee table.

Minimizing his interactions with the guests to avoid personal questions, Jim spent most of the cruise on the bridge. The system operation was flawless but on successive radar scans it was evident dead zones occurred due to structural ground plane interference. Collier came to his side with two of the guests and described the system capability in surprising clear detail. He gave Jim the credit for his education. Later in the day, one of the guests asked Jim for his contact information.

At the end when the guests had departed, Collier approached Jim. "Here's the $200. By the way, I thought you looked comfortable talking with the guests. I know they enjoyed you."

Jim replied carefully. "Thanks, Mr. Collier. They're nice people. Mr. Wallsky asked me for my phone number."

"Bob Wallsky has a smaller boat here at the marina. Perhaps he needs a little work done on it."

"One other thing; I noticed the rooftop antenna installation does generate a degrading effect on the radar's performance. You should consider getting it raised when you have a chance."

"Nick, How about personally seeing it gets modified? I have open accounts at Halyard and Dockside Marine. I'm leaving town for several days and it'll be sitting here. You'll need a pass to work on it. I'll stop by the Harbor Master's office and leave your name."

Jim agreed and gave his goodbyes. As he strolled away, he felt a little envy. These people had achieved a successful career without fear of reprisals. He wondered if he would ever regain his old life again. He lost everything because he let his greed override his good sense. It felt good mingling with Collier's guests and operating the electronics. He looked forward to seeing what he had to do to change the antenna's position.

Monday, May 13

Jim arrived at the marina and went straight to the Harbor Master's office to register for a dock pass. The receptionist asked him for his name and ID. Flustered by the question, he hastily explained. "I'm Nick Germain. I lost my wallet a couple of days ago with my entire ID." He pulled out his recently purchased wallet to illustrate his statement.

The lady in a sympathetic tone assured him. "That's okay. Mr. Collier vouched for you. Please sign here for your cardkey and pass."

Jim signed and accepted the items.

Jim had already determined the radome assembly alteration had to be performed by people familiar with the nuances of fiberglass structures. He decided to talk to Mike Sweeney who was surprised to see him so soon. He related his encounter with Wayne Collier and the required change in the yacht's antenna installation.

Sweeney sent George Volmer, a boat carpenter, with him to obtain the necessary modification information. As they climbed on the roof of the bridge, Jim judged that a twelve inch platform mounted above the roof would allow the antenna microwave beam to freely pass over the boat without obstruction. Volmer stated it could be built out of fiberglass and painted within a few days. The existing holes would be filled and painted at the same time. Jim emphasized he wanted the entire assembly and installation to be undistinguishable in appearance. Volmer nodded his agreement and left. Jim took the additional connector length dimension to Charlie Ford to order new cables.

These tasks accomplished, Jim had another important element in his strategy to address; he left the marina and took a cab close to the address listed on the Spanish tutoring card. The man who answered the door had a slight build, glasses, thin mustache, and an articulate manner. He gave his name as James Ortega and revealed he was a local high school music teacher who gave language lessons on the side. Jim was informed the lessons would cost $10 an hour. He asked if Jim spoke any Spanish at all and was told some brief conversational phrases. Depending on his school schedule which normally kept him busy in the morning to mid-afternoon, Ortega agreed Jim could take lessons at his convenience with an advance phone call.

Sweeney called him after a few days to tell him the antenna platform was finished and ready for installation. Jim stopped by Dockside Marine to pick up the new cables and met the carpenter at Collier's boat. Between the two of them, the antenna housing and cables were installed and the holes professionally filled and painted. Jim turned on the radar and noted with satisfaction the bothersome blind zones were gone and the radar returns were sharper. He called Collier's office number and left a message with his secretary. When Collier returned and visited his boat, he looked at the job and noted with satisfaction the quality of the modification and the radar's performance enhancement. Jim was chagrinned and secretly pleased to get $150 for what he perceived as a simple task. More importantly, he learned a little about marine electronics and modifying boat structures. It appeared he could maintain his cover while learning a little tradecraft.

Chapter Thirteen

ANXIETY FOR ALL

Monday, May 13
Newport Beach, Caliornia

A week had passed and Diane still had not heard from Jim. She became concerned and went back to his study, searched his desk and turned towards the safe. She was surprised when she found it unlocked. She felt a little guilty but looked in. She saw the combination taped to the inside of the door. In it was his wallet, ring and watch. The wallet had his IDs and credit cards but no money. She looked through the papers, took the combination and locked the safe. All of this was strange. It was obvious Jim left on purpose but where and why. Although it was like Jim to keep business matters from her, it was unlike him not to call or send an e-mail to let her know he was fine from wherever he traveled. If she hadn't heard anything by tomorrow, she would go to the police.

Tuesday, May 14

Diane described the events of the preceding week including her discoveries in the safe. No, she had not seen any signs of a struggle. Sergeant Todd Green-well from the Newport Beach Police Department had arrived on the scene as a follow up to her visit to their station. He was sympathetic and thorough inquiring about marital problems, money issues, failing business, and health concerns. Diane had to laugh however painful the questions seemed because their parents, relatives and friends would probably ask the same things in a more delicate manner. She could not tell if and how much money was missing from the safe. His business papers were kept under lock in file cabinets in the study. Jim had the only combination because of his business dealings. She inventoried his clothes closet and drawers but wasn't able to determine what was missing. She gave him photographs of her husband.

At the same time the investigating officer was at the Factor residence, Sergey and Petra were getting ready to pose as utility men to gain access to the house and perform a complete search. As was their habit, they used a phone card to call the house to make sure no one was there. On the second ring, a woman answered. Sergey heard some sounds in the background.

He asked. "Is Mr. Factor in?"

He was shaken when a male voice with an authoritative air came on the line and asked who it was. Sergey hung up and stared at Petra.

"We got trouble," was all he could say. Their easy job just got complicated.

Within days the NBPD ran a check with U.S. Customs Service and found Jim's passport had not been used since he arrived back in the U.S. the day before vanished. At the same time credit card records showed no recent transactions. He had not appeared on airline passenger lists. Taxi companies had no record of picking up anyone either at the house or in town fitting his description. Sergeant Greenwell's check of hospitals and the morgue came up empty. The Factors' bank accounts revealed no withdrawals or cashed checks for over two weeks prior to his disappearance. Greenwell examined phone logs and Jim's computers for clues into his whereabouts but without success.

Chapter Fourteen

ANOTHER MARINA JOB

Thursday, May 16
San Francisco, California

As Jim was leaving, Marie Queterras informed him he had received an earlier call from Bob Wallsky asking him to phone. Jim called back and a meeting was set at Wallsky's boat later in the morning.

Bob Wallsky was a slightly portly man with a contagious smile. He wore a tee-shirt, cargo shorts, sockless loafers and sunglasses. He escorted Jim up the gangplank to the aft deck of a cabin cruiser smaller than Collier's. However, whereas Collier's boat was for pleasurable use, it was obvious Wallsky's passion was fishing.

Wallsky confided. "Your attitude and the results with the electronics impressed Wayne. He thinks you have a lot on the ball and he's a good judge of people. My boat's a thirty-one-foot Pursuit, specially equipped with Lee outriggers, marlin tower with controls, rod holders, pulpit, sixty-five-gallon bait tank, transom fish box, and extra fuel capacity. I take my investment clients out for fishing mixed in with a little business so I want them to catch something. I monitor the fishing fleet frequencies but I really need to get an edge by installing a good fish finder. I've talked to a few salesmen but I can't tell if they're peddling smoke. Do you think you can make sense of their products and advise me on it? I'll certainly pay you for your time."

"Mr. Wallsky, I'll research it. Let me have the literature they left."

Jim walked away troubled and wondering what he unexpectedly had gotten into. He felt uncomfortable about getting involved in a situation employing his technical knowledge. Perhaps he was too cautious because the tie-in was a reach. He shrugged off the uneasiness and headed for the marine hardware store.

Charlie Ford informed him fish finders are sonars with a plastic transom transducer. The transmitted signal keyed a timer that stopped upon the reception of a reflected signal. After evaluating several models, they decided a Furuno FCV667 was best suited to Wallsky's conditions. Jim had no idea of the cost Wallsky had in mind. In order to explain the selection process, Jim compared the various models in a table with cost as the last entry. At the bottom he inserted his recommendation. Satisfied, he set out to attend his first Spanish lesson.

Friday, May 17

Jim met Wallsky near the marina at the Bayfront Restaurant and gave him the table summarizing the evaluation of the applicable fish finders. "The cost on the best choice is $545 not including installation."

Wallsky concurred. "Nick. How about taking care of it? Make sure it's installed and running properly when it comes in. Use my accounts at Halyard and Dockside."

After the meeting, Jim was surprised Collier and Wallsky hadn't raised the issue of a fee. Well, after all, he was doing it for the education so he'd take what was offered. Frankly, he was intrigued by the level of sophistication and the amount of technology the marine systems had adopted from military counterparts and the eagerness of boat owners to acquire them. He ordered the fish finder from Charlie Ford. Then, he went to get another Spanish lesson and see about the self-defense course.

Newport Beach, California

By the end of the week Sergeant Greenwell called Diane Factor to say, lacking any indication of foul play, she should file a missing person report. Her husband's picture would be distributed to other law enforcement agencies.

After Greenwell's call, Diane went back into the study and sat in one of the armchairs. She felt Jim was in trouble and was tackling it the way he always did with everything, by himself. She regretted nothing about her marriage. She recalled their college days when he would prefer to study alone and hard, made few friends and did not mind the isolation. She attributed it to his youth and his parents' preoccupation with running their business. On the other hand, he admired her social skills and the many friends she had acquired and kept in touch with throughout the years. Jim appeared to others to be self-absorbed and uncomfortable with small talk and to a degree it was true. He was always good to her and their respective families and friends. He just kept to himself and avoided confiding in others. Diane rose from the chair and left the study closing the door unconsciously behind her. She went into the living room, pulled the window curtains closed, curled up on the sofa and cried herself to asleep.

Chapter Fifteen

SELF-DEFENSE

Friday, May 17
San Francisco, California

The self-defense class was located in a martial arts studio converted from a retail store. The front windows were papered to ensure inner privacy. Men and women, young and old entered and left the premises most often in white karate outfits with white sash belts. A sign advertised martial arts and self-defense, listing jujitsu, aikido and tae kwon do. Jim walked into an open room with wood floors and padded mats in three main areas separated by freestanding six-foot high screens decorated in white rice paper and with red Japanese characters. There were three small groups per area each with an instructor. One of the groups was listening to an instructor, the other were going through arm and leg movements.

The third group was breaking up and their instructor returned their bow before waving goodbye. He was the only one wearing the white two-piece outfit with a black belt. The other two instructors were wearing brown belts. The black belt was in his thirties, about six-feet tall with blond hair and a modest beard on a handsome if rugged face. He walked lightly like a dancer. He lacked large muscles but his arms showed definition like a wrapped steel cable. He approached Jim and inquired with a trace of humor. "Hello, big guy. How can we help you?"

"I saw your ad and it intrigued me. People always assume a tall man can take care of himself but I rather doubt it if I came across someone who knew what they were doing."

"True enough. My name is Chris Muncie. And you are?"

"Nick Germain."

"Well Nick, there's self-defense and then there is self-defense. We start teaching defensive tactics ranging from the use of non-lethal force to survival tactics. The method is based on instinctive movement, practical concepts and sound principles. This is coupled with the ability to develop skills from an individual's natural defensive and offensive movements. These skills are thoroughly enhanced through training scenarios against grabs, strikes, weapons and ground attack. Through the training scenarios, the individual is better prepared both physically and mentally to function during the pressure and distress of a violent attack."

Jim replied. "It sounds like what I'm looking for. Do you work with individuals or just groups?"

Chris looked at Jim more closely before he spoke. "I recommend you start with a group for the initial stages and then, depending on your development, we can advance to individual instruction."

Jim looked about the large room and pointed. "There are two harnesses at the end of the room hanging from the ceiling and on pegs to the side; what are they for?"

"It's an idea I came up with. The more advanced students use them to learn balance awareness while executing their moves against an opponent. The braces on the harnesses are rubber which allows up and down as well as side to side motion. At the beginning only the combatant has it on for their movements against the opponent. It's interesting because at first the non-harnessed opponent has the edge. Eventually, the harness becomes familiar and the wearer uses it to escape the opponent's thrust and parry back with speed and agility."

"It seems the wearer might adjust to being on his toes more to push off and keep balanced."

"Very good observation Nick. It's exactly what happens. We then take the wearer off to be the opponent and the other puts on the harness. When both have picked up on the nimbleness and movements it affords I put them both in the harnesses to go against each other. When they get too good at it, which doesn't take long, they go off of the harnesses and back to the mats. The results have been outstanding for accelerating their training and efficiency."

"I can see it would happen. It's a terrific concept."

"Tell you what; I'm finished for the evening. Let's grab a beer and I'll tell you more about the class."

* * *

As Jim and Chris walked down the block, Chris explained. "Beginning students are introduced to the fundamentals of the art. This consists of blocking, striking, rolling, falling, footwork and basic self-defense. Physical fitness, exercise and flexibility enhancement are a major part of the curriculum. Once confidence sets in, the student's mental attitude undergoes a transformation as well."

Jim asked. "What's that outfit you wear?"

"It's called the Do-Gi or just plain dogi. It comes in different weights depending on the individual's skill; lightweight for children and beginners, medium weight for tournaments and heavy weight for serious practitioners. The belt is an obi and the color designates the advancement and skill level of the wearer. The common colors are black, brown, green, purple, orange, blue, yellow and white. You'll see other forms of martial arts with other colors such as red, gold and silver."

Chris pointed to the entrance of the Foggy Bottom Bar. They entered and sat in a booth. A pretty waitress with a ponytail approached. She smiled at Chris. "Beers?"

Chris nodded and pointed to Jim. "Connie, meet Nick Germain. He's considering a karate class."

She examined Jim appreciably, "If anyone can teach you, it's Chris." She went back to the bar.

Chris smiled. "Connie enrolled at the studio a year ago and can now handle herself. As for me, I was a Navy Seal for over twelve years and decided I wanted to do something else. I got out and opened the studio. How about you?"

Jim carefully chose his words. "I'm fairly new in San Francisco. I just started doing boat jobs at the Pier 39 Marina and stay at a house not far from here." He caught Chris examining his hands and added. "The work deals with boat accessories like electronics as opposed to scraping barnacles. Before that, I spent a little time in prison." Jim thought it necessary to maintain the same background he gave the Queterras. To his relief, Chris changed the subject.

"Getting back to martial arts. Students learn proper training skills utilizing the five components of fitness; cardiovascular strength, flexibility, muscular strength, muscular endurance and body composition. Intermediate and advanced students are taught more detailed and intricate movements."

"Chris, suppose I am interested in making sure the guy who attacks doesn't disable me and when I counter, he doesn't get up to try again. Then what?"

"We can make sure your individual training encompasses striking methods with restraining tactics, ground fighting skills, weaponry and more. Our method is meant to be gentle on the victim but devastating on the attacker. The techniques are swift and powerful while exhibiting gracefulness and balance." Chris took a drink of beer, paused and added. "Are you in some kind of trouble?"

"No, nothing like that. I just want to make sure I can defend myself. Can I take as many classes as I want?"

Chris shrugged. "The lessons on a group basis are reasonably priced but the individual lessons cost more. You can take them at your pace and, of course, your expense. When you sign up, you'll get fitted with a dogi."

After chatting awhile, they left the bar and went their separate ways. Jim found himself taken by the gentle and open nature of Chris although he knew he'd be a dangerous adversary. He was also impressed with the training rigor available. Intrigued and determined to start preparing for an unpredictable future, he made up his mind to start the lessons in the mornings before going to the marina.

As Chris climbed in his car he reflected on Nick. For all his appearance and stated background, he talked and behaved like an educated man.

Saturday, May 18

The next morning, Chris was surprised to see Jim waiting for the studio to open. "Hey Nick. I guess I didn't scare you off last night by telling you about the training involved. Come on in and I'll fit you with a dogi. You're the first one so I'll take you through some basic movements once you've changed."

Jim felt he was fit enough to take the training in stride and was shocked to be breathing hard after only ten minutes of warmups. He noted Chris was a patient and observant teacher who slowed down the lesson to coincide with his pupil's energy level. After the hour was up and other students started arriving, Chris closed the lesson by instructing Jim in the traditional bow. Jim paid for the lesson in cash. Chris watched him leave after changing back to his street clothes and thought, he won't be coming back.

On the way to the marina, Jim could feel the stiffness and soreness of his legs and shoulders after the session. "So much for thinking I was in shape."

Chapter Sixteen

CHRIS MUNCIE

Sunday, May 18
San Francisco Suburb

Chris drove into his condominium complex and admired the well kept appearance of the surrounding grounds. People would say it appealed to his neat, orderly military background and was a major reason for buying it but basically he hated to do any yard work. He remotely opened the garage, parked and let himself into the house. He had a three-bedroom unit because he wanted the extra space. He had converted a bedroom into a combination office and den. The other smaller room remained a guest bedroom. He looked around the living room as he went into the kitchen.

It definitely had a man's touch with a dark leather couch highlighted with brass buttons next to a sturdy wood coffee table. He checked the answering machine in his office. The mail consisted of two bills and advertisements. He sat in the office chair and used a remote to turn on the TV. His mind was on the dinner he had with Nick. The guy was strange, no, not strange but withdrawn and private. He couldn't tell if he was hiding something or just reluctant to discuss anything of a personal nature. He seemed to be a nice guy and had been comfortable in his presence. He tried to suppress a smile. There was a time the same description fitted him right down to his spit-shined combat boots.

Born Christopher Daniel Muncie, he lived in Wichita, Kansas until he was seven. His father's job as an aircraft mechanic took them to San Diego, California. There, the ocean waves rising and falling in rhythm and throwing themselves against the shore while wet-suited surfers rode their surfboards held a unique fascination. He watched them enviously for hours from the pier and beach. He satisfied himself with body surfing and swimming under the watchful eye of his mother. On his ninth birthday, he received a surfboard which kept him in the water through school. In high school he made the swimming and water polo teams. He tried out for football but lacked the bulk that distinguished the punisher from the punished. This led to an interest in judo and karate. His wiry frame and endurance was suited to track. His grades steadily improved.

After high school, he was recruited by a naval officer from the Navy Special Warfare Command in Coronado next to San Diego. For eighteen months, he was trained in unconventional warfare, direct action and specialized reconnaissance. Afterwards, he had been assigned to a sixteen man Seal platoon deployed in small units worldwide in support of fleet and national operations. He was involved in covert operations in Bosnia and reconnaissance operations in Afghanistan and Iraq. After twelve years, he had felt a need for a different type of life style.

He moved to San Francisco and completed his training in martial arts resulting in an instructional certificate. He used his savings to rent a store and turned it into a martial arts studio. In three years, he managed to build up a clientele from mostly word of mouth referrals and hired a staff of three instructors. He had developed the harness but he lacked the funds necessary to obtain a patent and get it on the market.

He was still single. Women acquaintances had drifted in and out of his life. The only one he now dated on a regular basis was Connie. He was too occupied with the studio to devote the necessary attention needed to foster a close relationship. He shrugged. He didn't need to look for company; he'd let it find him. How did he get into this melancholy? Oh yeah, thinking about his evening with Nick.

Monday, May 20

On Monday morning, Chris was once again surprised and pleased to find Jim waiting at the studio. "All right, Nick. So you're still interested after that workout. Change and let's go through more of the lesson." After a half hour, Nick was sweating but kept up until the hour was over. Chris remarked. "The lesson will be cheaper for you if you join a group at a later hour."

"Chris, I kind of like it this way if it doesn't bother you. I'll pay as we go along."

"Not at all, see you next time." When Nick had left, Chris again wondered about Nick's life and why he felt it important to learn to defend himself.

The lessons started first thing every morning and lasted for an hour six days a week. Chris observed Nick always paid cash for the lessons and quietly speculated about his background. He didn't seem to fit in with the laborers, blue-collar workers and the health conscious crowd frequenting the studio. He worked hard during the lesson and was progressing rapidly through the basic movements. He remained, for the most part, quiet and reserved. He took Chris's banter during their sessions in stride but never responded in kind. He made up his mind to ask Nick to dinner the next time he came in.

They went out to a nearby Asian restaurant where he was surprised by Nick's knowledge of the Chinese dishes and his adeptness at handling the chopsticks. He observed his table manners and noticed he was growing a beard but kept his hair short. Chris brought up a number of topics to obtain his reaction but they were deflected by neutral comments. It was only when Chris brought up the Iraqi response to the United Nations' resolution on arms inspection that Nick became animated by the discussion. Chris mentioned he had seen action as a Seal in Kuwait and Iraq during Desert Shield and Desert Storm in 1990 and 1991. Nick was going to add something but caught himself. On the whole, both men enjoyed the evening and each other's company and parted pleasantly.

Chapter Seventeen

INITIATIVES

Same Day
Newport Beach, California

Diane Factor woke up to a state of depression which had consumed her ever since the telephone call from Sergeant Greenwell. She took a long shower to clear her head. It was obvious the police had more to do than worry about a possible missing person. She realized she couldn't let it go without taking some kind of action. She inherited her stubbornness from her father who had built a small general store into a large retail chain. After high school, she went to college and graduated with honors. Eventually, she had risen to the post of Director of Communications for a large biotechnology company. By then, Jim was making a good income and they had enjoyed each other's company when traveling together. She maintained her athletic figure through tennis and exercise class.

She thought, this won't do. I am not going to wait around and mope. She wrapped herself in a bath towel, went to the phone and left a message for Sergeant Greenwell. Within the hour he returned her call.

"Sergeant, I want to pursue another avenue to find my husband. Do you know a good private investigator I could contact?"

Greenwell hesitated momentarily. "Mrs. Factor, I happen to know an excellent one. This fellow worked with the Los Angeles Sheriff's Department and later here as a detective. He's tough, stubborn and smart as they get. His name is Adam Weatherly and he has an office nearby in Santa Ana."

Diane dialed the number she received from Sergeant Greenwell.

A woman answered, "Weatherly Investigations."

"Mr. Weatherly, please."

After a moment, a man came on. "Hello, this is Adam Weatherly."

Her first impression was he had a low no-nonsense voice. She blurted, "Mr. Weatherly, I was referred to you by Sergeant Todd Greenwell. My name is Diane Factor and I would like to talk to you about my missing husband."

"How long has he been missing?"

"Going on two weeks," she replied.

There was a pause. "Mrs. Factor, let's meet in an hour. Give me your address and phone number."

When the doorbell rang, Diane opened the door and was surprised to see a man neatly dressed in a well-fitting suit with a white shirt and a fashionable tie. He was five-foot, ten inches with a muscular build and a nose that had been broken sometime in his past. He had a small diagonal scar on the left side of his rugged face. His size belied the quiet force emanating from him. His eyes held an intelligent gleam. He introduced himself and she invited him into the house. Diane showed him into the living room where they sat across one another. She folded her hands in her lap and looked straight at him.

"Mr. Weatherly, tell me about yourself."

Weatherly was taken aback by the unexpected question. He had expected to be confronted by an angry or despondent wife not one who wanted to probe his background. He smiled. "Would you like the Readers Digest version or?"

"The version you feel describes you best, Mr. Weatherly."

"Okay, let me know when I begin to bore you. I'm originally from Los Angeles. My father worked as an insurance investigator so you might say it runs in my genes. I studied criminology and law at the California State University at Long Beach. When I graduated, I joined the LA Sheriff's Department. After six years, my interest and success led to an assignment in investigations. They had a problem with me, I didn't know when to quit a case. I was offered a similar position with a promotion with the Newport Beach PD and took it. I had more freedom but the story was the same after a while. After four years I left to start my investigation agency. At the beginning it was touch and go but my former colleagues were generous with referrals I hired two former law enforcement nerds and we've been busy ever since. We are generally successful in finding people within thirty days although there's no guarantee it'll always be the case."

Diane nodded. "Thank you for your candor. Let me bring you up to date on my husband's disappearance." As they sat in the living room, Weatherly was walked through all of the events of that first day and the subsequent police activities. He asked to see Jim's study and the police report. She opened the safe and he examined everything and made notes. He saw that the papers in the safe were personal to them; mortgage, loan, car registration, insurance, a will and the savings account.

"I don't see his business papers."

"They're over here behind the cabinet doors in locked filing cabinets."

"Mrs. Factor, you seem to suspect your husband may in some sort of trouble which would make him run off like he did. Why?"

"I think because he left all of his IDs and the open safe. Jim isn't your everyday kind of professional. He's an arms dealer and has been very successful through the years. I see your frown. Not that kind. He's brokered large weapon systems for Northrop Grumman and Lockheed Martin although over the years he preferred to have the European aerospace industry for clients. His customers are mainly in the Middle East. He wasn't always in the business. He previously worked in the corporate world. He just preferred to be independent. Jim's profession took him into rather precarious situations like Desert Storm. I gather he associates at times with less than respectable customers. I can also tell you it had to be something drastic to make him react like he did. I am not being overly emotional. There is something else I think is important. It is in his character to face problems himself rather than confide and ask for assistance particularly if there could be trouble. This is the reason I'm seeking help."

"You should know before we continue, my fee is $500 a day plus expenses with a $5,000 retainer. The sooner we can begin, the better it'll be. Two weeks have passed and the scent has to be faint."

Diane took a checkbook from her purse and wrote a check. "Do what it takes."

"Mrs. Factor, to continue, do you have any idea why your husband might have left or been kidnapped? Usually, a woman, finances, health or danger are a reason."

"Mr. Weatherly, we have adequate finances, our health is good and my husband is devoted to me. I believe something particularly dire and serious must have occurred for him to leave suddenly."

"Okay, I see the phone logs showed no calls that morning. Did your husband have a cell phone? There's none listed in the police report."

"Good heavens, I completely forgot all about that. When he travels he carries a satellite phone. I picked it off his desk when it happened and left it in the bedroom in case he called." She went away and came back with the phone.

"Let me have it. I'll return it in a few days. I'll also contact Sergeant Greenwell. Then I'll be back in touch. In the meantime, please let me have photographs of your husband in casual clothes and in a business suit."

"Mr. Weatherly, one more thing. I want to be brought up to date right away when there is any progress."

After Weatherly left, Diane pulled out her telephone list. It's about time to bring both their parents in on her suspicion and action. She informed them about the events which had transpired up to her hiring a private investigator.

"No, it wouldn't do any good to come here. The police will do what they can but I believe this investigator acting on my behalf will be more effective."

She promised to keep them informed. She hung up the phone. She was thankful they hadn't inquired about personal problems. They had also taken it as something involved with Jim's business dealings.

Sergey and Petra listened in on Factor's wife telephone calls regarding his disappearance and hiring a private investigator. Sergey observed. "Well, we know it's useless to get into the house now that the son-of-a-bitch has taken off without leaving a clue where he's going. It makes the job tougher for us. The PI could be a break if he tracks Factor down. I say we hang around and monitor his progress through the calls. Let's find his office so we know where to find him."

When Adam returned to his office, his two associates greeted him. They were always curious and eager when they took on a new client. Elaine Marks handled the phones and computeroriented information searches while Marty Burns specialized in all types of surveillance technologies. Both college graduates were working for police departments when Adam had recruited them.

Adam ran down the information he received from Diane Factor. He handed Elaine the satellite phone and number. "Let's get the phone records for the last two years. Do the usual stuff on repeated numbers tracking down callers and their location. Let's scan these photographs and generate copies with a beard and moustache. Make a set with and without a hat."

He addressed Marty. "I need a wiretap placed on the Factor's phone. We'll monitor calls in case he tries to contact his wife or if she gets a threat or ransom demand. Place a video camera somewhere near the front of the house to keep an eye on the street. In their upscale community, we'll be able to observe any unusual traffic. I'll contact Todd Greenwell and get his insights on the matter."

When Sergeant Greenwell came on the line, Weatherly thanked him for the referral and quickly got down to business. "Todd, what's your impression of the Factor woman? Is she genuinely concerned and more important, do you think she is holding back anything?"

Greenwell sighed. "She feels there's more to it than a simple disappearance and it definitely has her worried. Did she tell you he's an arms dealer? Maybe something went wrong."

"I'm going to look into that angle. Thanks again, Todd."

"Adam, keep me in the loop. I don't want to get egg on my face."

When he got off the phone, Adam related what Greenwell said. "Elaine, make sure we check out all international calls to and from the home and compare them with the cell phone calls."

Chapter Eighteen

MARINA WORK

Monday, May 27
San Francisco, California

After a week, Bob Wallsky's fish finder arrived and was installed by the manufacturer's representative under Jim's watchful eye. The technician described the sonar's characteristics, the different features and options, and demonstrated the operation. The sophistication, details and the resulting performance were impressive. When the job was completed, Jim called Wallsky with the news. Wallsky asked Jim to meet him at the dock for a trial run.

Wallsky was excited about testing the system. Jim explained how the fish finder functioned. They headed west as soon as they exited the marina and entered San Francisco Bay. Within fifteen minutes they passed under the Golden Gate Bridge into the open choppy water of the Pacific. Both men put on windbreakers. Wallsky turned north along the California coast and reduced the speed to a slow cruise. Jim activated the fish finder. Experimenting with the settings, they were enthralled by the returns on the display.

Wallsky stopped the engines, went to the rear of the boat, pulled a fishing rod from a holder and took a fresh fish from a bait tank. He skillfully put it on the hook, settled into a large swivel deck chair bolted to the aft deck, lit a cigar, and dropped a line in the water. Jim noted the fish finder gave returns in their vicinity when Wallsky yelped with pleasure. A few minutes later, a ten-pound sea bass lay on the floor of the boat. Wallsky grabbed it by the gills, expertly removed the hook and released the fish into the water.

"Perfect!" He yelled and slapped Jim on the back. He started the engines and returned to the marina. Wallsky asked him to wait a moment.

He returned with some money, counted out $250 and placed it in his hand. "Thanks. Nick. It's exactly what I wanted."

Jim's experience with Collier and Wallsky led him to contemplate putting out a circular targeted at selective boat owners about his availability on sophisticated marine accessories questions or problems. This type of work appealed to his technical nature and seemingly would pay more for less time than other types of marina jobs. He became friendly with Miguel Rodriguez, a Mexican immigrant who had grown up performing boat-related jobs at the Cabo San Lucas, Baja, Mexico marina and moved to the U.S. as a young man. He had tried his Spanish on Miguel and could actually understand his response. Jim decided to find him and discuss the possibly of helping each other at the marina.

It didn't take long for Jim to locate Miguel who was polishing brass and scrubbing the topside of a twenty-nine foot Monterey 296.

"Miguel," he called out. "Can you take a break any time soon?"

Miguel grinned. "I'm ready now." He wiped the sweat off his face with a handkerchief and climbed down to the dock.

They sat on a nearby boat locker while Jim summarized his thoughts. "Miguel, I've done work for a couple of boat owners involving a degree of technical knowledge." He described the jobs he did for Collier and Wallsky. "I figure there are more like them with similar needs. Perhaps their systems aren't working well, they're not using it correctly or they want to upgrade to bigger and better. I'm willing to pay a finder's fee if you run across someone like that. If it requires more than I could handle, I'll hire you to work on it with me. What do you say?"

"It sounds better and more exciting than the stuff I usually do. I know the other guys working here who may want to get in on it too. I'll talk to them."

Jim walked away thinking about the problem with expanding his activity. He only accepted cash although some of the boat owners might attempt to pay by check. He needed a bank account but the lack of a social security number was an obstacle. He had to get false ID. He heard undocumented immigrants had sources. Asking the Queterras' was out of the question. As he walked, he suddenly thought of another possibility. The subject was too sensitive to discuss in the open. He turned around and went back to the boat where Miguel was working.

"Hey, Miguel," he yelled, "do you have time later on for a beer?"

Miguel motioned with his hands, twenty minutes.

At the nearby Bayfront bar, Jim drew Miguel over to a quiet table. They talked about boats, jobs and pay. Finally, he broached the subject of cash and checks. "Miguel, I have a problem. People want to pay me with checks and I have no way of cashing them. Any ideas?"

Taking a drink, Miguel slowly replied. "Do you have any ID at all?"

"No, I lost it all a while back. Can you help me with it?"

"Let me make some calls and get back to you."

Miguel sought out Jim the following day. "Nick, I know a guy who will do it but if you approached him he'll spook. He charges $300 for a good ID."

"I want to go ahead with it."

"You went out of your way to include me in your plans so here's what I'll do. Write down your full name, place of birth and birth date. I'll give it to him with your payment and he won't have to meet you."

Two days later, Jim had a social security number and a false birth certificate. He chose a different birth date to make him three years younger and listed Boston as a place of birth in case his accent was noticed. He used the ID to open a savings account in a bank blocks away from the marina. After this, he had business cards printed with his name and the Queterras' phone number. He let Marie know he might get some calls at the house. He assured her if it got too annoying, he'd get another phone line installed with a voice mail option.

Chapter Nineteen

THE INVESTIGATION BEGINS

Wednesday, May 29
Newport Beach, California

Adam was on foot canvassing the neighborhood around the Factor residence with the photographs when Marty called on his cell phone. "Adam, get back to the office quick. We have something to show you." He returned to his car, made a U-turn and raced back.

They were both waiting when he came through the door. "You're not going to believe this." They voiced in almost unison.

"Okay. Elaine. You first."

"The satellite phone and home phone had several repeat numbers but the one most interesting occurred on the satellite phone the morning he disappeared. The number shows up again almost six months earlier and continues back nearly a year. It's from a cell phone and the last call was from Costa Rica. Before that, the calls on the number were from Florida, and various European countries including Bulgaria."

"Good work. Do a crosscheck with the names and numbers in Factor's organizer. The police report has this list. Okay, Marty, your turn."

"Adam, I went to the Factor house to install the phone tap this morning and almost had a heart attack. Someone's beat me to it. If it wasn't the

NBPD which I seriously doubt, someone else is very interested in the Factors. I planted ours in a way where I can monitor their pickup while we independently eavesdrop."

Adam stared at both of them. "That's some kind of news and it may be a big piece of the puzzle."

Marty continued. "I placed a MiWatcher II color digital camera in the tree on their front lawn facing the street. By the way, after I found the other tap, I placed another camera facing the house in case our friends get careless when they return. A motion detector will trigger the cameras. The MWII automatically transmits the digital images with date and time stamp. A dedicated phone line isn't necessary; it'll use normal phone lines for transmission. The outputs will be transmitted from the Factor's garage by a cell phone connection."

"Good work you two. It's beginning to appear our Mr. Factor has gotten himself in trouble serious enough to deliberately take off. Now besides looking for Factor, we have another party to find. I'll keep up the canvassing while you two work out why he skipped. I'll work on how he did it. I'll ask Mrs. Factor not to use her home phone line if the call concerns her husband."

Adam performed a sweep of stores in the Factor residential vicinity. He noted the nearby gas station. Factor would have needed some quick transportation. He called his office. "Elaine, didn't the police report say there was a cab driver who thought he had a passenger that resembled Factor? Where did he pick him up and drop him off?"

"The police report says that he was picked up at the corner of San Joachim Hills Road and Marguerite Parkway. The taxi dropped him off not far from the Santa Ana Greyhound Bus Terminal. It was about nine-thirty in the morning."

"Bingo. The pickup occurred within a block from me. What did the police check at the bus station reveal?"

"Nothing. No one identified his picture."

"I'm on my way there now."

He drove around the area containing the Greyhound Bus Terminal carefully looking over the types of shops. He stopped when he saw the novelty store. The clerk thought he recognized Factor but couldn't recall a purchase. Weatherly surveyed the shelves and found a variety of beards and moustaches. He thought, if it were me, I'd want to alter my appearance before traveling.

When Adam entered the bus terminal, he went straight to the manager's office. He showed his badge and told Ray Gomez, the manager, he was trying to get information on a person who caught a bus over two weeks before. "Look, I know it's a long shot someone will remember him but maybe something about the man stuck in their mind and it'll jog their memory."

Gomez asked the ticket sellers to come into the office. Adam wed them the pictures of Jim Factor. Both tellers shook their heads.

Adam persisted. "Maybe there was something odd about the man like nervousness or overly cautious that might have seemed suspicious."

One of the tellers thought a moment and turned to Gomez. "There was something but I can't think of when it was. I sold a ticket to this guy and later he came back and bought another ticket. I thought it was strange he didn't exchange the first ticket because it wasn't cheap. Then I saw him at the other ticket window. I figure he was buying tickets for people with him but as far as I could see he was alone."

Adam pressed. "Can you at least remember the destinations?" The teller shook her head. "Sorry."

Gomez thought a moment. "Hey, if he didn't return the unused tickets, I can check which buses were one passenger short. The time will tell us what other buses went out around then." He sat at a computer terminal and checked the passenger sales and numbers for the date and time. "Okay, both the San Diego and the Phoenix buses was one passenger short. The only other bus at the time went to San Francisco and the passenger number matches the ticket sales. The bus driver was Jerry Spears. He's due here tomorrow afternoon. I'll call you when he gets in."

Chapter Twenty

MEASURES

Friday, May 31

For three weeks Sergey and Petra maintained constant vigilance over the Factor's house with the planted wiretap monitoring the progress of the police effort and Mrs. Factor's call to the private investigator. They located his office in the phone book. Factor had not tried to contact his wife. Her call to the private investigator was troublesome.

"Damn it, this isn't getting us anywhere, Petra. My gut tells me he's cut out for good. We may do better to concentrate on the PI to see if he gets anywhere."

"Why don't we personally find out if she knows anything?" Petra asked.

Sergey rolled his eyes upward. "Let me know when you have something useful to add."

Sergey called Borichov and informed him that the recent events placed their continued phone monitoring at risk. Borichov's response was predictable.

"Damn it. You took too long to get there and now this. Sooner or later, he's going to surface. Keep watching the wife and investigator. I want him found, I don't care how long it takes." Borichov slammed the phone down.

They packed in silence and checked out of the motel. They made it a rule never to stay in one place for long. There were plenty of motels that suited their needs. Petra took the wheel as Sergey made a call to the Factor house. When there was no reply, he told Petra to drive by the house. There was no sign of activity so he continued around the corner and parked.

He instructed Petra. "Go get the tap. It's too risky to leave it while the police and the PI step up the search. We'll monitor the house for short periods."

Within minutes, Petra returned and they drove off. "What's our next move?" Petra asked.

"Let's find out more about the PI and see if he'll lead us to Factor."

The retrieval of the listening equipment was heard and captured by Marty who promptly contacted Adam. He downloaded the video from the two cameras into their computer system. The camera facing the house did not show any intruder. The streetfacing camera, however, captured the passage of a car with two occupants a few minutes before the tap went dead. Elaine used computer enhancement on the passenger. The license plate was caked in mud probably deliberately and could not be read. The car was an older model dark Chevrolet sedan. When Adam arrived and viewed the results, Elaine had already made prints of the car and the passenger.

"Good work. It's time to have a talk with Todd Greenwell and see what they can turn up on our friends."

Greenwell was impressed with Adam's progress and entered the photographs into the FBI database. "I'll call you if we come up with a match."

In less than a day Sergeant Greenwell was contacted by the FBI who wanted to know where he obtained the photographs. He gave the details and ended by revealing their contact was lost. The FBI agent informed him the men were known members of the Russian mafia and considered dangerous. "We've been trying to get these guys for some time. We'll send out a bulletin on their car. If they keep to their pattern, they're on the road returning home. Unfortunately, we believe they'll switch cars before heading out." Greenwell filled Adam in on the conversation.

Adam called on Diane Factor and delivered a progress summary on the investigation.

"There are two avenues I'd like to pursue. The first deals with the circumstance of Jim's disappearance. There's reason to believe he felt his presence would a pose a serious danger to you. We need to find out why. The second avenue will be harder. We have to find him and he doesn't want to be found."

Without hesitation she authorized him to continue the search.

Chapter Twenty-one

THE INVESTIGATION CONTINUES

Monday, June 3
Newport Beach, California

Adam developed a time line of Jim Factor's actions since he walked out of the house. Jerry Spears, the bus driver, did not remember seeing Factor as one of his passengers but mentioned a person who sort of fit the description was involved in an incident during the trip. Adam was sure San Francisco was Factor's next stop. The question was; did he get off along the way or did he continue on? It would have been late in the afternoon when the bus arrived in San Francisco. Given the day's hectic events, Adam would bet he decided to stay put and hide. Traveling presented a certain risk. Hotels were easy to check but on the other side of the coin, boarding houses were impossible. He had to hand it to Factor. He showed no sign of panic and was thinking on his feet.

Not for the first time, Adam reviewed his own life. He was in his late thirties and in law enforcement since graduating from college. He maintained his fitness proficiency at the police gym and regularly frequented the gun range. Once married, his wife had difficulty adjusting to the long hours of detective work occupying his time and filed for divorce. She met a land developer while selling real estate and now had both time and money.

He wrinkled his brow, rubbed his chin and thought, "Okay, put yourself in Factor's shoes. It's getting towards dusk and he needs a place to stay for the night. He's been careful all day and won't be lulled into going to a hotel no matter how safe or easy it may be. He probably won't take a chance on sleeping on the streets if he has cash on him. It leaves him looking for a room but where? Assume the guy's resourceful and finds a room, location unknown, where they don't keep records and don't ask for ID; maybe a bed and breakfast or rooming house. Factor thinks he can get lost in San Francisco. Why not? It's a large city with a diverse ethnic population. He'll want to get a job although with his cash he doesn't need to. No, he'll get a job because he has the semblance of a plan by now. He'll be analytical and thorough, say a menial job where he can get paid in cash because he doesn't dare use his identity. It's time to talk to Mrs. Factor about her husband's hobbies and interests to obtain a further insight into him."

Adam called his office and asked Elaine to put the speakerphone on. "I'd like you both to put on your thinking caps. Let's say Factor landed in San Francisco and wants to find work for cash because he has no ID. What kind of work would be available? He doesn't need or want steady work. I'm willing to bet he'll try to revert to something a cut above the norm. I mean he won't wash dishes or pick crops. He's smart so he'll more than likely try to get something which suits his temperament. We have to secondguess this part." He paused, then added. "Marty, we need to follow up on the Russian mafia angle, namely, who issued the contract. Running a background check on everyone on the phone records may turn up something."

After the call, it occurred to him Factor would probably put a premium on getting false ID when he had settled into a routine. There were plenty of opportunities in a state with so many illegal immigrants. San Diego would have made a better choice in this respect since documents are peddled on both sides of the U.S./Mexican border. There might not be as many choices in San Francisco. The SFPD may be able to help him there.

Chapter Twenty-two

INSIGHT INTO JIM FACTOR

Tuesday, June 4

At the Factor residence, Adam pulled out a notebook, leaned back on the sofa and explained, "Mrs. Factor, I'm trying to develop a profile of your husband to help me in finding him. To tell the truth, I'm discovering Jim is an unusual person. Let's speculate he was informed he'd been earmarked for violence or death. He realizes if he stays, it places you in danger too. He doesn't panic. Instead, he calmly executes a successful disappearance and is a few steps ahead of us. I need to know about the man, who and what he is, and how he thinks."

Diane Factor sat down on the chair opposite him. She paused to collect her thoughts, cleared her throat and addressed him. "Mr. Weatherly, my husband's full name is James Thomas Factor. He was born and raised in New York City. His parents are retired and live near Clearwater, Florida. Up to two months ago we enjoyed a normal existence in Newport Beach. Jim is forty-two, six-foot two, around two-hundred pounds. with brown hair and gray along the temples. He's slightly overweight but tries to keep himself relatively fit when he's home. He makes an above average income which allows us to enjoy a leisurely life with occasional travel. As you already know, Jim has a military background and degrees in electrical engineering. What you don't know is he obtained two degrees in three years and still graduated with high honors. His previous occupation was as a weapon systems engineer for aerospace companies and involved extensive overseas travel. While employed, Jim was involved in U.S. and foreign military systems. He regularly interfaced with an Air Force intelligence agency and the Defense Department.

"This background enabled Jim to move into his current profession as an arms dealer. In our personal life he resolved not to call attention to this aspect for obvious reasons but rather to refer to himself as a marketer. His efforts are associated with the larger, more sophisticated arms. His customers are third world governments and militaries. In the Middle East, he works with a Kuwaiti partner from an established family with considerable holdings and wealth. His partner has extensive contacts and friends throughout the Arabian area which has proven to be mutually profitable. We vacation at least twice a year in Europe favoring Provence in Southern France and Tuscany in Northern Italy. It may surprise you to know, although I can recite his professional background, Jim kept his business dealings private. The products are weaponrelated and as a rule his clients and customers prefer not to publicize their activities."

Diane stood up and moved to the window. She continued. "As you have observed my husband is an intelligent, thorough man. When Jim starts something, he stays rigidly focused to the exclusion of external disruptions. Once he has an objective, he will develop a strategy to achieve it. He is a stickler for details. He has an aversion to becoming personal with people. He can be sociable since he is well read but prefers to keep his distance from relationships. To be perfectly honest, I believe Jim must have inadvertently crossed a line to get into this situation. Wherever and whatever Jim is up to right now, it's no accident. He believes someone is trying to kill him. He's made it his responsibility to keep me from being involved by taking such a drastic measure. My greatest concern is his ingrained behavior won't allow him to seek outside help. He may even consider doing something about it. It's one of the reasons why I decided to hire you."

She turned away from the window and sat down again. "Mr. Weatherly, you have done more than the police and you have good insights. I want you to continue to find Jim. However, as you have stated, we must find out who is after him and how to stop them."

Adam looked up from his notebook. "Mrs. Factor, suppose your husband has a plan and furthermore, suppose he is in San Francisco. You know him better than anyone else. Do you think there's a chance he'll stay there and bury himself in the city?"

She shook her head vigorously. "I don't believe he'll stay there long.

Knowing Jim, it's the first phase, to borrow one of his expressions. I think it's a matter of time before he leaves."

"If he did where do you think he would go? Does Jim favor any city, state or environment?

"Oh no, I don't believe that Jim will go anywhere but out of the country. He is very comfortable traveling abroad."

"Where? Are you thinking Mexico or Canada?"

"Jim is very familiar with Europe and the Middle East but my personal feeling is he would choose Europe. Yes, I am almost sure of it."

Adam thanked her for her time and candor. Driving back to his office, he pondered the conversation he just had with Diane Factor. It confirmed his earlier estimate of the man. Whatever Jim Factor is doing, it has a purpose. Let's hope we don't run out of time before we figure it out. Something else bothered him, something she said. No, it was in her description of her husband. Suddenly it came to him and he reacted with a start. He pulled over to the curb. She could have been describing him as well. Is this why he had uncannily been able to find the loose thread of Factor's disappearance? Is this why he was drawn to San Francisco for the next step of the search? Let's see what Elaine and Marty have come up with.

Diane Factor watched Adam Weatherly return to his car from the front window. His progress and interest in finding Jim gave her hope and feeling she was doing something to help Jim rather than sitting and waiting.

Chapter Twenty-three

THE SEARCH SHIFTS

Wednesday, June 5
San Francisco, California

Adam pulled into downtown section of San Francisco late in the afternoon. Elaine had provided him with a centrally-located hotel with reasonable room rates. Marty continued to track down information on the activities of the Russian mafia in the U.S. and, in particular, the connection to the hit men.

He assessed the surroundings. San Francisco sat poised on the forty-seven square mile fingertip of a peninsula. The city had much to offer from rugged coastline and tranquil bay waters to rambling, fog-capped hills, steep streets and a cluster of distinct neighborhoods lined by rows of preserved Victorian houses. This was the city where blue jeans, mountain biking, car chase movie scenes and topless waitressing first took off. Despite all of its activity, San Francisco maintained a small town mentality where having a car was a liability due to traffic-jammed streets and a dearth of parking spaces. Provided you don't mind the steep hills, every major sight in the town was a short walk, trolley or bus ride away.

It was a large city where anyone could get lost if he wanted to escape from his past. Yet, Adam strongly suspected this might not be as easy as it sounded for a person like Jim Factor. He had a starting point; Factor needed to assume another identity and somehow obtain false ID. Sooner or later he would get a job where payment would be made with a check. He would definitely require documentation if he planned to leave the country. Adam decided to see a former colleague, Detective Ray Peterson of the SFPD Investigations Division. He picked up his cell phone.

"Ray? This is Adam Weatherly. I just got in town. Any chance we can get together today?"

Peterson gave him the precinct address and directions. At the front desk, Adam was directed to his friend, a burly man with a blue suit, police badge suspended from a chain around his neck, tie hanging from an open collar and black shoes with rubber soles. He was hovering over a desk with two In-baskets filled to the brim, and a paper-strewn desktop with a computer terminal and keyboard on a side stand. They warmly exchanged greetings. Peterson motioned Adam to a nearby chair.

Adam opened the conversation. "Thanks for seeing me, Ray. I can see things are busy as usual."

"Hell, Adam, what are old friends for? I should have done what you did but," he shrugged, "a wife and two kids. You know how that goes. What can I do for you?"

He explained he was looking for a missing person who didn't want to be found. "I suspect he's here in San Francisco and he's going to get, if he already hasn't, false ID."

"Adam. That's a pretty thin conjecture. What makes you think he'd stay put in our fair city instead of heading for other parts?"

"Oh, I think he'll leave all right but I'm gambling he's orchestrating the departure. This is a thinking and deliberate person. He'll want papers to lessen the chances of being caught."

"Okay, to start with, we have on file over a hundred people who have been caught with their hand in the inkwell so to speak. I don't know how many more there are we haven't got to. My guess is another hundred."

"Could we narrow it down somehow? Are there any differences or trends we could start with?"

"Actually, there are. The IDs sold can consist of social security numbers, birth certificates, immigration papers, and driver's licenses. Most of these people provide the Mexican and Central American community with false IDs. The Asian community runs a distant second. Then there's the good ID versus the bad and the ugly; a cost of $500 compared to $100."

"I would think it'll be hard for him as a white American to access the Asian paper pushers especially since they'd be paranoid about an INS sting. I'd bet on the Mexican angle."

"It's not so clear either. They're just as worried about the INS and wouldn't cater to anybody who wasn't referred. The best I can do is give you a list of the ones we have. I wish I could help with the leg work but I'm up to my neck with cases."

"Ray, you've done me a favor as it is. I'll see where it goes from this point."

They shook hands and Adam left.

On the way to his hotel, Adam tried again to place himself in Factor's shoes. He would want a quality set of IDs; he would bet on it. It would minimize suspicion and attention. If he was paid by check, he could cash it at a bank once he opened an account. Otherwise he could do it for a fee at a check cashing service. It was time to get to the hotel, settle in and get some supper. Tomorrow he would start the search. It was liable to be in some rough areas so he would carry his gun.

Thursday, June 6

In the morning Adam bought a detailed street map of San Francisco's surrounding communities and organized his search off the list he had received from Peterson. The Mexican angle still on his mind, he deferred the Asian-associated names to the end. It still left him with a large number. He took along a number of photos of Factor. He also made sure he had a pocketful of ones, fives and tens. From experience, he knew bribes went a long way to ensure he was not the law and to get cooperation. He called his office for messages before getting in the car. The weather was comfortable and he wore a sport coat over a casual shirt to hide the shoulder holster. He drove off to the first stop on the east part of San Francisco.

The first name on the list was José Lopez who lived in a three-story walk-up apartment building with better days but you had to go back fifty years to have seen it. The hallways were cluttered with trash, the walls with graffiti and the air smelled of garbage and urine. He knocked on the door and heard footsteps come close to the door before he heard a raspy voice.

"What is it?" came from beyond the door about the same time an eye peered out from the peephole.

Adam held up his PI credentials. "Are you José Lopez?"

"So what? Get lost."

"I'd like some information on a possible customer."

"Does this look like the goddamn library? Go away." The eye left the peephole.

Adam raised his voice. "Wait a second. I got an incentive for the answer."

The eye returned. "Like what?"

"Like I'll stick around and chase away your customers. Then when I get bored, I'll raise the ante."

The deadbolts were slid back and the door opened as far as a chain would go. "Okay, what is it?"

Adam passed the photos through the door opening along with his card to a seedy-looking little man. "Does this guy look familiar? He would have tried to get some papers within the past month."

The photos were returned. "I ain't seen the guy before. He sure as hell don't look Mexican."

"You sure about that? If I locate him, you could be in for a big reward. Call my number if he does come by."

The door closed and the locks were reset. "Never seen him," was the fading reply.

Adam got in his car and entered the outcome in a notebook. The next stop was about a half hour away. He checked his watch with a sigh; at this rate he'll be lucky to hit three names a day. He wondered if the counterfeiters networked with one another. That could be good news and bad news. He'd find out before the week was over.

At the end of the third day and the seventeenth name, he had encountered resistance, caution, obstinacy and fear. It was always the same response. No one recognized Factor. If they had, he was sure they would have demanded a price for the information. He kept in touch with his office. Marty was making slow progress at tracking down every call Factor had made on his home and cell phone for the past eighteen months. The bulk of the calls were international which added to the complications. The repetitiveness was being used to develop a pattern. At this rate, he was going to wear out shoes and patience tracking down every name on the list. worst part was he could wind up empty handed after he finished.

Chapter Twenty-four

SECOND MONTH

Monday, June 10
San Francisco, California

A month quickly went by and Jim found himself busy with jobs around the marina four to six days a week. He religiously maintained a schedule of spending his early morning at the martial arts studio and late afternoons with the Spanish tutor. He didn't mind keeping busy, it took his mind off Diane and his predicament. Within days Miguel and a co-worker had referred two specialized jobs. He made arrangements to give them a finder's fee and restated his offer to employ them if the job warranted. In spite of previous misgivings, he was starting to enjoy the new experience. He had a one-page flyer printed advertising his services. Wayne Collier saw it and recommended him to fellow boat owners. His referrals were providing opportunities for higher caliber boat work than the pickup jobs. What he couldn't do alone, he coordinated with Mike Sweeney and Charlie Ford. The income was decent and it allowed him the time to pursue his other interests.

As Jim walked down the street from the martial arts studio to catch the bus to the marina, he spotted an older car for sale by owner for $500 in a driveway. He walked up to the front door of the house and knocked. A man with two-day growth of beard in coveralls answered the door.

"I see you have a car for sale. Does it run?"

"Yeah, it runs. I just need money right now. I'm Bob Nagel." They shook hands. Nagel pulled a set of keys out of his pocket and both walked over to the car. He got behind the wheel and started the engine. "Hop in; we'll go around the block."

When they returned to the house, Jim introduced himself as Nick Germain and told him. "I'm on my way to work. I'll give you a $25 deposit to hold it until tonight. I have a favor to ask. I don't have a driver's license yet. I'd like to leave the registration in your name and park it on the street in front of your house until I get a permanent address. I'll give you $25 per week like I was leasing it. If I miss a payment, you can take it back."

"That's fine with me."

After work, Jim went over and paid Nagel $475 in cash and got a receipt. The next day, he drove to a Department of Motor Vehicles office and applied for a driver's license. He filled out the application and saw he had been too forthcoming with the information. He ripped up the application and looked over to where they were being processed. The teller didn't pay attention to the information she was typing from on the form. This time on the application, he wrote his birth date according to the false birth certificate, and gave a false address on a known busy street. He lied about his height by four inches and his weight by twenty-five pounds. After he passed the written and driving test, he received a temporary driver's license. They didn't seem to be concerned about his head being lowered in the picture. The permanent one would be mailed out in sixty days.

Jim marveled his cash reserve had only minimally been reduced. He developed a friendship with Jimmy Queterras who acquainted him with the Mexican area. He was slowly grasping Spanish while gaining a proficiency in karate. He became a morning fixture at the martial arts studio. He had lost over fifteen pounds and become not only trimmer and lighter but faster on his feet. In deference to his increasing skill, Chris offered an opening in the advanced section. To Chris, Jim remained a mystery. He dressed like a laborer and lived in the Mexican area but his bearing and articulation was of an educated man. He observed that in a short time Jim had established a business at the marina which apparently yielded a good return. Both men had taken to each other and they often went out after the studio closed.

There were nights at the house when Jim looked in the mirror at an unfamiliar lean dark-skinned face with a beard stubble and short hair. He thought about his wife and their parents and wondered how they were coping with his disappearance. He took solace in the fact they were safe as had no knowledge of his existence.

Jim responded to a call at the house by another Collier acquaintance, Max Ahrens. Complaining about the lack of speed of his thirty-two-foot Bayliner cruiser, Ahrens asked Jim if he would look into it. Intrigued by the challenge, Jim contacted the boat's manufacturer to determine the maximum safe speed dictated by the design. Next, he asked Jimmy to come out with him to the boat and evaluate the engine.

Jimmy noted the engine was a seven-year-old 5.7L, 260-horsepower Mercury Mercruiser. He explained. "The age of the engine results in wear and reduces the speed sometimes up to twenty-five percent." He took measurements of the engine hold and checked the transmission. "Give me a couple of days to research the options." He told Jim.

Jimmy came up with a solution to the problem. He explained to Ahrens and Jim when they got together. "The Mercury engine upgrade capability is restricted. When new it probably hit twenty to twenty-one knots. My recommendation is to replace it with the Crusader 5.7 MPI. The engine actually would be smaller in length and width by a few inches but higher by six inches. It adds seventy pounds of weight which will slightly increase drag. The boat would have to be pulled out of the water for the overhaul." He added as if anticipating their question. "You're going to have to sink around $18,000 into the swap-out. The old engine might be sold for about $1,000. The boat would come to my garage for the work which could take a month including the time to get the new engine and parts." Jim was taken aback when Ahrens gave the job to Jimmy. He would have bet the cost would have dropped the subject.

At the end of the fourth week, the boat work was completed and ready for a test run. Jim and Jimmy accompanied Ahrens out of the marina and into the bay. The engine made a deep throat sound as the throttle was advanced. Ahrens headed west into open water. Once they passed under the Golden Gate Bridge he eased the throttle forward and soon the speedometer was showing eighteen knots. A frothy wake emanated from the churning propeller.

"Okay, let's see what she can do," Ahrens told them, and pushed the throttle up to the limit. The boat speed soon registered above twenty-four knots. After five minutes Ahrens pulled back the throttle and turned towards them. "You did it. It's terrific." When the boat was tied up, he gave the final payment to Jimmy and gave a check for $1,000 to Jim.

That night at the Queterras dinner table, Jimmy was telling his father and mother about the boat engine switch out and the resulting speed performance. Jim joined in the lively conversation pointing to Jimmy's expert solution to the customer's problem. The men drank beer and relaxed comfortably together. He was taken with the impression he was considered a friend and they were like a surrogate family.

Chapter Twenty-five

INTERACTIONS

Friday, June 14
Newport Beach, California

Sergey and Petra initially divided their drive-by surveillance between Diane Factor and Adam Weatherly. When it became obvious she had no knowledge where her husband was, they focused on Weatherly's agency. They discovered it was alarmed and followed the two employees to their homes. After three days of not seeing Weatherly's car in the building's parking garage, they surmised he was out of town on business and they assumed it probably had to do with Factor.

"Sergey, I'm sorry now I didn't place a tag transmitter on his car."

"Don't sweat it. How the hell did we know he would take off after Factor? We have to watch and let him do our job for us."

"I could always tap the office phones."

"Petra, does that seem like a smart thing to do? One of the employees is an expert in that kind of thing. You can bet he's rigged up an automatic sweep in their offices. On the other hand, you might have something. Let's tap their home phones. Neither of them will be expecting it."

"We could break into the agency too and see what we can find. The alarm system wouldn't be a problem."

"I don't want to do anything to tip our hand. Besides, I bet they have intruder surveillance cameras which would take too long to find and disable. Relax. After all, Borichov's paying for our time."

"Sergey, you know as well as I do he's going to get impatient. I'm surprised he hasn't already been on our case."

"Yeah, you're right. I better cover our asses. I'll call Mr.Federov and let him know where we stand just in case."

Later in the evening, Sergey spoke to Dimitri Federov about the events of the past month. "We're keeping a low profile and letting the PI find the target. It means staying here until something happens. The point is we don't know how long it'll be."

Federov's demeanor was of extreme irritation. "Damn it. I knew this was going to happen if I gave in to Borichov. I don't have anything for you right now so we're not pressed for time. Stay on it and I'll get a hold of him."

Sergey and Petra looked at each other. Sergey exercised his shoulders and rotated his head around his neck to loosen it. "Petra, go out and buy us some vodka. I'm stiff all over. Tomorrow, let's find a gym around here where we can work out."

Petra smiled for the first time in weeks, picked up the car keys and went out.

Moscow, Russia

Federov slammed the phone down on its cradle. Two men in the room glanced at each other. One nodded his head towards the door and they beat a hasty retreat from the room shutting the door and leaving the mounting fury behind them. Federov sat down behind the desk and called Borichov's private line. He poured a glass of vodka while he waited for the connection to be made.

"Hello," was the reply in Bulgarian.

Federov responded in Russian. "Borichov."

The voice changed to Russian. "Dimitri. What do I owe this extreme pleasure to?"

"This is not a pleasure call. You're aware my assets have run into a problem locating your person."

"Yes, yes. A little inconvenience I'm sure, nothing more. I'm certain they will come across him shortly."

"I want you to understand they're waiting for him to be found and it may take a lot more time. I don't want them to be told to do anything which would jeopardize their existence. Are we clear on that, Borichov?"

"Yes, of course. I'm sure they'll use good judgment since they work for you."

"One more thing. I don't have any jobs for them right now but when I do, I'm pulling them off."

Federov hung up the phone without any further word. That imbecile Borichov better let the team choose the best tactics. He couldn't afford to have them exposed. He regretted again he had agreed to his request. Brother-in-law or no, he swore it wouldn't protect him if things went wrong.

Varna, Bulgaria

Borichov bristled when the connection was broken. Common sense replaced his anger. That Russian son-of-a-bitch would have me killed and not think twice. It sounds like his team knows what the hell they're doing. How in the hell did Factor wise up to my move? He can't stay hidden forever. Sooner or later he'll try to contact his wife. It's ironic that his wife is paying some investigator to find him. When he does, I'll be there.

Chapter Twenty-six

SAME OLD, SOME NEW

Tuesday. July 2
San Francisco, California

Adam walked down the stairs leading from the last counterfeit ID supplier on the list. Unfortunately, Ray Peterson had been right. He wiped the sweat off his forehead. The Asians were certainly much more sensitive and careful than the Mexicans when it came to providing bogus papers. He doubted they would give up their security for any amount of money. It left someone out there not yet on a police blotter. Now this was really going to get harder. He needed to come up with a backup plan for locating Factor. He had to hand it to the guy. If he went looking for false ID, he would have sooner or later dealt with someone on the list. Adam was positive he had obtained false ID; it would have been a priority for me. Let's say Factor had someone's confidence to get them from a source. It implied trust or a relationship which seemed unlikely given the man's character. Shit, this has evolved into a real challenge. The more he thought about it, the more he wanted to find the guy.

Adam checked out of the hotel and quickly found the highway south. He thought about his schedule for the next few days. I have to check with the office, bring Mrs. Factor current, and recharge my batteries. It wouldn't hurt to get another approach going as a backup. He yawned. I haven't taken a day off since this started. He'd go back to San Francisco at the end of the week, get together again with Ray Peterson and exchange ideas. Maybe having the grisly veteran as a sounding board would give him a fresh outlook. At least I'll get to enjoy the holiday.

Wednesday, July 3
Newport Beach, California

When Adam walked into his office, Elaine and Marty rushed up to greet him. "Wow, Boss. It's been a while. We thought you didn't like us anymore."

He smiled at their excitement. "I missed you two birds too. Pour us a cup of coffee and let's cover everything we have on the Factor case. After that, bring me up on our other business."

They spent almost two hours covering the aspects of the Factor disappearance. Adam summarized his search among the false ID merchants and the implication of the failure. "I was counting on this approach to verify Factor is in San Francisco."

Elaine took his detailed notes and entered them into their computer system. Marty described his efforts to locate and identify callers on the phone records. His work was slow and methodical. After all of them had completed their reports, Adam leaned back on the conference room chair. "Okay, where does that leave us? Are we any closer? Are we barking up the wrong tree? What's our next step?"

Elaine was the first to speak. "Adam, Marty and I think you're on the right track. You have an eerie feel for Factor and how he thinks. If he has to have false ID as you say to stay hidden and gain some security, they had to come from someone. Finding the person would give us the name he's using."

Marty spoke up. "I'll keep going with the phone logs. Whoever is trying to kill Factor has to be drawing blanks as well. They don't have any of the information and contacts we have. It will keep buying us time. I'm running a crosscheck of all the domestic calls against the State Department's registered arms dealer list. So far, I've only got one match, Carlos Sengretti out of Tampa, Florida. Unfortunately, the list only consists of U.S. arms dealers. My next step is to try to get to the Norwegian Initiative on Small Arms Transfer. The other group that may have information I can use is the International Peace Research Institute in Oslo or PRIO as it's known."

It was Adam's turn. "His wife thinks he'll be laying the foundation to disappear again. We don't know how much time that gives us. Two months have passed. How long will he stay around? We're pushing the clock."

Elaine speculated. "Adam, let's go with your hunch he's already obtained false ID. He would have got them to cash checks. It's a long shot but maybe we ought to check all new bank accounts in San Francisco over the past six weeks. Maybe we could narrow it down to saving accounts at the beginning with a minimum balance. We could throw in a safety deposit box rental with the new account for the cash we believe he has with him."

"Nice thinking on the banks, Elaine. How about running a list for me? However, I'll wager he'll hold on to his cash in case he's forced to make another sudden move."

Marty joined in. "How about checking new registrations on used cars in the area over the same time? He may have bought himself a car to get around."

"It's something to consider especially if he had to anticipate a quick getaway. The problem is I doubt that he would re-register it and I bet he paid cash too. On the other hand, he may have applied for a driver's license to get a car. I'm heading back to San Francisco on Sunday. I'll ask Ray Peterson to run me a list of all new drivers' license applications in the city. I'm going to give Mrs. Factor our progress or lack of this afternoon. She may want to back out of her arrangement."

Sitting back on the sofa in the Factor house, Adam opened his notebook and summarized the results to date. He searched Diane Factor's face for disappointment and resignation. Instead, she surprised him.

"Mr. Weatherly. It appears you've made good progress so far. After all, you are covering the possibilities and ruling out the improbable. Please continue your search and I am grateful your reputation is well justified. Find him, Mr. Weatherly. Jim may well be planning to leave again but his insistence on thoroughness will not allow him to rush the process."

As they both came up from their chairs, Diane Factor surprised him again when she added. "Your intuition Jim may have developed a relationship which gave him an access to a counterfeiter is a very astute observation. I have never seen the quality come easy to him but I know he has it. Thank you."

Adam left the house and drove deep in thought which is why he failed to notice the car pulling out from the curb behind him im to his house. The two occupants noted the car and the address and drove on.

As he turned the corner, Sergey put a stick of gum in his mouth. After a quiet moment, he said to no one in particular. "We just got another shot at Factor."

Sunday, July 7

When Adam left early Sunday morning for San Francisco, he didn't see the dark car trailing him up the coast. There was no need for Sergey to maintain a visual distance with the planted transmitter underneath Weatherly's car sending out a tracking signal. When they arrived in San Francisco, they noted the hotel where Weatherly stayed and went to find one with their requirements. They would start taking turns following him in the morning.

Monday, July 8
San Francisco, California

Adam woke, exercised, showered, shaved and dressed. He made a phone call to Ray Peterson. After a few moments, a gruff voice answered. "Peterson."

"Ray, this is Adam. Yes, I'm still at it. Do you have time to get together after work for dinner?"

"Adam," Peterson replied in a friendly tone, "of course. I'm anxious to hear what's been happening. Pick me up at my house around six this evening." Peterson gave him the address, home phone and directions.

Adam opened his briefcase and pulled out the package from Elaine. The list of financial institutions in San Francisco offering bank accounts was staggering. There had to be at least two banks on every block in the city. Besides the logistics in canvassing the banks, he had to contend with privacy laws if he inquired about the amount in each account. He opened a street map of the city, placed the list next to it, and used a color marker to place the bank locations on the map. It was close to two hours when he finished. He estimated that there were over three hundred banks. At least he only had to talk to the New Account persons.

Adam was glad he chose to leave early for the East Bay where Ray Peterson lived. The traffic exiting the city was just as bad as Los Angeles. He followed the directions and located his two-lane street within a condominium complex. He parked in a visitor stall and walked to the house. Peterson opened the door before he released the doorbell. They shook hands and went inside to the living room. The room had a piano in the corner with small, silver framed pictures on the sideboard. A flowered-print sofa complete with large, tasteful throw pillows occupied the opposite wall with a mahogany coffee table stylishly containing magazines, a lacquered box and a vase with three roses. His flabbergasted expression drew a laugh from Peterson. A slim, petite woman in her late thirties with natural red hair came into the room when she heard their conversation.

"Adam, meet my wife Janyce. She's the one responsible for this décor."

He recovered from his initial surprise and extended his hand. "I'm very happy to meet you. I've known Ray since our days with the LA Sheriff's Department."

Janyce smiled. "It's always nice to meet Ray's friends. I understand the both of you are going to have a men's night out so I'll say goodnight."

When they were in the car, Adam turned to his friend. "Ray, I can see why you stuck with the force. You have a beautiful wife and home."

"Now don't get sentimental with me." Peterson replied secretly pleased with Adam's reaction. He gave the directions to Roma d' Italia, a family-owned Italian restaurant. "You'll like this place. Waiters shout above the talking customers and mouth drooling aromas fill the room."

Peterson claimed his reservation and they were shown to a table. Ray ordered a carafe of Chianti and they were supplied with warm bread while they talked. Adam briefed him on the developments of the case, his lack of success with the false ID approach and his assumptions and inferences.

"If you haven't found this guy after two months, it's really something. He's either not here or he's really, really good at covering his tracks."

"This guy has my respect and awe, Ray. He's adapting on the wing and doing a hell of a job at it. Anybody else would have called his wife, charged a credit card or something. He's given up the past."

"Nobody totally abandons his past. So you think he's still here in San Francisco?"

"I'd bet the house on it. The question is for how long." He mentioned Diane Factor's feelings about her husband's flight. "I have two other paths to try. Tell me what you think about them."

Adam described the bank account and driver's license approaches. "I struck out with the false ID but one of these avenues could come up with something. Could I ask you to get a dump on the drivers' license applications in San Francisco over the last two months? That will leave me free to cover the banks."

Peterson frowned. "The driver's license applications may not help if he lied about his height and weight and changed his appearance. The fact the photos are in color may help there. He probably gave a false address. The best we can hope for is to know he's here and discover his identity. I can do it but you're going to have a problem with getting the banks to give personal account information. If you run into a snag, have them call me at the station. I hope you have a comfortable pair of shoes with you."

They were observed leaving the restaurant by a dark car parked towards the back of the restaurant's parking lot. "Petra, tomorrow go back to the address and find out who he visited. I figure he's done for tonight. We'll go back and get something to eat."

Tuesday, July 9

Adam dressed comfortably with slacks, a sport shirt and walking shoes. On the way to breakfast he deposited his gun in the hotel room safe. He planned to strike out on foot across the route he had outlined. The only thing he needed was the map, notebook and photos of Factor.

Two blocks away, Petra observed the tracking signal was static. "It looks like he's not going anywhere. I'll take the car and check out the East Bay address."

Sergey nodded. "Call if you run into anything, I'll walk by his hotel later on and make sure he's there."

The first bank building on the map was down the street. People came and went through the heavy glass double doors set in a baked brick exterior. He found the New Accounts desk and waited for an elderly man to complete his application. The desk sign read Desmond Morris. He was a thin young man wearing glasses, wrinkled white shirt and plain tie. He sat down on the just vacated chair in front of the desk. He took his PI credential out of his pocket and placed it on the desk with some photos.

"Mr. Morris, I'm a private investigator and would like to ask you a question."

Morris stared at the credential and looked up. "Yes?"

"I would like to know if the man in these pictures has been in here during the last month or so to open an account, possibly a savings account."

Morris went through the photos. "I haven't seen him."

"Is it possible someone else at the bank waited on him?"

"Oh no. If I leave for even a moment I close the desk. He doesn't look familiar at all."

Adam thanked him and left the building. The next bank was half a block away. At this rate it was going to take him a month to hit every bank on the list. He wondered if he should have Elaine and Marty fly up to San Francisco and help him but decided against it. They had little experience reading the nuances of a reply in the event something struck a chord with a bank employee.

Thursday, July 11

Sergey and Petra stopped around noon at a small café and ordered sandwiches and coffee. They had been taking turns at a tandem tail of Weatherly switching off and on at designated intervals. In between bites, Sergey mumbled. "The way I see it, he thinks Factor is here and is checking banks for a sighting. This can go on for some time and my feet are getting sore."

Petra nodded dispassionately. "This isn't much fun and sure ain't getting us anywhere. Sooner or later, Borichov is going to get really pissed. The problem is we don't have any choice. If the PI can't find him, we sure as hell aren't going to do any better. Think Borichov will call the whole thing off?"

Sergey shook his head. "Borichov doesn't give a shit how much it costs him. It's the principle of the thing. He won't pull us off no matter how long it takes. It leaves us caught in the middle between and him and Mr. Federov. Our only hope is Mr. Federov will need us for another job. I think we stop following Weatherly before he gets wise to a tail. Let him run and we'll use his hotel and car to keep an eye on him."

"Okay. What say we head for the gym?"

Monday, July 15

The distributed circulars and word of mouth around the marina had produced an increase in jobs and calls to the house. Jim, after getting approval from the Queterras, installed a voice mail feature offered by the phone company with a separate number. Marie Queterras was a saint but even her good graces were being put to the test with the calls.

It helped the bulk of the calls dealt with less challenging work easily handled by Miguel and a couple of his friends. They were busier than ever. Jim steadfastly refused to take any money from them. Rather, he insisted they do the best job possible. He never wanted to deal for any length of time with people but to his surprise he was comfortable with it. The more sophisticated jobs requiring his personal intervention were less frequent but better paying. He didn't mind the arrangement; the jobs were interesting and required his interaction with other companies. It gave him time for the early morning martial arts classes. His Spanish had significantly improved from dealing with Miguel and he kept on with the language lessons after work.

He still had one issue he didn't quite know how to handle. Sometime, the boat owners paid with checks made out to him. He had avoided opening a bank account in order to minimize any attention. He mentioned the predicament to Chris one night after they had met for dinner. The reason he gave was he didn't want the responsibility.

Chris laughed until his eyes watered. "Nick, I don't know about you."

Jim somewhat taken aback with Chris's reaction annoyingly asked. "What's so funny?"

Chris wiped his eyes. "You are. On one hand you tell me you don't want the responsibility. On the other, you're generating jobs and income for what, three or four people? You have a small company going and it sounds like it's somewhat successful."

Jim stared at Chris with mouth agape and with a shock realized the implication of the statement. The reality of the situation caused him to spill his beer.

"Hey, Nick. You all right? I didn't mean to laugh. It's just that you've gotten to know the Pier 39 Marina people, you've printed circulars, employed a number of people, got a separate business line, and have a decent income."

Jim just stared at him. My God, Chris was right. He had done all of that. What in the world was he thinking of? "Sorry, Chris. I guess I didn't look at it that way. I thought I was being helpful."

"You have been. What you have accomplished in a short time is remarkable. Look, there is a way around the check situation. I have an accountant who can take the checks after you endorse them, cash them and write checks out to the people you designate. That way you won't have to worry about it. I'm sure he'll charge a small fee per check but it'll save you the time and trouble."

Jim toasted his companion. "Chris. Thanks. I don't know what I'd do without you."

Later that night as Jim prepared for bed; he wondered if he should tone down his activities. He looked at the accountant's name and phone number he had received from Chris. On the other hand, the suggestion was a good one and would keep him in the background.

Tuesday, July 16

The next day, Jim met with the accountant. He had an office in a two-story, stone-front office building. The sign on the door read George Marx, CPA. The receptionist was an elderly woman with a bright smile and motherly eyes behind horn-rimmed glasses. The wall by her desk displayed Marx's framed diplomas and certifications. Jim introduced himself and was led into an office with large bookcases containing wide three-ring binders and a row of five-draw filing cabinets. An over-crowded desk by the window was accompanied by a side console holding a computer, monitor, and fax machine. Marx rose to greet him and directed him to a chair. He looked to be in his late forties with an easygoing manner. He wore a pair of jeans and a brown long sleeve shirt with the sleeves rolled up to his elbows.

Marx initiated the conversation. "On the phone you mentioned Chris Muncie referred you to me. How can I help?"

Jim had thought about a story stressing a truthful portion to give it plausibility. "I recently moved to San Francisco and had some success putting together a small business at the Pier 39 Marina. The problem is the bookkeeping task ties up my time because I'm personally involved with the work. I need someone who will deposit my payments and write checks to the contract labor helping me. I have a bank account but I prefer you open an account for me allowing you to access it. You can take your fee from the account."

Marx asked cautiously. "How much money are we talking about?"

Jim understood the inference of the question right away and laughed. "No money laundering I assure you, not with an amount probably around $2,000."

Marx grinned. "You have yourself an accountant. Fill out the form my secretary will give you and we'll start things going. It'll take a couple of days. The checks will be written on my letterhead for convenience and you'll get a monthly statement."

Jim thanked him and left. As he walked away he congratulated himself on a perfect way to avoid any frequent contact with his own bank.

Chapter Twenty-seven

ANOTHER INVESTIGATIVE APPROACH

Wednesday, July 17
San Francisco, California

Adam was climbing up one of San Francisco's famous steep hills enroute to still another bank. Why was it he seemed to go uphill more than downhill? He was about to answer his own question when his cell phone buzzed. He answered. "Adam."

A voice chuckled. "How are your feet holding out? Any luck?"

"Hi Ray. I haven't done this much walking in years. Nothing has come up yet. I think you have more banks in San Francisco than pigeons. What do I owe this honor?"

"It took a while but I got a copy of all the drivers' license applications from the Motor Vehicle Department. Want to know how many?"

"Spare me the depressing details. When can we get together?"

"How about coming in this afternoon?"

The Investigations Division of the SFPD was housed in a four-story, graystone building that resembled a fortress with wire mesh covering its lower windows, a double entry foyer and a gated entrance to an underground parking structure. Ray Peterson left Adam's name at the front desk where he was given a visitor badge and assigned a visitor's parking space. He took the elevator to the second floor where Ray waved him over. He explained. "I have an office at the station where we met the last time. This building is where we get our real work done." He led Adam to a filing room with a conference table and straight-back chairs. Ray laid a thick folder down on the table. "Knock yourself out. No one will disturb you in here. Coffee's outside if you want some."

Adam sat down and opened the folder. The applications were in chronological order. He saw they included male and female applicants. "Hey, Ray, we could have trimmed down this pile by specifying males only."

"Tsk, tsk, Adam. Didn't you tell me this guy changed his identity? Who's to say he's not only careful but cagey."

Adam laughed. "Ray, I take it back. You're worth your weight in gold."

Adam sat quietly and carefully examined every application. He sorted them into three stacks; no-way, maybe, and could-be. He placed the no-way pile back in the folder and went through the maybe applications trying to associate the photo with the height and weight datum. He paid particular attention to those men with beards and moustaches. He reclassified the maybe applicants into no-way and added them to the folder. He saved the could-be stack for last. Adam stood and stretched. He glanced at the wall clock. He had been at the table for over two hours. He needed a break and got a cup of coffee. He came back and sat down. "Okay, Factor, are you here?" He took his time on the applications studying the faces. He found some credible matches but most were eliminated when their height and weight or age were completely unreasonable. At the end, he narrowed the potential field to two individuals and entered their address into his notebook. He pushed back the chair and massaged his shoulders. He had now been at the table for almost four hours. He gathered up the folder and walked over to Ray Peterson's desk.

"That's it, Ray, only two out of the pile look good."

He held out his hand for the folder and glanced at Adam's notebook. "The addresses are within a couple of miles of each other. Do you want me to tag along?"

"No, thanks. I appreciate everything you've done for me. I'll let you know what I come up with."

It took Adam over an hour to determine the two men on the applications were not Jim Factor. He called Ray at his office to let him know he struck out with this approach. Somewhat philosophically, he documented the negative results in his notebook. He knew Factor had out-foxed him so far. He was chasing what he would have done. Maybe it was time to try to second guess his next step. He still had another two or three weeks canvassing banks ahead of him. After that, he'd see.

Thursday, July 25

Adam was now working his way to the northeastern part of San Francisco. This area was tourist-oriented with Telegraph Hill and the surrounding Lombard Street and the Embarcadero to the east. He had already visited over one hundred and fifty banks and credit unions with no success. He entered the lobby of The First National Bank. It had the familiar trappings of a savings and loan. He proceeded to the New Accounts desk. The woman at the desk looked like all of the rest he had encountered. Conservatively dressed, reading glasses perched at the end of her nose, a name tag on her lapel that read Marge Santos, and poised in front of the computer catching up on entries.

"Good morning, may I help you?"

Even the question, the body language and tone were the same. "Good morning to you. My name is Adam Weatherly and I'm a private investigator trying to locate a man who we believe is in San Francisco." He held out his credentials so she could read them. Satisfied, she leaned back. "What does he look like?"

"I have some photos here. Please look them over carefully. He might have changed in appearance. He is tall, about six-foot two inches and weighs around two hundred and five pounds."

She placed them in front of her and studied them. "I may have seen this man." She said after a while.

Weatherly's heart skipped a couple of beats. "What did you say?"

"I think I've seen this man." She pointed to a picture of Factor that Elaine had doctored with a slight beard. "I'm sure he opened an account here but I can't remember when. It can't be that long ago."

"What was his name? Was it James Factor?" Adam was sure Factor didn't use his real name but he had to make sure.

"No, that doesn't sound familiar. The problem is I see so many people who come in and start an account."

"Is there any chance you could go through all of the recent applications?"

"I'm afraid not. People who have started and used their account are under a confidentiality umbrella restricting even bank employees."

"Ms. Santos, here's my card. If you see him come in, please call me. I am staying in town."

Adam walked out of the bank exhilarated and relieved. Finally, a break! He took out his cell phone and called his office. Elaine answered.

"I got a hit." He could hear her call Marty and both excitedly came to the phone before he could expand on his news. When they both were on the phone he explained what he had been doing and the results of his canvassing. He read them the name of the bank and the employee who identified Factor. "Elaine, we still don't know the name he's using but we now know he has a slight beard. Maybe he's letting it grow more. Let's concentrate on generating several versions of Factor's photo with a beard. I'll run it by this bank employee and see if we can get a better feel for his present appearance. Let's also try to get an idea of the neighborhood makeup within a mile or two of the bank."

The next call Adam made was to Diane Factor. "Mrs. Factor, this is Adam Weatherly."

"Mr. Weatherly, any news? Are you still in San Francisco?"

"I am, and I do have some news." He summarized his activities and the successful identification. He could hear her let a deep breath out.

"Mr. Weatherly, that's wonderful! What's your next step?"

"Up to now, I have avoided jumping ahead until we could be sure he was here. We have more options. Let me think them out and call you back."

The last call was to Peterson. "Ray, I got a hit." He gave an overview of the search and named the bank.

Ray replied. "Adam, I knew if anyone could do it, you would. Congratulations! This opens up new territory for you. Let me know when you want to get together."

"Thanks, Ray. I'll get back to you."

Adam put his cell phone away and started back to his hotel. He was going to change and get a steak. He would think about the next move as he relaxed. It wasn't lost on him it was a week short of three months since Factor had gone. How much more time did he have?

Monday, July 29

Adam returned to The First National Bank with the doctored photos of Factor sent to him by Elaine. Marge Santos picked one of them out as definitely like the person who opened the account. She still could not recall anything associated with the transactions. He thanked her and again reminded her to call if the man came back to the bank. If Factor were working, he would have to cash checks, which meant using the account on a weekly basis. Damn. Somehow though he again had a feeling Factor had thought through this possibility as well. He grudgingly continued to admire the man. However, we'll see. If he didn't get a call from the bank within two or three weeks, he would assume Factor remained a few steps in front of him.

Chapter Twenty-eight

AN UNEXPECTED INCIDENT

Friday, August 2

Jim drove away from the marina later than usual after a meeting with Miguel and three other men who were kept busy at the marina during the summer when boat owners were enjoying the weather and the constant breezes. Miguel had turned out to be an astute and observant businessman. Jim gladly partitioned the work to give him more of the better paying assignments. That afternoon, Miguel had asked if they could get together at the Bayfront Bar after things quieted down for a discussion. To his surprise, Miguel was accompanied by two other workers when he entered the bar. They sat in a semi-quiet table at the back and ordered beers.

Miguel spoke first. "Nick, we want to thank you for what you have done for us. We have been getting steadier and more regular work since you came. You are an honest and gracious man."

Jim was chagrinned and visibly touched. "I didn't offer anything you couldn't have done by yourself but I'm glad I could help."

"This is not the only reason we wanted to talk to you." Miguel continued. "We have an idea based on our previous experiences with marinas in Mexico."

Jim put down his beer and listened attentively.

"Most boat owners are people working during the week who come to the marina maybe two to four weekends a month. They probably have something to take care of on the boat so they do it in the little time they have which cuts into their play schedule."

Jim nodded and could see this would be the case.

"Here's what we think. If someone could offer a service for scheduled maintenance to repair or modify or even clean the boat for the owner while it was idle, then we could keep busy without being pressured and have the boat waiting for the owner. He could pay us after he inspects the job to ensure it was done properly."

Jim replied. "Miguel, it's a great idea. Why come to me? After all, this is something all of you can do."

"Ah, now we get to the bottom of the pail. Nick, you have established yourself with some of the large boat owners. Also, the other boat owners have seen your flyer and heard about you. We think if you were to organize us, we could approach them under your management."

"Miguel, I think you overestimate me and underestimate yourselves. I can see how it may work but let me think it over for a couple of days."

Jim drove away thinking about the possibilities and the logistics of the business proposition Miguel had laid out. He parked his car in its usual place in front of Bob Nagel's house and was on the way to the Queterras residence when he heard a muffled cry for help. He saw a young woman being dragged into the shadows between houses across the street by two men. He raced without thinking across the street and dove directly at the man holding the woman. He released her and turned towards him extending his arm in a short sweeping motion to allow a knife to open and snap in place. The other man had a sawed-off pool cue with tape wrapped around the handle. Jim had the element of surprise and the fact he was taller than the men caused them to hesitate before they attacked. He quickly spun in front of the one with the club, dropped his shoulder and caught the end of the club as he pivoted on one foot to position himself in a rising crouch. The aggressive movement caught the man by surprise and he instinctively extended his leg to get away from the contact. Jim seized this moment to plant a kick to the man's knee that snapped the bone. The man screamed in pain, releasing the club as he grabbed his knee and fell to the ground in pain. Continuing his motion Jim dove to the left as the knife sliced across the space he just vacated. He reached down and picked up the club. He rose to his feet and struck the man's wrist hearing the bone break. He pushed the end of the club into the man's abdomen and then swung it across the back of his leg. Seeing the man drop to the ground incapacitated, he picked up the knife, closed the blade and put it in his pocket.

The woman who had shrunk back against the building came out and surprised him by throwing her arms around him, both crying and thanking him. By now, someone from the house had heard the struggles and screams, put on a light and called the police. Jim heard the approaching siren and disentangled the woman's arms. He glanced at her and was stunned by the beauty of the woman. The long dark hair framed her light blue eyes and sensuous features. It would not pay to stick around this scene. He simply nodded his head, and said goodnight in Spanish.

He ran down the street and into an alley leading to the Queterras. Christ. What in the world was he thinking of, taking on those two guys? But he couldn't stand there and do nothing? The woman would testify against the two guys and he would be just a vague memory. What a day. The good news is he couldn't be identified and in a city like this, it would soon be forgotten. He threw the knife and club into a storm drain after wiping off his fingerprints. He hoped he could sleep after this. Maybe he ought to mention it to Chris. He walked up the porch steps to the house and felt better. It was ironic he was more concerned about being identified than the danger he had been in. "Whew, what an evening."

At night in his room, Jim recalled the events of the day and thought about Diane. The moments they had shared seemed more precious to him now than they had been. He thought of the companionship and warmth and her silly expressions. He missed them more then he thought ever possible. He wondered how she was taking his disappearance. He smiled sadly when he recalled her stubborn nature. I bet she's not sitting still but she'd be limited in what action she could take. Forget it, he reproached himself. It was the sight of the woman tonight. Keep in mind; get exposed, get expired. Concentrate on this life for the time being and get ready for the next one. It's going to be tough enough. With this in mind, he fell into a restless sleep.

Saturday, August 3

It was a slow news day, as they like to say in the media, and the episode dealing with a heroic figure saving a damsel in distress became the centerfold of everyone's Saturday morning news. It was particular newsworthy by the reluctance of the woman's savior to stay around and obtain his due accolade. She described him as a tall Mexican man with a beard and fearless against two men armed with knife and club. The police found none of these weapons. She could not give any details except to say he may have used karate. The men were taken into custody and transported to the county jail hospital to get treated for broken bones and abrasions before they were charged.

Chris read the news account and heard the TV commentator describe the encounter of the evening. It was interesting to him because it had occurred within a mile of his studio. It would be satisfying if it had been one of his pupils who had applied the martial arts training.

Adam sat down to breakfast nursing a slight hangover from the night before and unfolded the newspaper. His attention focused on the article describing the heroic efforts of an anonymous stranger who disappeared shortly after confronting two men assailing a young woman. Some kind of guy, he thought, not to stay around and bask in the admiration of the grateful public.

Sergey and Petra were in the corner café enjoying a filling breakfast. Sergey had taken a newspaper off the bench and was going through the news. "Petra, listen to this." He read aloud the exploits of a man who appeared out of the night to save a woman from two thugs and then disappeared just as suddenly. "It is this cowboy mentality I find intriguing. Only in the West." Petra nodded in agreement and continued eating.

Ray Peterson read the daily newspaper over a cup of coffee while his wife was in the shower. His eyes fastened on the writeup of a stranger coming to the rescue of a young woman who was being assaulted by two armed men. He'll have to get more of the details from the responding patrolmen. At least someone had stood up to these young punks. "They ought to pin a medal on this guy."

Jim had gone out on the porch and picked up the newspaper. As was his early morning habit, he perused the front page and business section before heading to the marina. The article on the attack was given front-page coverage. He read the accounts and breathed a sigh of relief. There was no description of the man who had come out of nowhere and had gone without being thanked or identified. The woman said she was sure he was Mexican. It was a lucky break. He still couldn't believe he had his life in danger without a second thought.

Chapter Twenty-nine

A SHOCKING DISCOVERY

Monday, August 5

Adam was thinking about his next move. He was convinced Factor was in San Francisco. The question was; when would he turn up? He was tired of following the trail. Why can't I anticipate this guy? He was covering his tracks beautifully. He had little reason to believe Factor would brazenly go into a bank to transact business. "If it were me," he thought, "I'd apply for a credit card and make the payments by mail." No, he had to think farther ahead. How about the bank's location? It wasn't in the outskirts but then perhaps he counted on safety in numbers. He'd have to think more about it. It was time to bounce some ideas off Ray. He couldn't stop reminding himself three months had passed and Factor must be getting restless. He probably already has an exit strategy in place. His wife knows him well and her feeling was he's biding his time. Damn it. The guy's already accomplished more in losing himself than anyone would have given him credit. In midmorning, he responded to a call from his office.

"Adam," came from an excited and high-pitched voice. "Are you there?"

"Marty? What's the matter?"

"Are you sitting down?"

"Marty, what's the matter?"

"I'll tell you what the matter is. Adam, my house has been bugged!"

"Wait, calm down. Are you sure? How do you know? Who did it?"

"Adam, I know it may seem like I've become paranoid but I took the scanner home this past weekend to check the house. I've been working the Russian mafia angle and those guys scare me. Anyway, I scanned the entire microwave band and I came up with a subtle wiretap of the same type I found outside Factors' house."

"When could it have been planted?"

"Adam, you still don't have it all. I went over to Elaine's this morning and used the scanner. Adam, she had a tap on her line as well!"

He held the phone in front of him and stared at it not believing what he'd just heard. "Marty, are you there?"

"Yeah."

"Have you checked the office?"

"I do it twice a week. It's clean."

"Marty, let me call the both of you back. I have to think about it."

He hung up the phone. Shit, he had gotten careless. They would have known about him from their earlier wiretap. Did this mean they followed him to San Francisco? He doubted he'd placed Elaine and Marty in danger but he didn't want to take any more chances. He had underestimated them. They were smart enough to leave his office alone and bug his people's home. What else had they done? His pulse rate had climbed during the conversation. He dialed Ray Peterson's number.

"Ray? How's your schedule today besides busy?"

Peterson, noting the anxiety in Adam's voice replied. "I can make time. Come by in an hour."

Ray got in the car when it pulled over. "Adam, make a right and go about a mile. At this time of day, the most private spot is the Barbary Coast Bar."

Adam parked the car on the side lot and both men entered a bar dark with age, tobacco and beer smells amidst subdued lighting. They sat down in a corner booth. Ray waited patiently for him to start. When two beers were on the table, Adam covered the Russian mafia angle, the initial tap on the Factor's home and the wiretap discovery of his employees' homes.

"You have a sharp kid there, Adam. Not many people would consider using the scanner on their own home."

"The thing is I determined early I would have two investigations going but I didn't anticipate I'd be targeted."

"Why not? Didn't you tell me the Factor wiretap was there before you came on? They probably kept track of Mrs. Factor's calls including those to you. It's logical they would use you to find Factor. The question is, 'Where are they now?' I'd watch your back from now on. Are you carrying?"

"Yeah. Okay, let's change the subject to Factor. I checked the bank's location but it doesn't give me any insight into where he is. I guess I could place circulars in the area but I'm concerned about tipping these guys off. It's been over three months since he ran and pretty soon I'm going to run out of time."

"I think you've done a hell of a job tracking him here. What do you have in mind?"

"If Mrs. Factor is right and I have to agree with her, Factor is biding his time until he leaves again. She thinks he'll head for Europe."

"If that's the case he's going to need better papers than what he's been able to get. He'd be dumb to use his own passport and this guy been doing smart things. I'll bet he goes after a convincing passport next if he hasn't done so already."

"Ray, assuming he hasn't done it yet, it may give me a chance to get a step in front of him. I need to get information on counterfeit passport vendors. How tight are you with the local Immigration and Naturalization Service office?"

"We work with them regularly. Let's go back to my office and I'll get you Lt. Frank Malone's contact information. We've traded information in the past."

Adam drove in the underground parking structure and into a visitor's slot. As they were leaving the car, a thought struck Ray and he halted him.

"Adam, get back in the car and drive over to that closed police area. I'll follow you on foot and let you in."

Puzzled, he followed Ray's instruction and parked in an area where police technicians were milling around a vehicle.

Ray called to one of them. "Joe, got a second?"

Joe Banks broke away from the group and came over and shook Peterson's hand. "Joe, meet Adam Weatherly, a PI but he was one of the best police investigators you'll ever find before he went private." He motioned towards Adam's car. "How about doing a sweep on his car?"

"Sure, Ray, what are we looking for?"

"The usual if I wanted to be able to track it."

Banks went over to a bench and came back with a microwave scanner and a look-up mirror to pass under the car. Within minutes, a return signal was observed. The mirror isolated the tracking device next to the rear shock absorber.

"God damn it." Adam uttered. "I was a fool not to think of the possibility. This means they probably followed me to San Francisco."

Peterson directed Banks. "Move the tracking device to where Adam can remove it at will."

He turned to Adam. "As long as you leave it alone, they'll be content to track you. My advice is to watch your back. See if you can spot them."

"Ray, I can't thank you enough. Joe, I appreciate what you did. As long as I'm looking, I doubt that they will do anything but watch. They think they're running a bird dog. I'll let them keep that notion. Now let's see about that INS contact." As he followed Ray back to his office, Adam made a mental note to start carrying his gun all the time.

Petra had been monitoring the tracking device on Adam's car. They followed his car to the police station. "What do you think?" he asked Sergey.

"He's been on foot for three weeks checking banks and now he's stopped. I bet he's found something or something's turned up. Either way, we keep watching him. It's too early to shake him down. We have to wait until he's found Factor. I don't like the idea he's interfacing with police. I better call Mr. Federov and Borichov to fill them in. Remove the tracking device tonight."

Petra entered the room at their hotel. Sergey asked, "Well, did you get it?"

"Sergey, we have us a problem. The bug was there under the car but it was moved near the right rear fender. You know what that means."

"Yeah. He found it. Did you leave it there?" Petra nodded.

"Okay, we're gonna have to be careful tailing him. We'll monitor the car and when it's removed, we'll know he's close to Factor."

Chapter Thirty

RESCUER SEARCH

Tuesday, August 6

As was his daily regimen, Jim was at the martial art studio door when Chris approached to open for the day. They both changed and Jim was put through movements containing thrusts and strikes. At the end of the hour, they decided to meet in the evening for dinner.

Patrolman John Boyer was one of a number of police officers whose beat included the area around the street location where the attempted assault on the young woman had been foiled by the actions of the rescuer. He had been on the force for seven months and this was the most exciting assignment thus far. The mayor's office had relayed orders down to the Police Chief to find the hero. In turn, these instructions were passed down to the beat cops. They had a very limited description but if he was on foot, he probably lived close to the neighborhood. After he stopped for lunch, he decided to drop in on the two martial arts studios on his beat.

Patrolman Boyer opened the door of the martial arts studio and saw Chris Muncie with a group of students. When Chris glanced in his direction, Boyer waved him over. "Hi Chris. We're looking for the guy who saved the woman the other night. Seems like the mayor would like to honor him. We have a rough description and sketch and little else to go on other than he's Mexican."

Chris studied the description and curiously inquired. "Is he in any trouble?"

"Nah, it's the other way around. City Hall would like to give him a medal. The woman mentioned he used karate so we're visiting martial arts studios on the off chance he's a regular. Do you have anybody that fits this description?"

Chris looked up. "Sorry, I don't see any resemblance with our students."

"No matter. It was a long shot at best. I'll check the other martial arts studio as well." He put on his cap and went out.

Chris looked after him deep in thought as Boyer walked away. *That description could fit could fit Nick except the Mexican part. I think I'll mention it when I see him tonight.*

Jim went to the marina after the workout. He had deliberately stayed away from Miguel to consider the possible ramifications of the business proposition. He could understand the merit from his brief marina experience. The busiest times at the marina normally were during the weekend and holidays when boat owners showed up to get something done to their boat before going out. He knew it annoyed some of them who would prefer to boat during their excess time rather than take care of some item. An ability to call and dictate a repair or other work to be done while the boat sat idle during the week would generate a lot of interest. He grudgingly admitted his presence would give the boat owners a sense of security and trust having strangers unattended on their property. He could set material and labor costs. However, it would require an office with phone, scheduling board and a set of books. Additionally, for convenience he would have to open accounts with Halyard and Dockside Marine. It might be useful to talk over the concept with Mike Sweeney and Charlie Ford before making a final decision.

Sweeney listened as Jim described the business approach. After he finished, Sweeney was excited about the prospect. "Nick, it's a terrific idea. The plain fact is the boaters hit us up at the last minute too and want a quick turnaround. It would work well for all of us. Do you know where you would set up your office?"

"I haven't got that far yet. Somewhere around the marina would be my preference."

"I can offer you an office here at Halyard. We have plenty of space. It would be during our business hours. I can make you a good deal on it if you're interested."

"I am very interested, thank you. That's a very tempting offer. Let me talk to Charlie Ford, get his opinion and I'll get back to you."

They sat in Charlie's office at the rear of the Dockside Marine Hardware showroom. As he had done with Sweeney, Jim outlined the proposal including the offer by Sweeney to provide him with an office. Charlie was as positive as Sweeney. "I'm surprised no one has thought of it before now. It makes a great deal of sense and doing the work at our pace makes it cheaper for the boat owner. I'd say you have something there."

Jim sauntered down to the docks. He had money to start the venture but he had to be careful not to reveal too much of it. He could get it started and have a separate phone line with an answering machine. He needed to speak to Miguel about the arrangements and price structure. Jim expected it would take a little time to build up the business. A set of flyers would help in this regard.

Jim joined Chris at a nearby restaurant after work. They chatted about the local news and sports. During a break between the courses, Jim told him about the expanded business he was planning with the help of the other men that worked in the marina. Chris shook his hand. "That's some plan. Any idea how long it'll take before it catches on?"

"I really couldn't say. Sweeney's offer lets me finance it on a shoestring to see if it catches on. Miguel and the other men are excited. I'll get the phone line in with an answering machine and we'll see where it goes from there."

"Hey Nick, guess what happened to me today. I got a visit from a cop who was looking for the guy who saved that woman this past weekend. They even have a rough description and sketch."

Jim stared at him before he replied. "Do they have any leads?"

"No, and I told him I didn't have anybody with the description at the studio. Except for the Mexican angle and the fact this guy decided to take on two armed men, I might have figured it was you." Chris studied Jim's reaction to this comment.

It was Jim's turn to examine Chris's expression and attitude. "Chris, I'm going to level with you because we're good friends. It was me Friday night. I can't understand what would make me take such a chance."

Chris nodded knowingly and chose his words. "Nick. That was an incredibly brave thing you did ignoring your own personal safety and coming to the aid of someone in danger. You handled it efficiently and effortlessly from all accounts. I'm proud of you for reacting as you did. I don't know why you prefer not to come forward but I'll respect and go along with your decision."

Jim let out the deep breath he didn't realize he was holding. "Chris. Thanks again. It seems as if I'm always grateful to you."

Chapter Thirty-one

EVENTS PROGRESS

Thursday, August 8

Adam set up an appointment with Lt. Frank Malone by referencing Ray Peterson. The INS office occupied the 16th floor of a modern office building located in the downtown section of San Francisco. The lobby featured a marble floor, a large table with an elaborate flower arrangement under a chandelier and two large paintings of early San Francisco; one with a city scene highlighting cable cars pulled by horses and the other of the rocky coastline. Twin banks of elevators in the center were book-ended by a bank and a restaurant. Adam noted he hadn't made it to this particular bank.

The INS office was behind two large double doors. The young receptionist was equipped with a head set and stationed behind a walnut desk. The office area with black leather couch and matching chairs resembled a lawyer's waiting room. He spelled out his name and she efficiently checked a list and verified his appointment. She called a number and announced his presence. No sooner had he sat down when a side door opened and a large African-American man entered. He wore a white button-down shirt opened at the collar with a tie. His shirt cuffs were rolled up behind his thick wrists. A pen and a pack of cigarettes were visible in his breast pocket and a badge was fastened to his belt. He could have passed for a National Football League linebacker with a height of around six foot six inches, an eighteen inch neck, broad shoulders capable of supporting a bus and a shoe size over fifteen inches. "Mr. Weatherly?" He asked in a gentle low voice which contrasted sharply with his appearance.

He responded. "It's Adam. Lt. Malone?"

Malone nodded. "Call me Frank. Let's go back to my office." He led the way through a door with an electronic scan lock. "Let's stop here and get a cup of coffee." Coffee in hand, they continued to an office where the window faced the financial center. "One of the perks of this office is the view. What can I do for you? Ray's a good friend."

Adam described his search for a missing person from Newport Beach to San Francisco.

"I'm impressed." offered Malone. "It isn't often I encounter a PI who actually earns his pay or follows through in such a dogged manner. I can see why Ray likes you."

"The fact is I've verified he's in San Francisco but I've been in a tail chase mode. I hope to get a step in front of this guy. That's why I'm here."

"You're assuming he hasn't already obtained a passport. How do I fit in?"

"His wife has a strong conviction about her husband. She feels he's here temporarily and intends to leave the country. He's not using any of his own ID which means he has to get a passport. I would like to get information on all of the counterfeit passport suppliers you have in the area. I intend to contact them with a photo and offer a reward if they're approached by Factor. At the very least, I'll find out if I'm still chasing or ahead of him for once" Malone whistled. "We try to shut them down when we get a tip but they move around. The passports provided are just-get-by ones and good ones. The price varies accordingly from $500 to $5,000. Any idea of what nationality he'll try to assume if it's not U.S.?"

Adam snapped his fingers. "I didn't think about that. I just assumed he would try to get a U.S. passport."

"You're aware there are a large Mexican and Asian population in San Francisco. He could try for a U.S. passport but it'll be more difficult to obtain or get away with since we have so many checks and balances. Since he won't pass for Asian, you might assume he'll go for a Mexican passport. Unfortunately, they're relatively easier to obtain. If your boy is as sharp as you say, he may also switch to another identity rather than use his present one." He turned towards his computer and entered a few commands. The printer came to life behind the desk. "I'm printing what we have. If you should find out others as you check them out, I'd appreciate the feedback."

Adam agreed, thanked him for the information and took the elevator down to the lobby. He didn't notice the two men in a corner of the restaurant watching his exit.

* * *

Sergey put down the cup of coffee and turned from Weatherly to Petra. "Let's look at the building directory and see if we can figure where he was."

They stood in front of the directory and looked at the entire roster. Sergey mumbled. "Companies, professionals, financial advisors, consultants . . . Wait, here's the INS office. I don't see any other place which would interest him. Let's start keeping a tighter rein on him just in case he gets lucky."

"Sergey, I think this guy Weatherly's better than lucky; he's good. We can't get too close or he'll spot us."

"Petra, sometimes you surprise me."

Friday, August 9

While Adam ate breakfast, he recorded his activities and findings for the week in his notebook computer. He included the list of names he had received from Lt. Malone. Satisfied, he went on line and sent the report to his office. He checked his e-mails and saw a message from Marty to call when he found time. He leaned back on the chair, picked up his cell phone and dialed the number.

"Marty, I got your message. I planned to give you a call. What do you have?"

"It took time but I managed to get information on Factor's telephone contacts. The guy was keeping company with some very bad characters. The two men identified by the FBI as Russian mafia hit men report to a powerful Russian mobster by the name of Dimitri Federov. Factor was communicating regularly in the past year with two people. The first was Carlos Sengretti, a Tampa-based arms dealer. He's on the State Department registered arms dealer list along with Factor. The U.S. Customs Service raided his Florida office and home looking for him in early May. They haven't caught up to him yet but they've done a bunch of digging. Sengretti had set up companies in New York and Florida over the past ten months they think were part of an illegal arms transaction."

"It looks like Factor isn't so clean. What do they have on him?"

"Nothing. They haven't found any involvement except they knew each other and communicated. There's more; Sengretti's phone records and Factor's have a common name, Mikhail Borichov. You remember PRIO, the International Peace Research Institute I told you about? They steered me to IANSA, the International Action Network on Small Arms. They have a large file on Borichov which I'll e-mail you. The condensed version is he's a Russian national who calls Bulgaria home. He has a company there licensed legitimately to manufacture weapons from Russian designs. He's sold arms primarily into Central Africa and the Middle East and has ties to Moscow through Federov who, by the way, is his brother-in-law."

"So it looks like Sengretti and Borichov were in business together. We don't know how Factor fits in. He must know something or else he wouldn't be running. Track down photographs of all of these guys for me."

Adam then proceeded to fill Elaine and Marty in on his visits to Ray Peterson and the INS office. Before he hung up, he warned Elaine and Marty to exercise caution around and outside of the office.

"We don't know how dangerous or desperate these people may be so please be on your guard and call the police at the slightest hint of danger."

"Adam, we were about to tell you the same thing. They aren't interested in us, just Factor and you. We wouldn't want anything to happen to you."

He ended the call and reviewed the conversation. The people Factor had done business with were serious players with major backing. The fact they tapped the Factor residence, Elaine and Marty's homes and planted a tracking device on his car meant they were experienced and determined. He was now going to concentrate on finding Factor and the guys tailing him. For the first time, he allowed a thought in back of his mind to come to the foreground. Could there be a solution to Factor's problem? He was going to have to think about that one. It was looking like it just became his as well. He cracked a wry smile; God, it was good to be on the offensive for a change.

Wednesday, August 15

It was late evening when Jim completed and checked the installation of an upgraded radar, GPS and autopilot for a forty-two-foot Murray Peterson schooner. The twin-mast vessel had a rich mahogany interior and the care lavished on it by the owner was evident throughout. He had run the electronics until satisfied the system performed each of its functions. The sun had settled and the lights were on in the marina. He turned out the lights, went out on deck and locked the boat. He paused to appreciate the reflection of the lights on the water channels in between the docks.

A momentary sliver of light from a yacht across the dock caught his eye and made him back into the cover of the boat's bridge. There. He caught the reflection again. It came from the stateroom area of the yacht. No other lights were visible. Strange, someone on board was using a flashlight. Jim had met the owner when he had worked on the boat tied up on its port side. He cautiously moved over the side of the sloop onto the dock careful to let the boat shield him and kept to the shadows. He inched his way down the dock and moved up the pier to the next set of moorings. There had been a rash of break-ins at the marina but no one had been seen much less caught. Jim wondered how the intruder got in without being noticed.

Jim treaded carefully on his toes and moved along the edge of the dock to avoid loose or squeaky planks. A boat went by in the channel and the wake caused the boats to move up and down in the swell. He heard a gentle thump coming from the outer hull before he saw the small powerboat tied up to the yacht's railing. He crept up to the side remaining out of the light. He now could hear drawers opening and closing and felt the search rather than saw it. He looked around the dock and outside of the boat for any accomplices. He ducked when the thief came on deck and dropped a bag over the side into the smaller boat. Then, he disappeared down into the hold again. Jim climbed the boarding ladder onto the deck careful not to sway the boat and silently made his way to the door. The movements inside were clearer. If the thief was carrying stolen articles, he would have his hands too full to notice him and the surprise would be his. He heard footsteps on the stairs approaching the door and stood aside. The thief wore a black shirt and pants with a dark hat. When he straightened out on deck, Jim saw that he was easy over six foot with a muscular build. Damn, it was too late to back out now. Jim assumed a defensive stance and nonchalantly quipped. "Are you finished yet?"

Startled, the man let the stolen goods drop from his hands and whirled to face Jim. At the same time he reached into his waistband for a gun. Jim sprang and caught the man's arm while at the same time twisting and driving his elbow into the throat area. The man grunted and launched a kick at his leg. Sidestepping, Jim went down on one knee and swiped the man's other leg knocking him off balance. The gun toppled to the deck. Jim stood and moved in again. The suddenness of the man's fist caught him on the side of the face and he momentarily saw stars. He backed away and then quickly delivered a spinning kick across the man's head. The man yowled and raged forward at Jim. Again he sidestepped and used the man's charge to grab his hair and batter his head against the wall of the bridge. He then drove the force of his elbow against the man's face. The man flailed out his arms and fists. Jim caught his right arm and used the momentum to throw him across the deck where he came to rest in an unconscious heap.

The noise of the struggle attracted the attention of the marina security police who were now running across the dock to the boat. Jim quickly found the gun and pushed it out in the open with his foot. Then, he slipped as quietly as possible over the side into the water and shielded by the yacht quietly paddled away. He heard them stomp up the gangplank and find the thief. Their flashlights shined on the water looking for anybody else but by then he had reached the back of another dock and steadily worked his way to the shore. In ten minutes, the SFPD had arrived amid flashing lights and siren. He was soaked and the water had chilled him completely. He had to make it to his car and drive away. He hoped the marina security force would take credit for the capture. Right now he needed to get dry. He couldn't go to the Queterras' in this condition and raise suspicions. He wondered if he could impose on Chris again.

Once in the car, he turned the heater to high. He had to get out of the wet clothes. He drove to an isolated phone booth and called the martial arts studio.

When Chris answered, Jim confided. "Chris, I ran into a little trouble tonight and I need to have dry clothes. I'm not anxious to be seen."

"Come over here and park in the back. Follow me to my house and I'll fit you out."

Near Chris's house Jim parked on the street. He entered Chris's car and climbed out when they were safely in the closed garage.

"Come on in and get out of those clothes. I'll get some others for you. The shower is over there."

When Jim got out of the shower, dried and put on the clothes, Chris picked up the wet clothes and placed them in the dryer. He handed him a glass of brandy. "Okay, Nick, do you want to tell me what happened?"

They sat down in the living room and Jim related the account of the encounter on the burglarized yacht and his subsequent escape from the police by going into the water.

Chris shook his head in disbelief. "You could have gotten yourself killed. Did it ever occur to you to call the police and let them handle this guy? And why did you run away?"

Jim replied. "Chris, all I could think of is this guy has been ripping off the boats for some time and I didn't want him to get away. I had no intention of confronting him at the beginning. It just happened. I got lucky. He was a brute. I took off because I didn't want to get involved explaining it to the police."

Chris let out an exasperated breath. "This makes twice in one month you've been involved in a dangerous situation. Do you have a death wish or a hero complex? No, I take it back. A hero would have stuck around. Why didn't you want to be identified?"

"Chris, let's just say I'm publicity-shy. I appreciate you helping me out. I can't say what made me do it; it just seemed to be the right thing. You can bet I'll be a lot more careful from now on." Inwardly, Jim thought, I better be. I can't afford any more close calls.

The next day before Jim went to the marina he searched the newspaper for any accounts of the previous night. No need to take any further risks. There had been no mention of it on the morning news. When he arrived at his Halyard office, Mike Sweeney stopped him and related the excitement of catching the thief.

"How did they find him?" Jim asked.

"There was a loud commotion on a boat. The security people heard the noise and investigated. They found this guy knocked out on the deck and stolen property in his tied-up boat. He was armed. They seem to think he slipped on the deck and fell. The police say he told them he had a fight with someone but no one saw anybody else. A later search of his house uncovered a great deal of stolen goods."

Jim felt a sense of relief. "That's good news. More than a few boat owners were pretty worried about this guy."

Later, Miguel met him on the docks and they discussed the events.

"Nick, I have to say we're relieved he's been caught. I think some owners suspected it might be us."

"I doubt it but I'm glad it's over. We have a busy day ahead of us."

Friday, August 17

Jim was surprised to receive a call from George Marx early in the morning at his Halyard office. "Good morning, George. You're not calling to tell me I'm overdrawn already? I thought I was somewhat keeping track there was money in the account." The voice in his ear laughed. "No, nothing like that. Am I getting a list from you today for check dispersal?"

"Yes. I'll also be giving you some checks. Am I close to pushing the account?"

"Nick, remember when you told me we'd be dealing with about $2,000 or thereabouts? Well, presently the account is over $12,000." Jim gasped. "Are you sure?"

"You're asking an accountant if he's sure about accounting. Your business must be taking off. Does your list contain withdrawals close to that amount?"

"No, and the checks I'll be giving you more than cover the withdrawals."

"Well then, don't worry about it. I'll see you later on in the day."

Jim hung up the phone and stared out the window. How was that possible? What had he gotten himself into? He had no idea that the business with Miguel was doing so well. Thank God he had been using the accountant to funnel the money. Inwardly he was pleased the venture with Miguel was sustaining itself. The prospects for increasing the business were very bright. What amazed him was the enjoyment and satisfaction he was deriving from it. It could not have been more different than his previous life. With a tinge of sorrow, he would regret having to leave it behind when it was time to move on. In the meantime, the education he was getting would hold him in good stead at his next destination.

Friday, August 24

Adam checked his notebook and observed over three weeks had passed and he had not yet heard from the bank. He dialed the main number and asked for New Accounts. "Hello, Ms. Santos. This is Adam Weatherly, the private investigator. I talked to you last month about one of your accounts."

"Oh, yes. I still have your card. I haven't seen the gentleman since we talked. It's possible I made a mistake. If I do see him, I'll be sure to call."

Adam spoke to no one in particular after the call. "Why doesn't that surprise me?" He was chagrinned when he thought; Factor, I would have been really disappointed if you had finally slipped up.

Chapter Thirty-two

GUN CLUB

Marin County, California

Entering the fourth month, Jim assessed his progress in preparing himself. His Spanish lessons moved into reading and writing. He spoke and understood Spanish slowly albeit in an articulate manner. He was improving at a rapid pace in the martial arts due to the daily classes. He considered yet another aspect of his preparation. After another workout, he pulled Chris aside.

"By any chance could you teach me to use small arms? Of course I'll pay you for your time."

Chris looked at him. "You in trouble, Nick?"

"Not that I know of, Chris, but I think it would be prudent for me to be able to handle any situation. That marina incident kind of made me think."

"Okay, meet me here after the studio closes and we'll start more of your education."

As Jim went to the studio to meet Chris, he reflected on his experiences with small arms. He needed to get lessons on handling a gun in a crisis rather than from behind a gun club stall. It'll be best if I let Chris train me from scratch especially since he would be adept in firearms from his Seal days.

Chris drove them across the Golden Gate Bridge to a gun club located in Marin County. When they arrived, Chris was recognized and warmly greeted by Rod Boynton who Nick learned was a former Army Ranger. Inside the club he was led to a fortified room. Behind a thick wire mesh, there was a locked display of guns ranging from small arms to assault weapons. Chris checked out a pistol.

"I am going to start you off with an Austrian Glock Model 17. It's a 9mm pistol with a ten, seventeen or nineteen-magazine capacity."

"How about other pistols?"

"You'd be surprise by how similar they all look, feel and operate. The Glock is a good starting point because of its popularity."

Chris demonstrated the classic Weaver firing stance, the weight distribution on the ball of his feet, the shoulder turn, and the recoil-absorbing motion.

"Now we come to the important part, maintenance and cleaning."

"Where are your tools?"

"The only thing we really need is gun oil. Disassembly and reassembling is possible without tools. He disassembled the gun pointing out the chamber, firing pin, magazine feed, the cartridge ejection mechanism and the barrel rifling. He lubricated the components as he reassembled the gun. Then, he inserted ten rounds into the magazine.

"Actually, it can hold an extra round in the chamber; you need to cock it so a round gets injected into the chamber, then remove the clip and load another round in it. By the way, there are three safeties. Always hold the gun so it's pointing down and keep your finger off the trigger until you get set to use it."

"It sounds pretty important to know all about the gun."

"That's because it is. You're supposed to get so familiar with it you can disassemble, lubricate and reassemble it blind-folded within a short time."

"Let's go to the firing stalls and see how it feels to you. Some people never get beyond the first step because it frightens them or they get too nervous to hold it steady."

Both men accepted ear guards and eye safety goggles from the attendant. There were ten separate shooting stalls.

"Okay, now look at the stall's left side. The switch allows you to bring the paper target to any distance and the display tells you how far it is from you. Let's set it for twenty feet. I'll start it off first so you can get a feel for the position and noise."

Chris fired five consecutive rounds into the target. He brought the target in and the close spacing of five holes in the center was witness to his skill. He replaced the paper target and sent it out again. "Okay, you try it."

Jim positioned the gun in his hand, released the safety, went into a stance and slowly fired the rest of the magazine at the target. He was surprised at the small recoil. Chris brought the target to them and Jim saw he had missed most of the shots.

"The reason for the misses is the gun moves fractionally off on each shot." Chris added. "You have to make a barely perceptible adjustment to make sure it stays put. Let's try it again." He put another target in place and sent it out again, this time to thirty feet.

Jim removed the clip and loaded ten rounds from the box of shells. He assumed the stance, released the safeties and squeezed out five rounds. The spacing was more regular but off-centered.

"Now you're getting it Nick. The rest is practice."

After two more tries, Chris led them back to the gun cleaning area where the gun was broken down and lubricated. "This part is always important," Chris pointed out, "Dirt and dust are enemies of a clean shot." He reassembled the gun.

Jim returned the gun and paid for the session.

"Come here and practice on your own. When you feel you're ready for the next level, let me know."

Jim made time to practice at the gun club until and continued until he could center the patterns at fifty feet with quick succession shots. He found the acquired skill gave him a strong measure of confidence and satisfaction. He remarked to Chris on a visit to the studio he was ready for the next gun lesson.

They drove out that night to the gun club and Chris surveyed his progress with an appreciative nod. "You have a good feel for the gun. Put on this underarm holster and let me adjust it for you. I'm going to show you to react, draw and fire. For this drill, we are going to another area of the club. Without ammunition, I want you to reach under your arm, draw the gun and go into a firing stance. Do it slowly at first without looking at the gun. In fact, stare straight ahead. Go!"

Jim awkwardly followed the instructions for a time. After a half-hour, the action went a little easier and faster. Chris halted the drill at this point. "When this maneuver becomes smooth and fast, pull the trigger once at the end. I have a pistol with a holster in my home gun safe I can lend you for practice. You won't need any rounds. There's gun oil in there so you can keep it clean."

Jim managed to get to the gun club to practice the draw and trigger pull every other day. By the second week, he took the Glock, loaded the magazine, and went into a draw and fire routine ing range. He was pleased to note the bullet patterns were accurate and tight.

Chapter Thirty-three

SALES OPPORTUNITY

Friday, September 13
San Francisco, California

Jim observed both boat owners and merchants were anticipating fall-like change in the weather. The calls he received dealt with taking care of outstanding problems and preventative measures before some of them stored their boats. Miguel had mentioned the seasonal slowdown would occur and continue until spring. He and his friends were planning to move south in October to the warmer climate of Baja, Mexico and work marinas. Halyard was preparing their dry dock storage yard for owners who wanted to pull their boats out of the water.

Jim was approached by one of the yacht brokers at the marina to see if he was interested in a part time sales position. Steve Wilson was the owner of Pacific Coast Yacht Sales and an acquaintance of Wayne Collier. Wilson stood straight in spite of his years, had groomed white hair, and fancied cream flannel slacks and a blue blazer with brass buttons and a coat of arms on the breast pocket. His breast pocket handkerchief matched his open neck shirt. He completed the nautical ensemble by smoking a pipe.

"Nick, a few boat owners have spoken highly of your work for them. How about handling the floor with me? You can start tomorrow. My regular guy has decided to move away leaving me short. During the fall and winter I generally only stay open four days a week. Its part time work and you'll be on commission."

"Steve, my knowledge of yachts is rather limited. But if you're game, I'll take you up on it."

"Good. I don't require any type of business suit. It's too formal for what we do. Business casual is good enough."

That night, Jim opened the closet and pulled out the clothes and loafers he wore when he left home. They had been cleaned but left untouched in favor of the practical jeans and shirts. He made a mental note to buy another outfit the next day.

Saturday, September 14

In the morning Jim walked towards Nagel's house to get the car when he heard a woman's voice shouting at him. Curiously he turned around and found a familiar-looking woman staring at him with a smile. She jumped in between his arms and covered his mouth with a kiss. She then backed away and grabbed his hands. Tearfully she cried in Spanish. "Thank you for saving me." He looked around quickly to see if anyone had heard her.

Jim quickly answered in Spanish. "Senorita, it is not necessary. Please don't tell anyone you saw me."

"But you should be thanked. I am Angelina Alvarez. Here is my phone number. I won't tell anybody." She wrote on a piece of paper from her purse. "Please call me."

Jim took the paper and looked at her. She was more beautiful then he remembered. "Thank you. I must go."

"Wait. Before you go, what is your name?"

"Nick. I really must leave."

He ran off clasping the paper not waiting for a reply. Once he was safely out of sight he slowed down and resumed walking. Goddamn. What are the chances he would run into the girl on the street and how did she recognize him when it had been dark that night? He put the incident aside, placed the paper in his pocket and resumed his walk to the car and the task of getting new clothes.

Jim's first day casual business attire garnered guffaws from Jimmy but Marie thought it a nice change from the usual jeans and faded shirts. She commented. "Nick, don't pay any attention to them. You look very nice."

Pacific Coast Yacht Sales was in a large building with two large roll-up doors in the rear. The yachts were placed on metal frame beds covered by a navy blue curtain suspended from each hull. The boats were lined up in a row against a raised platform so an interested client could size up the boats and easily board them from the stern. Steve Wilson was a walking encyclopedia on boats which Jim found the information interesting and informative. Wilson pointed to the building interior. "We keep all of our boats inside. A potential customer has a comfortable environment to spend as much time as they want going through the various models. You'll notice most of our competitors display their boats in an open parking lot." He continued to talk as they strolled through the building. "Pacific Coast Yacht Sales represents seven lines of U.S. manufacturers. We specialize in cruisers and yachts from thirtyfoot to over eighty-five feet. We offer cruisers with the features of a luxury home. A few people choose to live aboard such boats. They're mostly deep-vee hull designs to ride smoother in choppy waters. The cockpit and deck is formed in one piece for beauty and easy maintenance. Hulls are custom-engineered. Their cavities are filled with structural foam to add flotation and integral strength. There is another advantage; the ride is quietly solid while boats without foam have a hollow, drumming sound going over waves."

He pointed to the items as he talked. "There's a lot of detailed engineering that goes into the boats. For example, the curved tempered windshields are correctly angled to deflect the rush of air from your eyes. The basic cost range from $125,000 to well over $1 million. A place like mine averages about $12 million in annual sales. Accessories like VHF radiotelephone, GPS navigation system with chart plotter, cable TV, telephone, entertainment center, cockpit and deck enclosures, and lifeboat are sold separately and installed by nearby marine supply companies. We'll take trade-ins but only on a case-by-case basis." Wilson's vast experience was evident in his tutorial as they walked around the premises.

"Nick, at the beginning when you see a family of two to three people enter, come and get me. Those are serious buyers. They'll spend two or more hours going through the boats they're considering purchasing. Look at their shoes. They'll wear loafers they can kick off or deck shoes so they can walk on the boat's deck. Solo visitors mostly are dreaming and looking until they hear the price. You walk them around and if the discussion gets serious, bring me into the action. Many of the customers come from the hot inland areas like Palm Springs, Phoenix and Las Vegas. They want to get out of the heat and it's cheaper having a boat to stay on anytime they want than buying a place along the coast."

* * *

Within three weeks, Jim managed to make one sale and set up two others by applying his new knowledge with his practical experience with marine electronics. His time with Wilson at the yacht sales office gave him an opportunity to appreciate the lines, construction and nuances of various boats and their manufacturers. The cruisers ranged in price with the electronics and engine selection pacing the expenses. Depending upon the options and size, the yacht manufacturer could take six, twelve months or as long as three years to deliver a yacht. A broker made a commitment to the manufacturer to buy several boats a year as a condition of distributorship.

Wilson took him to Seattle for a yacht pickup right at the shipyard. They ran a checkout test for two days before taking the yacht down the Pacific coast. The gas tanks were topped off in port and then they were underway. He went through the navigation chart plotter and radar, became acquainted with the rules of the sea, and given a tour of the operational console where engines, weather conditions, communications, and pilot position were located. The manufacturer representative who was a seasoned pilot besides Wilson, an engine technician, and the new ownerr were present during the non-stop trip to San Francisco.

Chapter Thirty-four

PASSPORT

Saturday, September 21

Since the dinner with Chris three months before when Jim had realized the depth of his involvement at the marina, it had been on his mind to plan the next phase of his flight. He decided to wait until the weather turned cooler. This would give him close to six months to complete the preparations to leave the U.S. He had some ideas. On the whole, it would be safer traveling through Mexico. There was a steady flow of people coming and going at all times. He was going to need a passport to get to a major city in Mexico where he could take a flight to Europe. He decided a counterfeit Mexican passport might be easier to obtain and attract less attention at the border. He ruled out going to Miguel's source where he had obtained the birth certificate and social security number. There would be too many questions raised. This left him with finding another source. His conversational Spanish was now passable and the accent could be explained by virtue of Spanish rather than Mexican parents. He had located a church mission a few miles away catering primarily to Mexican immigrants where he would make discrete inquires. He did not want to test his friendship with Jimmy for fear he might be traced to the Queterras.

Jim made it a point to drive by the mission for three days on the way to and from the marina. Generally ten to fifteen people seemed to be normally engaged in conversations with a small mission staff. On the fourth day, he parked the car down the block and ventured into the doorway. He looked around an open dining room. A female mission worker beckoned him and in Spanish kindly inquired. "Can I could help you?"

"I have a problem of sorts." Jim responded in Spanish in a whisper. "I want to go back to Mexico but I lack a passport. Do you know someone who could help me?" He searched her face for a sign she would be indignant or hostile to a possible unlawful request.

Instead, she responded in a low voice. "I know a few persons have been able to get documents. I think they talk to . . ." She paused and searched the interior of the room and motioned with her head at an unkempt man sitting alone at a corner table.

"Gracias."

Jim slowly shuffled over to the man having a cup of coffee. His appearance belied his intelligent eyes and cautious manner. In spite of the ruffled appearance, Jim observed his clothes were of good quality and the man was clean-shaven.

"May I sit down?" He asked in Spanish.

"Of course."

Jim paused, then ventured. "I would like to ask you a question on a delicate matter."

The man turned towards him and critically examined him from the beard to his hands to his clothes. Satisfied, he replied. "I am listening."

"I need to get to be able to get into Mexico and stay awhile without attention. I have heard a Mexican passport can be obtained by some people."

"I have heard it too. I have also heard the quality is related to the price."

"I am curious. What is obtained with quality?"

"I am informed a real passport can be obtained through channels but the price is high due to expenses."

This statement did not surprise Jim. He had read corrupt Mexican officials had been involved with issuing passports but he had not believed it until now. He felt his pulse increase. A real passport would eliminate the risk of going into and out of Mexico. It was better than he had imagined.

Reading his reaction, the man went on. "I see you are interested in quality. I assure you it is not cheap."

"Go on."

"The price is $5,000 in cash. Half when it is set up, half when you receive the passport. Is this agreeable?"

Jim hesitated. "Are you certain it is real?"

"I assure you it is the real thing." He glanced around the room and reached into his inside jacket pocket. He passed a passport across the table. "Here, look at mine. You see where I have a valid visa stamp on this page. This is how your passport will be."

Jim made up his mind. "What do I have to do?"

"You are to come to this mission in three days at the same time in the evening. Someone will approach you and ask you to join them on the street. You will sit in their car while a microscanner is passed over you to check for a wire and weapon. You will be blindfolded and driven to a house and into a garage. Please follow their instructions. They will need to have a name, place and date of birth and, of course, half of the payment in cash. Adios for now."

Jim stood up and walked out the door. He thought, the passport was expensive and would take almost half of his reserves. If it was real, it could eliminate a lot of problems. Did he trust this person? He could lose $2,500 if it was a hoax. On the other hand, what choice did he have? He already knew he would take the chance. He had three days to select another identity. He had now been in San Francisco over five months and had deliberately delayed getting a passport to avoid detection. It was time to move on. He had to be ready.

Over the next couple of days, Jim was apprehensive about the passport meeting but knew he had to assume the risk. He selected a new name, Tomas Cassandra. He opted for an older date of birth. As far as a birthplace in Mexico, his first inclination was Mexico City.

He arrived at the mission on the third day in the early evening and went into the dining room. He had a coffee in his hand when a dark-haired woman with sharp features and a scarf on her head asked if she could sit down at his table. He nodded and looked around discretely for his contact. He was distracted from his thoughts when the woman addressed him.

"Do you come here often?" she asked.

Startled, he turned to her. "This is only my second time. And you?"

"I come here occasionally. Would you like to go outside for a while?"

Jim mistook the invitation. "Sorry, I'm not interested. I'm waiting for someone."

"I am the person you were told to expect. Wait two minutes and go outside to the curb."

She got up and left. After a few minutes, Jim followed. The woman pulled up in an older model car. "Please get in." A block away, she pulled over again and had him sit back in his seat. She used the scanner. Satisfied, she gave him a black bag to place over his head. They had driven for twenty minutes when he felt the car go up a driveway and heard a garage door open. The car entered the garage and the overhead door closed.

"You may remove the bag. Please follow me." She showed him to a room with photographic and computer equipment. To one side, there was a stool in front of a white screen. "My purpose is to take your picture, get your information on an application and collect a payment."

Jim handed her the money and gave her the passport information. "When do I get the passport?"

"One week from today, go back to the mission at the same time and wait. You will need to have the final payment."

When the photo was taken, she motioned him to the car. He was instructed again to put on the bag and was driven back to the mission where he was dropped off.

As Jim lay in bed, he considered various ways of getting to his destination. He thought of flying directly from San Francisco to Mexico City but rejected the idea in favor of caution. It would be prudent to take a train to Tucson and a bus to the U.S./Mexican border. He could walk across the border to Nogales and get a bus to Mexico City. Once in Mexico City, he would arrange a flight to Europe.

He was suddenly and unexpectedly saddened to leave the good people who had taken him at face value and given him friendship, trust and respect. He'd say goodbye on the pretense he was heading to Seattle to inquire about a job opportunity. He'd wait until he had the passport before returning the car, making the final arrangements and giving his farewells. It was time to select a final destination in Spain.

Chapter Thirty-five

DEPARTURE PLAN

Wednesday, October 16

At the public library, Jim initiated a search for the Spanish destination. His first preference was Costa Blanca, the east coast of Spain. This area allowed a seaward interaction through the Mediterranean with Spanish coastal cities, the French Riviera, Monaco and Italy. Across the Mediterranean, on the North African coast was Morocco and Tunisia, and to the southwest of Spain were Gibraltar and Portugal. The islands off the northern coastline, Mallorca and Menorca were within reach. As Jim read further, he was drawn to Alicante, a typical Mediterranean town situated on the Spanish coast south of Valencia. It was the tourist capital of the Costa Blanca with a population of three hundred thousand and had an important role in the region's economy through its port which handled produce, wine, almonds and grapes. The city's Esplanade d'Espanna was considered the most picturesque promenade in the region with its multicolored marble pavements adorned with geometric designs and its magnificent palms providing shade besides the pleasure boat harbor. Ironically, it was laced with reminders of California; a major street named San Francisco, a fortress called Castillo de Santa Barbara and a church, Iglesia de Santa Maria. The clincher was its latitude of 38.5 degrees, about the same as San Francisco.

To take his mind off the passport during the wait, Jim kept himself busy. At last the day arrived. At dusk, he strolled to the mission and entered the crowded dining hall. With a cup of coffee in his hand, he settled into a seat at the back of the room and waited. The woman was nowhere to be seen.

"Tomas Cassandra?"

Jim was about to shake his head when he realized the significance of the greeting. "Yes?"

It was the man he had met earlier and with whom he made the arrangement.

"I believe I have something of yours. Would you care to examine it to make sure?"

A passport was slid warily across the table. Jim cautiously opened the cover and saw his picture with the personal data and official stamp. He looked at the man inquisitively.

"I assure you it is real. You have something for me."

Jim reached into his jacket and discretely slid a paperwrapped package in front of the man. He opened the package and counted the money.

"Everything is satisfactory. Please wait until I am out the door before you leave."

Jim nodded. This had gone easier than he had thought. Had he missed anything? "Wait." He heard himself say.

The man sat back down. "Is something wrong? I assure you it is the real thing."

"No, I believe you. I have another question."

The man raised his eyebrows. "Si?"

"Suppose I want to get another different passport."

"What do you mean different? A different name or a different country?"

Jim thought fast. "Both. Can you do it?"

The man looked carefully at him before speaking low.

"I have access to a person who can provide a Canadian passport. It would pass a close scrutiny."

"How much?"

The man shrugged. "Let's say $2,000. Once I have the information, it can be produced in twenty-four hours."

Jim thought for a second before replying. "Okay. This time I'll supply the photo and the essentials. I'll give you half at the time and the other half when I get delivery."

"When will you have everything together?"

"Tomorrow at this time. Is it satisfactory? It means in two days we can conclude our business."

The man nodded. "Please stay seated while I leave."

A few minutes later, Jim finished his coffee and walked out of the mission. He expected any minute to be stopped on the street but nothing happened. On the way to the house, he held the passport in his hand. What made him think about getting another passport? Was he being too careful? No, he thought, I can't afford to place all my eggs in one basket. The extra $2,000 is easily replaced by the marina maintenance profits. I've got to think about a backup route north to Canada; probably nothing more complicated than a flight to Seattle and a bus to Vancouver. He realized there was nothing to hold him in the U.S. any longer. He would leave during the weekend, after almost six months in San Francisco. It would give him time to say goodbye to everyone. That part was going to be the hardest one of all and again filled him with sadness and regret. He had developed a deep fondness for everyone who had encountered during his short stay. He had not realized until now the depth of his feelings. He knew the smart and safe approach was to leave without a word as he had previously done from home. Somehow though, he found it difficult to think he could do it again. Besides he reminded himself, there was nothing in the gesture that could jeopardize his safety.

Rosa Munoz sat in the kitchen of her house and placed the business card on the table. She picked up the phone and dialed the cell number on the card. It would not have done to call before Juan had delivered the passport and obtained the final payment. She had been patient and waited for three weeks so there could be no tie-in with the rest of their operation. She recognized Tomas Cassandra from the photo shown to her three weeks ago by the man who gave her the card. This way she received her commission for the passport and the reward money from this man. She smiled as she held a passport picture in front of her.

When the phone was answered she told him. "Mr. Weatherly, I believe I have some good news for you but it won't be cheap. It will cost you $500 for my information. Shall we meet tomorrow morning say, at nine, at the Vanguard Coffee House at the base of Telegraph Hill? Sit in the rear and read a newspaper. Please have the headline facing the door. Oh, and don't forget the money."

Chapter Thirty-six

MORE PUZZLE PIECES

Thursday, October 17

When Adam went to the parking garage to get his car, he approached the rear fender, reached under, and removed the tracking bug. He looked around and placed the bug on a water pipe hanging from the ceiling. This way, they would think the car was still in the garage. He drove off and carefully checked the rear mirror for a tailing car. After driving a random pattern for a few blocks, he was satisfied he was clean. He wanted to arrive early for the meeting to check for a trap. He grimly thought, If there was ever a time to get paranoid, this was it.

He drove slowly pass the Vanguard Coffee House and saw it was all it seemed to be. He parked the car down the street in a lot and walked to the store. He located an empty table at the rear with a view of the front of the shop. With minutes to go, he opened the newspaper and folded it so the front page was in the direction of the door. He spotted the woman entering and looking around. When he caught her eye, she glanced cautiously about at the other customers and made her way to him. He was relieved she seemed suspicious; it ruled out anything but the business of the call. She sat down in the seat opposite him.

"Mr. Weatherly?"

He nodded and reached in his pocket for his credential. He gave it over to her. She stared at it and him. Satisfied, she returned it to him.

"I am Rosa."

He opened the conversation. "You said you have something for me."

"Yes. You have something for me."

He asked. "Are you certain it was the same man as this picture?" He passed the doctored picture of Factor to her.

She studied the picture. "He looks a little different but it's the same person."

"What information can you provide?"

"Exactly what you need, a name and a recent photo."

"How much did you say you want for the information?"

She licked her upper lip with the tip of her tongue. "Let's not play games. It will cost you $500."

"Do you have the information with you?"

She looked nervously around the coffee house at the people thronging the tables and nodded. Adam reached in his pocket and extracted the money from his wallet. She reached to retrieve it but he withdrew it from her grasp. "It's all here. The information first, please."

She reached inside her purse. "Here is his picture. His name is on the back of the photo." She pushed the photo over to him.

He took a look. Satisfied he slid the money to her. "What kind of passport did he get?"

"He bought a Mexican passport."

"Where did you meet him?"

"I was instructed by phone to pick him up at a certain location. The details are not important. My part of the arrangement was to take him to my studio. I took the passport picture and obtained the necessary information such as birth date and birthplace in Mexico. The information is written on the back of the photo."

Adam turned over the picture and read the name. "Out of curiosity, what made you think he was Mexican?"

The woman stared at him. "He speaks only Spanish."

Now it was Adam's turn to be surprised. He pushed over the money.

She stuffed it in her purse and got up from the table. "I won't get into any trouble, will I?"

He shook his head. "This is a missing person not a criminal."

Relieved, she turned and exited the coffeehouse. Adam stared at the picture of Factor. He took in the short haircut, light beard, darker complexion, and lean facial features. "God, I would have passed him by if I had seen him. I wonder if I overlooked him in the driver's license applications. Now I have a solid lead in the form of a recent picture." He became aware Factor waited until now to get the passport indicating time was close to running out for him to be found. Amazing, he thought. Factor has picked up Spanish to the extent he can converse in it and pass as a native without attracting attention.

He shook his head. The guy is incredible. Without Mrs. Factor hiring him to find her husband, he would certainly have disappeared without a trace. The fact he'd eluded his best efforts for almost six months was a tribute to the man's deliberateness. He had to be realistic; any time now Factor would take flight. If it happened, Adam knew he wouldn't be found. He had to figure out what to do with the picture. He couldn't make and distribute circulars because it would place Factor's life in danger. How much time do I have? My best bet is around two weeks which is cutting it very close. If Factor is precise in his timetable and there's no reason to think otherwise, he'll leave around the six-month anniversary of his disappearance. It doesn't leave me much time. He left money for the check on the table. He had to talk to Ray Peterson.

Adam drove over to the police building where Peterson had an office. When they were together, he related the events leading to getting Factor's passport picture. He noted Ray had also taken an interest in finding Factor if for nothing else than to find the man who had eluded Adam so successfully.

"So that's the story behind my getting this picture."

He handed Ray the picture. He turned it over and read Factor's passport information.

"You finally have a name for him."

"Maybe, I don't know. It would be smarter for him to come up with a different one than the one he's using."

"I got to hand it to him. And you say he conversed in Spanish to the girl and she didn't give it a thought. I'm glad this guy didn't take up a life of crime although I'm anxious to hear just what he did to get in this mess." He stared at the picture. "Say, he looks familiar."

"What are you talking about? Familiar how? Wait, you think you've seen him before?"

"No. He resembles someone. Hold on a minute."

Ray got up and went to another office. He returned with a file and pulled a sketch from it.

"Adam. Look at this and tell me he doesn't look like a dead ringer for this guy." He turned the drawing so Adam could see it. "Do you see a similarity between Factor and the sketch or is it just me?"

Adam stared at the sketch and the picture, than looked at Ray. "Good God. You're right. Who's the person in the sketch?"

"Over two months ago, a young woman was accosted on the street by these two guys." Ray pulled the mug shots of the assailants from the file. "Some passing guy heard her scream and jumped the guys in an alley. They were armed and he still managed to disarm and disable them. She ran and called the police. We literally picked them up off the ground and took them to the hospital. They had rap sheets which included assault and armed robbery. They're awaiting trial."

"I remember reading the account in the paper. At that time, you hadn't identified him because he ran away. Did you ever find him?"

"No and we tried after the mayor thought it would make a great human-interest story. He would have given a medal to the guy. Anyway, we had an artist do up a sketch from her description and gave it to the cops on the beat. We never located him."

Adam observed. "These guys had medium builds and are around six feet. They look too tough for them to be taken down by one man and they were armed besides."

"That's what we thought too. The woman claimed he did it using karate."

Adam shook his head. "Am I now to believe that Factor has not only learned Spanish in the short time he's been here but also karate? I can't believe it."

"Hey, you're the guy who has told me about his resourcefulness. Who's to say? The martial arts studios in the area were checked and we came up empty. The feeling was the rescuer was just passing through and left right after. The woman had not seen a car but with her emotional state could have easily overlooked it. Did Factor have any history of karate in his background?"

"None that I'm aware of. Ray, I have a map here. Show me where this took place."

Ray took a marker from the desk and outlined the block. "This is in a predominantly Mexican section of the city."

"Is there a church mission around there which provides aid to Mexican immigrants?"

"I believe there is. It's a popular place for those seeking help or work. I think you may have something there."

Adam copied down the rescued woman's name, address and phone number.

"Ray. Any problem with me calling and visiting her to see if she remembers anything else?"

"She doesn't want to be publicized, otherwise no. Just keep me informed. I'm really interested in what comes up next in your search. And don't forget to watch your back."

Adam glanced at his watch as he left the police station. He dialed the woman's phone number on his cell phone. An older female voice answered.

"Hello."

"Hello. I would like to speak to Angelina Alvarez please."

The voice turned cautious. "My daughter's not home from school yet. Who is this?"

"My name is Adam Weatherly. I was just referred to Ms. Alvarez by Detective Ray Peterson of the SFPD. I would like to stop by and ask her some questions regarding her rescuer."

The voice softened a little. "Mr. Weatherly, she'll be home around five if you wish to come by at that time."

"Thank you, I will. It won't take long."

Adam thought. "I better not push my luck with whoever is out there. I have to get back to the office one last time before I start my search." He parked in the hotel garage and replaced the tracking device. He went up to the room and stretched out on the bed. Before long he was asleep. When he woke up it was late afternoon. He took a shower and changed. He packed his suitcase and went down to pay the bill. He placed his suitcase in the trunk and looked around at the cars. He took the tracker and placed it under a delivery truck. There. It should keep them occupied for a while.

He drove to the girl's address and parked on the street. A large burly man opened the door. "Yes?"

Weatherly showed his investigator's license. "I'm Adam Weatherly, a private investigator. I was referred by the SFPD. I'm searching for Ms. Alvarez's rescuer and I would like to ask her some questions about him."

The man took the license and compared the picture with the man in front of him. He handed it back. "I'm her father, John Alvarez. Sorry, can't be too careful." He stuck out his hand and beckoned him inside. Adam entered the house and was directed to a chair in the living room. "I'll get Angelina." Within minutes, a pretty woman stood in front of him.

"You wish to speak to me?"

He stood up and introduced himself. "I'm looking for a person who disappeared and have reason to believe was your rescuer. The police don't want him if that's what you think. We feel he was scared into disappearing because he feared for his family's safety. I was wondering if you would tell me the story. Afterward I'll show you a photo to see if you recognize the man."

* * *

The girl indicated for him to sit down and she sat opposite him and related the incident.

"Did you get a good look at the man? How tall was he?"

"He was a little taller than the two men and he was faster too."

"What do you mean?"

"When the man with the club swung at him, he moved aside and took the club from him. Then he kicked him in the leg. I looked back as he hit the other man with the knife on the arm with the club. I didn't see what happened after that."

"You mentioned he used karate. Did it just look that way? After all, it was dark."

"Oh no. He held his hands in front of him and crouched before he moved so fast and took the club."

"I have a picture here. Would you look at it and tell me if it was the same man?" Weatherly handed her the photo of Factor he received earlier in the day.

She took the photo and stared. Her expression was one of recognition. What should I do? It is him. "Yes. This is the man who saved me. Who is he?"

"I can't say who he is right now but I will when I find him." Adam stood. "One other thing. You told the police he spoke in Spanish. Would you say he was Mexican?"

"Yes."

"Ms. Alvarez, thank you again for your time. I am happy that things turned out well for you."

She looked at him and hesitated. "Yes?"

"I accidentally ran into him on the street a month ago. I told him how grateful I was for his courage and his help."

"What?"

She nodded. "I asked him his name and he said Nick. After that he ran away."

As he drove away from the house, Weatherly had a number of mysteries on his hands. The information she gave didn't fit the Factor profile. The man's name was Nick, not Tomas. If she hadn't identified the picture, he would have had more than his share of doubts. He dialed Ray Peterson's home number as he drove from San Francisco.

"Ray, I just left the Alvarez girl. She positively identified Factor as her rescuer. She was adamant he used karate and certain he was Mexican. She mentioned she ran into him on the street and he said his name was Nick."

"Makes you think about the guy doesn't it. Here's a guy running for something he might have done and takes a chance on exposing himself. What's next?"

"I'm heading back down to Santa Ana for a couple of days. I have to clean up a few things at the office before I come back." He told Ray about placing the tracker on the delivery van.

"Adam, I wouldn't stay at the same hotel when you return."

"Actually, I was thinking about it. I'll let you know. Thanks again for all of your help."

After he hung up, Peterson could have sworn he just heard Adam imply he was going to go back and stay at the same hotel.

As Adam swung onto the highway south, he reflected on what he had told Ray. Was he really thinking about going back to the same hotel? Maybe, came the answer, but on his terms.

Chapter Thirty-seven

IMPATIENCE ALL AROUND

Friday, October 18

Sergey and Petra pulled alongside the vehicle they had been tracking. It had been parked in the middle of a side street so they had no problem finding its location. Sourly, they stared at a florist delivery truck. Petra got out of the car and looked up and down the street. Then, holding a handheld tracking monitor, found the bug under the rear bumper. He palmed it and returned to the car.

Sergey asked. "You got it?"

Petra muttered. "Yeah. The bastard caused us to run around all day. Let's get him and sweat it out of him."

Sergey raised his eyebrows. "And where do you suggest we start? By now he's checked out of his hotel. We could keep tabs on his police pal or we could go back to his agency. I figure he's getting close to Factor and is trying to get us out of circulation. We need to split up and keep a watch on his buddy until he makes contact. We also know the PI's car so we can keep searching for it at another hotel. Either way we need another car."

"Borichov isn't going to like this. He already believes we've been living it up on his money."

Sergey turned serious. "Neither is Mr. Federov."

* * *

In the evening Sergey dialed Federov's private number and took a deep breath. "Mr. Federov? It's Sergey."

An angry voice replied. "What is it? Are you finished?"

"No, we temporarily lost the PI. He got wise to our tracker, removed it and checked out of his hotel."

"God damn it! All I need is to have you two made. What do you think he'll do next?"

"He's been keeping company with a cop friend here so we figured we would split up and wait for him to make contact again. We doubt he's found the guy yet. If he did, he'd head back to his e an easy target. Trouble is it'll take time. Our best guess is he'll show up again."

Federov demanded in a chilling voice. "Sergey. Stay put. You'll hear back in a half hour." Then the line went dead.

Sergey replaced the receiver.

Petra looked at him. "What he say?"

"I don't need to call Borichov. He's gonna be hearing from Mr. Federov."

Varna, Bulgaria

Borichov answered the persistent ringing on his private phone. "Yes?" The Russian voice at the other end dripped with venom. "Borichov." Came out as a curse.

Borichov answered calmly although his stomach became tied up in knots at the tone of the voice. He forced himself to stay calm. "Dimitri, what can I do for you?"

Federov relayed the news he received from Sergey. "You've had my two men tied up for almost six months on this petty revenge of yours. Understand this, Borichov. You wind up your business fast. In two weeks I pull the plug."

Borichov hung up the phone and raged around his office. He hadn't made much off the Igla missiles and now this. Fuming, he called a travel agency he used in Varna and made arrangements to fly to San Francisco by way of Toronto. Then he called Sergey.

San Francisco, California

When the phone was picked up, Borichov roared. "Sergey?"

Sergey almost dropped the phone and mouth lipped 'Borichov' to Petra. He replied hesitantly. "Yes?"

"I just heard from Federov because of your incompetence. I won't have it. This fucking assignment should have been handled months ago. I have made travel arrangements to get there. I will send you my arrival information and you will pick me up at the airport. Do you understand?"

Sergey gulped. "Da." He gingerly put the phone down and delivered the disturbing message. "Borichov is on his way. Best I can tell he'll be here in two days. We better prepare and get another car. We'll concentrate our surveillance on the PI's pal."

Chapter Thirty-eight

WEATHERLY'S DILEMMA

Friday, October 18
Newport Beach, California

It was after midnight when Adam drove into his driveway. He rubbed his eyes and opened the trunk. He carried his suitcase into the bedroom, took off his clothes and collapsed into bed. The last thing he did before he fell into a deep sleep was to place his gun under the pillow.

The glaring sunlight and a distant car horn woke him. He looked at the time, yawned and rose. After showering and shaving, he put on a clean suit. His gun went into a belt holster. Adam headed directly to his office. Elaine saw him first and shouted to Marty. They were anxious for some news. He poured a cup of coffee and they gathered in the conference room.

Adam opened his notebook and started his review. "Okay, I'm going to back up a bit so you can see where I was coming from with my actions. I'll first say a lot of credit for my progress to date goes to Ray Peterson of the SFPD. As you are aware, it was Ray who had the notion to check my car out in the police garage and discovered the tracker. Needless to say, this verified our suspicion we're under surveillance by the same people who want Factor."

While Adam was relating his accounts of the past month, Elaine took notes on a laptop computer in front of her. Neither one interrupted him with questions or comments.

After he finished, Marty spoke first. "Adam, that's the most fascinating story we've ever heard. You're saying Factor learned Spanish and picked up karate in the last five months."

He smiled and nodded. "You got it. He's also got two identities going. Instead of laying low and biding his time to take off again, Factor has been preparing himself from the day he disappeared. You recall his wife told us he possessed these tendencies."

"That guy is something else. What now?"

Adam noted the hint of admiration in Marty's voice. "This is where you two come in. Take a look at this map of San Francisco. The neighborhood is highlighted. The black circles indicate the church mission and the rescue locale. The third circle is the bank where he was seen. It's not very close to the other two sites. I need some work done before I leave again for San Francisco on Sunday. Do a search for martial arts studios, rooming houses, bars, night and adult schools offering language classes, low rent hotels and the like."

"Adam, what about the Russians?"

"Oh yes, I'm coming to that. I checked out of the hotel and got rid of the tracking bug but you can be sure I left some pretty pissed off people back there. I believe finding Factor isn't enough. We have to deal with the mafia problem or else we'll just place him in danger when we find him. Unless something can be done about this threat, we run the risk of him leaving again and this time he's well prepared."

This time Elaine spoke up. "Are you saying we have to somehow neutralize the threat? You're not serious?"

"Oh, but I am. I don't know how yet but it has to tie in. While you two are working on my search, I am going to brief Mrs. Factor. One more thing, since Factor now has a passport, we can figure he'll leave the country soon. It's like him to self-impose a six-month limit and from what we now know, this time he's ready. I'm convinced if he takes off, we won't see him again. You can bet he already has a plan in place. When I get back from Mrs. Factor, I want to review the status of our other clients."

Adam telephoned ahead and set up the appointment with Diane Factor. He barely rang the doorbell when the front door opened. "Please come in Mr. Weatherly."

As before, he was shown to the living room where she had coffee waiting.

"I'm anxious to hear your progress." She confessed.

He nodded and opened his notebook. "Mrs. Factor, I'll give you a detailed account of my activities since our last meeting. Please interrupt whenever you want."

With that, Adam recounted the events of the past month. He covered his discovery that not only did Jim acquire Spanish, he could and did pass for Mexican. Additionally, he learned karate and obtained a passport. Adam withheld his brush with the Russian hit team and his belief there was little time left. Mrs. Factor remained quiet throughout the entire discourse. He finished, closed the notebook and looked at her.

She chose her words carefully. "Mr. Weatherly, from what you say, Jim must be close to leaving the country."

He looked at her, nodded his head at her astuteness, and answered truthfully. "I believe from his achievements we may only have a two week window left to find him."

"What is your next step?"

"We've isolated the neighborhood where we think he lives but it's still a large section. I plan to go back on Sunday and canvas the area."

She stared at him perceptively. "What about the cause of his disappearance? What happens when you find him?"

"You mean if I find him."

"No, Mr. Weatherly. I know you are going to find him. In case you hadn't noticed, you're both cut from the same cloth."

He was taken aback. She had stated in simple words what he had felt when he started this case.

"Adam. Thank you for your persistence and resourcefulness. I find it comforting."

She watched at the window as Weatherly got into his car. She thought, "There must be something more I can do. Maybe I should go to San Francisco and make myself available if anything develops."

As he drove back to his office, Weatherly reflected on the conversation. She was a remarkable woman. Then he realized she called him Adam for the first time. Perhaps she sensed danger and wished to reassure him by her confidence in him. Or, was she telling him to be careful?

Adam realized as he sat and listened to the accounts of their other cases Marty had matured and become an experienced investigator. Maybe all he needed was to fend without me. Marty had assumed the legwork with Elaine providing the backup assistance and between the two of the agency business was under control.

"Marty, I am very impressed. You've picked up the investigations end and done a superb job. You and Elaine have become a formidable team."

Both employees beamed.

He added. "I'm thinking when this is over we may need to get another electronics geek and get you started on the outside work with me. That is, if it's all right with you."

Adam barely managed to keep a straight face when Marty broke into a broad smile as Elaine patted him on the back.

Saturday, October 19

Adam felt well rested after a good night's sleep. He had the day planned before he was left home. He went straight to the office where Elaine and Marty were waiting for him. They had a search area map laid out with a list of businesses in each block. They had color coded the appropriate stops on each street. There were extra prints of Factor's passport picture on the side.

Marty pointed to the map. "Adam, these are only the ones we could find in the directories, business license files, and the Internet. There is probably twice the number not listed. In a ten-square block area there are three churches, one church mission, two martial arts studios and a number of rooming houses and hotels."

Elaine added. "I've input the information on your laptop computer so you'll have it in two forms. It's a lot of territory to cover in less than two weeks."

"It's the only lead we have. I'll keep you posted daily on my progress. If you come up with any ideas, let me know right away."

Marty asked. "Can you do it alone?"

Adam smiled. "I'm afraid I'll have to. Quite honestly, there's a big risk here in more ways than one. I'm going to try to find the Russians as well."

Elaine and Marty were stunned and replied almost in unison. "What?"

"Look, finding Factor started out to be our primary concern but it's grown larger than that. If and when I find him, we both become targets. I've got to neutralize them some way. That's why I'll need you both here as my backup."

Marty cautiously asked. "How do you intend to do it?"

"When I find Factor, I intend to move back into the same hotel I just left.

I'm sure they have it under surveillance. If these guys are as good as I think they would have Ray Peterson under surveillance too. It's what I would do in their shoes."

"Do you think Ray's in danger from them?"

"No, I'm sure they have little interest in him except to get to me. I'll make sure they do when the time comes. I'll have to wing it at that point and see what happens. I'm going home to pick up some things and then drive back. Initially I'll stay at one of the low rent hotels in the neighborhood. I'll call you when I pick one."

"I'm guessing you don't want to notify the authorities when you find them?"

Adam shook his head. "It wouldn't solve anything."

After he left, Elaine and Marty discussed Adam's intention in hushed tones. "Let's keep very close tabs on him, Marty."

Marty nodded. "If we find out he's in danger, we may have to call Ray Peterson."

Adam drove back home and backed his car into the garage. He went into a spare room where he unlocked a closet. In a hidden compartment behind the rear wall, he pulled out a duffel bag and brought it into the room. He took out a pair of automatic assault rifles outfitted with sniper scopes, several pistols, ammunition and a set of night vision goggles. Hanging in the closet he had a black jump suit with Velcro slots for magazines and the halogen Surefire flashlight. A Kevlar vest hung to one side. He had no idea what he would need but more was better than less.

He took the equipment to his car and opened the trunk. He placed the weapons along with a SWAT Pro Med first aid kit into a steel box welded to the car frame. He padlocked the box and closed the trunk. He went into the bedroom and packed. He'd leave very early so he would get into San Francisco by noon to allow time to find a hotel.

Chapter Thirty-nine

FINAL EFFORTS

Sunday, October 20
San Francisco, California

It was close to noon when Adam pulled into the search area in San Francisco. The day was overcast with low gray clouds and a slight drizzle. The temperature had dropped into the 50's and he could hear a foghorn echoing in the distance. He pulled the car to the curb and pulled out the map. Several hotels and motels were in the vicinity. He decided to drive around the area before checking into one of them. The area consisted of two-lane streets, rows of narrow houses, and clusters of small shops. To his dismay, there was an occasional house advertising a room-to-let. He winced as he thought. If I were Factor, I'd pick one of these. He finally chose a motel with parking on the side next to the room. There was a corner bar and a restaurant within walking distance. Once inside the room, he set up his laptop computer and e-mailed his location to the office. He opened the map, obtained his bearing and selected a walking route for the morning. He planned to center his search from the neighborhood where the rescue took place.

Sergey and Petra were on the highway heading south to San Francisco Airport. Borichov was due to land within two hours and they wanted to be on the arrival side of the terminal waiting in the car. Sergey noted the worn seats and the rough engine performance. He observed sarcastically. "Petra. Couldn't you have picked a better car?"

"Sure, I could have ripped off a luxury model but then the police might have an incentive to look for it. Anyway, this will convince Borichov we're not frivolously spending his money." They both laughed when they thought of Borichov's expectant reaction when he saw the car.

Sergey's countenance returned to business. "Tomorrow we'll split up. You head out to his cop friend's house until he leaves. Call me when he does. I'll cover his precinct station soon after. Then you head back and cover the hotel where the PI previously holed up. Right after noon we'll switch places."

They were parked outside of the airport for twenty minutes before Borichov came out of the terminal with his luggage. Petra got out of the car and approached him on the sidewalk. He noted that Borichov was dressed in an expensive but wrinkled suit and had an expensive suitcase. Borichov in turn looked at the heavyset man in ill-fitting clothes coming towards him. He then glanced at the car and saw Sergey at the wheel. He nodded, passed his suitcase to Petra and climbed into the front seat. Petra sat in back seat with the suitcase. Sergey started the car and drove away from the airport. Borichov took the time to look with disdain at the interior of the car. Sergey looked at Petra in the rearview mirror and saw a slight grin. He looked away and gritted his teeth to keep a straight face.

Borichov broke the silence when they were on the highway heading north to San Francisco. He demanded icily. "Tell me exactly what you have been doing and what happened."

The trip and the narrative took up the time until they drove into their motel.

Sergey remarked. "I've taken the liberty of getting a room for you next to us. What name are you using?"

Borichov replied. "My passport reads Mikel Bronkovsky. What is this place?" He looked around at the surroundings. "This is our motel. It is nondescript is it not?"

"Maybe for you. Take me to a luxury hotel where I will stay."

Sergey shrugged and got back in the car. "One of the best is the Inter-Continental Mark Hopkins Hotel at the top of Nob Hill."

Borichov took out his cell phone and contacted information. He was soon connected with the hotel's front desk. "Do you have a suite available?" He listened and nodded. "It will be fine. I am Mr. Bronkovsky. I'll be checking in shortly."

Sergey drove up the circular driveway to the entrance. Before Borichov left the car, Sergey gave him his cell phone number. "Call me when you wish to get together. Do you wish us to pick up a car for you?"

Borichov glanced at him as if he had heard a sarcastic remark. He turned his back, walked up and signaled a porter to take his bag. Sergey watched him strut into the hotel with the air of a Russian aristocrat. Sergey had no doubt he would get a room to his liking.

Factor had spent a peaceful Sunday jogging and walking around San Francisco. The rolling hills were as much a signature of the city as symmetrical houses and pricey restaurants. He felt he had spent a fruitful five months and knew it was now getting to the time he had allotted. The passport was the final key. He chuckled as he thought he had accumulated more money than when he had arrived. He would miss the marina, the Queterras' and, most of all, Chris. He hadn't counted on the friendships he had formed. They all had taken him at face value. He still found it surprising. Diane was always so good at it he marveled at her natural ease with people. He smiled at how she would react to his accomplishments. He wondered what she was doing and how she was coping. He desperately wished he could hear her voice. He turned around and headed for the house midst the blaring of a foghorn in the bay.

Chapter Forty

COUNTDOWN

Monday, October 21

Jim, as was his habit, woke up at the crack of dawn. He slipped on jeans, a sweatshirt and sneakers and quietly let himself out the door. There was a mist in the cool morning air as he walked briskly and then started his running. It took him ten minutes to make it to the martial arts studio. He smiled as he noticed he beat Chris to the door. They greeted each other warmly and entered the studio. Jim changed into the dogi and went through the warm-up movements loosening up his muscles and joints.

Chris approached and they bowed to one another. "Jim, there's no one here so let's do a little assault and counter-assault tactics. I'll play the aggressor. Are you ready?" Before Jim could reply, Chris raised his arm and thrust his leg and foot at his midsection.

Surprised by the sudden movement, Jim's instinct moved him into the charge at an angle with an elbow parry of the thrusting leg. He let his forward movement take him by Chris as he dodged and somersaulted into a ready position. Chris had already turned and was striking out with his foot where Jim's head would appear when he raised up. Jim surprised him by somersaulting towards him and kicking out a foot to the back of Chris's leg. Both tumbled and got to their feet. They crouched towards one another when the front door opened and a student entered and stared at them. They looked at one another and laughed. They continued the pattern of parrying and thrusting for an hour. Bathed in sweat, Jim bowed to Chris and went to change. Chris followed him to the locker room. Chris patted him on the shoulder. "Jim, you did a nice bit of improvising on my sudden attack move. You took me off balance with your unconventional counter."

"Thanks, Chris. Actually it was fun to see the expression on your face. How about a beer tonight?"

"Sounds good. Connie asked about you the other night. Do you want to double date with her and a girlfriend?"

"I'll pass on the date but not the beer. See you later."

Jim jogged back to the house and climbed the stairs to the bedroom. He grabbed a towel and shaving kit and went to the bathroom. Afterwards he put on his newly acquired business casual clothes and went downstairs to the breakfast table. The Queterras' were already there.

Jimmy remarked with faintly disguised humor. "If it isn't the famous broker of yachts, ships and other sea-faring crafts."

Jim laughed. "Hey, a guy has to earn a living." He sat down with them and had breakfast.

When he finished, he left the house to pick up the car and drive to the marina. Today was a Pacific Coast Yacht sales day. He enjoyed the dry wit of Steve Wilson and looked forward to the tutorials on ship construction throughout the slow intervals of the day. He was to meet Miguel for lunch to talk about the boat repair schedule. Both of them were surprised at the number of jobs awaiting them. At this rate, even Miguel's friend José who in the past went south into Mexico during the fall and winter months, would be kept busy.

Jim turned at the sound of a person entering the front door. His acquired customer evaluation quickly assessed the man's attire and the boat shoes. The man slowly gazed over the boats on the floor and settled on the thirty-one foot Maxum 3100 SE yacht. Jim thought, Steve should get this guy. He edged to the office side and knocked gently on the window; their signal of a real prospect on the floor. Steve looked up from his coffee and paperwork. He motioned with his hand; take care of it. Jim was surprised as he strolled to the yacht. The customer had already climbed the platform and was in the stern reading the placard with the specifications. He looked down at Jim. "What can you tell me about this beauty?"

Jim answered authoritatively. "The layout alone is worth the investment. My preference would be to add radar to the system for extended motoring. A cockpit cover with a front, side and aft canvas enclosure is also available matching the hull design and interior decor providing an all-weather operating capability."

The man stuck out his hand. "I'm Frank Spencer."

"Nick Germain. I'll leave you alone so you can check it out. Give a shout when you have a question."

Spencer nodded. Jim climbed down and headed for the office. He sat down and was reading the manufacturer's description on the model in case other questions arose. He didn't notice Spencer until he came in and sat in the chair opposite the desk. Jim asked. "Any questions?"

"Yes, how much with the radar and enclosures?"

Jim consulted the computer and gave him the cost. Usually this is when they thanked him and pulled the plug. Instead, Spencer surprised him by pulling out a checkbook. "What's the deposit and when can I expect delivery?"

Jim checked the inventory list. "Depends on the colors and fabrics you want. We may have to order it and it could take thirty days."

"I like the colors of the one on the floor. Is it available?"

Jim nodded. "We'd have to install the radar and navigation system and order the canvas enclosure. Both only take a few days. We'd need the time to prepare it for you and haul it to the marina. Were you going to get a berth around here while you wait for a slip?"

"Can I get you to set me up with one, have it placed in the water and delivered it there?"

"Sure. You need to get enrolled in the U.S. Power Squadron class if this is your first boat of this size."

Spencer shook his head. "No. I've been doing boats since I was a kid." He wrote a check and handed it over. Jim completed all of the paperwork and finally the process was finished. They both stood up and shook hands. "Thanks for your help. I appreciate you didn't push. I like to make up my own mind." With that, he turned and left the building.

Wilson stuck his head through the door. "How did you do?"

Jim placed all of the paperwork and the check into a folder and handed it to him. "This was by far the biggest one I've sold."

Wilson reviewed the entries and nodded approvingly. "Nice job, Nick." He handed the folder back to him. "You have a good sales and marketing instinct. Go ahead and follow up on the options and find a slip for him."

Jim couldn't resist smiling at the compliment.

Adam awoke early and had breakfast at the nearby café. He dressed in casual slacks, rubber-soled shoes and a sweater covering his belt holster. His jacket held the map and Factor's picture. He never expected results to break right away and was accustomed to the slow methodical process of a search. He knew he could just go to the selected target places but he had to systematically move towards that direction by process of elimination. This was a lesson learned early in the investigative work which escaped the young impatient rookies. It appeared Marty had absorbed this training lesson. Adam put on a hat noting it would soften the sight of a white man asking questions in a Mexican area and help stave off any hostility. He'd concentrate on businesses such as bars, restaurants, shops, stores, rooming houses and hotels. He knew from experience the unconscious reaction he'd get if there was any recognition of the picture. He turned up the collar of the jacket and entered the first establishment. The proprietor looked at him with suspicion. Adam thought, "Oh boy, this was going to be a long day."

Sergey and Petra hadn't heard from Borichov and assumed he was trying to shake off the jet lag by sleeping late. They split up with Sergey going early to the cop's house and Petra taking over the hotel surveillance. For now it was the only thing they could do to reestablish contact with the PI. He didn't doubt Weatherly would turn up. Once Borichov contacted them, it was going to be a trying time.

Petra strolled down the street giving a sideward glance at the hotel front doors. He noted the parking garage to the right of the building. The access to the hotel was the connecting door near the front. Positioned somewhere in front of the hotel, both entrances could be observed at the same time. He turned into the parking garage and walked towards the back. There were no exits except through the attendant in the entry booth. He walked back out and went to the end of the street. He turned left down the side street and paused when he came to the alley. He looked around and went into the alley. When he reached the hotel rear door, he saw it was a fire exit and allowed no outside access into the building. He turned around and walked back to the main street. He crossed and searched the shops along his path for a likely surveillance spot. He came upon the Internet café with its computer screens on the tables isolated by low partitions to give user privacy. He went into the café and found the attendant.

"How does this work?"

The attendant looked up from his paper. "Find an open station anywhere and sign on. It'll ask you for a screen name and password. After that, it'll request a type of payment."

"Can I pay cash?"

"Sure. You leave a deposit with me and I'll give you a time span for your computer from my station. If you hit any porno sites, the tally keeps count."

Petra was about to register indignation when he realized it provided an explanation for a long session at the terminal and kept quiet. Wait until he told Sergey in the evening. He searched the room for a computer screen whose back faced the street and where the user had a view of the window. He could see people passing by. Some paused and peered in drawn by curiosity before continuing down the sidewalk. He chose a spot and pointed it out. The attendant made note of the number and pointed to the rate schedule on the sign behind him. Petra paid for four hours and stuck the receipt in his pocket.

At the terminal he followed the instructions to sign on. Immediately the screen displayed an array of icons and he signed on to the Internet. The reflection in the monitor of the attendant ay the back of the room showed he was occupied and never looked his way. Petra slid his chair to the side to get a better view of the hotel across the street. He chuckled inwardly noting he was going to be able to brush up his computer skills while keeping an eye out for Weatherly. He saw a couple of fellow customers had notepads and made occasional notes. There were a few who just stared at the screen. No one took any interest in their neighbors. This was a perfect spot to watch the hotel. He could even get coffee and something to eat.

Adam looked at his watch. It was after five and getting towards dusk. He pulled the map out and marked the spot where he was. He'd start from this point tomorrow. He turned around and started towards the hotel. Once there, he turned on the laptop and e-mailed his office the day's status. He undressed and changed into casual clothes. He closed the door and walked toward the Chinese restaurant down the street. After he ate, he planned to visit some bars in the hope that someone saw Factor.

Petra informed Sergey about the Internet café across from the hotel. Sergey nodded his approval. They were comparing notes when the phone rang. It was Borichov asking if there had been any results. "We're keeping surveillance at three places looking for the PI. He's got to turn up in one of them. When we find him, we'll call you."

Sergey hung up and shrugged. "Let's go eat."

Jim met Chris at the Foggy Bottom Bar. He was already settled in a booth chatting with Connie and Kate, another waitress. They called him over as soon as they saw him walk through the door.

Jim sat down in the booth. "Hi girls. How was your weekend?"

Kate frowned and waggled her hand. "So, so. Why didn't you come in for a beer?"

Jim grinned. "I worked Saturday and took in the sights on foot yesterday. I'll take a beer now."

Kate walked away with a hint of a pout. "I think she likes you, Nick." Chris said.

Jim gave a little shrug. "I'm too busy right now. Let me tell you what happened today at Pacific Coast." He described his yacht sale.

"It sounds like it sold itself. Do you get a commission?"

"As far as I know."

Chris laughed. "It must be nice to have so much money in your pocket you don't care."

They ordered off the bar menu and relaxed. Around eight, they called it an evening and left.

Chapter Forty-one

ROUTINES ARE MAINTAINED

Tuesday, October 22

Adam sat in a booth at the rear of the hotel restaurant and looked around the room. He could see the familiarity between the customers and the waitresses. Even the young policeman who had arrived after him was recognized by a couple of the regulars. That's the way to run a beat, he thought, have everyone comfortable with your presence. The kid will do all right. He glanced at his watch. It was time to hit the pavement.

Jim went to the Halyard's to review received calls and parcel out the day's activity. He saw Miguel and waved. They entered and went back to the small office. The answering machine indicated four messages. Three dealt with maintenance and repair. The other was from Wayne Collier. Jim rose from the chair and went to the wall where he had hung a whiteboard. He had made a table containing boat location, owner, date of the call-in, job description, assignment and status. With the four new ones, there were nine entries.

"Miguel, this is my first time for this but it seems we're busier than ever."

"I have never seen it like this. Boat owners seem to be finding more time to go out since leaving the time-consuming cleanup and straightening to us. May I make a suggestion?" Miguel asked.

Jim nodded. "Of course. Are we running out of manpower to do the work?"

"The inside cabin cleaning could be done by less skilled workers who know what to do. What do you say if I ask a cleaning lady to loan us the service of one of her girls? I can train her on the details. In this way we can stick to the actual boat maintenance work."

"Good idea. Go ahead and hand the work out. Collect the bill and leave it on the desk so I can pay it over the weekend."

When Miguel left, Jim wondered how to tell him about taking over the operation when he left. He noticed Miguel had absorbed the logistics of running the business from the office. He had not yet introduced him to George Marx although he and the others received checks from him. He didn't see it as much of a problem. The boat owners seemed comfortable with the arrangement. Jim knew it was his friendship with Wayne Collier which put them at ease. Speaking of which, he picked up the phone and called Collier's office. His secretary recognized his name and asked him to hold.

Wayne came on the line. "Good morning Nick. Keeping busy?"

"I am. At last the weather has improved."

"That it has. I'm going to take a couple of clients for a ride and thought you'd like to come along. It'll be toward the end of the week and be a three-day trip."

"Where are you going?"

"I'm taking them down the California coast to Newport Beach. We'll stay overnight on the boat during the trip."

Nick's heart skipped a beat when he heard Newport Beach. Talk about an eerie invitation. He knew he couldn't take any chances. "Thank you very much for the invitation. It sounds like fun but I have a few things requiring attention. I'll take a rain check if you don't mind."

"I don't mind. We'll have another outing soon."

They exchanged pleasantries and hung up. Jim continued sitting for a while. Talk about a freaky coincidence. On the other hand, he was pleased that Wayne had offered him the opportunity. He wondered what Wayne would think when he disappeared. He was thinking of leaving letters for Miguel and the others explaining he had a job opportunity to check out in Seattle and saying goodbye. He had a couple of weeks to think about the wording.

Jim looked at the board. One of the entries was a problem with a boat's navigation system. He noted the mooring location and left the office. Wayne's call was still on his mind. It made him think his six-month deadline was aptly chosen. Then again there was the mafia. How long would they continue to look for him? Forget it, they weren't about to give up on him if he knew Borichov. They'd have a hard time making a connection between San Francisco and Spain. He was going to check schedules and develop an exit route on Saturday. He'd use the library's public computers to go on the Internet and get the necessary details. He could write his letters while there. He made the decision to leave the following week. He closed the office door and headed for the docks.

Wednesday, October 23

Adam checked out of the hotel and placed his suitcase in the trunk of the car. He settled behind the wheel and checked the map. He'd start where he left off last night.

In the afternoon, Adam came to the first martial arts studios. When he entered, a slim Asian man wearing a karate dogi with a black belt walked up to him. "Hello, I'm John Chen. May I help you?"

Adam nodded. "Can we talk in an office?" He was led to a small room with a desk and chair. When he had sat down, he showed his ID. He explained. "Mr. Chen, my name is Adam Weatherly. I'm a private investigator from Southern California. I'm looking for this man." He handed over the picture of Factor. "I have reason to believe he's the one who rescued the young woman last month near here."

John Chen closely examined the picture.

Adam continued. "The girl told the police he used karate on the two assailants. Naturally, it made sense to check to check establishments like this one."

Chen nodded his agreement. "Over the month we also received a visit from a policeman who asked if we could identify the man. He didn't have a picture, just a sketch and description. Are you sure this is the man?"

He replied. "Pretty sure. Do you recognize him?"

"I'm sorry, I do not. Thanks to the publicity, we did get an increase in students."

"As a former police officer, I am aware of the martial arts since they were part of our training and we practiced at the police gym. This particular man fought two armed men and disabled them. Do you teach attack skills?"

"Yes. Some of our students wish to rise to the advanced ranks and participate in tournaments. This requires a mental transformation not all of them can make. They are taught restraint on their strikes, naturally."

"What do you mean by a mental transformation? I haven't heard of the term."

"Just because a person is proficient at karate, it doesn't make them want to go out and take on the world. The initial purpose is self-defense. Let's say they learn the aggressive movements. Does this mean they would intercede on the street if they witnessed something like the girl was going through? Most certainly would not. Mental conditioning is important and takes time to evolve."

"So you are saying an instinctive reaction like what occurred indicates a more unique mindset and back up experience."

"Just so. Most people would hesitate and consider the consequences of any action. It appears this man acted like he was conditioned to hostile encounters."

Adam thought for a moment. "A policeman would act this way. Who else?"

"A military man, perhaps."

"Mr. Chen. Thank you for your time. I found the discussion very informative."

Chen bowed. "You are welcome, Mr. Weatherly. I hope you find your man."

As Adam walked down the street, he reflected on the conversation. Where would have Factor obtained this mentality? Wait a minute, I'm wrong. That's not the question. I've been shortsighted. I should be asking why he obtained this mentality. To leave home on the spur of the moment was one thing; to get into a dangerous confrontation with two thugs was another. Besides, Factor would be trying to do everything in his power not to bring attention to himself; certainly not going after two guys who were armed. He shook his head. Maybe it made sense if he was confident he could maintain his anonymity. Did he still doubt Factor was the rescuer? His gut told him he did it. How did he make the transformation? Further, how did he have the presence of mind to speak only Spanish during the entire encounter? I have to find him if only to meet him. He knew it went beyond the assignment. Factor had become an enigma if not an obsession with him.

For the rest of the afternoon. Adam could not get the meeting with John Chen out of his mind. He took a break and called his office. He related the entire conversation to Elaine and Marty. "What do you think?" he asked.

Marty spoke first. "Adam, can it be the same guy? After all, we're talking about a family man whose idea of exercise was golf and an occasional stint in the gym."

"I know on the surface it sounds farfetched but I know this guy and I believe it's him."

Marty added. "I think you have him pegged. Now we have to find him and there may not be much time."

"That's my job. I'm a third of the way through as of today. I'll keep in touch."

Elaine turned to Marty after she hung up the phone. They both glanced at the wall calendar. "If Adam is right, we have less than two weeks. I wish there was more we could do."

"Elaine, he's the best there is. If he can't do it, no one can. Look what he's come up with so far. We'll take care of business for him here until he finishes. It sounds like it's not going to be much longer."

"Marty, we're forgetting something. Did you notice that Adam never mentioned the Russians?

Jim settled into the old desk chair in his Halyard office and stared at the to-do list in front of him. He glanced out the window at the boat yard and took a deep breath. The phone jarred his thoughts. It was another boat owner looking for assistance. He picked up the list, tore it in shreds and dumped the pieces in the trash. He went to the whiteboard and made the latest job entry for Miguel.

Saturday, October 26

Jim went to the library to use a computer and its access to the Internet. He searched the train schedule for the following Saturday. He would take the train to Tucson. From there he could take the bus to Nogales. Once across the border, there would be transportation to Mexico City. He had already checked out flights from there to Paris. He logged out and left the library. He stopped at a second hand store and strolled the aisles searching for an old but usable travel bag. He found a suitable soft carry-on suitcase and made the purchase.

He was thinking about the dinner with Chris that evening. Maybe it would be a good time to tell him of his intent to leave. As he exited the store he narrowly missed bumping into a man intently looking down at the map in his hand. He grinned and thought, This isn't a great tourist area, buddy.

Adam was getting tired and impatient. He had covered over half the area and still had gotten nowhere. What was he overlooking? Stop and think. Put yourself in his shoes. You're getting set to run again. How would he leave? Plane, bus, train, car? He would avoid a flight from San Francisco. He'd have to present identification and use cash. How about bus or car? Too slow for large distances. It left the train; no ID requirements, frequent departures and he could pay in cash. Train to where? Maybe to Mexico. He might consider Tijuana, Nogales, or El Paso. The possibilities in between were endless. He could request the passport identity be watched for but doubted he'd get much cooperation. Keep thinking. Factor's a careful planner. What would I do? How about travel agencies? He had included them in his search but nothing came out of it. He could get the information off the Web if he had a computer. If he's holding up in a rooming house, he might not have one to avoid suspicion. Where else? Internet cafes? Possibly. He smacked his forehead with his open palm; a library, of course. Where did he see one? He pulled out the map and was so intent he failed to see the man leaving the store and almost ran into him. "Sorry." he muttered as he located the library's location. He put the map away and hastily walked down the street.

Once in the library, Adam went to the reference section and located two public-use computers with Internet connections. Okay, this was probably where Factor got his travel information. Damn, he was still playing catch-up. He left the library and returned to the search. By the end of the day, nothing turned up. He headed back to the hotel. He anticipated a shower and a steak that night. Tomorrow he'd sleep in since businesses would be closed for Sunday and send in a report to Elaine and Marty.

When Jim walked into the Foggy Bottom Bar, he saw Chris sitting at the booth having a conversation with Connie who was standing by him. Chris saw him first and waved. Connie turned around and smiled. When Jim drew near, Connie pleaded. "Nick, will you tell this guy to ask me out sometime?"

Jim looked at Chris who pretended not to hear. Chris pointed to Connie. "Nick, would you ask this lady to adjust her schedule for earlier hours?"

He laughed. He had heard this banter between them before. He suspected they were secretly seeing each other regardless of the display they threw up when he was present. He sat down in the booth opposite Chris and ordered a beer. When they were finished, they paid, waved goodbye to Connie and left for the restaurant.

Chris drove down to the Embarcadero to one of the popular seafood restaurants in the city. When the waiter came to take their drink order, Jim asked for a dry gin martini.

Chris stared at him quizzically. "Martini?"

He recovered and smiled sheepishly. "I just felt like something different."

Chris asked for a beer and they settled back in their chairs. "How's the marina business going? The weather must have slowed things down."

"Actually, Chris, we're staying busy. How's your studio doing now with the cooler weather?"

"This is the season we get busier. The cooler weather has people go inside for their exercise."

The drinks arrived and each toasted the other. Jim figured that now was as good a time as ever to tell Chris the news.

"Chris, I've got something to tell you."

Chris studied Jim's serious expression. "Oh?"

"I'm going to leave San Francisco in a week."

The statement took Chris by surprise. "What's that? Why?"

"A job opportunity has come up in Seattle and I want to look into it."

"I thought you were doing all right at the marina. What are you going to be checking on?"

"A marketing job but it's not definite. I want to see what it's all about."

"I'm really shocked. You've done a lot here and thought you enjoyed it. Have you told anyone else? When are you planning on it?"

"In a week. I have to get some things straighten up in the business while I'm gone. It's just an exploration trip. You're the only person I've told. I don't want to stir up a fuss."

"Nick, you got a few people here who will care if you take off without saying goodbye."

Jim felt tears come to his eyes as the remark made him think about Diane. "It may not be permanent. Who knows, I might not like the proposition."

"Nick. Are you in some trouble?"

Now it was Jim's turn to be surprised. "No, nothing like that. Why?"

"I saw Rod Boynton this past week and he tells me you're a frequent visitor to the gun club."

"I just found the gun practice an interesting diversion. That's all there is to it."

"Okay, Nick. The fact is you'll be missed but I can understand you wanting to check out opportunities."

"Thanks, Chris. I would appreciate it if you didn't mention it to anyone. I'd rather tell them myself."

"How about a going away party?" Chris asked watching Jim's reaction.

Jim squirmed. "No thanks. You know me. I hate the limelight."

"All right. Here comes the food."

The evening ended in general conversation. Jim knew Chris did not believe his story; at least he had told him and he felt good about it.

Chapter Forty-two

AN EVENTFUL DAY

Monday, October 28

Adam saw the sun had broken through the clouds for the first time in days. Maybe it was an omen. He rose and went to shower. He thought, do I have five days left? Maybe less. Probably less. Well, it wasn't the first time he had been under the gun. He dressed and walked to the restaurant. A good breakfast is all I need. I'll skip lunch to hit more places. He pulled out the map. The second martial arts studio was on this morning's route. The last one was informative. Perhaps, this one will be just as interesting. He hadn't contacted Ray Peterson since he started his search in this area. Oh well, time enough for that.

Jim woke up and dressed. He usually went to Chris's studio at this time in the morning so why stop now? He jogged down the street and met Chris as he opened the door.

"Hey, I thought you might take a break seeing as how you're leaving."

"Nope, old habits die hard. Besides I have to keep in shape."

He worked with Chris for an hour and then left to shower and change. As he jogged back, he thought about introducing Miguel to George Marx around mid-week. He wondered how much money he had in the account. He had asked George to deposit his commission check from Steve Wilson. The $5,000 amount was a huge surprise.

Segrey and Petra had already performed their exercises in the room. They both showered and dressed. Sergey remarked. "So far our search for the PI has been useless. I wonder if anybody is ever going to find Factor. For all we know, he's already flown."

"Do you think he'll go back home?"

"Nah. He's scared and will stay on the run. We'll give it one more week. After that, I'll call Mr. Federov and tell him it's a lost cause."

Adam neared the martial arts studio and observed people going in and out. The windows were covered so he couldn't see what was going on inside. He followed a young man through the front door into an open room. There were three groups going through a series of movements. A man wearing a black belt around his waist broke free of one group and came over to him.

"Hello. I'm Chris Muncie. And you are?"

"Adam Weatherly. Is there any place we can talk in private?"

Chris now paid more attention to the man. He was shorter than Chris but his shoulders and arms belied a muscular build in spite of the soft tone of his voice. His face showed a slight scar of a fight. He'd bet this guy won it. "Are you a cop?"

Adam pulled out his credentials and gave it to Chris. "No, a private investigator."

Chris examined the photo and ID closely, then handed it back. "We'll go in the back to my office." He yelled at the group to continue the movements until he returned. They walked back and sat. "Okay. What can I do for you?"

"I'm looking for this man who disappeared from his home around six months ago." With that, he passed over the recent picture of Factor to Chris.

Chris looked at the picture and stared. My God, it's Nick. Careful to keep any sign of recognition or reaction from Weatherly, he curiously asked. "What's he wanted for?"

Adam noticed Chris didn't say he never saw him. He relaxed in his chair and replied. "He's not wanted for anything. I was hired by his wife to find him. It appears he was threatened and in danger as a result of some business he conducted. He apparently felt his life and his wife's were at risk so he ran away."

"Interesting story. What does that have to do with our studio? "You probably heard about the man who rescued a girl from two muggers not far from here a couple of months ago."

Chris nodded. "So?"

"The girl said he used karate on them."

"Was he hurt?"

"No. I can't say the same about the two guys. They were laid up in the jail hospital after he got through with them."

"I've had the police come in after that and ask questions with a sketch. I couldn't help them and I can't help you."

"I talked to the girl about two weeks ago. She identified the photo you have in your hand."

"I didn't see anything in the papers about it."

Adam nodded. "That's true. I didn't tell anyone except my office about it."

Chris handed the photo back. "I don't know I can help you." He asked bluntly. "Is he a student here?"

"I'm afraid not." He rose from his chair. "Now, if you'll excuse me."

Adam stayed seated. "May I tell you a few things about him starting with his name? Maybe it will remind you of someone."

Chris sat back down. "If you like."

"His name is Factor, Jim Factor. He lives in Southern California with his wife Diane. He was a former aerospace engineer who turned into an arms dealer."

Chris listened quietly.

Adam continued. "I think he was somehow involved in an illicit arms transaction which soured. As a result, one of the principals sent a Russian mafia hit team to kill him. He found out and took flight. His wife filed a missing person report with the local police department but hired me when she wanted to do more. I followed his movements to San Francisco and been searching for him ever since."

"What makes you think he's still here?"

"Ah, now you've put your finger on one of my two concerns. His wife feels he would stay in one place to regroup since he is methodical in that respect. By the way, I'll vouch for that. He's evaded me for almost six months. I know he has obtained false ID and a counterfeit passport. He's learned karate and Spanish since he's been here. I believe he's getting ready to leave again. And I know deep down inside if he does, no one will ever find him again."

"Spanish?"

"Yes, does that surprise you? He can pass for Mexican. He apparently speaks fluent Spanish and I bet he can read it as well."

"You mentioned two concerns."

Adam's expression became serious. "I have a big predicament when I find him. I've been tailed to San Francisco by a Russian hit team. They had gotten away with bugging Factor's house and the homes of my two employees. They also placed a tracker on my car which I didn't discover until a friend on the SFPD had my car checked. I'm sure they're still here looking for me to lead them to Factor."

Chris filled in. "So you're worried if you find this Factor, it will place him in imminent danger."

"Count on it."

"It's an interesting story. I still don't understand why you're so concerned with this hit team if your job is simply to find him."

Adam leaned towards Chris. "It started out that way. Now, it's gone way beyond it. My hat's off to this guy for the decision he made to abandon his life for his family's sake. He's done everything right. I don't know what kind of work he's taken on while here but I wager he's picked up a skill he can use somewhere else. I'll tell you something more; he has my admiration and respect for what he has accomplished. No one in my professional lifetime has ever eluded exposure with more skill than he has. Getting back to your question, I'm not finding him so he can be set up for these guys. Somehow, they have to be neutralized."

"You mean turn them over to the police?"

"No, I mean that won't do. After I find Factor, I've got to deal with them directly."

"How many are they? Aren't they professionals?"

"There are two I know about. Yeah, they're professionals and deadly."

Chris shook his head. "It's a hell of a story."

"Have you seen him?"

"I'll have to think about it. Do you have a card?"

Adam handed him his card and wrote his cell phone number on it. "Before I leave, mind telling me something about yourself?"

"Nothing much to say. I'm a former Navy Seal who wanted to get out of the violence game and into business for myself. I've had this place for a few years."

Adam rose and put out his hand. Chris shook it and started to show him to the door. "Chris, I believe we don't have much time." Chris almost said something but held back. "Goodbye, Adam."

Chris watched Weatherly leave the studio and walked over to one of his instructors. "Dean, take over my group for me. I've got some paperwork in the office to catch up on."

He walked back to the office, closed the door and sat down.

Did he believe the story he just heard? It was fantastic yet rang with an element of truth. It would be just like Nick. Or was it Jim Factor? He was leaving this Saturday. He could vouch Jim had picked up the boat business and martial arts, even handling a gun. God, he had picked up Spanish too. He could recall his time with Jim when he harbored a curiosity about his manner, articulation and background. Somehow his story about prison never seemed to fit the man he called his friend. He had more questions than answers. Did he believe Weatherly? If he stood by and did nothing, Jim would simply disappear and no one would find a trace. Everybody would be safe. But if running was Jim's simple solution to this threat, why had he bothered to learn the martial arts and handling a gun? Maybe Jim was preparing to draw a line in the sand on his own in the future.

What about Weatherly? Did he have his own agenda? Was he serious about taking on the hit men once he located Jim? Why would he even think about doing it and placing himself at risk when he had never met Jim? Damn, what a situation? Yet, he felt the sincerity of Weatherly. Was it just a performance? He didn't think so. And what about himself? Didn't he get out of the Navy because he was tired of all the violence? Yet, here it was staring at him in the face. Wait a minute. What was he thinking? He's not involved in any violence. How did the thought jump into his head? This is scary. I don't have to make a decision now. Hell, I don't have to make any at all. Still, he glanced at Weatherly's card. I've got some thinking to do.

Adam walked out of the martial arts studios immersed in his own thoughts. He strolled along the sidewalk oblivious to the surroundings. He reviewed the conversation he just had with Muncie. He didn't say he knew Factor or of him. He asked a lot of questions. Curiosity? No, he didn't believe it. Muncie knows him, I'm sure of it. Although, for sure he didn't know Factor picked up Spanish. What else is out there Factor has kept from everyone? How does Factor keep everything straight? Does Muncie know Factor is close to skipping again? Factor would be cautious about disclosing his plans. He opened his car and sat in the driver's seat without starting it. He suddenly realized he was through with canvassing. Okay, my gut says I found him. What's my next step? He pulled out the cell phone and called his office.

Elaine answered with the usual greeting.

"Elaine, it's me. Get Marty on the phone, please." Marty piped in from another phone before Elaine could answer.

They chimed in. "Adam, have you found him? Any news?"

He brought them up to date on the conversation with Chris Muncie. He kept his opinions and thoughts out of it instead preferring to hear their views.

"Adam. That's great! What now?"

"Suppose you two tell me. What do you suggest?"

Elaine spoke first. "I'll run a background check on Chris Muncie and his martial arts studios."

Marty interrupted. "Adam. It sounds like you're thinking of going to go back to Muncie and somehow enlist his support. I suppose you could conduct surveillance on him to see if he leads you to Factor but I'm guessing he'd be expecting it. Anyway, it may backfire and turn him off from helping you. What's your impression of him? Will he think about it and get back to you?"

Adam smiled at the insight Marty had just shown. The kid's learning fast. "Marty, that's good thinking, I hope so. Elaine, please get what information you can and e-mail it to me."

Elaine turned towards Marty and silently clapped her hands.

Marty grinned and both turn to the phone.

"I'm terminating my search. The next step rests with Chris Muncie. I need some exercise so I think he's going to get another student for a couple of days. He has to make up his own mind. He said he was formerly a Navy Seal."

"Adam. It fits in with your previous conversation at the other karate studios."

"Yes, I know."

"Adam," It was Elaine, "What happens when you find him? You know what I mean."

He paused before answering. "That's the million dollar question. But first things first."

"Adam, you'll need help if you're going to do anything. Were you thinking of enlisting Ray Peterson?" Marty asked.

"I don't think he would approve of any independent action. Besides, I want to sleep on it. Get me the information as soon as you can."

Adam hung up, started the car and drove back to the hotel. Once inside his room, he laid the map down and looked through his clothes. It's time for some exercise. He changed into a sweat suit and sneakers and went to his car. He drove back to the martial arts studios and parked. Muncie was conducting a class when Weatherly walked in the door. He looked up with surprise. He left the group and came up to Weatherly. He asked suspiciously. "What are you doing here? Did you forget something?"

"No. I figured I'd see if I could work out with one of the instructors while I had the chance."

Chris took in the sweat suit and beckoned him. He went to the group and told them to continue to practice with each other. Then he directed Weatherly into a vacant part of the room with a practice mat. "Will I do?" He asked with a slight smile. Weatherly nodded. Weatherly stood to the side and did stretching exercises to loosen up. Satisfied, he turned to Muncie. "Okay."

Weatherly bowed. Chris returned the bow. Then, they settled into defensive positions and circled each other. Weatherly dropped fast and lunged with his legs to ensnare and trip up Chris. No sooner had Chris evaded the maneuver than Weatherly somersaulted in and kicked out. It narrowly missed Chris. He took the initiative and feinted to make Weatherly shift his feet. Instead Weatherly came inside of his attack and pushed out with his hands. Chris moved away and circled Weatherly. Weatherly mounted an open hand attack which Chris repelled and countered with a pivoting kick. The sudden change in tactic caught Weatherly by surprise and he went down. He jumped to his feet and circled Chris.

The group of students halted their practice when they heard the combatants' grunts and hovered with fascination as the contest unfolded before them. Both men were inflicting blows. The stranger was the more aggressive of the two but Chris was clearly the superior fighter. Both men were sweating profusely. After fifteen minutes the stranger threw up his hands and bowed. Chris returned the bow. The students applauded until a stern look from Chris sent them scampering to their practice areas.

Weatherly caught his breath. "Whew, I'm a little out of practice. You're very good. Usually, I can bull my way through and catch an opening or two."

"You've had training and developed a unique style. Where did you learn?"

Weatherly wiped his face with a towel. "I started in college through my stint with the police. I appreciated the lesson. What do I owe you?"

"Nothing, the first one is free." With that, Chris turned away and went to the group. He half expected to hear Weatherly ask a question but was surprised when he saw him go out the door. He nodded with approval; the guy is both smart and tough.

Weatherly returned to his hotel and checked for e-mails. Nothing yet from Elaine. He took a shower and checked his body for bruises. He felt a little sore. Boy, I'd hate to really tumble with Muncie. He would be a dangerous handful. He did find out one thing; he had not displayed any hostility towards him during the exercise. He thought, maybe, just maybe. Here's where patience and a leap of faith are really needed. If he doesn't come to me, Factor's gone. He pondered calling Diane Factor but decided there wasn't much to go on. Besides, he didn't want her to come up to San Francisco and get in the way. With a start, he asked himself, get in the way of what?

Chris drove into his garage and headed straight to the kitchen. He reached in the refrigerator and took out a steak and opened a beer. He placed the steak on the grill. He prepared a potato with vegetables and tossed a salad. While the steak was cooking, he took a drink of beer and thought through the events of the day. It kind of boiled down to this; did he believe Weatherly? Was Nick this guy Jim Factor? Would he really be in danger if he were discovered? Sure, Weatherly had a stake in finding him. After all, he was hired by Factor's wife.

The timer went off reminding him to turn the steak and stir the vegetables. He took another drink of beer. What was Weatherly insinuating when he said he would have to take care of the second problem? His adeptness and ferocity on the karate mat made Chris think that this was no idle chitchat. Weatherly had something on his mind. He hated to say it but he wanted another talk with him. Usually, he'd eat in the kitchen with the TV on to catch the news of the day. This time, he sat in the living room to eat and think. He glanced on the coffee table at the picture of him in his Seal days. When he finished the meal, he walked into his home office. Behind a panel, he dialed a combination and opened the gun safe. He stared at a Sig-Saur P226 9mm pistol with full capacity clip and an ammunition box. He took it out and cleaned it becking it up. He closed the safe and the panel. He decided to sleep on it.

Chapter Forty-three

EVERYONE'S UNDER PRESSURE

Tuesday, October 29

Chris spent a restless night thinking about Jim and the decision confronting him. When he neared the front door of the studio he saw Jim waiting as usual. He unlocked the door and turned on the lights while Jim went to the corner and proceeded to perform warm-up exercises. He hoped his apprehension didn't show. He went over to where Jim stood and they both bowed. They assumed the opening combat stance and went into defensive and attack movements. Before they knew it, the hour was up. The other students were coming in the door.

"Beer tonight, Chris?" Jim asked.

Chris nodded and waved goodbye as he turned to meet the group of students.

Later on, Chris was shocked to see Weatherly standing inside the door with a grin.

Adam walked up to him. "Hello. To tell the truth I had so much fun yesterday I was hoping we could do it again."

In spite of himself, Chris laughed. "You're a glutton for punishment," he replied, "this time it'll cost you."

Adam nodded. "I figured that. Lead the way."

Chris turned to his group. "Please go through the exercises and movements for a while."

A few of the students though were looking at Adam remembering the karate combat they witnessed the day before. Reluctantly, they started their exercises. Chris motioned to Adam to follow him to the other mat area. Both went through a short warm up and then turned and bowed. They circled each other as before. This time Chris knew to expect an unorthodox beginning attack. The attack, defense and counterattack movements of both men continue until Chris noticed his students starting to leave. He put his hand up to. Adam to take a break. Both men were breathing heavily.

Chris walked over to the students and inquired. "Why are you leaving?" He was surprised when they pointed to the clock. "The hour's up."

They bowed and he returned the bow. He walked over to Adam. "I'm afraid that's all the time I have to spend with you."

Adam declared. "Just as well, you're too good for me. I have to rest these weary bones. How much do I owe you?"

Chris cited a figure and Adam reached into his pocket and paid.

"You're quite unorthodox in your selection of moves but you have a good martial arts instinct which serves you well."

"Thanks for the compliment. You wouldn't be so generous if you knew how sore I was yesterday after our session."

Chris smiled. "Pain is gain," he said.

"Right. Well, thanks again." Weatherly walked away towards the door.

Chris made up his mind and called out. "Adam." He looked over his shoulder and replied. "Yes?" Chris heard himself saying. "You busy tonight?"

"No. Why?"

"Maybe we could get together. Say, the Foggy Bottom Bar at six-thirty?"

"Sounds good." Adam opened the door. "You need directions?"

Adam shook his head. "I'll find it."

Adam walked to his car feeling the soreness with every step. He thought, finally I caught a break. It hadn't come too soon. He couldn't have managed a third encounter with Chris. God, that guy was good. As he drove he decided now he could really go for some breakfast. After that, he'd call his office and take a rest. He made a mental note to hit the gym more often if only two karate sessions made him so sore.

When he got back to the hotel room, Adam checked his email messages and saw Elaine had sent a file on Chris Muncie. He scanned it over and was impressed with the combat actions and evaluations listed on his service record. The background check on the martial arts studios showed it to be debt-free and pay its bills on time. He took off the sweat-stained warm-ups and threw them in the corner. He gingerly walked to the bathroom and filled the tub. Forget the shower. He was going to soak a long while and follow up with a nap. Tonight was going to be an interesting. He wondered what Chris would tell him. He planned to arrive a little earlier so he could survey the bar's exits just in case anything went wrong.

Jim was in the boat's cabin troubleshooting a navigation system aboard one of the smaller cruisers. The owner's complaint was it wouldn't overlap the boat's position on the monitor although it did allow the local chart to be entered and displayed. From the bridge he could see the other boats and the open bay. Ah, here was the problem. The owner had loaded the navigation chart but inadvertently input the option to base the position reference from a point down the coast rather than his own frame of reference. He inserted the proper frame of reference before he turned off the system and left. He still had to tell Miguel he was taking over the business. He also wanted to introduce him to George Marx.

Sergey read the newspaper for the second time as he drank a cup of coffee across the street from the hotel the PI had stayed in when they had lost him. He wondered how Borichov was keeping himself busy during this time. If they didn't find Factor by this weekend, the job was over. He was already thinking about Miami. He glanced discreetly at the hotel entrance. It was time to stretch his legs. He was stiff. The exercises in the motel room were limited. He longed to go to the gym but he knew it had to wait. Petra had the car at the police station. Maybe they'd get lucky today. Somehow, he doubted it.

Newport Beach, California

Diane Factor had just gotten off the phone with Jim's parents. She wished she had something more to tell them. She trusted and believed in Adam Weatherly's dogged determination to find Jim. It was almost six months since Jim had left without a word. Was he still in danger? She had read enough to know hardened criminals had revenge on their mind for years. She shuddered. I have to be patient and believe, well believe anyway.

My darling, I miss you very much. However bad it was for her, it had to be more difficult for Jim wherever he was. He had to maintain a false identity and constantly look over his shoulder. How long could he possibly hold out without funds? She mentally reproached herself. She knew better than that.

He would hold out until it was time to move again. In spite of her anxiety, she felt a strange sort of pride in her husband. Weatherly had determined Jim was in San Francisco and felt he was closing in on him. She was mindful Jim would leave once he had accomplished his purpose. His purpose, why had she used that term? Something was eluding her. It had come down to days. What could she do about it? She had been patient for these six months but she wanted to do more. She would go to Weatherly's agency to see if there was any more information.

Chapter Forty-four

DISCOVERY AND RELIEF

San Francisco, California

It was not yet six in the evening but Chris wanted to get to Foggy Bottom first. He was willing to bet Weatherly had the same thought. He kept himself busy all day to avoid thinking about what would happen this evening. He didn't know what he would say or do or even accomplish.

At the same time Adam was thinking. What would be Factor's reaction to his presence when it was explained? Would he bolt for the door? He had looked forward to this meeting right from the very beginning. It had nothing to do with the job. He wanted to meet this man face to face. It was hard to explain and he wouldn't try. He knew Factor had made a tough decision and left a life behind. He had evaded exposure by his wits. And, he had gone beyond that. He had acquired skills and what else? Another livelihood? He'd bet on it. He located the Foggy Bottom Bar on the street map and saw it wasn't far from his search pattern. He closed the door to his room and left the hotel.

In the parking garage he opened the trunk and deposited his gun in the lock box. Satisfied, he closed the trunk and got into the car. If it weren't for the persistence of Diane Factor, he would never have put in the time to find him. Anxiously, he drove to the bar. He circled the parking lot and saw only one rear exit. He parked the car near the entrance and went in.

He spotted Chris Muncie at one of the booths. He walked up and Chris motioned him to sit.

Chris spoke first. "I've been having second thoughts about this meeting all day."

Adam nodded and understood. "I would have in your shoes too. What happens next is really up to Jim Factor or Nick as you know him. What's your relationship with him?"

"He's my friend," was the short reply.

Adam reflected, Diane Factor was right when she said Jim had hanged. He asked. "Chris, how do you think he'll react when I reveal who I am and what I'm doing? Will he run?"

"Nick. Damn it, I got to get used to his real name, Jim. Anyway, at times he's impulsive but the right way. Other times he's deliberate. I'm wondering myself."

They both turned and looked towards the front door when they heard it open. Chris saw it was Jim and waved.

Jim saw that Chris had company at the booth and strolled over saying hello to Connie as he passed the bar. He came over to the table and sat down alongside of Chris.

Adam stared at the man he had been hunting for six months. If he had passed him on the street, he would have had trouble recognizing him.

Chris motioned at Adam. "Nick, meet Adam Weatherly. Adam, this is Nick Germain."

Both men shook hands. Connie came over and took their drink orders. When she had gone, Chris took the initiative. "Nick, I met Adam at the studio where he's given me a battle for two straight days."

Jim laughed. "Chris, I doubt anyone could take you close to your limit. But it's a fine compliment to your skill, Adam."

Adam smiled. "I have to say I agree with you. I couldn't take him on my best day and on his worst one."

They laughed as Connie returned with the beers. When she left, they toasted and took a drink.

Adam declared. "Jim, I'm a private investigator hired by your wife Diane to find you."

Both Adam and Chris looked apprehensively at Jim expecting an eruption of motion and sound.

Instead, Jim calmly took another drink of his beer and put it down. He replied in a low voice without rancor and with appreciation. "You're very good at your job, Adam. How is Diane?"

Adam answered, relieved at the response. "Safe and worried. She hired me two weeks after you left. You covered your tracks very well. If Chris hadn't chosen to help me, you would have remained gone without a trace and I would never have found you." Adam turned to Chris. "Is this a good place to talk or should we leave for a quieter spot?"

Chris suggested. "I have beer, liquor and food at my place. I suggest we move this meeting there if it's all right with you, Nick?"

"It's Jim, Chris, and it's fine with me. I think there are some stories to tell." Jim saw Adam hesitate. "It's okay Adam. I'm not running. I'll even ride with you."

Adam nodded. He put some money on the table and the three walked out the door.

They made themselves comfortable in Chris's living room with mixed drinks in their hands.

Adam initiated the conversation. "Jim, if it's all the same to you, I'd like to start at the beginning and tell you what's transpired and my steps to find you."

Jim nodded, leaned back relaxed and listened.

At the conclusion of Adam's story Jim interjected. "I figured the threat was real when I received the no-nonsense warning. It's why I didn't hesitate to pack up and leave on the spot." He provided the details of his encounter with Carlos Sengretti and subsequently with Mikhail Borichov. He described his consulting role in the illegal arms transaction. "Sengretti called me at home to tell me the deal was blown. He said Borichov blamed me and made arrangements to have me killed. My guess is Sengretti got careless and had to take off in a hurry. Have there been any inquiries by any federal authorities at my home?"

Adam shook his head. "It appears all they have and are interested in are Sengretti and Borichov."

"Anyway, I figured if I disappeared cleanly without a trace, I'd be safe and they would leave my family alone."

Adam added. "It did work out that way to a point. They placed a wiretap on your house and a tracking device on my car." In answer to their unspoken question and concern, Adam continued. "I have a friend, Ray Peterson, on the SFPD. His people located it. I took it off the car so our friends are blind. But I'm getting ahead of myself. Let me go back to where my search led me to San Francisco." Adam described his search in San Francisco covering rooming houses and hotels, banks and fake ID merchants. Drivers' license applications were also reviewed with no success.

Jim confided. "You're a very thorough person, Adam. I doubt anyone but you would have had the patience to carry it off especially in light of the disappointing results you were getting. By the way, how did you pick out San Francisco from the other two places?"

Adam told him of the computer search for a missing passenger in the three buses.

"Nice. I should have thought of it but time was getting away from me."

Jim, Adam and Chris took turns completing the narration. Jim looked sheepish when Chris told of his encounter with the two assailants on the street. Adam recounted his luck at finding out Jim had obtained a counterfeit Mexican passport.

"Actually Adam, the passport is real. It's why it cost so much. I felt it was a must if I was to successfully leave the country."

"Jim, tell Adam about your present business."

Adam raised an eyebrow. "What business?"

Jim related the events at the marina which led to the start of a business serving boats owners.

"Jim, you don't cease to surprise me. Did it make any money?"

Jim was chagrinned. "More than I ever thought. My own personal account has around $15,000. The business supports four people."

Adam just stared at him. "You've accomplished a hell of a lot in six months, and hardly a way to be hidden from view. On the other hand, I'd never have thought of a business angle."

It was three in the morning and they sat in silence with coffee when the story was finally completed. Adam commented. "I would guess your plan to leave is on hold."

Reluctantly, Jim shook his head. "I still have a problem." Adam rubbed his hand over his chin. "Ah yes. The problem. I've been giving it a lot of thought. Let me tell you something. The undertaking to find you has evolved in my mind into two parts. Finding you, of course, was the top priority. The second part was how to deal with the mafia team who I strongly suspect are still here searching for the both of us. Without taking care of this critical issue, I don't see myself revealing your existence."

The statement took Jim and Chris by surprise.

Jim finally spoke. "Adam, you're the amazing one. I appreciate what you just said more than you know. I have come to expect I would have to confront Borichov. It's why I started with the martial arts classes from Chris. You mentioned the FBI's interest in finding these guys. Couldn't we just turn them in?"

Adam shook his head. "It would get rid of your near-term problem, not the overall one."

Jim considered his options for a moment. "I'll have to deal with the hit team before I leave and then go after Borichov. I worry that in frustration they'll retaliate against my wife. Adam, you suspect they're looking for you. That's how I'll find them first."

Chris intervened. "Hey, wait a minute. You're not seriously thinking of tackling them by yourself?"

"I don't see I have a choice. It'll get rid of the immediate threat. I just have to work out the logistics."

Adam slowly interjected. "Maybe there's something else that can be done about it."

Chris picked up on the inflection of Adam's voice and the nuance in his statement. "I got a feeling you have a solution. Want to let us in on it?"

Hesitantly, Adam looked at each one of them. "Yes. I figure they couldn't be ignored, bribed or scared so as I see it there are two options; let Jim proceed with his risky intention and stand down, or take them out with him."

After a stunned moment of silence, Chris asked. "Did I hear you right? Are you suggesting you engage them? You do realize they're professionals not to mention armed and dangerous."

Adam replied. "I guess I'm saying I'm counting on it."

It was Jim's turn to be amazed. "You mean like a gunfight at the OK Corral?"

Adam shrugged. "It's the only way. If we can do it in a way where they disappear, we're all home free."

The realization of their intentions and the extreme risk and danger suddenly overtook them. Silence filled the room as their thoughts muted any sounds.

Jim admonished them. "I can't let you get involved. I'll stick to my original plan to leave the country. There's no reason for the both of you to place your lives and careers in jeopardy. This started with me."

Adam answered his objection. "I appreciate what you're saying but, speaking for me, I'll be damned if I'll let scum like them get away. They've done this before and should you escape, they'll continue to do it."

Chris slapped Adam on the back. "What Adam said goes double for me. When I left the Seals, I had a bellyful of war games and covert missions. Now I realize they're necessary if we're to be free from intimidation. What you did, you'll have to face another day. I can't believe there would be any witnesses against you. I want you to know I consider you my friend."

Adam added his Amen. "Jim, I've gotten to know a lot about you. I could say it's my job but the whole thing has become personal to me."

Jim stared at both of them. "My God. Yet, I know these guys won't go away."

"The question is how and where."

They all quietly thought about this angle. Chris looked at them. "Alcatraz Island?"

"The Rock? What about it?" Adam asked.

"Think about it. It's relatively near, isolated, and closed in the early evening. It's full of hiding places and no one will hear anything. Further, there is only one way by boat to enter and leave the Rock. And, the currents will take anything dumped out to sea. The distance from the Alcatraz dock to the building complex at the top of the island is about a quarter of a mile. It has a decent elevation which gives an overall view of the island except for the buildings."

Jim considered the idea. "It's just north of the Pier 39 Marina. I don't know. It means we would have to find these guys and then decoy them to the island. Once there, we would to have to fight them at night."

Adam shrugged. "As far as locating them, I think they're waiting for me to turn up again at the hotel where I first stayed."

Chris added. "I can come up with the right equipment from friends around this area."

Adam smiled. "I also brought a bunch of toys with me."

Jim glanced at Adam. "You thought about this possibility?"

Adam nodded. "Or something like it."

Chris yawned. "I don't know about you two but I'm bushed. Let's continue this discussion after we get some sleep. We don't have much time to plan. Let's use my studio as a rendezvous point at noon tomorrow."

They all got up. Jim asked Adam to drive him back to the bar where he had his car. Adam stared at him, grinned and shook his head.

"Jim. See you at Chris's at noon?"

"Don't worry, Adam. I'll be there."

Chapter Forty-five

A STRATEGY DEVELOPS

Wednesday, October 30

Jim rose a little later than his usual schedule. Marie Queterras heard his footsteps on the stairway. He explained. "A little too late partying. I decided to sleep in."

"Do you want anything to eat?"

"No thank you. I have to get to the marina."

When Jim arrived at his office at Halyard, Miguel was waiting for him.

"We got another two calls yesterday. I've passed them out already."

"Great. I can't believe we're so busy. I have some business to take care of this afternoon and for the next couple of days. Can you take care of everything until I get back?"

"Sure. Anything serious?"

Jim sat down in the chair. "No, just time consuming."

Adam woke up to a ringing phone. He remembered requesting a wakeup call. He yawned and walked over to the table holding his computer. He checked for messages. Seeing there were none, he stretched and went to take a shower. When he got out, he called room service for breakfast. This was going to be a busy day.

* * *

Chris glanced at the clock on his night table. He knew one of the other instructors would open the studios and start the morning sessions if he wasn't there. He entered the kitchen and made a protein drink. Then he went back to the bedroom to get ready for the day's events. As he showered and dressed his Seal experience recognized the need for a plan to be quickly fabricated. It had been e had visited Alcatraz and certainly not for the purpose they had in mind.

At noon as was agreed upon, they met at Chris's studio and went back to the office. Chris had a video camera and knapsack. He inquired casually. "Do the both of you have jackets and walking shoes?"

Puzzled by the question, Jim and Adam nodded.

"Then, let's get in my car. I've got reservations for the tour of Alcatraz Island." Chris explained. "We're going to Pier 41 adjacent to the Pier 39 Marina to catch the ferry to Alcatraz Island. The National Park Service maintains the Rock. If we're going to consider a stand, we need to get a firsthand look at the territory."

They parked then wandered to the pier where Chris collected the tour tickets. They were surprised by the number of people waiting to go to the island. Chris explained the Rock is a popular attraction in San Francisco. Adam bought a throw-away camera for still pictures. Jim went to a souvenir shop and picked up literature and a walking guide of the island. As they stood at the landing, they stared at their objective. Alcatraz Island in San Francisco Bay lay about one and a half miles north of them. Its southern side could be plainly seen against the background of Angel Island.

Jim read them an excerpt from the guide.

There are treacherous currents in San Francisco Bay, a major factor in its past selection as a high security prison. It is an inhospitable island. It sits directly in the path of fog-bearing, chilly westerly winds blowing through the Golden Gate Bridge, particularly during summer afternoons. Visiting Alcatraz means carrying a sweater or jacket and wearing comfortable gripping shoes as many paths are steep.

When their turn came, they boarded the ferry.

Adam observed as they sat inside. "With all of these people going there, we won't stand out."

Chris nodded and declared. "There's no hurry to come back right away so we can inspect every part of the island."

The ferry took less than twenty minutes to make it to the Alcatraz dock. They looked at each other when the ferry circled the island. The landing wharf was on the north side of the island hidden from the San Francisco coast. Chris went outside to video the ferry's approach and the building to the right of the dock. They left the ferry with the rest of the visitors but hung back to examine the setting in more detail. A cool wind blew across the island. Jim continued to read the guidebook out loud pointing out the salient features of the island. In between, Chris and Adam discussed tactical positions that would yield a view of any boat coming into the dock.

The dock tower is to the right of the wharf and the old barracks build-ing is to the rear and right of the wharf. The four-story barracks build-ing today houses the bookstore, exhibit hall and theater. The ground floor of the old structure has enclosures called casemates where can-nons were supposed to be placed to protect the wharf.

Chris exclaimed. "The docks can be seen from the casemates. If we were to have an early warning station, it would be there."

They walked to the rear of the barracks building and up the slope to the cell house. Farther up the path they spotted the water tower. Adam grimly observed. "It has a good overall view from the top but anyone on the upper walkway perimeter is exposed and vulnerable." As they walked closer they saw the side ladder leading up the water tower had rusted away. Adam said what they all thought. "The water tower's out of the question."

Chris had them stop. "Let's backtrack to the docks and take the other path."

From the wharf they moved straight up the path and noted the stairs leading to the first level. Standing in the center of the level and looking up towards the right they could see the imposing eighty-four foot reinforced concrete lighthouse. It was on the next level. The ruin of the warden's house was ev-ident on the right. They walked on and came upon a slope on their right leading up to the level where the lighthouse base and the warden's house were situated. The warden's house was a fire-gutted structure with four deteriorating walls. Chris pointed out it lacked a vantage point for a sniper or firefight stand. The lighthouse interior was inaccessible. Adam mentioned it probably contained intruder sensors. To the rear of the lighthouse was the imposing three-story cell house building with its many cellblocks and floors. Chris offered the roof would provide a good view and shooting zone with protection. The problem was accessibility and the possibility of being similarly sensor-protected. There were no outside fire escapes and the windows were barred. Built to keep people in, it had the added benefit of keeping people out. They looked past the water tower to the rear of the island and the New Industries Building. Jim read again.

At one time it housed workshops and a large laundry. The buildings and adjacent areas were closed to visitors early on because the state of deterioration made them a hazard. Later, this part of the island was designated a bird sanctuary and closed even to the National Park Service.

The three men looked at one another. Chris shrugged and slithered through a rusted chain link fence. Jim and Adam searched the grounds for prying eyes. Soon, the three men were walking towards the rear of the building. The entry was open. The huge laundry with its equipment in a rusting condition was on the ground floor. They passed by the rows of dryers against the wall and the row of washers on the floor on the other side to a set of metal stairs. The second floor was an open bay impressive in size with narrow pillars standing in two paths in the center of the structure. There was no hiding places and a lethal fire zone for anyone unlucky enough to be caught in it. They collectively came to the same conclusion. The laundry was a perfect final stand location.

Chris took a video of the approaches and entrances to the laundry, and the positions of the rusty but sturdy equipment. Chris cited another advantage, no electricity. "We'd have a good view with night vision equipment."

Adam agreed. "We'd be able to spot them way before they could see us."

Jim added cautiously. "Unless they're similarly equipped."

Chris nodded. "We had better consider the possibility. These guys are pros. They won't hear us on the concrete floor if we move some of the debris from our path."

Adam voiced their concern. "If we're in here, we'll need to have some way to track their movements. I'm thinking we set up motion detection video cameras around the island and monitor them through a cell phone connection."

Chris opened his knapsack and brought out a note pad and a tape measure. He tossed the tape measure to Jim. "Let's get some ideas of the distances between the equipment and entrances for a ground plan. Include the windows just in case. They're at ground level and we don't want them to fire in at us. The thick wire mesh screens on the windows will prevent them entering from there."

While Jim measured, Adam took pictures of the laundry room carefully to sequence each picture with respect to the ground plan being drawn on the note pad by Jim. Chris videotaped the doorway approaches from several vantage points. Finally, they met in the middle of the room.

Chris addressed them. "I think we got what we came for. Let's go outside one more time and check the water's edge. I don't believe anyone could make their way by boat from there because of the swirling current and steep craggy outcrop but let's make sure."

Chris's observation was proven correct.

Adam summarized the situation. "There are three paths available to get them here. It places us at a disadvantage although we can count on them splitting up. With communication gear they'll keep track of each other. We can mount video cameras with motion detection triggers and monitor all of the paths. We have to come up with a way to let them know we're in the laundry area. I'd hate to mark time while they break into the cell house looking for us."

Chris grinned. "It won't take them long but we have to draw them in and not expose ourselves. Actually, not all of us will be in the laundry area."

Jim and Adam looked sharply at Chris. "What?"

"We can't all be here. We'd be trapped and at the mercy of their firepower. For example, what if they have grenades? If I had them I'd toss them in from the open doorway behind us."

They were silent for a moment contemplating the implications of the threat.

Jim frowned. "I see your point. We need someone out there watching our backs."

Adam looked at Chris closely. "I think he means more than that, Jim."

Chris nodded. "We'll need an outside person in any event. The outside person will be responsible for ensuring the enemy's attack unfolds the way we dictate. He'll double as a sniper."

"Won't they first go after the outside person?" Jim asked apprehensively.

"Not if they think it will expose them. The outside person will have an advantage but will have to move once his position is compromised. If two of them go after the outside person, one of us will have to go out to support him."

Jim thought for a moment. "This isn't a cut and dry case of setting up an ambush, is it?"

Chris reminded them. "It never is nor should we expect it to be. Remember we're dealing with deadly professionals. We just have to keep thinking faster on our feet. We'll have one big advantage. We'll know the terrain ahead of time. Their advantage is they're skilled and experienced. We can count on them to be heavily armed. They aren't going to back down from trying to kill us. They'd probably face a similar fate if they don't succeed. Let's go around back. We haven't checked the power plant and there's a perimeter path hidden from the tour area. At the same time, we can survey the best spot for the outside man."

Chris stored the note pad, tape measure and camera in the knapsack. They made their way back to the second floor and went outside by the edge of the building and up the path to the power plant complex. Jim glanced at the layout map in his hand. "This suggests there's a four-story abandoned building on the other side of the smokestack. There's a rocky outcrop across the way from it."

Mindful of the barracks building where they could hear the milling visitors, they reached the building unobserved and entered. Diesel generators deteriorated by rust and age lined the bottom floor. They climbed the stairs to the next floor. After walking down the corridor and peering into two large rooms, Adam observed. "It looks like this was used to house the power control and monitoring equipment." They retraced their steps and climbed to the third floor. They walked past what appeared to be offices.

Chris went to the windows and waved them over. He pointed to the pathways and the other buildings. "Although we're lower in elevation than the rest of the island, this place has possibilities. The rocky knoll is right across the way." He took out the video camera and recorded the scene.

They walked to the end of the building. Debris from broken and vandalized walls and doors filled the corridors. They peered out of the end of the building past the husk of the old Post Exchange and Officer's Club. They could see the barracks building hundred feet away where a park ranger and tour group were visible.

Adam nudged Jim. "Do you see what I see?" he asked. Jim and Chris looked and saw the wharf and docks. "Thanks to the burnt out Officer's

Club, the docks are in plain sight from here. We're on the north side and unlikely to be seen or heard from the San Francisco shoreline." Chris filmed the view from the end window.

When they exited the east entrance of the building, they saw the perimeter path on the north side leading to the docks past the ruins of the Officer's Club and the guardhouse and alongside of the barracks. They backtracked one more time. Adam pointed to the path leading past the water tower. "It goes directly into the entrance of the New Industries building. If they wanted to avoid being seen on the main two paths, they'd have to take the same route we did."

Chris studied the slope between the water tower and the power plant building. "There's a rugged and rocky outcrop next to the water tower and in front of us. It's higher than this building and has a commanding view where an outside person can roam." Adam and Jim both looked at him with skepticism. "Of course, we're going to have to hide him pretty good but it's a perfect spot." He pulled the video camera out of the knapsack and videotaped the surrounding. Satisfied, he put the camera away. "I think we've seen enough. We're lucky no one has spotted us moving around. Let's not push our luck."

They walked back keeping the buildings and terrain in between them and the tour area until they neared the docks. They mixed with the visitors who were waiting to board the return ferry. As the boat docked at Pier 41, Chris took out the video camera and the throwaway camera. "I'll get this film into an overnight photo developer on my way home. Let's plan on getting together in the morning for breakfast at my place." Jim and Adam nodded their agreement and headed for the car.

Sergey shuffled his feet and rolled his head around his shoulders trying to get loose. He was bored and he was angry, something he never thought he'd admit to while on a stakeout mission. This was different than the jungle and other jobs he had been involved in. He had never had to spend this much time on any job. Borichov was crazy to lay out all of that money for what seemed like a petty revenge. Even though he exchanged positions with Petra at noon every day to break up their patterns, it had done little to relieve the tedious effort he expended making sure he moved to different locations. He glanced across the street at the hotel entrance. Petra and he had agreed whoever had the police station under surveillance would have the car to attract less attention.

Sergey thought not for the first time. Damn Borichov and his obsession.

Factor's probably far away by now. To compound their discomfit, Borichov had to call every night and become abusive at their lack of progress. If it had been anybody other than Federov's brother-in-law, he would have arranged an untimely accident for him. He wondered how Petra was taking it. At least this job was coming to an end in three days. Let Borichov and Federov argue about it then. He wondered what Borichov hoped to accomplish coming here. More than likely, he took the job personally whereas with Federov it was always business. He sighed and ribbed his eyes. It would be good to get back to the heat of Miami.

Chapter Forty-six

THE PLAN

Thursday, October 31

The men met in early morning at Chris's and were greeted by the smell of brewed coffee. They hungrily set upon the pastry and toast while laying out the developed pictures on the dining room table and going through them and the drawn up layout of the New Industries Building. A television with a VCR was in the corner of the room. Chris started the video taken the previous day. Jim and Adam were impressed by Chris's detailed narrative as he filmed the scene. "We're approaching the wharf. This boat is about one hundred feet long and needs its engines to keep it steady and controlled from the strong current swirling around the south edge of the island."

The camera panned to a building on the right of the dock.

"This is the barracks." Jim was heard to say. The camera pointed at several visible openings on the ground floor. Jim continued. "Those are casemates where cannons were placed to defend the island from unwanted intruders."

The camera moved to the dock tower and slowly moved up the structure. They heard Chris comment. "It has a good view of the wharf and the nearby area but is vulnerable. It has a wooden floor and anyone on the ground being cautious might fire a few rounds through it."

Chris stopped the video. "We'd need to get some idea of the force against us and their armament. This is the best spot because it's the only way in and they'd be together before separating."

Adam nodded. "We could have one of us viewing the dock from above the knoll or plant a remote camera with the monitor back at the laundry room. I don't know if the dock is lighted at night. I doubt it. We'd need to have an IR and optical camera triggered by a motion detection sensor."

Jim spoke as he wrote on a pad. "I'll keep track of the requirements as we go along."

As they completed the arrangements Adam stated the obvious. "We should verify they're here before we go any further." He looked at each of them.

Chris replied first. "Are you planning what I'm thinking?"

Jim joined in. "You don't mean you're going to deliberately show yourself to them?"

"Look, you two. I don't see any other way around it. I don't think they'll come after me until they're sure I'll lead them to Jim. Let's say they're watching my old hotel. I'll check back into it. It will give them time to pick up on me. Chris, what about backup surveillance on me so we can spot them and see how many there are?"

Chris nodded. "They'll be so busy keeping an eye on you they'll never think about watching their backs. The danger is if they decide to grab you and beat the information out of you. Then we'll have to move in prematurely."

"I'll keep my distance. What we now need is electronics and weapons. I brought an assortment with me but we're going to need more."

Jim and Chris looked at him with questioning expressions.

Adam shrugged. "As I said before, I figured finding you was my job until I realized there was more to it. I appreciated the sacrifice you were making and it got personal. I agree with you. Someone's got to make a stand."

Chris volunteered. "I have some weapons here and in a locker at a gun club. I think I know where to get more."

"I don't know what to say." Jim said.

Adam spoke to Jim. "You should sit on the sidelines. Chris and I are experienced with this type of action."

Jim smiled. "You want to tell him, Chris?"

Chris slanted his head towards Jim. "I introduced Jim to my gun club some time ago and he's been practicing with firearms. I hear he's pretty good from my friend who runs the club."

Adam shook his head. "Jim, you're something else. Okay, then. It'll be the three of us against the two of them. I would say we can use the edge."

Chris pulled out a pad and a pencil. "We need a timetable. I'm thinking we'll set it up for Saturday night. That gives us the rest of today, Friday and Saturday morning. Adam, tomorrow afternoon you'll check into that hotel. Wait until four. Jim, I need you to search the marina tomorrow for a boat suitable for us to stow equipment and get to the island on Friday and Saturday nights. Oh, one other thing. When you're picking out a boat, make sure there's one close by it our friends can steal as well. We'll spend the rest of today inventorying what we have and making a list of what we'll need."

"I can call my office and have my people overnight any electronics." Adam said.

Chris nodded agreement. "Okay. As for me, it's my job between now and Saturday to do the shopping for weapons and anything else I can think of. Jim, you and I will have to finish by three tomorrow afternoon to keep tabs on Adam. Saturday, we'll finish up stocking up the equipment and get some rest. Adam, can you sneak out of the hotel around nine tomorrow night?"

"I'll recon the roof, fire stairs and back doors after I check in but I don't see a problem."

"Okay. Jim, we'll pick Adam up around eight and head for the marina with the equipment. We'll load up the boat and go to Alcatraz from there. The trip will serve as a dry run and allow us to set up cameras and establish our positions. Saturday, Adam will check out of the hotel in the early evening in a hurry. Adam, eat supper prior to leaving the hotel and keep looking at your watch. It should get their attention. I figure they'll put two and two together and follow you thinking you're going to lead them to Jim. In the meantime, we would have gotten to the boat and be hidden in it. Park your car and run for it. Untie the boat and slowly ease it out into the channel. Make sure they're following. Fake engine trouble if you have to until they get the picture."

"I am concerned about Adam." Jim said hesitantly. "We're assuming those guys won't jump him and try to force him to talk."

Adam replied with a grim smile. "I'll be careful. Besides, I'll have a gun on me. I really don't think they'll want to tip their hand until they know where you are. They've been at it for so long they won't risk a slipup. Anyway, you two are going to babysit me. Make sure you can identify them. I have pictures of two of them but who knows, they could have been replaced or there might be more of them. To get this information and decoy them is worth the exposure."

Chris asked. "Adam, you wouldn't happen to have a Kevlar vest you could wear?"

Adam grinned. "It just so happens I do."

"Okay, let's start making a shopping list for me tomorrow. The way to do it is to consider the mission from beginning to end and the tactics to be employed." Chris paused and noted the smiles from Jim and Adam. "All right, you guys. I admit my Seal training is taking charge." He shrugged. "What the hell! I didn't know it would ever come in handy again. I'll start it off."

Chris picked up the VCR remote and rewound the video they had taken the day before until it stopped at Pier 41 where they had boarded the ferry to Alcatraz Island. "We went during the daytime and needed the windbreakers. At night, we can't use reflective clothing. We'll keep warm with black jumpsuits with Velcro tabs and outside pockets. We'll need black non-slip, rubber sole shoes, knit caps and gloves. Shoe polish will take care of darkening our faces. The communications gear will be a headset over one ear with a mouthpiece. We'll all wear Kevlar vests under the suits."

The video was fast-forwarded to their arrival. They saw the dock tower and barracks and at the right corner of the screen was the power plant building. Chris paused the video. "This confirms we can cover the approach from the upper floors of the building. What we could use is a night vision telescope. Ordinarily I would have said we need to take out any dock light but it'll give us a chance to size them up."

Adam spoke up. "We still want to know the path they take from the wharf. It'll take a motion-activated camera with a monitor setup."

Jim added his input. "The outside person will need some sort of ground pad and thermo camouflage that won't reveal body heat in case they're using NVGs."

Chris nodded approvingly. "Now you're into it. Let's go on. We can be sure they're armed and I don't mean with just pistols. This crowd will have some heavy pieces. We can assume they'll have silencers. They'll be looking for a trap and be extra careful. What we want to avoid is a situation where they'll try a flanking maneuver. You can bet they'll have communication between them. I'm thinking we're going to need some heavy-duty military-grade equipment." Chris looked straight at each one of them. "We're going to need a good medical kit too just in case."

"I have a Pro Med kit used by SWAT. It's pretty complete."

"We'll need rations like water and energy bars. We should have cell phones."

Adam frowned. "Chris, I don't know about you but some of the items on the list aren't at your neighborhood Wal-Mart. There's a waiting period to buy guns in California. I brought some weapons but . . ."

Jim answered. "I think I know where Chris expects to shop for gun supplies."

Adam looked at Chris. "What's Jim talking about?"

"I mentioned a friend, an ex-Ranger, who has a gun club in Marin County." Chris stated. "I seem to remember he has quite a collection locked up in his building. I think he'll be agreeable."

Adam shook his head in wonderment. He offered. "I can handle the electronics and a police equipment store will have the tactical jumpsuits and other articles. Give me your shoe sizes and I'll pick them up."

"I'll pick up waterproof duffel bags." Jim volunteered.

Chris partitioned the list and gave each a segment, a key to his house and the burglar alarm code. "Gather all of the supplies and bring them there. If you have a problem getting anything, let the rest know. Let's try to have everything all together by Saturday morning. Adam, park your car in my garage to unload your equipment. Jim and I will check the inventory on Saturday morning. Adam, you're going to have your hands full keeping those guys off your back. Jim, buy three disposable cell phones with Bluetooth ear pieces right away so we can keep track of each another." Chris extended his hand palm down. Jim and Adam each covered it with their hand. "Good luck, everyone."

Sergey picked up Petra and drove to a convenient restaurant midway between their respective stakeouts. When they had been seated, Sergey turned to Petra after searching the faces of the diners. "Petra, we've wasted six months on this fucking job for Borichov. I don't think I can hold out another week."

Petra, surprised by the uncharacteristic admission from the stoic man in front of him was taken aback as if he had just heard blasphemy. He took a drink of water and set the glass down carefully in front of him. In a lowered voice he agreed. "Sergey. I too am tired and counting the days. Do you believe Factor is still here? It's crazy. I wouldn't be."

"Here or not, we have Borichov on our backs."

They ate quietly, each man with his own thoughts. When they finished, they left to resume the surveillance.

Chapter Forty-seven

THE PREPARATION STARTS

Same Day
San Francisco, California

Chris raised his garage door so Adam could back into the spare parking space. When the car was in, he lowered the door. Adam went around and opened the trunk. Chris peered in and saw a steel box welded to the frame with a tempered steel lock. Adam spun the dial to the preset numbers and heard the release. He lifted up the lid and stood aside to give Chris a view of the contents.

Chris whistled. "Jesus, Adam. You weren't kidding! I don't recognize some of this stuff but these weapons can't all be standard police issue."

"Actually, Chris, a couple of these items are SWAT specials like the Armor Express body armor, tactical vest, and stun and sting grenades. The M24 rifle and Uzi I picked up over time. Let's take them inside." He saw Chris examining the sting grenade. "They're based on the design of the frag grenade. Inside are many small, hard rubber balls. When released they pelt anything within range. They're ideal when the target is hiding behind cover."

When they had finished, Adam took out a Beretta 92F 9mm semi-automatic pistol in a DeSantis shoulder holster and put it on. "I also wear an ankle gun. The best ankle gun I've owned so far is this S&W Centennial Airweight. It's light and fires a reasonably powerful round with the .38 Special +P and has a largely closed action." He put on his sport coat. "I think we all had better be extra careful from now on. I have to send a message to my office for the electronics. I'll keep in touch."

Chris opened the garage door and watched Adam drive away. He could feel the familiar anticipation return and the nervousness hit his stomach like the old Seal days. He closed the door and went back in the house to get his shopping list. He had, check that, they all had a busy couple of days in front of them.

Adam arrived at his hotel and went straight to his room. He turned on his notebook computer and checked for e-mails. He had a couple from Elaine and Marty. He went through the one summarizing the agency's clients' dealings. He noted with satisfaction Marty had handled the outside work with confidence and achieved success. Elaine was overseeing and directing his activities from the office. Marty was interfacing with a Palm Pilot and copying him. He smiled. Both had certainly proven themselves while he was in San Francisco. Okay, now to give them a call.

Elaine picked up the receiver on the first ring. "Adam?"

"I see Marty must have installed the caller ID interface with the telephone directories. How are you doing?"

A concerned voice answered him. "We're going out of our minds worrying about you."

"I'm fine and made a lot of progress. I'll fill you in a couple of days. Is Marty around? I need some supplies."

"Marty's on the way back. Let me place you on hold for a second."

After a pause, Elaine came on the line. "Adam, he's minutes away. Have you found Factor?"

"Elaine, I have to be careful with what I say. I have had my moments. There's a little unfinished business and then it'll be over."

"Adam, here's Marty. I'll put you on the speaker phone."

"Adam?"

"It's me, Marty. I'll get to all of your questions in a few days. I need some of your special electronics sent overnight to me."

"You got it. What do you need?"

Adam went through the mental list he put together emphasizing remote night surveillance and detection equipment. "Marty, it can't be too bulky. Mobility is important. If we don't have it, buy it."

"Anything else?"

"Yes. I want equipment with no fingerprints on them. If you need to rely on anything from the office, wipe it down thoroughly and use gloves to handle them. Remove identifying labels. Take them out of their boxes and bubble wrap to conserve space. I'll also need a package of zip or cable ties."

A note of concern entered Marty's voice. "Adam, you need help over there?"

"Thanks, Marty. I appreciate the offer but I can handle it. I'll be in touch. Overnight the package to this hotel."

Adam hung up and leaned back in his chair. When he received the electronics gear tomorrow, he would take it to Chris's for assembly and testing. He wondered how Jim and Chris were doing. He thought about the plan. He was to be the tethered goat after tomorrow. He hoped the Russian bastards would take the bait. He relied on them being patient enough to cut him some slack rather than try to take him. The fact is, the plan depended on it. He took his gun from the underarm holster and set it on the table. He went to the closet and returned with a gun cleaning kit. He laid a newspaper on the table and began disassembling the Beretta. He stared at his hands. They were steady so far. He breathed deeply and lost himself in his thoughts.

Newport Beach, California

Elaine Marks took the call from Diane Factor. Diane came right to the point. "I would just like to talk about the progress in finding my husband. I've been patient and hopeful for six months and I want to get some reassurance things may be happening soon. Would you have some time today to sit down with me?"

"Of course. When would you like?"

"I'll be there at one."

After Elaine hung up she called Marty and related the call. "What do you think?"

"Adam keeps her posted but he's up to something right now we have no idea about. We can tell her everything we know but let's leave our speculation and Adam's recent request out of it. We do know he's close to Factor."

"Should we call and tell him about Mrs. Factor's visit?"

"Adam is more than likely busy at his end and probably doesn't need the interruption. Let's handle it ourselves."

Diane Factor, Elaine and Marty sat together in the conference room. After introductions, Marty began the conversation. "Mrs. Factor, before we begin, do you have specific questions for us?"

She looked at both of them. "I have been briefed by Mr. Weatherly but perhaps there are more recent developments you are aware of. Let's start with that."

Marty nodded. "We'll tell you all we know but it won't be as much as what Adam knows. We believe he knows where your husband is. We don't know if he has made contact with him. Adam is also conscious of the Russian hit team's presence and the danger it presents to Mr. Factor by exposing him. He has said it'll be over soon but he has not told us what that means. We would be remiss if we speculated because we too are in the dark as to what is currently going on."

"I appreciate what you just said. Mr. Weatherly is a resourceful man. Would it serve any purpose if I flew to San Francisco?" Diane asked anxiously.

Elaine looked at Marty before replying. "I'll be honest with you. It could interfere with his initiative and distract him. He is the type of person who would call you to be there if he felt it was in your best interests. Marty asked him if he needed his assistance and Adam declined the offer."

Marty continued. "We're sitting tight ready to give Adam any backup support. Our suggestion is to be patient for the time being until we learn more."

Diane smiled. "Mr. Weatherly has two very fine employees. Thank you for your candor."

Marty turned to Elaine after Mr. Factor had left the office. "What do you think?"

"It depends. Do I think she shares some of her husband's qualities? You bet I do. She revealed that by coming here to pursue more information. I'm glad we were up front with her. I think she would have seen through us if we hadn't. I'd say it was better than even chance she'll go up there anyway to await results. She doesn't know where Adam is staying so she'd just get a room and wait."

"My gut tells me Adam doesn't need to know about this possibility yet. I'm sure he has a lot on his plate. I've got to assemble the equipment he asked for if I'm going to get it overnighted."

San Francisco, California

Jim went to the marina and strolled through the B and C docks where the smaller boats were berthed. He looked up at the gray sky and felt the stirring of a cool breeze. Near the end of the C dock, he saw an ideal boat for their needs. It was a twenty-seven-foot Boston Whaler recognizable by the center arrangement for the boat controls. It had a blue canvas overhead cover and a matching tarp covering the bow and aft areas. The boat's stern proclaimed the *Tailwind*. He peered down at the boat's interior. The deck was clean and opened. He looked around at the other boats. Satisfied he was not seen, Jim climbed into the boat. He opened the recessed door in the bow and found it contained an anchor and rope. On the side was the ignition key. Just to be sure, he inserted it into the dashboard and turned the ignition switch. The engine roared to life. He noted the gas tank was almost full. He cut the engine and returned the key to the locker. He climbed out of the boat and let his glance fall on the nearby boats. There it was. Two boats away was another open cockpit boat. He went over and checked for a key. He made sure it could easily be found. He left the dock and walked back to the wharf and stood on the sidewalk by the railing. Anyone standing here would have a clear view of the boat.

Jim walked to the marine accessory store down the street from the marina. He found three sturdy waterproof duffel bags long enough to hold a rifle. He located a black woolen sweater and a black knit cap. He made the purchases and went to his car and locked the items in the trunk. He walked a block and found a cell phone store. He bought three cell phones. Once outside he called Chris's cell number. Chris answered right away.

"It's Jim. I have a cell phone number for you." He gave Chris the number and told him of his progress. "Anything I can help you with?"

"Check the hardware stores for SureFire tactical flashlights. Get two. You can drop off the equipment at my house anytime. I'm on my way to the gun club. I'll see you later."

Marin County, California

Upon crossing the Golden Gate Bridge into Sausalito, Chris took the route into the rural countryside leading to the gun club. He had called ahead to find out if Rod was working at this time of day. The club was generally opened from eight in the morning until ten at night to accommodate most of its patrons work schedules. The traffic was reasonable this time of day. He pulled into the parking lot and walked in the entrance. Rod was describing the gun club's services to a prospect. He waited until the man left and approached the counter.

Ron glanced at the arrival and smiled. He caught the seriousness in Chris's expression and lowered his voice. "Hi Chris. What's up?"

"Hello Rod. Can we go to your office and talk?"

He nodded and led the way back into the club's interior. When Chris entered the office and was seated, Rod pulled the door closed and went behind his desk. "Okay, Chris. What's going on?"

"Rod, I need some equipment but it has to stay between us."

"You mind telling me what it's for? Or don't I want to know?"

"You don't want to know." Chris confirmed.

"Meaning the equipment has to be clean?"

Chris stated emphatically. "Squeaky."

"Okay. Are you going to give me a list or lay out the scenario so we can see what fits?"

Chris moved his chair closer to the desk. "Rod, I need your expertise and what you can gather up but I can only deal in generalities. It's to protect the both of us."

"How much time do I have?"

"Today and tomorrow."

Rod thought for a moment. "That will narrow it down. Go ahead."

Chris explained. "I'm thinking of a scenario where it's three on three in rough terrain. The other guys are real pros and could have a diversity of weapons."

"How diverse?"

"Automatic assault rifles maybe with night sights, semiautomatic pistol, knives and ammunition. I doubt they have RPGs with them but I can't rule out grenades."

Rod whistled. "Shit, Chris. This sounds serious. You're talking a night time encounter, I take it?"

Chris nodded. "Likely."

"How prepared will these guys be to take you on?"

"I doubt they'll be expecting a concerted effort if that's what you mean but they won't be taking anything for granted and it won't take them long to adjust."

Rod ran his hands over his head and leaned back. "The element of surprise and comparable firepower can be on your side. Let's start at the beginning. You'll need night vision to keep track of them. I take it you've thought about the tactical jumpsuits with the usual trimmings. Do you have the ear communication covered?"

"Yes, along with motion detectors. Do you have a heat absorbent camouflage blanket?"

"You plan on setting up a point man?"

"It's on my mind." Chris responded grimly.

"Okay. On short notice you can forget silencers. It's a tall order anytime."

"It's all right. I doubt anyone will be around to hear or care."

"Right, I'm thinking three Heckler& Koch MP5 submachine guns each with a night vision gun scope. I can only get you one Kevlar vest. What about pistols?"

"Just one; the Glock 17 with holster."

"Supplying the ammunition is no problem. Conserving it is. Those MP5's are capable of eight hundred rounds per minute on full auto. I suggest a small portable pull cart or backpack for it."

He noticed the question on Chris's face and answered. "I'm talking stopping power ammo."

Rod thought for a moment. "Hollow points I have. Grenades?"

"Got it covered."

"Are you bringing anything back?"

"Don't count on it."

"I'll give you the bill when you pick up the goods. I hate to say this but . . ."

"It'll be a cash deal. I'll have it with me." Rod paused.

Chris seeing the hesitation asked, "Something on your mind, Rod?"

"You in serious trouble?"

"I'm helping some friends."

"Do you need another body?"

"Rod, I appreciate the offer. Thanks, but no. I'm grateful for what you're doing for me." Chris stood and held out his hand. Rod shook it warmly.

"Give me until tomorrow afternoon to get everything together. Drive your car around the back when you get here."

Chris left the parking lot and drove back over the Golden Gate Bridge. There was an Army-Navy surplus store outside the city where he knew most of his other requirements could be found. He breathed deeply. He wondered how Jim and Adam were making out. Adam would have other things on his mind as well. He most vulnerable one right now, at least until they could watch his back.

Chapter Forty-eight

THE PREPARATION CONTINUES

Early Friday Morning, November 1
San Francisco, California

Jim woke up early and glanced out the window noticing the gradual buildup of gray clouds. He got ready while thinking about the upcoming series of events. He felt apprehensive about placing Chris and Adam lives in danger. Since he arrived in San Francisco his focus had been in preparing to take on Borichov on his own terms. He looked up at the ceiling light where his cash and passports lay hidden. He considered his options. Before he could be missed, he could go to the bank, take out the money earned at the marina and afterwards go the Amtrak train station for a ticket to Tucson. Why involve two good people in his battle? Another part of him told him if he ran he'd lose a near term opportunity to reclaim his former life. He missed Diane. He didn't kid himself. He knew the planned undertaking would lead to a loss of lives. He was the least experienced on both sides. He wasn't as concerned about himself but Chris and Adam were risking their lives and, let's face it, their futures. He glanced at the ceiling again. No, damn it. He refused to run. He had known and had taken steps to make a stand someday. Now was as good a time as any. It was too early to go to the marina. He decided to go to the martial arts studio and work off his anxiety. Before he left, there was something else he had to do. He placed a chair under the light and unscrewed the fixture. He reached around and collected a large portion of the cash he had in reserve. He replaced the light and got down. He put on his windbreaker and shoved the money in the pockets.

Jim was surprised to see Chris opening the studio. Chris looked at him, smiled and waved him into the room. "Feel like going through a few paces?" Chris asked. Jim grinned and nodded. After a half-hour, both men were soaked in sweat.

The door to the studio opened and Adam stood watching them. In a hurt tone he asked, "Hey, can I get in some exercise of my own?"

Jim and Chris laughed and motioned him in.

Later Jim spoke in a low voice. "Chris, I have cash on me to pay for the weapons." They all walked into the office and Chris opened his safe. When Jim pulled out the money, Chris raised his eyebrows. Jim answered his unspoken question. "It was part of my running money." Jim patted Adam on the back as he walked out the door. "I've got a few things to do. I'll see you both later on."

Jim drove to the marina and went to the office. Miguel had not yet made an appearance. Jim saw the board with the maintenance schedule had additional jobs and assignments. He sat down behind the desk and debated telling Miguel about taking over the business. Better not, he thought. There's no telling if their plan would come to pass. Adam would be heading for the hotel where he might be seen if the Russians were still around. Once that occurred, there would be time to clean up the loose ends. He wrote down the boat and slip location where Miguel had entered Jim's name. He might as well keep busy before he met with Chris in the early afternoon.

Adam left the studio after an hour and drove back to his hotel to shower and get something to eat before he packed and checked out. He'd meet with Jim and Chris and they would drive to his previous hotel. His hair was up in the back of his neck. He knew the hit team would be watching and waiting for him once he checked in. They would be on edge and damn mad. If they followed him they were real pros and very dangerous. He felt better knowing Chris and Jim would be watching his back while he was making like a decoy. What if the Russians had reinforcements?

He stared at the lap top computer on the desk. He wondered about bringing Marty and Elaine up to date on his developments. They were terrific kids. He knew they were anxious to hear from him but disciplined enough to keep from contacting him. One way or other, it will all be over in forty-eight hours. He wanted to call Diane Factor and tell her of his progress but he held back as well. Who knew what the outcome of their plan would be? It was important that the knowledge of the upcoming conflict reside only with them. It was crazy what they were planning. He was a former law enforcement officer sworn to uphold the law. Never had he let a case affect him like this one had. He shrugged off the apprehension. There were times a person had to get off the sidelines and into the game.

Chris called one of the other martial arts instructors over from his small group. "Dan, I've got some things to do for the rest of the day. Run things and close it up tonight." Dan nodded and went back to his group of students. Chris went out to his car and drove home. He would get cleaned up first and then inventory what had been assembled. Later, he'd drive to the gun club and get the weapons. He was the only one experienced in the type of battle about to occur. He had a good feeling about Adam. He was sticking his neck out too. He was a strange guy and smart as well. He had been hired to find Jim and had done so skillfully and doggedly. During that quest, he had come to know and respect Jim and become one with them. Jim had shown himself to be a good man and a friend. Certainly he had proven to be resourceful and adaptable. What a threesome they were. He was realistic. One or more of them could be seriously hurt or killed. It was up to them to use his experience to keep them all alive. Chris climbed in his car and took a look at the dash clock. He had around four hours to get everything done before he picked up Jim and they headed for Adam's hotel.

Sergey sipped his coffee in moody silence with a scowl on his face. He casually scanned the diners in the restaurant and turned back at Petra. "This is the last day. I hope Borichov realizes it so we can make arrangements to leave."

Petra lowered his head over his coffee and grunted. "I'm not taking anything for granted but I worry Federov will hold this failure against us."

Sergey angrily pounded the table causing nearby diners to glance at them. In a low whisper he concurred. "This will be our first failure but I'm sure we'll hear of it. That's reason enough for us to have found Factor." He slid the chair back and got up from the table. "Take the hotel and I'll take the police station. We'll switch as usual at one."

Chapter Forty-nine

THE IMPLEMENTATION STARTS

Late Friday Morning

Adam sat at in his hotel room and made a mental note of his activities for the day. He was interrupted by a call from the front desk informing him a package had arrived. So far, so good. The plan called for him to show himself later on once Chris and Jim were in place. They had no idea if the hit team was still there searching for Jim or himself. He was ingrained with the lessons of patience and resourcefulness. He'd give odds they hadn't given up. The uncertainty of his having found Factor should hold them at bay until they knew for sure. He needed to stay hidden until the evening when he would meet up with Jim and Chris to head for Alcatraz Island. He wondered how they were doing with their part of the plan. He thought about having the package delivered to his room but thought better of it. He'd take it out to his car when he checked out.

He couldn't stop the flood of thoughts. What had really prompted him to plan such a course of action? His wife had left him years ago for greener pastures. At least he didn't have guilt, children or alimony to contend with. He was content with relationships for mutual romantic gymnastics. Who was he kidding? He liked his present involvement with Nancy for her shapely figure and contagious laughter. It was his choice to stay away from steering the relationship into a more serious direction. Maybe it was time to reconsider. After this was finished, he might look her up. It was worth a try.

Then again was there another reason? Did he miss the element of danger in his work? It was part of it but not all. Jim Factor had impressed him from the day he took the job. He expected to face his vulnerability one day; it was inevitable considering the actions he had undertaken. And then there was Chris; the former Seal had encountered violence in untold numbers of operational confrontations. He left a military career and opened a karate studio. He had a lot to lose. Hell, they all had plenty to lose. Yet, Adam felt a close bond had been established between them. Three men had converged in a suburb of San Francisco and found something in each other. It was not too late for them to back out but he knew it wouldn't happen. In any case, the forthcoming chain of events was set in motion way before now. It was almost noon and o check out. As soon as he was in his car, he'd contact Jim and Chris.

Chapter Fifty

THE IMPLEMENTATION CONTINUES

Friday Afternoon

Adam drove slowly mulling over the uncertainty waiting at the hotel. Although he deliberately chose to place himself in jeopardy, there was no need to close his eyes to the imminent danger. Before he checked in, he would park a block away and make a walking sweep of the entire area around the hotel. Since it was a little chilly, he would wear a windbreaker to alter his appearance. He removed his shoulder holster and placed the gun in the jacket's pocket. He stowed the holster under the seat. As an afterthought, he put a baseball cap in the other pocket. If they were watching, odds are they would cover the garage and lobby of the hotel and pay little or no attention to any passersby.

Adam found a parking space. He'd concentrate on the area in back of the hotel before crossing the street and searching the other side for them. He had the advantage of knowing what the two goons looked like and it gave him an edge. The dark gray sky helped to diffuse the lighting available to the observer. They could use field glasses but it would be conspicuous and they were sure to be obsessed with maintaining a low profile. He crossed the street leading to the front of the hotel and walked around the block. The side street was one-way towards him. He saw an alley running down the back of the hotel. He didn't want to walk down it for fear they were watching the rear as well.

He noticed a dumpster in the front of the alley and ambled nonchalantly to it. He peered inside and spotted a cardboard box. He emptied the insides, folded the top flaps down and hoisted it on his shoulder. This should do very nicely. I'll keep it on my right shoulder with the hotel rear on the left. That should block anyone's view of me from outside of the hotel. He walked slowly for two hundred feet before reaching the perimeter of the hotel property. He noticed there was little cover for a person to watch the back of the hotel. The alley was wide enough to accommodate trucks. There was a loading platform and two fire doors. A fire escape with a pull-down ladder covered the second floor up to the roof. He continued walking until he reached the end of the alley. He left the empty box in another dumpster and walked towards the street in front of the hotel. He made a note the side street was one-way in the opposite direction.

He crossed the street staying on the same side as the hotel and moved slowly away from the hotel. He viewed the opposite side of the street in the shop windows. There were several alternative places to keep the front of the hotel under surveillance. He'd pick a restaurant, a parking place, rooftop and a room across the way be it a hotel or an office. He'd check those possibilities when he doubled back on the opposite side of the street. His cell phone alerted him to a call with its vibration.

"Adam here." He answered.

"It's Jim. Where are you?"

"I'm a block away from the hotel checking the area before I went in. I'll feel better knowing the layout in case there's trouble. Besides, I have to slip out unnoticed tonight to meet with you. I'll pass on the information then."

"Good idea. Any chance they may see you?"

"Actually, I was hoping to spot one or both of them. I have the advantage of knowing what they look like. I'll keep in touch and call after I check in. It'll take me another hour to make the rounds."

Adam put the phone away and continued his deliberate pace down the street. It was now time to double back on the opposite side. He crossed the side street and walked with a lazy lope back along the block. He kept an eye on the front of the hotel and its parking structure. When he could see them, he would be close to the hit team's position if they were at ground level. He paid attention to businesses.

He suddenly halted and read the sign on a store twenty feet away almost directly across from the hotel. It was an Internet café. What better location to sit all day without attracting attention? The hairs in back of his neck started tingling. He stood still pretending to read his paper. He didn't dare go on or get close to the window. No use taking chances. He could stand around for someone to leave but that wouldn't be smart. He decided to resume his search and walked back towards the alley entrance. He retraced his steps and crossed the street so he was on the same side as the hotel. He walked down the street looking where an observer might position himself to watch the hotel. It was clear there weren't any practical locations except the Internet café. A second or third floor hotel room facing the street would give him a view of the café customers as they entered and left.

He circled the block and made his way to his car. He took out his cell and called Jim. "I've finished canvassing the area. I think I know where they could be in order to watch the hotel without bringing attention to themselves." Adam described his search and the preliminary conclusion. "Rather than parading around and letting them take the initiative, I have in mind to check in on foot by going in the rear hotel door. I'll get a room overlooking the street and start my own surveillance. I have equipment in the car. Sooner or later they'll rotate or quit for the night. Then I'll bring my car around with my luggage. This way, you and Chris won't have to watch over me. I'll sneak out the back tonight and you can pick me up in the alley. We'll take care of business and I'll get back here before morning."

Jim replied after a pause. "Adam, are you sure this approach is safe? These guys are dangerous. What if they're not there but inside the hotel somehow like guests or employees?"

"I would think they'd stick out like sore thumbs. Let's try this way and see what happens. It'll be perfectly safe and, anyway, I'm taking precautions. I'll call you back when I'm settled in. I figure it'll take a half hour."

Before Jim could answer, Adam hung up and turned off his phone. He got out and opened the trunk. The box Marty had sent was still unopened. He cut the tape and looked through the electronic gear until he found the high power binoculars. He stashed it inside of his jacket and walked back to the hotel's rear entrance. When he reached the locked door, he pounded on it until it was finally opened by a hotel employee.

An aggravated man inspected him. "The entrance is around the front."

Adam nodded apologetically slipping through the door. "I'll use it next time pal, thanks."

When Adam was settled in his room, he locked the door and moved to the window. Perfect, he thought. I can see the café across the street. He slid a chair to the window careful to keep behind the thin curtain. Using the binoculars he scanned the front of the café. There was just enough glare generated off the dirty window to prevent him from seeing into the interior. He just had to wait it out. In the meantime, he used the cell phone to call Jim.

The phone was quickly answered. "Adam?"

"Yes, I'm settled in the hotel in room 207. I have a view of the street. I've been giving this some thought. If they are watching the hotel entrance, the night time will give them trouble. They're either going to move to this side of the street or the hotel itself or quit until tomorrow. We've got to know if they're here and I have to let them know I'm back."

"You mean you're going through with letting them see you?"

Adam chuckled. "I'm afraid I am. I plan to go down to the restaurant and keep an eye on the street. When I see any of them, I'm going to step outside and go down to my car. I can get away before they can react fast enough. At least they'll know I'm here. I'll meet up with the both of you at Chris's house and we'll take care of the necessary arrangements tonight."

"What if you miscalculate and they catch up to you?"

"I won't let it happen. I'll call you as soon as anything develops."

Adam pocketed the phone and checked the time. It would be dusk in another hour. He'd go down to the restaurant before then. Suddenly aware of a growing feeling of anxiety, he reached for his shoulder holster.

Sergey was bored dividing his time between the computer screen and the hotel entrance across the street. He rubbed his eyes, stood up and stretched his legs. How long have they been doing this? It was a good thing there were two of them alternating on a daily basis. Once more he looked around at the people seated in front of other terminals. Not one looked around. They were all engrossed with their computers. Some even mumbled while they interfaced as if the object in front of them was human. He looked out the window at the pedestrians. Seldom did anyone look inside the café. It was if they respected the privacy of the people at their stations, except he knew better. They were too engrossed with their own business. One more day and they could pack up and leave. He figured Factor had left San Francisco but the PI's whereabouts disturbed him. He was still away from his office. Was he still in San Francisco or had he left the city on a new lead?

One more day and it wouldn't matter except Sergey felt the repressing frustration of his first failure. This was not good for his future. He didn't realize he had struck the keyboard with his fist in frustration until he saw the faces peering at him from around their computer monitors. He ignored them and stared at his screen. He could use a drink but instead got up and settled for the water fountain. He anxiously looked at the clock. He'd rather be in the African brush for hours and, if necessary, days in order to wait for his prey. At least he'd have a weapon in his hands and control over the situation. He wondered what Borichov was doing with his time. Probably on the phone conducting business or maybe with a woman while smoking a cigar and holding a drink. He went back to his seat and checked the time. With relief he noted Petra would be coming by within the hour.

Petra walked nonchalantly to the car and looked around the street. "Strange," he thought, Sergey and I have been keeping watch on a police station for days and no one has made us or even cared to check the area. This America is so foolish to take no mind of people walking around a police building. He scowled. This wouldn't be the case in Russia. On the other hand, maybe it's not so bad to be allowed to go anywhere and not have to worry. He drove back to the downtown section. He was glad it was almost over.

Adam nursed his coffee and decided it was time to leave the restaurant. He got up and walked outside the front door of the hotel. He casually stood and examined the passing traffic before turning his attention to the other side of the street.

At that moment Petra pulled in front of the Internet café to pick up Sergey. Aware he was in a no-parking zone, he kept a watch for police. It was then his eyes took in the man in front of the hotel. He couldn't believe his luck. He undid the seatbelt and opened his door, got out and stood frozen in the street. Sergey walked to the car and took in Petra's reaction. He yelled at Petra and climbed into the driver's seat. A passing motorist blasted his horn and almost hit Petra in the narrow street.

Adam heard the horn and glanced across. There they were. He was sure of it. He willed himself to remain calm and ignore the surge of adrenaline raising his pulse. Ignoring the man on the street, he turned and headed nonchalantly for the parking garage. Once inside the door, he ran to his car and, as soon as it started, slammed the car into gear causing the screech of the tires in the close area. He exited the garage in the opposite direction assuming the driver in the other car would not risk a U-turn on the busy street without bringing attention to them. His heart was pumping. He felt his shoulders tightening up as he maneuvered the car away from the hotel and down the side streets constantly checking his rear view mirror. Once he saw he was in the clear, he called Jim.

Jim answered right away. "Adam?"

"It's me and you're not going to believe this." Jim gasped. "You saw them?"

"They saw me first. I barely got away. I think we can safely bet they're in a frenzy looking for us. My feeling is they'll head for the hotel and see if I'm checked in. Then they'll lay low and wait for me to return."

"Adam. Are you sure you got away? What if they had started shooting?"

"They didn't which tells me they want you badly."

"They have been waiting and watching all this time. That thought alone is enough to chill me. It's started now hasn't it? There's no turning back."

"This is it. Tell Chris I'll meet you both at his house and we'll head for the boat together. Everything going okay at your end?"

"Yes. I'll let Chris know right away. See you in a little while."

Petra ran to the passenger side and jumped in the car. He repeatedly pounded his fist on the dashboard cursing in Russian so loudly close-by pedestrians turned in alarm to see where the vehement ranting was coming from. Sergey spun the wheels and accelerated dangerously down the street. Petra continued his tantrum, spittle running down from his mouth. When Sergey was far enough from the scene he pulled the car over and slapped Petra hard across the face. "What the fuck were you doing, you idiot? Everybody on the street was staring at us."

Petra stunned by the blow stopped his yelling and sat back. Soon he collected himself. "Sorry Sergey. I lost it. Did he make us?"

Sergey looked in his rear view mirror and shook his head. "I don't think so but it was close. He walked into the hotel parking garage. What we don't need is to blow this chance. Let's check the hotel."

"How?"

"I'll make a phone call to the hotel and ask for him. We'll find out if he's registered."

"What about Borichov? He's going to get tired of waiting for us to have something?"

Sergey shook his head. "We don't tell him a thing until we know for sure." He pointed to a phone booth on the side of the street and got out of the car. Looking around he walked over and looked through the hanging phone book. He placed a call and spoke. Petra saw him nod and hang up. When Sergey got into the car, he anxiously asked. "Well?"

Sergey nodded and for the first time in weeks smiled. "He's registered. We'll forget the other targets. Let's get back to our room and decide what we do next."

In their motel room, Sergey put a bottle of vodka with two glasses on the table and poured each of them half a glass. "It'll help us relax and think. We can't botch this chance up. We now know the PI's here and he's located Factor. He won't suspect after all of this time anyone would still be looking for him. We don't know his room number and can't walk in and bug it anyway. We'll have to keep watch on the hotel until he gets back. Then we have two options; snatch him and make him talk or follow him to Factor. I say we follow him. It'll be less messy and quicker."

"Are we going to bring Borichov into this?"

Sergey sneered. "Yeah. If anything goes wrong, we'll place the blame on him."

"You know he'll say it was our fault and Federov may believe him."

"He won't be able to say anything if he gets killed in the process. I'll call and fill him in."

Sergey completed the call. "He says to keep a watch on the PI and call him if we think he's going out. He wants in on the action. You and I will start taking turns this evening. We'll wait in the parking garage to see if he's still driving the same car. Bring another tracking device for it. We're not taking any more chances that we'll lose him. Go get the guns from the car and let's get ready."

Petra came back in struggling with two heavy bags. He placed them on the bed and started extracting the guns. He pulled out three Kalashnikov AK-47 assault rifles. He placed the spare magazines and extra ammunition for the rifles and pistols on the floor. He removed gun oil from the bag. Sergey placed newspapers on the table and sat down. He took out a Yarygin Pya MP-443 Grach pistol. Petra sat across from him and both quietly cleaned the weapons. When they were finished, Sergey pulled out a metal case and opened it. Inside embedded in form-fitting cutouts were two stun grenades.

They completed the cleaning and carefully replaced the weapons in the bags. "We have a gun for Borichov. He's so anxious to get Factor, he can join us. Gather up your things and we'll check out. We won't waste any time heading for Miami after we finish the job."

Chapter Fifty-one

PREPARATION

Friday Night

Adam pulled his car inside the parking garage across the street from Pier 39. Jim, Adam and Chris reached inside the trunk and removed the three black bags filled with equipment. They left the guns inside the locked metal box. Each wore dark clothing and rubber-soled shoes.

Jim whispered. "Okay, I'll go first and make sure the C dock is clear. I'll leave the gate open for you. The watchman generally pays more attention to the larger boats so he won't be a problem." With that, Jim put on the black cap and walked away. Adam and Chris stayed back against the wall of the building and watched Jim make his way across to the marina. The darkness swallowed him up.

Chris glanced up at the sky. "The clouds keep everything in the shadows. Okay, let's go now."

Jim quietly went to the boat and climbed down. He stashed the duffel bag at the rear under the canvas tarp and listened for Adam and Chris. He saw their shadows cast by the marina lights before he heard the muffled footsteps. He waved them over and took each of the bags from them. They got in and sat down. "Ready?"

Adam and Chris gave him thumbs up.

Jim started the engine. "Chris, free us up." Chris reached across and released the mooring ropes. Jim slowly backed the Boston Whaler out of the slip and put it into gear. He edged the boat slowly and quietly past the other boats until it passed the end of the dock. He turned it into the marina channel and continued the pace until he entered San Francisco Bay. The swift current captured the boat right away and carried it from the marina. Satisfied they wouldn't be seen Jim opened up the engine and turned on the running lights. "Keep an eye out for other boat traffic. This time of night I don't expect to see anything except a large ship coming in from our portside using the channel. There's no fog so we should easily see their running lights."

Adam looked towards the island. "Hey, I never thought about the lighthouse. Its light is pretty bright even from the side."

Chris nodded. "It guides ships into the narrow entrance of the bay and around the rocks of Alcatraz. It won't take us long to get there at this speed. The landing wharf is just around the right side."

"I'm going to turn off our lights now. Chris, when I pull alongside, tie us up. From here on it's your show."

When Adam and Chris were on the dock, Jim handed over the duffel bags. Birds settled for the night around the wharf and the surrounding buildings were unnerving as they stirred, shook their wings and shifted in the shadows. The cool salt mist deposited a sheen of moisture on every surface. They walked carefully up the ramp to the path. Chris turned towards them. "Let's use the flashlights. With an entire island shielding us from the mainland, the beams won't be seen. I doubt if the inhabitants of Angel Island across the way will see or pay attention to this hunk of rock. The first order of business is the placement of the cameras."

Adam glanced around. "I'd forget the dock tower. We can fasten a camera on the barracks building side facing the wharf. The background shadows and darkness will easily hide it. Its motion detector will activate it. They have no choice but to come this way."

"Let's keep moving towards the water tower and the New Industries building. Adam, this path is probably a good one to monitor with a camera. Let's put one in the tree over there."

He glanced upward at the water tower. "I doubt if I'll ask for volunteers to lie on the topside walkway and look down on them. A wooden floor is no protection. However, Adam, place a camera on the rung of the ladder about ten feet from the ground."

Jim pointed to the location. "They're sure to spot it." He looked at Chris and a smile formed. "Oh, I get it. We're going to place another camera watching this camera."

Adam grinned. "Cute idea. We'll get a count on them and what they're toting." He reached in the duffel bag and mounted the two separated cameras.

Chris turned toward the New Industries buildings. They followed him to the front where they had encountered the section of rusting chain-link fence surrounding the complex. They entered through the torn section and carefully made their way. He peered over the island's edge. The tall fence and the rock cliff combined with the cold treacherous water with its rip currents were enough to discourage any escape attempts.

They picked their way around discarded equipment, rusting boilers, soiled sinks and tables in the laundry area. The wind passing through broken windows made an eerie sound and muffled any footsteps. The mood turned somber. Jim uttered what each had been thinking. "This place is creepy. I expect ghosts of the imprisoned souls to jump out. The constant gurgle of the water surging by the island gives me goose bumps."

Chris knowingly told them. "We get to experience it first. Imagine how our guests will feel when their feelings are bolstered by the knowledge we're waiting for them somewhere here. Having them on edge is to our advantage—until the shooting starts. There's plenty of cover for us and distractions for them."

Adam offered. "We should open all of the large circular doors of the wall-mounted washers and driers so they could act as shields. Chris, do you think they'll have flash-bang grenades?"

"If they do, it would be hard to throw them in these close quarters without the risk of finding themselves in the open. They'd have to get too close for comfort. If it were me, I'd use standoff automatic weapons with night vision sights. I hope to hell they don't have an RPG in their arsenal. However, your idea of the open doors is a good one. We can expect them to try to come in from behind us. Their concern would be the exposure on the sides of the building. They have the option of going up to the next floor and coming down to this end. It means one of us will have to be positioned to watch the back stairwell but not close enough in case they pop a grenade down the stairs as a precaution before heading down."

"I think they'd commit only one of them on the tactic. The other one will cover this area to see if we get up and move. They won't know how many of us are here."

Jim suddenly realized. "We don't know how many of them will be out there."

Adam answered. "This is where the cameras come in handy. Oh, oh. It just occurred to me if they were smart they would have a cell phone jammer with them. Hell, they ca't think of everything and neither can we."

Chris rubbed his chin and shook his head. "It's a two-edged sword. It would also disrupt their communication with each other." He searched around. "One of us should be posted here behind this large metal vat on the floor. There's sufficient room to lay behind it and it provides shelter for a move against the far wall. It has the view of the stairs behind it. The other spot should be farther up into the laundry room underneath the large metal sinks. It has the added benefit the person can keep low and scoot back under them to the back. We'll need to clean out the debris under them and push it into the aisle."

"Where's our other spot?" asked Jim.

"It'll be outside in a location to cover the front of the New Industries building and the lower entrance to the laundry room. He'll have an assault gun with a sniper scope and lay under a thermal-insulated blanket to hide his heat signature. Because there isn't enough cover on the hill, the blanket will have to function as a blind. Once he fires he'll have to move to a new position to avoid becoming a target. He'll have to pass by them somehow to join up with the other two in the laundry room. If he's successful, there'll be one less of them to worry about."

"Who do you have in mind to be out there?"

"Adam, I am the most experienced and I've put down people in the past. You'll be in here with Jim and handle who gets by me. If you have any questions or suggestions, now's the time to bring them up."

Jim looked hard at them. "I'll want the two of you to know I'll take care of my share of it."

"Anything else never entered our minds. Let's get back to the boat. All of us have to prepare for tomorrow and a good night's sleep is a must."

"I'll get the boat's gas tank refilled tomorrow when I get to the marina in the morning. The boat has a canopy I can put up so we'll be hidden tomorrow when Adam draws them down to the dock."

Chapter Fifty-two

THE LONGEST DAY

Saturday Morning, November 2

Jim woke up early, put on a pair of warm-ups and jogged to the martial arts studios. He was not surprised to find Chris already had opened up the room. Chris waved him over to the back area where the harnesses hung.

"Jim, let me get you into one of these. It'll get your thinking into a different mindset." With that, he fitted the harness on him. "It'll take a little bit of getting use to because the suspended weight of your body allows you to experiment with movements which may at first seem unwieldy. I'll keep off the other one for right now. I want you to come towards me but be aware that your feints, at first, may not be controllable. Your momentum will take you into harm's way meaning me."

Jim moved into several stances and realized he could use the toes of his feet more in the process. Finally, when he felt he had a semblance of the new capability, he nodded to Chris. "Okay, I'm ready. Who's the aggressor?"

"You start. I'm going to keep my position in one spot and only duck, parry and weave. See what you can do."

Jim moved in and suddenly attacked with a one-arm thrust. This time, instead of trying to gain an advantage he shifted back and exercised a kick. Chris had to back up and grinned. "That was pretty tricky of you. I didn't plan on your quick counter before you tried to get me off balance with a follow-up arm thrust. Now, I'll be the aggressor and see how you handle it."

Chris moved his arms and crouched. He suddenly elevated and kicked out. Jim was caught off balance but adroitly sidestepped rather than peel back away from the impact. Using his toes allowed Jim to step into Chris's space and deliver an arm thrust that made contact. Chris backed up. "Bravo, Jim. You have advanced much more than I've given you credit for. Did you notice the harness allows you to perform lateral countermoves with less preparation?"

Jim bounced on his toes. "It was better because I could recover my balance using my toes for a maneuver rather than plant the entire foot."

"Okay, let's continue with the contact exercise for a while."

Finally Chris looked up at the clock. Alright, let me remove the harness. You've had it on for a half-hour and seem to have gotten used to it. We'll continue the contact exercise again."

They circled each other and parried. Jim crouched and sprang at Chris with a right arm thrust causing Chris to initiate a defensive move. At once Jim pulled back, sidestepped and delivered a kick at Chris stopping it before it made contact with his chest.

Chris placed his hands on his hips and stared at Jim. "That was as good a move as I've seen from very advanced practitioners. You used your toes to get the balance rather than set your feet to shove off and more than that, you did it laterally to come in from my undefended side. Stay right here." With that he left and came back with an object in his hand. "Give me your green belt. Here, wear this one from now on. You've earned it." He gave Jim a black belt.

Jim looked at it in surprise. "Wow, I don't believe it. Are you sure?"

"I wouldn't have given it if I wasn't. Now get out of here. Both of us have lots to do today."

Jim bowed with a smile, changed back into his warm-ups and left.

Once Jim had showered and changed into his work clothes he left the house and went over to George Marx's office. Marx looked up when Jim came in. "Hi Jim, what can I do for you today?"

"I have some instructions for you. I'd appreciate it if it could be handled before noon."

"You got it. What do you need?"

"First of all, I would like you to get me $5,000 out of the account and into traveler's checks. I'm going to go to Seattle to look at some opportunities there. During my absence, I'm leaving Miguel Rodriguez in charge. I'll have him come in today and introduce himself. Would you initiate the paperwork so his signature is also on the account?"

"Consider it done. I'll have the money for you by noon."

Jim drove to the marina and located Miguel working on one of the boats. He waved him over. "Miguel, I need to get to Seattle for a few days to look over a few things. I know you can take care of anything that comes up. If anybody needs assistance with the electronics, go see Charlie Ford and ask him about it. I need you to go to George Marx's office, our bookkeeper, and get introduced. He pays the bills and does our payroll."

"Nick, how long will you be gone?"

"I doubt if it'll be more than a week but run things for us in case I hit a snag."

Jim went back to his car and checked his notes. There were some things he had to take care of before he could join Chris and Adam.

Sergey was startled to hear the phone ring in their room. Petra looked at him and the phone. "It could only be Borichov. What the hell does he want now?"

Sergey picked up the phone. "Yes?"

"This is Borichov. I am tired of waiting. Pick me up right away. I will keep watch with you."

Before Sergey could reply, the phone went dead. "He wants us to pick him up. He says he's tired of waiting. Can you believe it? We've been at it for six months and he's tired. We better get over there, then head for the PI's hotel to keep watch. Borichov knows it's now or never and wants to be in on it."

"Do you think he's smart enough to leave his personal items in his room?"

"He knows what has to be done. Remember, he was doing field and wet work before we even thought about it. We have enough firepower for the three of us. At least we'll outnumber them and Borichov will personally see the results."

Saturday Afternoon

Jim picked up the traveler's checks from George Marx and headed for the Queterras house. Once there he went to his room and locked the door. He had to consider the possibility something could go wrong. He couldn't afford to take any chances with the stakes so high. Even if everything worked out, he would leave this part of his existence behind. He changed into warm clothes and put the coat and hat aside. He pulled the travel bag from the closet and packed clothes. Lastly, he put the chair under the light fixture and removed his remaining cash and the two passports from the recess. He replaced the fixture and put the chair back. He slipped the cash, the traveler's checks and the passports into the bag. Satisfied he had everything; he unlocked the door and went downstairs. He walked down the block to his car and hid the bag behind the spare tire in the trunk.

Jim called Adam on his cell phone. "Adam. Any sign of our friends?"

"Hi Jim. I'm sure they're there watching. Are you ready?"

"I'm all set. I'm going to give Chris a hand to unload his trunk and take all of the equipment to the boat after dark. I gassed it up this morning and set up the canopy. The marina shuts down around six. As we planned, Chris and I will be hidden in the boat. We'll start up the engine and free it when you drive into the parking garage. Run across the street onto the boat dock. The gate will be open. We'll keep an eye out behind you. Jump on board and ease it out the marina. We'll turn on the running lights to make it easy for them to follow us. I hope they don't start shooting right away."

"I doubt it. They want you so they'll follow us. Is the other boat there for them?"

"Yeah, it's ready to go."

"Okay, that time of night it'll take me around fifteen minutes to drive to the marina from the hotel. I'll call when I check out with my luggage and go to the car. They should pick me up fairly rapidly. Up to then, I am going to relax and get an early dinner downstairs."

Jim placed a call to Chris. "I just talked to Adam. He's ready to go after dark. Shall we meet at the parking garage and get something to eat together by the marina?"

"Sounds like a good idea. I'm heading home to change my clothes. I'll meet you at the parking garage at five."

Saturday Evening

Jim pulled into the first level of the parking garage and found Chris standing by his car. He parked in the first open space close by and walked over. The sun was casting long shadows but still thirty minutes from setting when they entered a seafood restaurant down the block from the marina.

They sat in a booth by the window facing the bay. Chris asked. "Is everything all right Jim?"

"Yes, but I'm concerned for Adam. He's on the hook. We won't be there for him if they decide to grab him."

"Don't underestimate Adam. From what I've seen, they'd have their hands full if they tangled with him. I agree with his assessment. They want you very badly so all they'll do is follow him. We have to be ready when he calls. He should be at the boat dock by six-thirty which will be lighted enough for them to see him get in the boat and shove off. It'll be pretty dark when we get to the wharf at the Rock. After we eat we'll go to my car and haul everything to the boat."

Saturday Night

They stowed all the equipment in the boat under a tarp. Jim fastened the canopy cover about them as they sat at the rear of the craft. Jim noted. "Everyone here has gone home for the day. We'll be left alone while we sit and wait." He reached under the cockpit and found the key. He placed it in the ignition and turned it on. The motor came on right away. He saw the battery was at full charge. He turned it off.

Chris observed. "The wind is light right now with scattered clouds. We have almost a full moon tonight." They both sat quietly with their own thoughts. The water in the marina splashed against the hull and gently rocked the boat.

Adam carried his suitcase out the front door of the hotel and walked into the parking garage to his car. He threw the bag into the backseat and started the car quickly. He looked around before he backed from the space and put it in gear. He didn't hesitate but drove out the exit and turned down the street. Now where are they? As if by arrangement he saw a car turn his way and accelerate until it was a half block behind him. It was too dark to see the people inside. He reached for his cell phone.

The sound of Jim's cell phone vibrating broke the silence. He quickly answered. "Adam? What's happening? Are you on the road?" He placed the phone between them so Chris could hear the reply.

"I'm on my way and our friends are about two hundred feet behind me. I can't tell how many there are but they're sticking like glue. Are you in place?"

"We're here and ready. The first level of the garage has empty spaces. Hit the ground running after you park."

"You got it. I'm not sure they won't shoot to get my attention. I should be there in about ten minutes. I'm going to take a direct route to the pier so they won't have any trouble keeping up with me."

* * *

Sergey remarked to Borichov. "I can't believe our luck. It looks like he's checked out of the hotel and going after Factor."

"Pay attention to your driving. Don't lose him, you fool."

"I don't dare get any closer or he'll spot us. Petra, when he stops we'll get our things from the trunk." Sergey kept them ten cars lengths behind Weatherly.

Petra looked up from the map in his hand. "He's heading towards the waterfront if he stays on this street. It will make it easier to follow him a little farther back."

Sergey nodded. "Good."

Adam picked up the phone from the front seat. "Jim, I'm near the garage. Get ready." He put the phone in his pocket and sped up. He entered the parking structure with the tires squealing, found a space and jumped out locking the car as he ran towards the street. He could hear the other car race in the garage and the tires skidding as they pulled into a space. He ran over to the sidewalk and into the marina. The gate to the boat's anchorage was propped open. He jogged to the boat and jumped in. Jim started the engine under the canopy and slouched down while Adam took the wheel. All of them heard the footsteps arriving at the gate as they passed the entrance into the bay.

Chris put the binoculars on the moorings. "There are three of them and they're carrying duffel bags. They're trying to find an unlocked boat. They found it! Okay, here they come. Adam, turn on the running lights and give it the gas. No conversations, sound carries over water. We don't want to tip off our numbers."

The view around them was like black mirror. Behind the boat the city lights were reflected off the water. They couldn't see for any distance to the right or left, Jim mused, or the port or starboard sides. The green running light on his right would stand out to those following as they swung to the east of Alcatraz Island and its dock. He gave an involuntary shudder. Only large vessels would be traveling at night and when they glimpsed its running lights, it would be too late.

Borichov stood and watched as the other boat passed along the docks heading for the marina channel. He yelled. "Quickly, find another boat."

Sergey and Petra were jumping into different nearby boats looking for an ignition key. Petra found it first. "Here. Come here." He started the engine. Sergey handed down the duffel bags and climbed down ahead of Borichov. He untied the mooring lines and Petra gunned the engine in reverse to clear the dock. He aimed the boat towards the outlet channel and raced after the other boat. Sergey stood beside him pointing out the running lights.

Borichov moved next to Sergey. "Don't lose them. Where the hell are they going?"

Sergey stared ahead. "They're heading for Alcatraz Island. I can see their lights. It must be where Factor has been hiding. He reached behind into the duffel bag and brought out a rifle with a telescopic sight. He cradled it on the roof of the boat and searched the other boat. I only see one person."

Borichov pulled the gun down. "Don't shoot you idiot or we'll never find him. Follow him over. He'll never see us coming and the sound of the water drowns out our engine noise." He bent over and examined the contents of one of the bags. "Very good, we have enough here to take care of them." He straightened up. "What is this Alcatraz Island?"

Petra answered. "It was an infamous prison that was closed forty years ago. It's a daytime tourist attraction. At night there's no one there."

"How does Factor avoid being discovered?"

"There are buildings on the island closed from all visitors due to the rundown conditions. It's rather clever of him. He could mix with the visitors to go back and forth to get supplies."

Sergey pointed to the lighthouse beam. "The light shines over the western part. We have to make sure we stay in its shadows." Borichov assured him. "I can see their green running light. They're rounding the island on the right. The dock must be on the other side. Give him a few minutes to tie up before we go in the same way."

Chapter Fifty-three

FIGHT NIGHT

Saturday Night
Alcatraz Island

Jim took over the boat's controls and closed in slowly to the landing wharf. He turned off the running lights and guided the boat to the side of the dock. Chris jumped off and tied the boat to the mooring pylons. They handed the supplies over and climbed on the dock. Carrying the bags they walked up the ramp to the sidewalk. On the path to the New Industries Building they looked back to see if the other boat had pulled up. The lighthouse beam shone above them as they kept to the shadows. They only heard the sound of the rushing water around the island and the milling of the birds. The perpetual chill and mist lingered in the air.

Chris observed. "They'll make sure of the terrain before they rush in; probably split up to do a systematic search which will take them to the back of the island. It'll give us time to get settled in and monitor them."

They arrived at the knoll where Chris had indicated he would be located while the other two entered and positioned themselves in the laundry room.

Jim spoke up. "Chris, I'd like to offer an opinion. The person out here is extremely vulnerable if they're as good as we think they are. I'd like to suggest the three of us be together in the laundry. It's easier to defend against an all-out attack and you did say they'll come loaded for bear."

Adam nodded. "I have to agree. We now know there are three of them. We'll have our hands full if we separate."

"We'll all go in." Chris conceded.

They walked around the edge of the building and entered the laundry area. Chris positioned them on each side and took a high point on the wall-mounted equipment from where he could cover the rear and the floor in front of the room.

By this time Adam had the video camera monitor out and was viewing the coverage of the installed cameras. "The landing dock camera shows three armed men and they're carrying bags between them. You were right, they're splitting up. Two are going on the path we were on and the other is on the walk on the other side. It's a classic sweep maneuver."

Time slowly passed as Adam continued to watch the monitor and give a running commentary. "Two of them are at the water tower. They've spotted our camera. Oops, they just shot it out. I didn't hear any gunshot. They must have silencers."

"Any sign of the third guy?" Chris inquired.

"No. The two are now at the base of the knoll. Wow! One of them must have hurled a grenade onto the top of the knoll."

The sound reverberated into the open portion at the other end of the building.

Chris responded. "Shit. It would have caught one of us. Jim, good instincts. It also means we can't take anything for granted with these guys. Adam, any sign of the third one yet?"

"No, but I think it was him who threw the grenade. I can see one of them talking into a communicator. Here we go. One of them is pointing to this building. He's motioning to someone to look around the front. They're going to the top floor and work down. It'll be fairly quick search since the floors for the most part are wide open and stripped of furnishings or interior walls. They're out of sight now. The third guy will probably make his way along the front. He's been on the ramp side. If he crosses in front of the building to come from the sidewalk next to the water and the high metal fence, our camera will pick him up."

Chris advised them. "From my position I can monitor the mesh-covered windows on both sides. He'd have to crawl the length of the building on his stomach toting firepower if he wanted to stay out of sight under the window ledge. One more thing I want you to realize. This is for your benefit Jim. We must concentrate on head shots. We have to assume they are wearing body armor. They may not expect us to have any on so we'll have a slight advantage."

They stayed quiet trying to listen for sounds indicating the presence of the Russians. The slapping of water against rocks could be heard in the background.

Adam announced in a whisper. "Two of them are at the front of our level. It looks like they figured out where we are. They're doling out guns and other things from the bags. The third one just hooked up with them. He's shorter and stouter."

Jim swallowed. "It has to be Borichov."

"Perfect. It'll be a clean sweep. Okay. It's started. They're dividing up and coming on. Good luck guys." Adam closed the monitor and pushed it away from him. He cradled the submachine gun with its night vision scope and made sure the spare clips were in close proximity. He grimly noted the Kevlar vest was providing a degree of warmth from the cold night air. He wiped a drop of sweat from his forehead.

Sergey stood in front of the building. "We've covered all of the places they could be except for this building's lower level. One of us has to circle from the outside so he can enter from the rear. Speak Russian from now on."

Petra walked the front of the building from side to side and came back. "Sergey, there are large windows covered with heavy mesh on both sides running the length of the building. The left side sidewalk is in bad shape and has a chain link fence near the water's edge. The right path is in decent shape and slopes down to the lower level's entrance. The reflected light from the lighthouse makes it vulnerable. I'll go down the other side."

Sergey nodded. "Make sure you take enough magazines and two grenades. We'll wait until you tell us you've reached the end. Then we'll come in from the front and distract them with firepower. There is one other thing." Both Borichov and Petra looked at him. "The camera we shot out. The question is, who put it there? It probably was the Park Service but suppose they did it. It would mean they're expecting us. On the other hand there are only two of them and only one is experienced. Let's do this as fast we can and get the hell out of here."

Borichov halted them. "I want Factor alive. He's mine, you understand. No slip-ups and no excuses. You worry about the other guy."

Sergey glanced at Petra and shrugged. "And if they're both firing? Just how are we supposed to know who's who?"

"Just do it."

Jim waited behind the shelter of the metal vat on the laundry room floor. The feel and weight of the submachine gun was comforting. He checked to make sure the safety selector was on semiautomatic. It smelled of gun cleaning oil. It was hard to avoid the thoughts infringing on his concentration. His transgression had placed Chris, Adam and Diane at risk. He should have run again except this was the opportunity to restore his former life.

He shook his head. Damn it, pay attention. How's it going to start? Chris is right. It makes sense for one or more of them to come in from the rear. He couldn't see the doorway from where he was. Chris was back there on top covering them. What was that? Did he just hear a scraping noise outside by the closest window? He turned his head slightly at the direction of the sound. He heard Chris's whisper in his earpiece. "Steady now, no sounds and no firing until I give the word no matter what." Jim took his finger off the trigger.

Chris set his weapon on semi-automatic. Anyone coming around the side should be by their position anytime now. What would this guy do? A distraction is my guess. They don't know there are three of us and they can't say for sure we're hiding here, at least not yet. I'd waste a grenade if I were him. He clung to the top of the driers and waited for the telltale sound.

Adam made himself comfortable on the other side of the aisle from Jim. He cradled the automatic weapon and for reassurance passed his hand over the sight and magazine. He heard the instructions in his earpiece. He thought, Chris must have an inkling of their next move. He looked over where Jim laid behind the vat but the darkness hampered his vision. He was calm as he assessed the coming firestorm. Damn, I wish I had remembered to bring earplugs. There was going to be one hell of a lot of noise in the closed space.

The three of them heard the unmistakable ping of the released grenade handle as the pin was removed followed by a thud as it hit the outside of the doorway. Barely three seconds later the combined daylight-bright flash and the explosion simultaneously lit up and shook the laundry room. Chris immediately reassured them. "Stay still." The silence brought in the sound of the bay waves slapping the rocks below.

Sergey contacted Petra. "What's happening?"

"Nothing."

"What do you mean nothing? Are they in there?"

"What do you think?"

"Can you fire into the opening?"

"I'd need to get in back of the doorway to do it. If they're in there, they can pick me off."

"Shit."

Borichov spat and gave orders. "Stop screwing around. We'll go in behind any cover in there and open fire towards the end. If they're there they'll shoot back. Petra, when you hear them, go to the back and throw the other grenade." With that said he rushed the doorway of the building and went in until he was behind covering structure. "Get in here." He yelled to Sergey.

Sergey landed close to him and looked into the darkness. "I can't see anything with the night vision scope. Borichov, move to the side and fire a burst. I'll spot where they are by the return fire." Borichov moved quietly to the other side of the room behind metal equipment. He couldn't determine its usage but it provided solid shelter. He pointed his gun down into the darkness and pulled the trigger. The muzzle flash and unsuppressed noise heralded the stream of bullets which hit, penetrated or ricocheted off equipment, walls and ceiling. Borichov cursed and dove on the floor as his fire was answered by two returned volleys which passed through his vacated position.

"Petra, the two of them are located at the rear about waist high. We'll fire again to keep them busy so you can get in that doorway and throw the grenade."

"Okay, Sergey."

Chris inquired. "Jim, Adam. Are you okay?"

"Okay here."

"Same."

"All right, they didn't know we were here and decided to find out. We still have the third one somewhere outside. You two don't worry about him. Just concentrate on finding where they're firing from. Sooner or later they're going to get really impatient and raise the stakes. There's so much crap on the floor we should hear them when they move towards us. They probably have night vision scopes so keep hidden until you fire. Then scoot down."

The Russian's automatic weapons sent an unrelenting stitch of bullets into their location again until their clips were expended. Chris ignored the hail of bullets and sat still watching the rear of the building. He saw the dark figure leap on the rear platform and start to hurl a grenade. He opened fire and struck the man. The grenade dropped from his hand and rolled over the edge. The man regained his balance and jumped down the opposite side as the grenade went off.

"Chris?"

"I'm okay. One of them tried to throw a grenade in here while the other two raised a rumpus. I hit him but he managed to get away. I doubt he'll try it again. He probably figured out there's three of us. Adam, can you check the front camera to see if he got back to the others?"

Adam opened the monitor careful to shield the light and keyed in the camera. "Yeah, he just showed up and he's clutching his left arm. The others have come out of the building and they're talking. One is wrapping a bandage around the arm. I wish we had audio."

"They're probably speaking in Russian anyway."

Sergey keyed the communicator. "Petra, what's going on?"

Petra winced. "How many were firing back at you from in there?"

"Two. Why?"

"Because the third one fired at me when I climbed on the platform behind the doorway is why. I got lucky. The vest stopped all except one shot. The grenade went off outside."

"Where in the hell did the third person come from? This limits our options. At least we're smarter now."

Borichov angrily demanded. "Why do you say that? We still have to get them. I'm not leaving until Factor is dead."

Sergey patiently replied. "We know where they are and how many there are. They're way back in there and we have the entire perimeter and access through the second floor as well. They can't get by us. Petra, any ideas?"

"They're in a defensive position. Unfortunately, we don't have an RPG in our bag. But, we could do the same tactic. This time I creep up towards them from inside instead of outside. When I'm close enough, I'll throw the grenade. You would have to give me suppressive cover that will keep them pinned down."

Sergey turned to Borichov. "Now you'll get your chance. Instead of maintaining a constant covering fire, we'll do it in five second intervals. Petra, while we're firing, crawl closer and stop when we do."

Borichov barked. "Why stop? We keep it up."

"Because they'll mark our positions while we're firing. When we stop, we shift to a new spot and fire again. Okay? Get ready."

Chris noted the break in the firing. "Jim. We're going on the offensive. Are you game to getting out of here and going around them?"

"What do you want me to do?"

"Take your MP5 and spare clips. Go around the side of the building and head for the knoll in front. Take the thermal blanket to put on top of you as you lay down."

"Chris, what about the possibility they'll park another grenade there and catch Jim?"

"There's no cover in front of the building to allow them to do it. Jim could pick them off when they tried. With him there, we'll have them between us in a kill zone. Jim, use the concrete ramp on the other side. They won't be expecting it and you'll get to the front knoll faster."

"Chris. Why Jim and not me?"

"Adam, they're going to try to overwhelm us from the front. You've been through gun battles enough to ignore the turmoil and maintain your focus. Jim will be all right. Move back to his spot. They should be coming soon. Get going Jim."

Jim disappeared out of the rear doorway when the gunfire erupted from the front. Chris and Adam ducked behind their cover as bullets flew all around them ricocheting from the equipment and ceiling.

Jim heard the ear-splitting sound the bullets made as they struck anything in their path as he passed in a low crouch by the windows. Then silence. He continued along quietly. The firing resumed at the same high level as he passed by the front entrance of the building. He resisted a look when the firing stopped again. He stood still in the shadows. If they stepped outside they might see him. The firing resumed prompting him to run up the path and settle himself on the knoll facing the building. He unfolded the blanket and made sure it covered his body as he lay except for a small opening in front where he aimed the MP5. He peered through the night vision scope and took in the front entrance. He had a complete view if they came out except for the lower two feet obstructed by the terrain.

"Chris. I'm in position. What's going on in there?"

"Jim. Good. It seems as if two of them are providing a fire cover for the third one to come in towards us. They're smart enough not to stay in the same place each time. My guess is he'll try to get close enough to heave a grenade."

"Chris."

"Adam?"

"How about I creep up to meet him? He'll never suspect a thing."

"No, Adam. There's no telling when he'll throw the grenade. He knows he'll be vulnerable if the grenade doesn't work. I can make things uncomfortable for him from up here. I am going to walk single shots on the floor towards the front to try to unsettle him. By keeping my barrel pointing down, they shouldn't spot the flashes. I'll pause between shots. Listen for his movement."

With that said, Chris began a systematic firing pattern. From the other end came heavy firing towards where they estimated his position was. Each side stopped firing to assess the situation. Adam thought he heard a scratching noise coming from the front.

"Chris. Did you hear that?"

"Adam. I still have the firing in my ears. How far would you say?"

"Maybe fifty feet."

"Let's put a kink in their plans. How's your pitching arm?"

"Raring to go."

"Okay. Jim, have you been listening?"

"Yes."

"They may come out of the building when Adam heaves the grenade."

"All right then. Let it fly."

Adam straightened up and stood against the side of the equipment. He placed the grenade in his right hand and pulled the pin with his left. He planted his feet and flung the grenade as far as he could into the darkness. Quickly he crouched down behind his shelter and closed his eyes. The grenade's resounding clap of thunder reverberated throughout the area while at the same time illuminating all about it with the intensity of a giant flash bulb.

Just then they heard an object strike the floor up ahead of them. They ducked and covered their ears, opened their mouths and closed their eyes. Again a rumble and a flash occurred. They could hear someone scrambling away from their position.

"Chris. You guessed it right on the money. Whoever was out there has retreated."

"It was a classic case of you show me yours and I'll show you mine."

"Jim, are you there? Watch for them to regroup."

"I got it."

Petra called out. "Sergey, hold your fire. I'm coming out." He staggered over to them. He was covered in dust and dirt. He put his fingers in his ears to clear them. "Shit. Shit. Shit. Where in the hell did they get the grenade? Who are these guys?" He turned to Borichov. "You sonofabitch. You said this was a piece of cake."

Borichov aimed his assault rifle towards Petra with a killing look. "Who do you think you are to talk to me like that?"

Sergey yanked the gun from Borichov's hands. "Are you crazy? We have a job to do and we'll do it. What do you know about Factor? Your file said he was in the Air Force. Was he in Special Forces or something? Why is the PI defending him? Who in the hell is the third guy? Where did their weapons come from?"

"The guy was an arms dealer but not like me. He sold large weapon systems. There was nothing to indicate he's anything but a technically savvy broker."

"Okay. Let us alone to do our job. Take back your AK-47, stay here and watch our backs. Petra, let's figure out our next move."

"I don't see we have any choice. We have to go in after them. One of us has to be a decoy."

"We'll take turns at that. We'll each take a grenade. When we're close enough we'll use them. Borichov, we're going in."

"Don't waste time talking. Do it."

Adam whispered, "Chris, so far it's a stalemate. What's next?"

"They don't know that Jim's outside behind them now. It's our ace in the hole. They already tried to get someone behind us and it didn't work. They desperately want us so I figure they'll spread out across the floor and come that way. They'll count on return fire revealing our positions."

"It'll give them the advantage."

"Not that much. They have to be concerned we have night vision scopes and they now know we have grenades. Like us they have shelter from the leftover equipment scattered all along the floor. It's a problem but maybe the stings can help there."

Suddenly their area was flooded with automatic fire from one side of the building. As abruptly when the firing stopped Chris unleashed a burst towards the source. He crouched down as a burst came at him from the opposite side. Adam noted the direction and returned the fire almost before the firing subsided. He moved away from the cover as a burst raked his vacated position.

"Adam, they're closing in from two sides. I'm going to draw their fire. Don't fire; just throw a grenade at the spot."

"Go ahead."

Chris fired at the previous location of the muzzle flashes, than quickly retreated backward. In response a stream of rounds filled the gap. Adam got on his knees, pulled the pin and hurled the grenade over his head at the other wall. He ducked and waited. The sting grenade's rubber projectiles peppered the volume slamming against metal and walls. They heard a shout followed by a loud curse. They heard an object in front of them strike an open drier door and dropped behind cover. The flash of light and loud blast temporally disoriented their senses. It was followed by twin sets of automatic fire. Adam recovered first and pulled the pin from a stun grenade and threw it disregarding the stream of bullets. The grenade went off and silenced one of the guns. Chris recovered and went to full automatic with a fresh clip and sprayed the area. Adam followed his example and swept his fire along the base of the wall. He heard a cry. He crouched down and replaced his spent magazine.

"Adam. Good move, I think you got one."

"It leaves two to go. That was close. What now?"

"We don't know where the other two are."

"Chris, Adam. What's happening?"

"Jim, we're having a battle in here. Any movement outside?"

"Not yet. Do you need me there?"

"Stay put. Adam?"

"Yeah."

"I'm going after the one you hit. Can you alternate fire from two points?"

"Yes. Are you sure about this?"

"Let me know when you're ready. Go semiautomatic."

"Okay."

Chris crouched quietly down from his perch and slowly edged towards the Russian position. Adam watched his progress through the night vision scope but lost him as Chris made his way to the left wall. He gave Chris ten seconds before he fired into the right side of the building. He ducked and moved to the area where Chris had been positioned. He fired at the left side careful to aim high up on the wall. He barely had time to drop prone on the floor when a torrent of bullets struck his empty firing position. He saw it came from the right side. He nodded with satisfaction because he knew Chris had probably observed the location from where he was. No firing had come from the left side. He was suddenly worried the Russian on that side was playing possum to lure them into a trap. He was going to warn Chris but hesitated. Chris knew what he was doing. He waited another few seconds and opened fire again repeating his previous pattern. This time he selected a different spot on the other side. He dropped to the floor faster than ever as bullets sprayed the area. He had a thought; playing possum could work both ways if Chris had reached his objective. Adam cried out and pointed his gun at the ceiling and fired a short burst. Then he crawled back to his original position to wait. This time there was no return fire from either side.

* * *

Borichov tried to determine the status of Sergey and Petra. He heard Petra cry out and then only Sergey was firing at Factor's position. He resisted the thought of going inside to check on them. He cradled the AK-47 and moved from the inside doorway to the outside careful to stay in the shadows. He swept the night scope along the rear ridge as a precautionary measure. He put his hand inside his jacket and checked to make sure the pistol's safety was off as he moved slowly towards the path. He could hear the firing inside of the building and one definitely was the distinctively sounding Kalashnikov. The sound of the waves splashing against the rocks and bird sounds masked his movement.

Jim in his perch watched through his scope and caught a glimpse of motion in the shadow of the doorway. He blinked and concentrated on the edge of the building. There it was again. Someone was there. He shifted slightly and continued to stare afraid to blink. He breathed slowly surprised he was so calm. He took out the ear communicator out and laid it on the ground so he could concentrate. The figure had to emerge from the shadows if he wanted to come back up the path. He must be less than forty feet away from me. I can make him out now. He's carrying an assault rifle. He peered through the scope and put his finger on the trigger. He looks like Borichov but I have to make sure.

"That's far enough. Drop the gun and put up your hands." Borichov froze. The voice was familiar. "Factor, is that you?"

"It's me. Either drop it or I'll fire."

The cold timbre of Factor's voice halted Borichov's impulse to fire in his direction. He felt the weight of his pistol and managed a cold smile. "I'm putting it on the ground. Where are you?"

Jim stood shaking his blanket to the ground and keeping his gun trained on Borichov, his finger on the trigger. "Raise your hands."

Borichov obeyed looking at him in a rage. "You caused me a great deal of money and trouble."

Jim moved slowly down to Borichov. "Your problem was believing I turned you in. You're not too smart. What did I have to gain from it? You caused me to run away from my home and my life. Now it's my turn."

Borichov glanced towards the doorway.

Jim understood the inference. "I doubt your friends are going to be able to help you. They have their hands full inside."

"Who are those people with you?"

"Good friends. Now turn around. We're going back."

As Jim set foot on the path, the damp ground made him slip and the gun barrel flew up. Borichov saw his opening, reached inside of his coat and withdrew the pistol. Jim, trying to regain his balance, saw Borichov's move and let go of the gun. He reached inside his vest and in one rapid motion drew and fired the Glock. Borichov stared in shock as his chest exploded and he lost the strength to hold his pistol. He collapsed on his knees. "How?" He fell to the ground.

Jim kicked the pistol away.

He gurgled with an evil sneer. "It won't do you any good. Federov will avenge me." He took his last breath and lay still.

PART TWO

Chapter One

FLIGHT TIME

Saturday Midnight

Jim put his gun away and hastily looked back at the entrance to see if any of the others would come out when they heard the pistol shot. Satisfied he was unnoticed he went through Borichov's pockets. He found a hotel key and a roll of money. He pocketed them and stopped to think. He recalled Adam mentioning the hit team was affiliated with Borichov's brother-in-law Dimitri Federov who was in the Russian mafia. A shiver and anger came over him as he realized after what they had been through it wasn't over. "I've got to get out of here. I hate to do this but I've got to take the next step by myself." He could still hear the gunfire inside of the building.

He hoisted Borichov over his shoulder and picked up the guns. He struggled with the load and reached the dock where the two boats were tied up. He dumped Borichov into their boat and untied the lines. He started the engine and pulled out into the current. When he was far enough away, he placed the engine on idle and went to the body, stripped him and threw the clothes into the water. Next he dropped Borichov over the side watching as the current took him away. The guns, ammunition, knife and tactical vest went into the water. He searched the boat for any evidence. When he was done, he put the engine in gear and raced back to the marina.

Jim tied the boat in its proper mooring slip and left. He walked quickly to the parking garage and got to his car. He opened the trunk, wrote a note and placed it on Chris's windshield. He looked at Borichov's hotel key and hastily started his car. He proceeded out of the garage and drove to Nob Hill. He parked the car on the street and took his travel bag from the trunk. He walked to the Intercontinental Mark Hopkins Hotel and went directly to the elevator. Jim rode to the eighth floor and let himself into Borichov's suite. He went into the bedroom searching through drawers and a suitcase. He opened the closet and went through the pockets of the hanging clothes. As an afterthought, he put on one of the jackets. He returned to the suitcase and ran his fingers carefully along the inside lining. He found a small loose edge and pulled it open. It revealed Borichov's counterfeit and genuine passports, an address book and more money. He placed his bag into the suitcase, took it and left the suite. He rode the elevator down to the parking garage and went through a side door. He got in his car and drove to the San Francisco Airport.

Adam listened to the silence for a while and whispered. "Chris? Are you there?"

"Adam. It's all over. Come here. I'm going to need a hand." He turned on his flashlight.

Adam followed the bright beam until he reached Chris. He looked down at the body. "Where's the other?"

"Against the wall. You nailed him with the burst. Let's get them out of here. Collect all of the weapons."

"What about the shell casings? They're all around here."

"Leave them. It'll be sometime before anybody comes into this restricted area. Jim, are you there? Jim?"

"He's not answering. Let's drag these two to the entrance and look around. I don't see the third guy so be careful."

They brought the two bodies into the doorway entrance and called out. They went up the knoll and found the thermo blanket on the ground. Near the path they found a shell casing. Adam examined it under the light. "It's a 9mm shell."

"Jim has a 9mm Glock. The other two had Russian pistols on them. Let's carry them down to the boat and come back for the weapons. Jim may be down at the dock. We'll take each one separately using the blanket like a sling."

The body suspended between the two of them, they went to the dock and looked around.

"What the hell? Chris, there's only one boat here. Jim must have taken it."

"Let's not waste time. We'll go back for the other one and the weapons. We got to get out of here. I don't think anybody heard the racket but we don't want to stick around to find out."

With the two bodies in the boat and the weapons collected, Chris started the boat's engine and pulled away from the dock. "Adam, search their pockets and then take off their clothes."

Adam looked up. "Nothing, not even car keys. They probably left everything in their car."

"We won't worry about it. Chances are if it's anywhere unattended, it'll be broken into and cleaned out."

Shortly thereafter in the channel between the marina and the island, Chris slowed the boat. "Adam, pitch these guys over along with the clothes and guns and anything else incriminating."

That done, Chris advanced the throttle and they powered into the marina. They docked the boat in its proper place and Chris returned the ignition key inside the locker.

"Where could Jim be?"

"Let's check the parking garage and see if his car is there." They walked together across the street to the first level.

Chris checked the space. "He was parked here and he's gone. What could have happened? Let's go to my place and see if he's there. Wait, there's a note on the windshield."

Adam ran over. "Is it from Jim? What does it say?"

Chris read, "*Thank you. It's not over yet.*"

"He must have gotten some information from Borichov before . . ."

"It's the way I see it. You think it has to do with the Federov guy?"

"Yeah. Shall we go loosen up at your place?"

"Definitely."

Chapter Two

ON THE ROAD AGAIN

Early Sunday Morning, November 3
San Francisco, California

Jim arrived at the airport and drove into the long term parking lot. From there he took a shuttle to the international terminal. He saw there was a United Airlines flight leaving for Toronto in four hours. He went into a men's room and entered a stall. There he transferred the Canadian passport and traveler's checks to his pockets. He emptied the clothes except for a shirt from his travel bag into the suitcase. He put Borichov's passports and currency into the bag and carried it separately. He changed into his shirt and pants and placed the clothing he had worn into the trash. Satisfied with his appearance he went to the United Airlines ticket counter and handed over his passport.

"I want to get a one-way economy ticket to Toronto on the seven-fifteen morning flight."

"That will be $310, Mr. Moreno."

"While you're at it, how can I check the European international flight schedule? My company may want me to turn around and get on another flight."

"Any idea where they'll send you?"

"In the past I had to go through Paris. Please check that for me."

"Here's one that leaves at eight-ten this evening from Toronto on Lufthansa into Charles de Gaulle Airport. Shall I book it for you?"

"Yes, please. How much is that?"

"The total is $1,595."

"Fine. I'll check one bag straight through."

Jim left the area with his travel bag and went through security. He entered the departure area and made a phone call. In the terminal he found a seat that gave him some privacy. He reached in his bag and took out Borichov's address book. He thumbed through it and found Dimitri Federov's name and Moscow address. He thought, "I'll deal with him from a European location."

Monday Morning, November 4

Adam informed Chris he was going to stay in San Francisco a while longer to try to determine where Jim might have gone. He decided to backtrack each of Jim's contacts during the time he had been in San Francisco. He first made a call to Lt. Frank Malone and summarized his findings on Jim's acquisition of a Mexican passport under the name of Tomas Cassandra. He read off the passport information. "Frank, any possibility a search could be made to see if it has been used during the last couple of days?"

"Sure. We interface routinely with State and Customs. Let me check with them and I'll get back to you."

Adam next decided to ask Ray Peterson for another favor. He had the make and the license plate number of Jim's car.

"Ray, I found Factor and lost him again. I have the make and license number of the car he's using. Can you do me a favor and put out an APB on it?

"Sure. Odds are if he's going to ground again he might abandon it. Don't forget, he could always change the plates. I'll run it by the DMV and call you if anything comes up."

He then called his office. He smiled when he heard their voices.

Elaine spoke first. "Adam, are you all right?"

"I'm fine. As you are aware, I did find Jim Factor but as events would have it, he disappeared again out of concern for his and his wife's safety. I'm doing some follow up to understand what he did while he was here and try to figure out where he might go. In the meantime, I have to contact his wife."

"Adam, while you were there, she came here looking for more information." Elaine briefed him on their conversation with her.

"You both did exactly right. I'll keep in touch with you. I won't be here any longer than I have to."

He called Diane Factor. She answered right away.

"Adam Weatherly, Mrs. Factor."

"I recognize your voice, Adam. What news do you have? Did you find Jim?"

"I did and to my dismay, he's taken off again. However, there's more to this than I can say on the telephone. If you'll be patient, I want to try to locate him over the next couple of days. As soon as I finish, I'll drive down and give you a detailed account of my efforts. I will stay in touch."

"I'll wait until then. Goodbye."

Newport Beach, California

Diane slowly hung up the phone disappointment flooding through her. Stop it, she willed. Jim's alive but obviously something happened. He doesn't do anything without a purpose. What was nagging at her? Was it something about a purpose? Then it came out with a rush. Jim's going after them. It's the reason for his preparation. She had to sit down. She'll stay calm and wait for Adam Weatherly's report.

Monday Afternoon
San Francisco, California

Adam went through the newspapers to see if any gunshot victims had been recovered from the waters off San Francisco. He didn't even find news on any activity on Alcatraz Island, not that he thought he would. His phone rang.

"Adam. Ray here. I got a hit off the DMV check. The car is registered to Robert Nagel. You might want to talk with him."

Adam wrote down the address and drove over to the house. He noted it was in the same general area as Chris's martial arts studio.

When he arrived, he was surprised to see the car parked in front of the house. He touched the hood and felt its warmth. The front door was answered by a burly man with a beard wearing shorts and a sweatshirt.

"Mr. Nagel?"

"Who wants to know?"

Adam displayed his credentials and explained he wanted to talk about the man who drove his car. Nagel admitted him into the house. "Why do you want him? Has he done anything wrong?"

Adam explained his involvement in the search.

"I don't know what I can tell you about Nick. He bought the car from me several months ago but asked me to keep the registration for a while."

Adam interrupted, "How is it you have it here?"

"I got a call from him yesterday morning saying I could have it back and it was at the San Francisco Airport long term parking lot. I went there early this morning and picked it up." He smiled. "In the glove compartment I found a hundred dollar bill and a note that said 'Thanks.'"

"Was there anything else in the car?"

"Nope, I checked the trunk and it was empty." He chuckled. "Nick left it with a full tank of gas."

Adam thanked him and left.

Next on his list was the Queterras' home. He noticed the groomed yard and good condition of the house as he walked up the front steps to the porch. He rang the bell. A woman with an apron opened the door and peered at him through the screen door. "Si?"

"Mrs. Queterras, my name is Adam Weatherly. I'd like to talk to you about Nick Germain."

Warily, she asked. "Who are you?"

Adam told her his business and the search he conducted which resulted in finding Nick. "I know he left here a couple of days ago. What can you tell me about him?"

"Mr. Germain was a wonderful man. He came months ago and worked at his business at the Pier 39 Marina. He was courteous and respectful. Even though he was a border, my family and I enjoyed his company. The day after he left, I went to clean up his room and found he left me $200 with a 'thank you' note. He didn't have to do that but it's the kind of man he was."

Adam nodded. "Thank you for your time."

She wiped her eyes. "If you find him, you tell him he's welcome here any time he wants."

"I will. Goodbye."

Adam drove away shaking his head. All he could say was, "Remarkable." He drove to the Pier 39 marina and parked in the garage across the street. He walked down to the docks and encountered a locked gate. He waited until one of the workers came from inside the marina. "Pardon me, can you tell me where I can find Miguel Rodriguez?"

He pointed down the row of boats. "He is working on the cruiser, eighth boat down the line."

"Thank you."

Adam walked along the dock and came to the mooring. He saw a man cleaning the topside of the boat. He called out. "Miguel."

Miguel stopped his work and looked down. "Yes."

"My name is Adam Weatherly. Do you have a few minutes to talk to me about Nick Germain?"

Miguel climbed down from the boat and joined Adam on the dock. "Nick is gone up north for a while. I'm running things. Do you need help with your boat?"

Adam shook his head. "I'm a private investigator." He showed his ID. He proceeded to tell Miguel the purpose of his visit.

"That's a hard story to swallow. We worked together here for almost six months. He built up our business which is really doing good."

"Do you have the time to tell me about it?"

Miguel told him of the work on the vessels and Nick's involvement with Mike Sweeney of the Halyard Boat Company, Charlie Ford of the Dockside Marine Hardware Store, Steve Wilson, owner of Pacific Coast Yacht Sales, George Marx the book keeper, and boat owners like Wayne Collier and Bob Wallsky. Adam busily wrote the conversation down in his notebook. Finally, Miguel stopped talking.

Adam put his notes away. "Let me ask you something. What can you tell me about the man rather than what he did?"

Miguel took his hat off. "Nick was a special person. He didn't seek out all of these things. It came to him. He generously shared the work and the pay with me and the others here. He was a good man and everybody liked being around him. I am sorry he left. He said he'd be back in a week though."

"Where did he say he was going?"

"Seattle to look at another business opportunity."

"Miguel, I don't think he'll be back. I believe he handed you the business when he introduced you to George Marx. Thank you for telling me about him."

With that Adam shook hands with Miguel and left.

Adam redeemed his car and drove away in wonderment. How could a person touch so many people and accomplish so much in such a short time, especially given his past? I'll go back to the hotel and input my notes. It'll give me a chance to see what else to do.

When Adam was in his hotel room, he made a call to Lt. Frank Malone. "Frank, I have some news. Jim Factor parked his car at the San Francisco Airport yesterday morning. Can you run a check on the Mexican passport to see if it was used recently?"

"Easy enough to check. You might also want to run a search on the outbound flights both domestic and international."

"I'll do it. Thanks."

Adam dialed another number. "Ray Peterson, please."

"Hello."

"Ray, its Adam. I located the car. It was parked at the home of the registered owner. He received word from Factor yesterday that he left it in the San Francisco Airport long term parking lot and he could reclaim it."

"It means he took a flight out. Have you checked the airlines passenger lists yet?"

"No. Can you do that for me? Include domestic as well. One of his contacts mentioned he said he was heading to Seattle. We're looking for the name on the passport, Tomas Cassandra, but we should also include Nicholas Germain and James Factor in case he's remaining in the states."

"I'll get to it."

Paris, France

In a little over nine hours, the flight from Toronto began its descent into Paris Charles de Gaulle Airport. On arrival, Jim went through French Customs and proceeded to the railway station within the airport. Charles Moreno purchased a first class train ticket to Barcelona. Inside a closed compartment, he was able to rest during the trip. It would be over six hours before the train pulled into Barcelona, Spain where he could exchange more dollars for Euros and purchase another train ticket to Alicante.

Chapter Three

THE REIGN
IN SPAIN

Monday Night
Alicante, Spain

As the train pulled into the Alicante train station, Jim reflected that the trip from San Francisco had taken almost two days. He stretched his legs, took the suitcase down from the overhead, and stepped down to the platform. He had arrived at his final destination. He located the taxi stand and entered a vacant cab. Speaking Spanish, he addressed the driver.

"Take me to the Visitor Center so I can find a room."

"It's closed now but I can recommend a very clean hotel not far from the bay."

"Is there a marina nearby?"

"Si, Señor."

"Okay, let's see it."

The taxi stopped in front of a small, neatly landscaped hotel. The sign read Los Cantanos. Jim inspected the white building with the forest green trim with a large enclosed front porch. He thought. "Time for my new persona." He paid the driver and entered the lobby. The reception area consisted of a counter with a bell and numerous brochures of the local sights, activities and restaurants. A couch sat opposite the counter with a nearby table containing a newspaper and magazines. He rang the bell and an attractive woman appeared behind the counter wearing a colorful purple short-sleeve blouse and wide pleated green, red and white skirt. She had her hair tied back. Dangling earrings framed an oval face with blue piercing eyes and pink lipstick. She had no wedding band but wore a silver and pearl ring. She tilted her head to one side and inspected his appearance.

He shrugged to suggest the travel imposed the disheveled appearance before her. He smiled and greeted her in Spanish. Her only comment was, "Umm."

"I'm looking for a room for a few days."

"How few and how many?"

"Depends on the room and the hotel."

She smiled. "And how will I know when you are satisfied with the accommodations? Do you have special standards I should be aware of?"

He surprised himself by laughing. "Your sense of humor is all I require. How about a week?"

"Very well. There are only ten rooms here but they are comfortable and clean. I have only one vacancy. Each room has its own bathroom. The weekly rate is 210 Euros and it includes a continental breakfast. The bar on the enclosed porch serves traditional tapas and regional wines at four. Would you like to first see the room?"

"I trust it'll be nice. I'll pay in advance." He signed the register, C. Moreno.

"May I see your passport Mr. Moreno?"

"Of course."

"Charles is your given name."

"Yes. And yours?"

"Theresa Montoya."

"Thank you, Senora Montoya. One more thing; could you direct me to a nearby bar where I can get a drink?"

"Please call me Theresa. Down the street on the right is the Spanish Thorn. It is a peaceful place where the locals and the occasional visitor can get drink and food."

He touched his beard. "I might go there after I get cleaned up and change. Thank you again."

He was not prepared for what he found. The hotel room was spacious with an open window allowing a balmy breeze to come in passed lace curtains. It was decorated in neutral tones with bright splashes of Mediterranean colors. The bed on one side had a white wicker headboard with a set of red decorative pillows on clean white ones. He sat on the bed and enjoyed the feel of the firm mattress. There was an ample size bureau and a clothes closet with a door mirror. The bathroom was light and roomy with a shower and tub arrangement. A flat panel TV was on the wall opposite the bed. Two rugs lay on the polished hardwood floor. A phone was on a table by a small sofa. Jim found the room peaceful. He emptied the suitcase and wondered about his valuables. He picked up the phone.

"Theresa, is there a safe for valuables?"

"I have a safe on the premises by the front desk. If you want I'll bring up a box you can place articles in and lock. This I deposit in my safe and give you a receipt. Is that satisfactory?"

"Yes, it is. Thank you."

Shortly afterwards he heard a knock, opened the room door and received the box. When she left he emptied the contents of the travel bag placing the American dollars and the four passports inside. He counted the money. He was amazed to see Borichov had had over 10,000 U.S. dollars and another few thousand in Bulgarian currency. Including his own money, he had about $20,000 in cash and travelers checks. He also had 500 Euros not to mention his Swiss bank account. He closed the box and locked it. Then he turned towards the bathroom to shower and shaved off his beard. When he finished, he chose a light shirt with a pair of beige slacks and loafers. "I have to buy some clothes and shoes." He went down to the lobby and exchanged the locked box for a receipt. He then proceeded to the nearby bar to have a drink before returning for some much needed sleep.

Tuesday Morning, November 5

Jim woke up after sleeping almost twelve hours. He dressed in jeans and a faded shirt and went down to the lobby to thumb through the local brochures. He found a description of Alicante and read with interest about the boat harbor of the Marina de Alicante. He found pamphlets advertising fishing boats but nothing specific on the marina. I guess I'll have to find out for myself. He heard someone calling and didn't pay attention until he realized it was his new identity. He looked up suddenly with a sheepish grin to see Theresa glaring at him.

"You are so engrossed in reading you don't hear well?"

"No, I mean yes. Sorry. What did you say?"

"You are interested in fishing?" She pointed to the brochure in his hand.

"Actually, I am more interested in the marina. Do you have any information on it?"

"There is a Tourist Office by the entrance at the end of the promenade. It is a mile away. I'm sure you'll find everything there. How was Spanish Thorn last night?"

"Rather pleasant, actually. I didn't stay long. I was tired. I'll see you later."

Jim walked at a brisk pace to the marina and found the Tourist Office. He entered and went over to a blown up layout of the marina. He read the details and was impressed. It held seven hundred forty-four craft up to two hundred feet in length. He compared this to the San Francisco Pier 39 marina with three hundred-seven slips up to a length of sixty feet. The marina maintenance offered diver services, crane and launching ramp. He'd have to walk the perimeter to locate a marine hardware store, dry dock and yacht dealers. He realized he couldn't give the Pier 39 as a work reference but perhaps there was an opportunity in the future.

For the time being, however, he needed to get access to the Internet to learn all he could on Dimitri Federov before he could develop a course of action. He approached the information desk and inquired about computer terminal accesses. He was given a street map and directed to the Cyber Internet Café on Calle de San Vincente. It was back the way he had come.

He made up his mind to take a sightseeing tour the next day to become acquainted with the city. Calle de San Vincente was the major thoroughfare. He stopped at a bank and exchanged two thousand U.S. dollars into Euros. He wandered along the avenue and came across a men's clothing store where he bought pants, belts, shirts, shorts, socks and shoes. As an afterthought, he selected two pairs of pajamas. He decided on a new wallet and wristwatch. Next he went to a sporting goods store and purchased sport shorts, tee-shirts and running shoes. A block away he located the Cyber Internet Café. It had rental computer terminals on separate tables. He had to buy a notebook and bring it with Borichov's address book for his research. He had one last item on hi list, a martial arts studio, but he could look into it later.

Chapter Four

AN ATTEMPT
AT CLOSURE

Tuesday, November 5
San Francisco, California

Adam woke early, put on his workout clothes and ate breakfast in the hotel. Afterwards he drove to Chris's martial arts studio to relieve his tension. Chris took him over to the same hanging apparatus he had Jim try. Chris described the function and procedure to Adam. Then they both went into each other for almost thirty minutes. Finally coated in sweat, they unbuckled and went to the side for water.

"Chris, this is some kind of system you've put together. It makes you focus on stance, balance and motion. I'll need a couple more attempts to get to where I could give you trouble."

"Adam, I tried Jim out on it before we left. He defeated me the first time he used it."

"What? That's incredible. You gotta be one a hell of an instructor."

"Or maybe he was one hell of a student. I certified him a black belt right after it. How are you doing on your interviewing? Any insight into where he's gone?"

Adam shook his head in frustration. He related the conversations he had with Marie Queterras, Bob Nagel and Miguel Rodriguez. "It's hard to believe Jim did so much and affected every one. You know his wife repeatedly told me he was a self-centered person. How he unconsciously changed is beyond me. I'll tell you something else. The fact he was able to transform himself will make it extremely hard if not impossible to locate him again. He'll easily blend in like a chameleon in any surroundings. I'm going to talk to one or two more of his acquaintances today and check with my contacts in the SFPD and INS. I'll keep in touch."

Adam showered on his return to the hotel and went out. His first stop was the office building where he would find George Marx, Jim's book keeper. The receptionist showed him to Marx's office. Adam settled into a chair in front of the desk. He introduced himself and related the purpose of his visit.

George Marx smiled after he heard the story. "You know, when I met Nick or Jim I guess I should say, I found myself looking into intelligent eyes that belied the itinerant laborer he seemed to be. He didn't waste words and got to the point in an efficient manner. He was at ease talking to me not that I'm aloof. I mean he addressed me as an equal. At any rate, he wanted me to handle the transactions for a small one-employee business which I initially felt was overkill on his part. The business took off in a short amount of time and soon I was writing checks for up to eight people."

"George, when did all of this occur?"

"About four months ago in mid-July." Marx consulted his computer. "He opened an account with $2,000. Let's see, even with $5,000 withdrawal this past week, there is a balance of over $15,000. I gave it to him in traveler's checks."

"Wait, did you say he withdrew $5,000? Did he say what he needed the money for?"

Marx nodded. "He was going to look into a business opportunity in Seattle."

"This may sound like a strange question but what was your opinion of the man."

"At first he seemed purposeful and pleasant but not given to socializing, no joking and nothing personal. Later, he was friendlier and open. I got the impression he was comfortable conducting business."

"Thank you. You've been very helpful."

"Adam, I take it you don't think he was going to Seattle."

Adam thought a minute. "I think he believes he has a strong reason to leave and he may have done so already." He stood up. "Thank you for your time."

"I hope you find him and his situation gets resolved. The person he placed in charge, Miguel Rodriguez, seems to have a good head on his shoulders as well."

* * *

Adam reflected on the conversation as he drove back to the hotel. Jim had the foresight to make sure of ample funds in the event something went awry in their plan. How many people have the presence of mind to pay attention to contingencies? He hoped Ray Peterson and Frank Malone had something for him. He was starting to get an uneasy feeling.

Adam called Malone first to see if Jim had used his Mexican passport at the airport. Malone told him no one had used the passport anywhere in the U.S. Next, Adam called Ray.

"We went through all of the passenger lists from all departing flights on all of the Northern California airports and nothing came up. He could have left the car at the airport as a red herring and taken a train or bus as he did before."

"I don't think so. He found another way. Oh my God!"

"Adam. What?"

"Damn it Ray. I could kick myself for not thinking about it."

"What the hell are you talking about?"

"A second passport. He must have bought not one but two passports and I'll bet you each was completely different."

"Adam, nobody can be that devious or far-sighted."

"This man is. He withdrew $5,000 from an account he had a few days ago and converted them to traveler's checks. He could have taken a flight from San Francisco Airport after all and I'll wager it was an international flight. Now I've really lost him."

"Not necessarily. I got an idea."

"What do you have in mind?"

"I'm thinking we should see if we can get the video tapes from the airport to see if we can spot him and his outward flight. Let me call the airport security office and get you into there."

"Ray, you're a genius. Call me back when you have news."

Chapter Five

INFORMATION AND ADJUSTMENT

Wednesday, November 6
Alicante, Spain

Jim went jogging early in the morning before there was much activity in the streets. When he left, the reception desk was empty and apparently the hotel's other guests were still in their rooms. He was going to Calle de San Vincente during his run to investigate a karate studio listed in the city phone directory. He didn't have to worry about Spanish lessons anymore since he was passably fluent. His proficiency should increase by leaps and bounds during his stay. He'd have to remember to read the newspapers to enhance his education.

He saw the studio on the other side of the street nestled between two stores. He crossed over and peeked in the window. A sign indicated it opened later in the morning. He started running again and thinking about his abrupt flight from San Francisco. He was sorry to leave Chris and Adam without more explanation but there was no time to debate his views on the danger he would place everyone by remaining. At least Adam would have a devil of a time trying to track him here with his new identity. He had a three day start. He'd have figured out by now he had left from San Francisco Airport.

He suddenly stopped running. Would he think about checking the terminal videos routinely made as part of the overall security? Adam was resourceful and insightful not to mention persistent. What could he find out? Possibly his Canadian flight. He had made his Paris connection at San Francisco. He could determine his new identity but chances are he'd be stymied by the prospect of searching for a somewhat common Italian name in France, Italy and Spain. He wondered if he could doctor Borichov's Bulgarian orts. He could probably find the skill here in Alicante. He started running again.

He approached the hotel bathed in sweat. He sat on the porch stairs to rest. A familiar voice called out to him, "Buenos Dios, Señor Charles."

He saw Theresa inside the porch placing the breakfast items on the counters against the wall. "Buenos Dios, Senora Theresa."

"You are out early. Too early for a tourist I think. Did you enjoy your run?"

"Yes. The city is pretty this time of the day without the busy traffic."

"Come in and have breakfast. You can meet the other guests if they don't sleep in."

Jim entered the porch. He poured a cup of coffee and sat down at a table. He pleasantly inquired, "Do you work here full time?"

"Yes. The owner is a slave driver." She laughed and shook her head. "I own this hotel. What do you do in Canada?"

She had an infectious laugh and it made him smile. He had forgotten about a cover story. Then he recalled his short tenure with Pacific Coast Yacht Sales. "I'm a salesman on holiday."

"Really. What do you sell?"

"I sold boats."

"Sold?"

She was quick. He would have to be careful. "I decided to quit and visit Spain for a while."

"No family? No attachments? No obligations?"

"None."

Two guests came onto the porch for breakfast and she greeted them. They introduced each other. Jim read the newspaper. When he was through, he went to his room to freshen up. When he came down he picked up a flyer on bus tours.

Jim joined the tourists and locals strolling under shade provided by two rows of tall palm trees. The temperature was warming and the morning haze was dissipating. He bordered the bus and took a window seat. He relaxed and enjoyed the tour. At its conclusion, he walked back to the hotel.

* * *

He gathered up Borichov's address book along with his notebook and pen and went out. A brisk pace placed him at the Internet Café within fifteen minutes. He entered and requested a terminal four an hour. He settled in a corner of the room. There were only three customers in the room. His Internet search focused on thenRussian mafia and Dimitri Federov and revealed an interesting set of facts. When the Soviet Union collapsed Dimitri Federov and other Russian mafia bosses took advantage of the confusion and gained control of politicians and government resources. Soon their organizations owned banks, casinos, trucking, car dealerships, even a local airport. Operating from stylish headquarters along Moscow's Leninsky Prospekt, they controlled prostitution, gambling, drugs and weapons dealing. It declared Federov's Moscowbased Solsnetskaya Organization was presently the biggest and most feared criminal organization in Russia counting five thousand members. Its power reached from Moscow to Miami to Geneve and the Middle East. Federov sent his soldiers all over the world. He had a second residence in Israel, a popular retreat among Russian mobsters because of a certain rule: Jews from all over the world may return to Israel and cannot be refused even if they are on the run. As a result, many non-Jewish Russians obtained false passports. Federov appeared to be one of them. Whenever somebody had to be eliminated, Federov flew his professional hit team to the place. The team took care of the hit and then flew back to await a new assignment. Despite numerous attempts to prosecute Federov, he evaded conviction because the Russian government refused to turn over documents showing he was the head of a criminal empire.

Jim leaned back in his chair and considered the findings. He wanted to see the connection between Federov and Borichov. He searched for Cortex International and found it was an export company which supplied the Belgian peace-keeping forces in Somalia, Africa. It also sold arms to rebel soldiers and violent militants in Central Africa. The company had contacts with several Afghani groups and sold them tons of ammunition and weapons; soon after it had a new customer, the Taliban. It was rumored he used his position as Dimitri Federov's brother-in-law to expand his operation to the Middle East.

Jim needed to determine how he could neutralize Federov. He assumed Federov's phone number was a private line. I better pick up a cell phone. He signed off and left. I'll have to think about the best and safest course of action.

At the hotel, the late afternoon bar on the porch was already by several of the guests. He listened to the animated conversation Theresa was having with one of them. She saw him on the walkway and waved him inside where she asked, "Are you familiar with our local wines?"

He shook his head.

"In that case I shall educate you. These are from the village Jalon, about fifteen kilometers from Alicante. The famous Jalon wines are strong red and the sweet muscatel and sold by the liter. Every Tuesday the town has a popular market held in the square and the adjacent streets. You can get anything there."

"I'll try the red wine. Is there a nice restaurant around here?"

"You should try the Baydal at the port. They feature paella, our tradition-al dish. It's almost as good as mine."

"Really?"

"Yes. Mine is a variation. The original recipe calls for rice, rabbit, chicken, snails, green and yellow beans, tomatoes, olive oil, salt and saffron. It's way too much. I use shrimp, spicy sausage and fresh caught fish instead. You don't need a reservation but nine o'clock is a good time to go."

"You've convinced me. I'll try them tonight."

Jim went to his room and lay on the bed. He sifted through the facts he had acquired on Federov and Borichov. Theresa had mentioned the Jalon town market. He was familiar with these types of weekly local markets from his trips to Provence, France. It might be worthwhile to see if he could get in touch with a qualified forger. A balmy breeze eased its way through the win-dow stirring the curtains. He kicked his shoes off, closed his eyes and settled into a peaceful nap.

Jim woke up, took a shower and changed. He checked himself in the mirror. "I could use a decent haircut." He saw it was almost nine. He left the hotel and walked to the restaurant.

The restaurant was on the shore situated past the marina near the port entrance. A large red neon sign on the roof proclaimed Restaurant de Baydal. A large dark blue awning extended from the building to the sidewalk where a doorman opened car doors and greeted customers. He walked through the doors past the reception area to the lounge and sat down on a comfortable stool at the bar.

He smiled at the bartender. "Gin martini straight up with a twist, Tanqueray Gin if you have it." He swiveled around and glanced at the room. He thought, "God, it feels great to be civilized once more without worrying about being seen. I didn't realize how much I missed it." He turned back to the bar and found the frosty martini glass in front of him. He gingerly picked it up and stared at it before closing his eyes and taking a sip.

"You like to savor your drinks?"

He almost choked. He recognized the voice. "Theresa. What are you doing here?"

She gave a coy smile. "I thought I would come for dinner. Is it all right?" She fluttered her eyelashes.

He laughed. "Of course. Won't you join me?"

"Thank you for the invitation. I'll be glad to."

He looked at her closely. Her daytime blouse and skirt appearance had been replaced with an above the knee red dress that revealed a smooth neckline, an ample bust and a silk shawl around her shoulders. She also wore a white pearl necklace and a red purse. Her hair was down to her shoulders. On her wrist she had a white pearl bracelet. He had to work to control his hormones.

"Theresa, you're beautiful."

"Thank you. You look very nice."

"Would you like a drink?"

"A glass of white wine."

Jim hesitated. "How about a glass of champagne instead?"

"Delightful."

Jim ordered champagne and requested a table for two in the dining room. When they had been seated, he inquired, "Do you go out to eat often?"

Theresa gave a small chuckle. "Not this way. I just thought it would be worth it to see your surprised expression. I owed myself a night out."

"I'm glad you did. It's nice to have company."

Jim and Theresa continued in conversation through the dinner and coffee which followed. When they were finished, he paid and they left the restaurant.

"Charles, I drove here. I wasn't about to walk in high heels. I'll take us back to the hotel."

At the hotel, they climbed the porch stairs and stood in the foyer.

"Theresa. Thank you for having dinner with me. I had a wonderful time."

"I thank you too. I enjoyed your company. See you in the morning. Good night."

Jim undressed in his room thinking about Theresa and the dinner. His mood turned sad as he thought about Diane. "I really miss her. I've managed to put her out of my mind for too long. How can I get myself out of this mess? This Federov character is one dangerous guy. What are my options? I hide for the rest of my life or I confront him. Easier said than done. Anyway that's tomorrow's problem."

Wednesday, November 6
San Francisco, California

Adam received an early morning call from Ray. "We're all set. I'm anxious to see their security setup. I'll pick you up at your hotel and we'll go in a black and white to get around the red tape." Ray parked in a security zone and they were escorted to a closed area on the second floor of the main terminal. They were greeted by Mark Richards, District Director for the Transportation Security Administration. Introductions were made followed by Adam's request to see the video tapes associated with outgoing flights.

"I thought it would save time if we first looked at the international flights starting last Sunday morning. It's our best guess. Next would be domestic flights."

Mark Richards nodded. "It's helpful to narrow it down. There are less international than domestic flights. We can bypass the security detectors footage and just concentrate on the departure gates."

They assembled and sat in chairs in front of a bank of monitors. Richards had Eddie Post, the computer operator, place the departure flights and corresponding gates for the previous Sunday on separate monitors as he ran the video. "This camera recorded the passengers entering the gate from the terminal. Let Eddie know when you spot your man otherwise he'll keep it rolling. Boarding generally takes around an hour for the overseas flights. I'll leave you here. I have other business to take care of in the airport."

Ray and Adam occupied adjacent chairs and made themselves comfortable. They were on the third morning flight video when Adam had it stopped. "There, the tall man. Can you give us a close up?"

Ray agreed. "It does look like him. He's making no attempt to hide his features."

Adam asked. "What's the flight?"

Eddie looked at the edge of the monitor. "San Francisco direct to Toronto on United Airlines Sunday morning at seven-fifteen."

"Can we find out the passenger's name?"

Eddie worked at the keyboard. "I'll put the passenger list up for you."

Adam and Ray went through the names but none was familiar. "We have a problem. He's using an alias. Is there a camera at the United Airlines ticket counter?"

"There is but it won't help. You'll need to locate your man by process of elimination from the passenger list names and addresses. I suggest you go over there and talk to them."

Ray and Adam thanked the TSA staff and made their way over to the United Airlines offices. Ray made their requests and they were given a printout of the passengers and their addresses and phone numbers.

Ray checked the list. "Adam, there are about one hundred-eighty names on this list. If you eliminate the crew, women and children it may get a whole lot less. It seems you have a bunch of canvassing to do. Do you have anything else?"

"No thank you, Ray. The rest is up to me."

Chapter Six

MAINTAINING ROUTINES

Thursday, November 7
Alicante, Spain

Jim woke up to the makings of a sunny day. He lay in bed considering his day. He decided to put on warm ups and head for the martial arts studio. There he found a floor layout similar to Chris's studio. He met a black-belted instructor who introduced himself as Juan Ramairez and inquired about one-on-one training and signed up for a personal lesson.

Ramairez asked, "Charles, are you ready to start now?" Jim nodded.

Ramairez reached behind him into a cabinet and pulled out a dogi and black belt. "Here, go in the back, find a locker and put this on."

When Jim returned Ramairez led him over to a private area on the side of the room. "Start your warm-ups and then we'll go into some defensive movements."

They performed the traditional bow and then moved towards each other. Juan feinted and kicked out. Jim moved sideways and attacked with a kick of his own. He then sidestepped and thrusted, ducked and moved back. They proceeded to parry, attack, probe each other's strengths and weaknesses, and gradually elevated the thrust to fighting tactics and restrained attacking movements. Finally, after over an hour had passed, Juan threw up his hands. "Enough. Now join me in a cold drink and tell me where you received your training."

Jim described his daily regimen but situated the martial arts studio in Toronto.

Juan nodded. "He must be a good instructor. Do you have a job? I could use another part time instructor."

Jim shook his head. "I'm on an extent holiday. I'll be dropping in occasionally to keep in shape."

"Early mornings are the best. We get busy later on."

Jim went to get changed. As he dressed, the start of a strategy began to take shape in his mind.

Back in his hotel room Jim reread his notes on Federov. He needed to do additional Internet searches. He also wanted to go through the San Francisco newspaper Web site for mention of any bodies found in the bay. He doubted it. There was a strong likelihood Borichov had been swept out to sea by the strong currents. Federov should be wondering by now why he couldn't contact Borichov or his hit team. He'd return to the Internet café after he cleaned up.

Jim sat at the computer terminal first turning his attention to the San Francisco newspapers. He failed to turn up any homicides tied to a watery grave. He also failed to find a reference to any specific Federov company. Than an idea occurred to him. He researched car dealership businesses in Moscow looking for a status brand. There it was. A Mercedes-Benz dealer was located on Serafimovicha Street 2. From all accounts, the infamous Organization wouldn't miss an opportunity to have control over a prestigious dealership. He located its e-mail address and wrote it in a notebook.

The next challenge was to identify a meeting location. He wasn't anxious to fall into the practiced hands of ruthless men who had no compulsion in drawing out the information he possessed. He had to steer clear of Spain and Italy. What about Paris? Some place like the Eiffel Tower. No. He required an escape route where being followed would be almost impossible. He snickered attracting the attention of a nearby terminal user. He got it; dinner after ten at the legendary Maxim's Restaurant where crowded sidewalks, visitors to the Louvre, cafes, restaurants and underground trains created a natural diversion. He found the restaurant's web site and was pleased it took online reservations.

He had to get to Federov without raising the attention of any monitoring agencies. Would Federov recognize the alias used by Borichov in his passport? Possibly. He'd have to think about the wording for the e-mail sent to the car dealership and ensure the email could not be traced back to him. It presented a problem. Although he could set up a bogus e-mail account, he could not hide the transmission's origin. He would have to send the e-mail from a location preferably outside Spain. He ended the session and left the café.

Lost in thought Jim cut through an alley to avoid the street traffic. A threatening voice stuck a knife in his back and issued a warning, "Do not turn around. Hand over your money. Now."

"Hey, is this some kind of joke?"

The object's point pricked his skin. "I said now."

"Okay. Relax. I'm going to get it out of my pocket."

The knife's pressure eased. Jim withdrew his wallet and deliberately let it fall to the ground. He bent down to retrieve it, pivoted suddenly to his left and gave a vicious chop to the wrist holding the knife. The sound of the bone breaking was followed by the man's scream. Jim took his head and brought it down to his knee. The man staggered bleeding profusely from a broken nose. He collapsed and was still. Jim went through his pockets and took the man's wallet. He checked if anyone had seen or heard the confrontation. Satisfied they were unnoticed, he moved into the shadows exiting the alley and slipped away.

Jim locked the door to his room and went through the wallet. The driver's license gave the would-be robber's name and address. He was not from Alicante. He took the Euros and put the license back in the wallet. I'll get rid of this when I go out. He began to think about the message he would send to Moscow. A notion occurred to him. He went back to the wallet and removed the driver's license. Here's my e-mail identity. I wonder if this guy has an e-mail account. I'll check it out before I leave Spain to send the message.

San Francisco, California

Adam completed sending the list of names to his office with an explanation and instructions for Elaine and Marty. He walked around his hotel room and glanced out the window. It was a gray and cloudy day. Rain w as in the forecast for the next two days. He read his notes. No one had the slightest inkling where Jim might have gone. He was positive the Seattle trip was a ploy to leave without having to answer questions. Suppose he was heading for Europe. There was no doubt in his mind Jim could vanish there. It was time to have a meeting with Diane Factor to give her the details. It had been some job. He gave his thanks and goodbyes to Chris, Ray Peterson and Lt. Malone an Jim's cryptic note still haunted him. *It's not over.*

Newport Beach, California

Elaine and Marty split up the United Airlines passenger list and were using the Internet, phone directories and calls to verify names and corresponding addresses. A problem was encountered with foreign visitors and their overseas residences. In a few hours they had narrowed the search to seventeen persons. Telephone directories for cities with low populations were incomplete, a common occurrence in Canada and Europe. The widespread use and substitute for land lines by cell phones in many countries resulted in eight unverifiable persons; two Canadians, three French, two Germans and an Englishman.

Marty wondered, "Elaine, do you think we could call the authorities in those countries to verify the identities?"

She shook her head, "I think we'd run into opposition on the basis of privacy. There has to be a better way." She thought for a minute. "Marty. I got it. Let's use the search engine to access digital maps and check the authenticity of the addresses. If it's phony, we won't get a result."

"That's good. At the very least, it'll reduce the list."

They continued the elimination process until three names remained. Marty looked over them. "Now we're down to a Canadian, a German and a Frenchman."

"Why don't we further check if any of the three took a connecting flight from Toronto the same day?"

"Okay."

They accessed the passenger lists from all flights leaving from Toronto.

"We had to be stuck with one busy airport. The amount of domestic Canadian and international passengers is staggering. Let's try correlating names and let the computer do the search for a match."

They huddled in front of the computer waiting for the matching results. Finally Marty pointed at the monitor.

"Elaine, the three of them went to the Charles de Gaulle Airport in Paris on the same Lufthansa flight. My money is on the Canadian, Charles Moreno. The next question is; did any of these three make another connection?"

"Marty, now we're talking tens of thousands of passengers a day. We can try and see what turns up for the arrival day." Elaine accessed the passenger lists and resumed the matching program. The computer stopped the search and presented the outcome. "Here we go. Only the German continued on from Paris. It makes sense for him. The Frenchman departing also makes sense. It leaves the Canadian. It must be him."

"What do we do now? Do we assume he stopped or went on? I can't think of anything else we can do. You don't suppose he used his Mexican passport to go on another flight?"

"Let's try that match for Monday."

The computer search was unproductive. "We could try the same search for Tuesday."

Marty shook his head. "I think we're at a dead end. He could be in Paris or take a shuttle, bus or train from there to any part of Europe. Let's fill Adam in and see if he has any suggestions."

San Francisco, California

Adam answered the call. He listened while Elaine and Marty summarized their searches and the final outcome. "You two did a hell of a job. I've got to think it through but my gut says this time he got away clean. I'm going to write up all the events and results before I head back tomorrow. I have to brief Mrs. Factor on the findings. I hate to say it but Jim Factor has gotten away from us. Sooner or later he'll probably use one or both of his passports but we can't monitor every single flight in Europe much less the world. It'll be futile particularly since I figure he'll obtain another passport when he has a chance. He's got enough money to live on for a spell depending on where he is. And we know he's adept at finding employment. Anyway, I'll see you when I get back."

Chapter Seven

THE SYNOPSIS

Friday, November 8
Newport Beach, California

Weatherly sat in an arm chair in the living room of the Factor residence with papers in his hand and faced Diane Factor. "Go ahead, Adam."

"We last met about three weeks ago. A considerable amount of things occurred since that time. I did find Jim and then lost him. Here is a passport photo of him with his alias behind it."

Diane took the picture and sobbed as she held it against her chest. Adam stayed quiet until she regained her composure. After a few minutes, she dried her eyes and nodded to him. "I'm sorry. Please continue."

Adam proceeded with his detailed narrative describing his meeting with Chris Muncie which led to finding Jim. He described the events leading up to the encounter with the Russians. At this point he put his papers down. "Mrs. Factor, here is the part I will narrate for your ears only." He gave the account of the hostile action on Alcatraz Island the previous Saturday night.

Diane Factor clasped her hands over her mouth and listened intensely. She hadn't realized she was holding her breath until Adam mentioned they suffered only minor scratches. She exhaled slowly. He came to the part where Jim disappeared taking one of the boats.

"You're saying he left with one of them?" She questioned.

Adam nodded. "We're certain Jim killed him and carried him to one of the boats. We also believe he disposed of the body in San Francisco Bay."

"You think he learned something from this man, is that it?"

"Unfortunately, we think he found out another party is aware of him and would continue the retribution. It's the only reason for him to run again."

"What happened afterwards?"

Adam reached into his briefcase and took out a piece of paper in a plastic sheet. He handed it to Diane. She took it and read it several times, then handed it back. She wiped the tears from her eyes. Adam stayed silent. Finally, she looked up. "Please go on."

He picked up his notes and resumed, "I now believe Jim arrived in Paris under the name of Charles Moreno. Does that mean anything to you?"

"No. It sounds Italian. He loves Italy."

"Unfortunately, we have no chance of picking up his trail from Paris. He could be heading anywhere. Do you have any idea where he would go?"

"It could be France, Italy or Spain. I just don't know."

"Mrs. Factor, I would like to digress and tell you something I discovered about Jim. He made genuine friendships with whomever he dealt with and they thought a lot about him."

Diane Factor burst into tears. Adam silently waited until she became calm. She asked, "Do you have any guesses as to what he will do next?"

Adam chose his response carefully. "I'd say it was a matter of time before he will stop being passive and consider taking some kind of action."

"What do you mean?"

"He could have written the danger still exists or it's best for everyone if I leave or not say anything. But he didn't. He let it be known, 'It's not over.' I believe he's going to draw a line. These are very dangerous people with a great deal of resources."

"What do you think I should do now?"

"Wait. Sooner or later something will turn up."

"I can't begin to tell you how grateful I am for everything you have done. I feel I should go to San Francisco and meet Chris Muncie. Perhaps I will. Please send me your bill. Rest assured I won't quibble about it."

Diane walked Adam to the door and hugged him. After he left she went to Jim's study, sat in his chair and whispered a prayer to him to be careful wherever he was and whatever he was planning to do. I'll be here waiting for you when you finish. Adam Weatherly had just had verified an earlier suspicion her Jim had a specific purpose in mind and he would not let it rest.

Chapter Eight

A DANGEROUS
THRUST

Alicante, Spain

Jim returned to the Internet Café and used a search engine to discover if
the assailant had an e-mail address. He was pleased when one came up. He
copied it in his notebook and searched for the train schedule to France. He
found the next day's timetable for the express to Toulouse, France on the
coastal route which included Barcelona. It made a stop at the Alicante railway terminal. He visited Maxim's web site to check the reservation schedule
for the coming week and its Paris phone number.

At the hotel, he got out his notebook and began to compose a message
to send to the Moscow car dealership. He wrote several drafts until satisfied with the wording. He had determined a way for Federov to confirm the
meeting without exposing one another. He reviewed the final version:

> *A personal invitation for your executive management and a guest to be*
> *among the elite few to be given details of the new redesigned Mercedes-Benz*
> *E55 sedan for your security-minded customers. Please join me for dinner*
> *at Maxim's Restaurant in Paris in the evening of Friday, November 14 at*
> *10:00 p.m. Confirm through a notice on your dealership web site.*
>
> *Mikel Bronkovsky, European Vice President*

Jim closed the notebook. I'll send it when I get to France tomorrow. A week away gives me time to prepare. "Damn. This is the deadliest game of chicken I've ever played with the biggest stakes. What do you give to the person who has everything and can kill you? Oh yeah, in return I'd like you to forget I exist and let me live my life in peace without having to look over my shoulder. Good luck with that." He lay on the bed with his hands behind his head and studied the ceiling. He was interrupted by a knock on the door. He jumped up and looked around at his things. He moved to the door and called out, "Who is it?"

"Theresa."

"Okay, hold it a second." He put the notebook away and opened the door. "Hello Theresa. I've been meaning to thank you."

"When you ignored me, I thought you didn't have a good time."

"It was unintentional. I just had some things I had to do. Come in."

"You didn't even try to kiss me last night. Is there something wrong with me—or is it you?"

"No, no. I swear." Jim could feel his face getting red. He never gave his actions a thought. He stammered, "No. Really, are you kidding? You're beautiful."

She pouted. "That's better." Then she smiled. "I'm sorry. I'm having fun at your expense. Make it up to me and be my escort at a dinner party in town tonight. I know its short notice. Or do you have plans?"

"I'd be delighted to do so. I don't have a dinner suit with me but I can try to pick one up right now."

"That impresses even me. We have to be there at eight. Knock on my door downstairs fifteen minutes before."

"I'll be there."

She closed the door and left. Smiling, he put on a jacket and left the hotel in the direction of Calle de San Vincente.

Friday Night

Jim inspected his appearance in the mirror. He had purchased two expensive dark suits, white shirts and ties, socks, and dress shoes. The tailor was paid extra to do the alterations right away. While he waited he dropped into a salon and received a haircut, a manicure and pedicure. He arrived at the hotel, purchases in hand with an hour to spare. He showered, shaved and dressed. He couldn't remember when he had a suit on last. Then it came; the business meeting in Kuwait the day before he took flight.

He knocked softly on Theresa's door. She opened it and he stared at her transformation. She had on a shimmering silver clinging dress that ended at her knees and showed off her figure, silver earrings, a silver clutch purse and matching high heels. She gathered up a long silver coat and took his arm. She gave him an appreciative once over and they went out.

"I've called a taxi. I don't want to drive and we'll be drinking. Are you going to say something, anything at all? I'll even accept a whistle."

Jim laughed in spite of himself. "I'm overwhelmed by the vision before me."

"That's more like it. I approve of the way you've cleaned up. You have very good taste in clothes and you wear them well. I'm sure to be the envy of all the women there."

Theresa gave the taxi driver the address and they settled back for the ride. The cab took them to through an up-scale neighborhood to a recessed mansion surrounded by a ten-foot white block wall. A pair of iron gates in front of the driveway opened and a man with a clipboard stopped the car. He opened the rear car door. "Name please."

Theresa answered, "Senora Montoya and guest."

The security man found the name and checked it off. "Have a nice evening."

Jim and Theresa entered a large foyer. A coat check girl took her coat and gave him the receipt. They walked into a large room where there were already close to eighty guests. Jim inwardly thanked his impulse to get a dress suit. Theresa held his arm and guided him over to a group of guests. They turned and greeted one another. Theresa introduced Jim as Charles, her visitor from Canada. Jim noticed they were in their thirties and forties, tastefully dressed, and all exhibited a friendly and open manner. The conversations ranged from the weather to politics to the business climate. Waiters circled the crowd with trays of drinks and hors d'ouevres. Bars along the wall offered cocktails. Both of them took a flute of champagne and joined the group in conversation. Jim thought, "This is a night of firsts for me. Say, this is excellent champagne." He swept the room with his eyes. The room with sixteen foot ceilings easily accommodated tow hundred or more people. The walls contained both colorful modern and traditional paintings, and sculptures on marble pedestals.

He saw Theresa glance at him with a hint of mirth in her smile. He put his lips close to her ear and inquired, "Who's the host?"

Before she could answer, an announcement invited them to move to another room where there was a setting of round tables each with eight chairs. There were place cards on the linen tablecloths and bluish white chargers held white bone china dishes. The center of the tables held silver candelabras with long slender white candles. The ornate silverware glistened and Waterford water glasses and crystal wine goblets reflected the overhead lights. Waiters in traditional uniform circulated pouring wine from crystal decanters. Theresa located their seats and sat down introducing themselves to their companions.

"Theresa. What is this evening about?"

"This is an annual event held by the mayor of Alicante honoring the art and cultural patrons and benefactors for their efforts over the past year. He's quite a wealthy man."

The dinner ended and after a brief speech, they retired to the outside room which was transformed into a dance floor with an orchestra on a stage at one end. Jim danced with Theresa occasionally when she wasn't the object of other requests. Jim enjoyed the affair aware he had missed a social life in San Francisco. He checked his watch. It was close to one. Theresa came over to him.

"I think we can leave now if it's all right with you."

"Absolutely. I have things to do in the morning and I have to get up early."

Taxis waited out on the curb for the convenience of the guests. They stood in line and rode back to the hotel. Jim escorted Theresa to her room. At the door, she turned towards him and they embraced and kissed. "Thank you for a nice time, Charles."

"The pleasure was all mine. I have to get up early so I'll say goodnight."

Chapter Nine

THE DIE IS CAST, AGAIN

Saturday, November 9

Jim gathered up the material he wanted to take into France. The train departed shortly after six in the morning. At least he could catch up on his sleep during the trip.

When he exited the train in Toulouse there wasn't any difficulty finding an Internet café. He sat down at the computer, typed the message and took a deep breath. Here goes. He clicked the Send box. He signed off quickly and returned to the train station.

The train pulled into the Alicante railway terminal shortly before eleven at night. He picked up his travel bag and walked to the taxi stand. The driver was asleep in the front seat when Jim woke him up and gave him the address. In a short time, he was climbing the front stairs to the hotel. He was about to go up to his room when Theresa opened her door and startled him. "Charles. Come in." She opened her door wide.

"I won't be good company. Besides, I've been in these clothes all day. Okay, just for a few minutes."

Her room was more like a suite with a front room tastefully furnished. He walked in and sat down. "Would you like a drink or a cup of tea?"

"The tea sounds good. How come you're up so late?"

"I was waiting for you. I wasn't sure you were coming after a while. Did you complete your business?"

He nodded. "I have to see if it goes anywhere. There's a possibility I'll have to travel next week. Why were you waiting?"

"Charles, you can be so naïve. I thought you might like to rest here tonight."

He stared at her in surprise and was tongue-tied for an instant. "Uh, Theresa I appreciate the offer but I'm really afraid I wouldn't be up to it. Can I have a rain check?"

"Charles, this isn't an invitation to a bullfight." In a huff, she jumped up and opened her front door. "Go and get your sleep." He stood and walked out. She slammed the door behind him.

He climbed the stairs to his room shaking his head. What had he gotten himself into? He'd make amends tomorrow. He wondered if Federov would receive his message and understand it. How long do I wait until then? If he got it, no doubt he would think hard about responding. Well, I'll know within six days. He threw the bag on the floor, stripped and fell into bed. The last thing he remembered was the way Theresa looked in her satin and lace night gown.

Tuesday, November 12

Jim walked over to the Internet café after having another brutal martial arts session with Juan. The days, he noted, were getting colder with an increasing mid-day breeze blowing on shore from the harbor's direction. He sat down at a terminal and pulled up the Moscow Mercedes-Benz dealer's web site. He searched the site and found the insert. It read;

> *We expect to have the first details on the new Mercedes-Benz E55 luxury sedan for our security-conscious clients within a week. You can expect our executive staff to personally convey the news upon their arrival.*

There it was. The confirmation he was both looking for and dreading. He had to get airline and hotel reservations quickly for Thursday. He decided to use his Mexican identification. Since it's the real thing, I won't have to worry about being stopped. He still hadn't come up with a bargaining chip. I better come up with something good. He would pack up everything. There was no way of predicting what would transpire from the meeting but he had to anticipate the worst. He was sorry to leave such a pleasant, friendly city.

He also enjoyed the presence of Theresa and would miss her openness and easy-going manner.

Chapter Ten

THE GAMBLE

Thursday, November 14
Paris, France

Jim rrived at the Paris Orly Airport north of the city and took a taxi to the Hotel Du Louvre, a stone's throw from the famous Louvre Museum. The hotel was within walking distance to Maxim's Restaurant. He entered the hotel appreciating the colorful and tasteful décor of the lobby with the winding ascending staircase against the wall. He remembered the ornate iron-gated elevator on the side and the lounge down the hall. He gave the receptionist his confirmation number and handed over his Mexican passport. "Mr. Cassandra, how will you be paying for this room?"

"I'll pay in advance for two nights with traveler's checks and leave a deposit in the event I incur expenses in the hotel."

He accepted the room key and handed it to the porter who placed his suitcase on a trolley and led him to the elevator. Jim noticed the irony of having Borichov's expensive suitcase with him. He found the inside secret compartment useful for the passports and some of the monies. He tipped the porter and unpacked his clothes. He transferred passports and monies to the room safe and hung his top coat and clothes. He changed into casual clothes and a jacket and left the hotel.

Jim chose to pass in front of Maxim's to look for any changes. He needn't have bothered. The famous facade was the same as it had always been. He walked to the end of the block and turned the corner. He continued for a short distance and came to the open alley behind the restaurant building. He nonchalantly entered and passed a large covered dumpster behind Maxim's. There was an employee-only door and a fire escape against the wall above it. He resumed walking to the end of the block. From prior visits he recalled the bathrooms were in the rear hallway off the bar. If someone was after him, there was nowhere to hide in the alley. He would have to quickly exit the shorter side of the alley and get to the boulevard. He continued down the street to a café. He sat inside and, in French, ordered a baguette sandwich and cup of coffee. Tonight he'd eat in the hotel and retire early. Friday would be stressful while he waited for the dinner hour.

Dimitri Federov glanced out the window of his executive jet as it circled the city and proceeded in a gradual descent into Paris Orly. He stayed seated nursing a glass of vodka while the jet taxed to the corporate terminal hanger. As it parked he dropped his cigarette into the glass and put it aside. He was accompanied by three of his men. The leader, Viktor Kharkov, was seated across the aisle. He inquired. "Are we booked at the Ritz Paris with the Imperial Suite I requested?"

Viktor Kharkov stood. "All is ready." He waited for Federov to make his move. He adjusted his shoulder holster before donning his jacket. At six foot, three inches Kharkov had to bend his upper body to avoid bumping his head on the aircraft's ceiling.

"Viktor, leave the guns on the plane." Viktor nodded in deference to the order and took off his coat. He turned to the other two men. "You heard." The three took off their shoulder holsters and placed them on the seats. Viktor took off his ankle gun. He told his men. "Make sure you're clean."

Federov led the way down the front aircraft stairs to the interior of the building where he was met by a French Customs agent who recognized him from previous trips. "Welcome to Paris, sir." The passport was stamped and they left the hanger. Federov entered a chauffeured black Mercedes-Benz sedan while Viktor and his two men followed close behind in a black SUV. They drove to the Paris Ritz.

Federov made himself comfortable in the suite's front sitting area. He poured a drink from a bottle of vodka into an ice-filled glass. He waited impatiently for Viktor to complete a survey of the room with a microwave scanner. "Well?"

"It's clean, Mr. Federov."

"Sit. Have we heard anything from Sergey or Petra, or for that matter, Borichov?"

"No sir."

"Tomorrow night we will get answers."

"May I ask why you are certain this source is reliable?"

"Not many people know the identity on Borichov's other passport. This person does. I want to hear what he has to say. I don't like loose ends. He has deliberately chosen a very public place to meet. Viktor, you'll be coming in with me. Did you bring a good suit to wear?"

"Yes sir. Is it your intention I remain unarmed?"

"We will just talk. Your men will station themselves outside, one in front and one in back."

Friday, November 15

Jim reached into the room safe and withdrew Borichov's passports and two thousand Euros. He left his hotel at nine-thirty for Maxim's. He wore a top coat over his suit. He arrived at the reception desk and gave the hostess the name Mikel Bronkovsky. She checked his coat and escorted him to a table set for four at the side of the room. Jim followed paying close attention to the bar and restroom locations. The room was half full. He chose the chair with its back against the wall facing the direction of the dining room entrance. His stomach had butterflies although his hands were steady. On the hour, two large men were shown to his table. The leader was impeccably dressed in a navy blue double-breasted suit with faint white pinstripes, He was trim, black mustache with dark hair neatly groomed. The other was a refugee from an NFL team except his bulkiness was not due to fat but the way he wore his suit. All three stood and silently apprised each other before accepting the pulled out chair from the waiter.

Federov addressed him in a low voice in English with an accent. "I am Dimitri Federov. Before we say or do anything, I want to see the proof of admission."

Jim nodded and began to reach in his suit inside pocket when a large hand from the other man grabbed his arm and held it. Jim understood. With his other hand he opened the front of his jacket and showed the pocket. Then he slowly reached in, removed the two passports and slid them across the table. Federov carefully inspected them from cover to cover including the dates on the last stamped pages. He nodded to Viktor. "Okay. They're genuine. I'll hold on to them. One other thing before we start; Viktor will go with you right now to the Men's Room and examine you for a wire."

Jim got up and led the way. After a short while they returned and sat down. Viktor muttered, "He's clean."

"Excellent. Now we can enjoy a drink before we talk." He ordered three glasses of Russian vodka and Perrier water. When the drinks arrived, Federov took a sip and turned towards Jim. "Now, you will please introduce yourself."

Jim took a sip of vodka and set the glass down. "My name is James Factor." Federov raised his eyebrows at hearing the name. "Yes, I'm the person Mikhail Borichov wanted to terminate. He enlisted your two soldiers for the job. Before you judge, I would like to tell you the entire story."

"Just a moment." Federov called the waiter over and ordered a bottle of Russian vodka for the table. "Go on."

Jim began his narrative commencing with his first meeting with Carlos Sengretti at the Paris Air Show and the subsequent proposition. He gave the full account of his involvement and the decision to leave prior to the implementation of the arms smuggling scheme. He related Sengretti's phone call leading him to abandon his family and home without explanation and escape to San Francisco. He recounted the events leading up to and after the gun battle at Alcatraz Island including his deadly encounter with Borichov.

"I went to his hotel room where I found and took passports and money. Afterwards, I left for the airport heading for Europe with a counterfeit passport of my own. I was determined to find you and explain the situation."

Viktor looked at Federov and then back to Factor. Federov took a drink from his glass. "You know I can eliminate you for what you did. Besides killing my shit of a brother-in-law, you took out two good men. You have balls though, I'll give you that. Sergey and Petra were no amateurs and Borichov was no slouch himself." He looked at Viktor. "Impressive, huh Viktor? Okay. How are you called?"

"Jim."

"Okay, Jim. What am I to do with you?"

"I'd be willing to work for you for say six months as a consultant and advisor as long as it would be for legitimate matters."

Both Federov and Viktor laughed so loud nearby diners turned in their direction with both annoyance and curiosity.

"Do you know what it is we are, Jim? Our organization is hardly democratic or altruistic in nature."

Jim gravely nodded and added, "I am aware of it but you do have commercial interests such as the Moscow Mercedes-Benz car dealership."

"It was clever of you to contact me that way."

"I'm not saying you would come out empty handed. All I'm asking is a chance to redeem myself by being in your employ for six months."

"And after that?"

"I want to go home to my wife and resume what is left of my life."

Federov thought for a moment. "Let's order."

After the meal was over and coffee had been served along with brandy, Federov spoke. "Where are you staying?" Jim told him. "Do you have all of your things with you?" Jim nodded. "Tomorrow, come to the Paris Ritz Hotel at noon. You will then accompany us to Orly where we shall leave for Moscow." Jim could think of nothing to say. Federov turned to Viktor. "No harm is to come to Mr. Factor. Now may I have the check?"

Jim reached for it. "It was my invitation."

Federov smiled. "Ah, but it was for my benefit. We shall see you tomorrow." Jim noticed it was not a question. "I'll be there."

Chapter Eleven

IN FOR A PENNY

Jim arrived at the Paris Ritz Hotel well before noon and entered the lobby with his suitcase. There was no sign of Federov or his party. He went to the sitting area off the lobby and picked up an English magazine from the coffee table. He thought over the evening's conversation certain Federov had said noon. It was close to three when Federov walked through the front entrance followed by Viktor and two men. He motioned for Jim to come with them. He went out and saw Federov enter the Mercedes-Benz. Viktor and the two men went to the black SUV so Jim took his suitcase and climbed in with them.

The two vehicles drove straight to the airport and around to the corporate terminal. They went to a counter where a French Customs agent was posted. They gave their passports. Jim pulled out his Mexican passport and handed it to the agent. He stamped a page and handed it back without a word. Jim walked behind the four men and recognized the aircraft as a Gulfstream GV. They entered and moved to the rear while Federov went up to the cockpit to talk to the pilots. Viktor and the two men picked weapons off the seats and put them on. Federov came back and sat down. Jim selected an unoccupied row. The single seats were covered in classic ivory leather. A divan and a four place conference group were covered in a tan fabric. He noted the mid-cabin computer workstation with a twenty-one inch pop-up monitor.

An attendant appeared from the rear of the cabin with a tray holding a flute of champagne and one of vodka on ice with hors d'ouevres and set it on the table by Federov. The engines started whining and settled into a muffled roar. The aircraft began to move as the attendant asked Viktor and the men for their requests. Lastly she came to Jim. Viktor turned around and said something in Russian. She left as the aircraft started its roll down the runway. It lifted smoothly, turned and climbed. When it was in level flight, the attendant came with a tray with vodka and food for Viktor and the two men. She went to the rear galley and came back with a tray identical to Federov's for Jim.

Federov gave his attention to the computer and made several calls. He took a sip of champagne and swivel around to face the rear. "Jim, come up here and sit beside me."

The attendant rushed up and took Jim's tray. She placed it on the table near the chair indicated by Federov. Jim sat down and waited.

Federov advised, "Try the champagne. I picked up two cases while we were on the ground. I think you'll find it extremely pleasant."

Jim picked up the flute and drank. It was delicious and he said so.

"Are you familiar with this type of aircraft?"

"I know of it but this is my first time in a Gulfstream. It's a beautiful aircraft and appears to be very well equipped. It is the extreme long range model GV is it not?"

"Correct. We can certainly fly non-stop to Moscow if I desired but we are making a detour."

Jim wanted to ask about the destination but kept silent.

"You know how to be patient and silent besides having nerve and a sense of honor. These are good qualities. I have decided what to do with you. Viktor, come here."

When Viktor sat down, Federov continued, "We are on our way to Varna, Bulgaria. Yes, I see in your expression you recognize the city. I will leave you there with Viktor. You are to take over Borichov's entire operation. Viktor will inform them of my new ownership. Also, I noticed you have a Mexican passport. You will put it aside and receive a new passport. Pick a European country and name."

"I have a Mexican passport with the name Tomas Cassandra. I speak somewhat fluent Spanish. Can I use the same name with a Barcelona, Spain birth place?"

"Give the information to Viktor and he'll set it up. He will acquaint you with Varna and the region. He knows the language too. He will stay while you learn the ropes and set up your protection. There are unscrupulous men out in the world. I will expect you manage the company, maintain the books and make a profit."

"Borichov was going into an illegal arms transaction in South America. Are you expecting me to engage in that kind of business? I cannot do so in good faith."

"You will run a legitimate business and make a good profit. Failure is not acceptable, you understand? I will occasionally send clients and customers. My organization will audit your books at unannounced times. Are you clear on what I have explained?"

"Yes. Thank you."

"Save your thanks. I am not doing you any favors. I am doing it for myself."

Jim understood he was dismissed and returned to his seat. What had he gotten himself into? He was expected to run an arms business he had no doubt was totally illegal. He had pompously declared his aversion to breaking the law and thrust himself into a situation of his own choosing. He had to perform; there were no illusions about his fate if he failed. At least he knew the arms trade but how far would it take him? He settled back into the seat. He made progress all right, like jumping out of the frying pan into the fire.

Chapter Twelve

A NEW PLACE

Varna, Bulgaria

It was nighttime several hours later when the Gulfstream landed at Varna International Airport and taxied to the corporate terminal. Jim followed Viktor up the aisle and down the aircraft stairs onto the apron. They picked up their suitcases and walked through a terminal where a chauffeur waited with a black Mercedes-Benz sedan. They heard the plane taxi away behind them. Their luggage was placed inside the trunk as they climbed into the rear seat. Viktor conversed with the driver and leaned back.

Jim questioned Viktor. "We didn't have to go through Customs?"

He didn't turn his head. "They know Mr. Federov."

The drive took them through the city and into the mountainside. They drove up to a set of iron gates set into a ten-foot high, two-foot thick cinder block wall extending from both sides into the darkness. The driver pressed a button on the dash and the gates rolled back. The gates began closing as they passed through. The driver stopped in front of a large entrance where two men stood near large double wood doors. One hastened to the car and opened the rear door. The other went to the trunk and took the suitcases. Viktor got out and walked up the stairs without looking back. Jim followed him into the house.

He walked into a large circular room under a chandelier hung from a twelve foot high ceiling with five sets of doors along the perimeter. A wide carpeted stairway with a polished wood banister hugged the wall and ascended to the second and third floors. The man with the luggage climbed the stairs and disappeared into the second floor. Viktor motioned to Jim to follow him through the middle door. They went down a hallway into a large modern kitchen where a man dressed in white stood. Viktor said something to him and sat down at a carved wood table to one side with six chairs. Viktor pointed to a chair and Jim sat down.

"Viktor, whose house is this?"

Viktor raised a bushy eyebrow. "Yours."

"I don't understand." Then realization struck. He was taking over Borichov's estate too. Food and drink were placed in front of them and they ate in silence.

Viktor advised, "Monday morning we go to the plant."

When they had finished eating, a well-dressed man came into the kitchen and addressed Viktor. Viktor conversed with him and when the talking stopped, the man turned to Jim and said in English. "Mr. Tomas Cassandra, I am Ivan Covo, the master caretaker of the estate. Should you require anything, you have but to page me." He handed Jim a pager. "I will take you to your room now."

They walked out of the kitchen a short way and stopped. Ivan pressed a button on the wall and a door slid open to reveal a lift. The three entered and Ivan pushed a button on the side panel. Jim saw there were three floors. They exited on the second floor and walked down a long hallway. Ivan pointed at a door and Viktor went in and closed it behind him. Ivan continued down the hallway until they reached a set of carved double doors. "This is your suite Mr. Cassandra. We have already made room in the closet and hung your clothes. I will be removing Mr. Borichov's belongings tomorrow."

"Please call me Tomas." Jim said.

"Certainly Mr. Tomas. Would you want breakfast in your room or downstairs?"

"I'll get it downstairs."

"Will there be anything else?"

"Yes. I would like a tour of the estate in the morning."

"Certainly. Good night."

When the door closed, Jim inspected the suite. He quickly found his empty suitcase and checked the interior lining. He was relieved his money and passports were untouched. There was a large sitting room at the front with a television on the side. At the rear were another set of double doors which led to the bedroom. The bathroom was on one side facing the walk-in closet. On the other side, large leaded glass windows framed with deep red drapes looked out over the rear of the estate. There was another large TV on the wall. He yawned. He had to get to bed. On the night table wall he found a panel with buttons. He pushed several and the drapes closed across the windows and the lights were extinguished. Jim's thoughts drifted towards home and Diane. I bet Adam has briefed her on all that occurred in San Francisco. I wonder what Chris and Adam are doing. Within moments he was asleep.

Sunday, November 17

Jim awoke to sunlight dimly leaking from the edge of one of the drapes. He reached over and pushed a few buttons turning lights on and off until the drapes parted allowing the room to be flooded with sunlight. The opulence filled him with energy. He went to the windows and looked down at the grounds. He observed satellite dishes along the side of the house. His mood sobered as he watched a patrolling armed guard. He turned and went into the bathroom. He showered, shaved and opted for casual clothes. He went downstairs to the kitchen. On the way, he passed one of the men he had seen the previous night. The man bowed and continued on his way.

Jim finished breakfast and pressed the pager button. Ivan appeared almost instantly as if he had been standing nearby. "For the tour," Ivan informed him, "we will first go through the house and then outside." Jim was escorted through the entire house. When they were on the third floor, he was shown to the library. He was astonished by the tasteful furnishings and décor throughout. He had rather expected large oversized furniture and gaudy wall coverings. What he encountered instead was a tasteful and comfortable setting. When he mentioned it to Ivan, he was informed Borichov had the home decorated by an English interior designer.

They went outside and Ivan halted. He produced a communicator and spoke. Shortly, Viktor and an armed uniformed man joined them. Ivan introduced the head of the guards, Captain Anton Golarif. Viktor added, "The captain was formerly with the Russian Army. The estate covers over five acres. There is a tenman military barracks at the rear although many of his men live in the local area and commute. The grounds have the latest security technology including ground pressure sensors. One of Mr. Federov's companies did the work. I supervised."

Jim inquired offhandedly, "Is there an exercise room on the premises?"

Captain Golarif answered. "We have a very good one in the barracks building."

"Would you or your men mind if I used it?"

"We would be pleased if you did."

Jim thanked the men for the tour and went into the house. He wanted to do some exploring on his own in the library.

Monday, November 18

Viktor was already seated at the table drinking coffee and eating breakfast when Jim entered. The cook came over and placed waffles, syrup and coffee in front of him. Toast and jam were on the table along with a pitcher of orange juice.

Viktor threw his napkin on the table and stood. "We can leave for the plant whenever you want."

"How about fifteen minutes?" Viktor nodded and left. Jim reached for his coffee.

When he had finished, he pressed the pager button for Ivan. "I'm ready to go to the company." Ivan spoke into the communicator and the chauffeured Mercedes-Benz pulled out in front of the house. Jim and Viktor entered and sat in silence as they rode in the direction of the city.

A half hour later, the car turned on a street where an eightfoot wall, topped with barbed wire, was set back from the sidewalk. They drove for two blocks before turning into a large entrance with a guard house on the side amidst concrete cones. A steel barrier loomed in front of the car blocking entrance into the complex. Two guards with machine guns approached the car. The chauffeur talked to Viktor. Viktor rolled down his window and pointed Jim out to the guard. He issued a stream of orders. The men saluted and moved away. The steel barrier descended into the ground and the driver took the car into a parking structure. He stopped and opened the rear door allowing Jim and Viktor to exit. Jim looked up at the two-story building. There were a number of large single story buildings around them. He paused. "Viktor, it doesn't seem like a very large company."

Viktor gave a thin smile. "Mr. Tomas. Did you see the large walled areas we drove past before we turned into here?"

Jim nodded. "What of it?"

"They are the boundaries of the company. It covers a land mass of about twelve acres." Jim gasped to the amusement of Viktor. "Come. Let us go in so you can be introduced."

They entered through a bullet-proof glass doorway. A man in a well-tailored business suit waited. He handed Viktor a picture badge and motioned for Jim to follow. Jim sat on a stool and a picture was taken. He had Jim place a thumbprint on a form. He spoke in English. "If you please, write your name on this form. I will take care of the rest." He handed Jim a temporary badge. He put out his hand. "Mr. Cassandra, now that we have these formalities out of the way, I am Josef Amorusk, the general manager of Cortex International. I have already been informed by Mr. Federov of your position."

Jim shook hands. "I'm pleased to meet you. Please call me Tomas."

Viktor interrupted, "Mr. Tomas, I will leave you in Mr. Josef's capable hands. I have some friends here to visit. I will see you later."

Josef led Jim through most of the company complex. "I will leave you with my deputy, Hans Goethalz while I take some calls. We will get together for lunch in the executive dining room and I have my afternoon cleared for you. Hans was formerly president of a German manufacturing company before coming to Cortex and becoming the manufacturing department head. He speaks English as do most here. Mr. Borichov insisted on it for common communication. Hans will show you the manufactured products. He interfaces directly with the supervisors, foremen and the floor bosses."

Josef called over a heavy set man with large arms who looked as if he had been born with a scowl on his face. His demeanor was one of annoyance and hostility. He wore a shirt with the sleeves rolled up above his elbows and a nondescript tie in an opened collar. He didn't offer to shake hands and glared at Jim. They worked their way around the facility on an enclosed motorized golf cart. When they stopped, Hans led the way to the side of a building. He stopped and demanded of Jim. "What are you doing here?"

Jim taken aback replied cautiously. "I have been placed in charge of the company."

Hans moved closer. "What gives you the right to have the position I deserve?"

"Friend, whether you or I deserve this position is a moot point. I'm here and you're there. Live with it." He started to turn away. At the corner of his eye he saw Hans's fist launched at his head and managed to duck and escape most of the impact. He shook it off and backed away. Hans closed in caught up in his anger and frustration.

* * *

The encounter was witnessed by Viktor and Josef off to the side. Josef started to interrupt but Viktor held him off. "Wait."

Jim tried to reason with Hans. "Don't do something you'll regret."

The statement only served to stoke the fire within Hans. He came at Jim swinging a fist at his head. Jim dropped and pivoted letting Hans sweep by him off balance. Hans turned and rushed at Jim in order to grab and pin him. Seeing there was no other alternative, Jim went into a defensive stance and waited. At the last second, he sidestepped and struck out with his elbow making contact with Hans's head. Enraged and heedless of the blow, Hans went after him flailing his fists. Jim grabbed Hans's left arm and struck out with his foot into Hans's leg sending him to the pavement. Hans got up slowly and advanced more cautiously.

"Hans. I wouldn't advise you to come any closer." Jim entered into an offensive posture. His words bounced off the thick skin of Hans causing another violent eruption. Before Hans could close in within reach, Jim was spinning with his leg swinging like a scythe. His foot caught Hans on the side of his head and toppled the man in a heap on the ground. Hans painfully tried to get up. Jim extended his hand to him. Hans looked at him, smiled and accepted the hand. He stood unsteadily on his feet for a few seconds and wiped the blood from his mouth.

Finally he spoke. "Mr. Tomas. It appears you are the right man for the job after all. Welcome to Cortex International." This time he put out his hand and shook with Jim.

Josef turned to Viktor. "Well, well. That was a surprise." Viktor shrugged and walked away.

Josef escorted Jim to Borichov's vacated office after lunch. It was a singularly large office with an oversized desk and a conference table with eight chairs. A computer terminal sat to the side. "While you were off with Hans, I had Mr. Borichov's effects removed and stored. As you are aware, his only living relative is Mrs. Federov. How shall we start? This is new ground for me. How much do you know of Mr. Borichov's business?"

Jim replied. "I know very little about Borichov's past or current dealings or what his company does and I don't know much of small arms dealings.

My arms sales were all legal. My clients were large aerospace and defense companies. I sold major items such as airborne weapon systems, armed helicopters and such. My customers were third world countries' militaries."

"Mr. Borichov was close to Russian companies involved with manufacturing products for defense and exporting small arms particularly in Central Africa. He bought cheap and sold high. Soviet Union-financed armament companies with management willing to sell their machinery for almost nothing attracted him. He came to Varna where land and labor were cheap and set up Cortex in the mid-80s. During one trip, he came upon an abandoned Russian Illyushin Il-76 sitting at an Afghanistan airstrip and worked out a trade for it. After it was overhauled, it was used to transport machinery out of Russia and into Varna. It was also used to ship our products into Africa and the Middle East.

"The acquired machinery was associated with the precision manufacturing of small arms ordinance such as assault rifles, missile tubes, gun barrels, and artillery pieces. He took over a military light vehicle company outside of Moscow and moved their equipment here as well. We started with a version of the U.S. Humvee at first but later turned to missile and radar trailers and heavy-duty trucks. These were sold to neighboring countries and Africa.

"Mr. Borichov was heavily involved with arms dealings which were both questionable and profitable. The margins were astronomical and funded his acquisitions. Over a year ago he became occupied with one major transaction he believed had the potential for a significant gain. It fell through though he was still able to sell the weapons and settle for a small return."

"Thank you. I have some questions. What is the annual revenue and profit? How many people are employed? What sales are pending? What are the sales projections and what do they involve? What was Borichov's role in all of this?"

"First of all, in our business we deal with the USD not the local Bulgarian lev or BGL. The Euro and the English pound are acceptable currencies. Average monthly salaries are in the $250 to $300 range. The dollar is currently trading around 1.46 GBL. The company's revenue is roughly $90 million with a profit close to $20 million. Cortex employs three hundred-forty people and has a few subcontractors. We are predicting annual sales for next year of $110 million. I will have the marketing department give you the specifics later. As for Borichov, he was active in the acquisition of illegal arms deals. He wanted to get into electronics but it would have required a substantial investment. If we need electronics we contract with KAS Engineering's subsidiary, the Arsenal Company, another Varna-based company. He somewhat delegated the running of the company to myself and the executive staff."

Jim wondered. "How much of it is legitimate business?"

"I take it you're inquiring about illegal arms sales."

"I gather it represents a good portion of the overall sales."

"On a percentage basis, perhaps twenty percent. Those types of sales were fundamentally Borichov's contribution and he encouraged the marketing people to locate opportunities and pass it on to him. As I mentioned, the profit was greater for those types of sales as were the risks."

"I made it clear to Mr. Federov that I was unwilling to further pursue illegal arms sales."

Josef registered surprise, "And Mr. Federov agreed?"

"Conditionally. He strongly stated his concern is revenues and profit. Obviously, I didn't know at the time the extent of these sales and he did. Now it will be up to us to see how to change the mix. I'd like to set up meetings with the executive staff and marketing department. I want a meeting with the computer technology head. I would like to know what measures could be taken to reduce manufacturing costs. One other thing; Borichov has a large estate with servants and armed guards. What did he pay himself?"

"The expenses of his estate are funneled through the company. His personal salary was about five million USD with an expense account of two million USD."

"Let's change it as of now. Notify finance to make my salary $350,000 with a $250,000 expense account. That will be all for now. Let's get the meetings put together."

Josef reached into his pocket. "Before you go, here is your company picture badge. The blue background implies executive. I took the liberty of putting President under your name. If you wish a different title, I'll have it changed. Here is a cell phone programmed with my personal office and home numbers, and my cell phone. You will find phone numbers for Hans and Viktor and for the motor pool which controls your transportation. The security department has been informed of your position and given your photograph. Here is your new passport. Please wait a week to use it so we can enter it into the Spanish system. I neglected to tell you about the company aircraft. We'll get into that tomorrow as well. Will there be anything else?"

Jim's head was swimming with all of the information. "Forgive my manners, Josef. Tomorrow I would like to hear all about you and your background." He turned and went out the door. Viktor was waiting. "Ready to go?" he asked him.

Viktor nodded and led the way to the waiting car. Josef watched them go thinking things were going to be different for all of them.

Tuesday, November 19

Jim woke up early. He went outside and performed stretching exercises. Then he jogged around the back down to the barracks and walked in the building. He passed a recreation room with a TV and pool table and a kitchen area. The bathroom and showers were on one side. He found the exercise room. The equipment included weights and weight machines, treadmills and stationary bikes and mats. Two guards were exercising when he walked in. He got on one of the treadmills and set the speed. Soon he had increased the speed to a jog and then a run. After twenty minutes, he reduced the pace and stepped off. He went to the weights and lifted for another fifteen minutes. He moved to a rubber mat on one side of the room and began a series of martial arts stances and movements. He was bathed in sweat when he completed his regimen. One of the men in the room came over.

"Mr. Cassandra. Pardon my insolence. May I speak?"

Jim nodded.

"You know karate and such?"

"I have practiced these. Why?"

"Would you like to do the movements together? I lack a suitable partner."

Jim thought, he's setting me up. I'll bite. "It's fine with me. I haven't the time now but maybe within the next few days."

He walked away and bumped into Captain Golarif. "I see you have discovered our facilities."

"If there are no objections, I'll use it in the early morning."

The Captain was astonished. "You can use it anytime. They belong to you."

"Thank you." Jim left and went back to the house to get cleaned up and eat.

When Jim walked into the Cortex conference room the first person to greet him enthusiastically was Hans Goethalz. Josef stood to one side amused and impressed. Jim noticed Hans wore a clean suit with jacket and tie. Hans introduced him to the other men. When they were seated, Jim referred to his notes and reaffirmed his position and outlined his intent to make Cortex a legitimate business entity. They would honor existing commitments but decline any illegal arms sales henceforth. He understood the revenues and profits would suffer in the short term. They would have to attempt to recover some of the shortfall in the obvious ways; work on lowering costs, increase sales by adding to the marketing department, and developing new product lines. He welcomed their inputs and made himself available to hear recommendations.

Jim addressed the marketing department along the same lines. He challenged them to expand sales with existing customers, ferret out new opportunities, and gather information on improved and new products. He would announce a bonus system for their department within a few days.

He met with the computer technology and the manufacturing supervisors together. He reiterated the new direction of the company. Jim requested an inventory of the computer systems and software, and the manufacturing equipment with respect to increasing both quality and productivity while lowering manufacturing costs. He wanted recommendations accompanied with budget requirements. They were to consider equipment obsolescence, upgrades and new purchases. The resultant savings had to be quantified so the implementations could be prioritized.

The day had been busy and Jim sat in the president's vast office and entered his notes into the computer. The computer was brand new. He had one more item of business to attend to. He had his secretary ask Josef in for a one-on-one meeting. Josef entered and closed the door. Jim walked round the desk and sat on the chair adjacent to him. "I know I can read the personnel file Josef but I rather hear your story directly if you don't mind."

Josef sat back, crossed his legs and began his to relate his history. "I was born in the Sofia region in the eastern part of Bulgaria. I graduated from the Technical University in Sofia with a bachelor's degree in mechanical engineering and industrial management. Back in September 1941, the Soviet Union invaded Bulgaria which accounts for their influence and presence in this country. Under their umbrella, after graduation, I applied and was accepted for employment in Russia at a military arms factory where I became involved with not only development but operations. I advanced to the post of plant superintendent when I first met Borichov who was negotiating for manufacturing licenses. He offered me a management position in my native Bulgaria. This was in 1984. Eventually this company grew because of his African connections and corresponding illegal arm sales. I am married with a boy and a girl. My parents still are alive in Sofia. My salary is about 47,000 lev or 32,000 USD. Is there anything else you wish to know?"

"Have you been instructed to report on me to Mr. Federov?"

Josef nodded. "Viktor told me to send a detailed report to Mr. Federov at the end of each week."

"I see." He pulled out his cell phone and punched up Viktor. "Viktor, could you come into my office please? Thank you."

Viktor opened the door and shuffled in. "Yes?" Jim asked. "Does Josef work for me?"

"That's right."

"I see. And I work for Mr. Federov?"

"Yes."

"Therefore, any reports Josef writes go to me whereas my reports go to Mr. Federov. We eliminate the middle man. Do you wish me to inform Mr. Federov of the arrangement or. . . ?"

"I will do so."

"Thank you, Viktor. I will be with you later." Jim watched as he left and closed the door. He turned to Josef. "Now you serve only one master. Since we will be going through a transition period, I will raise your salary to fifty thousand USD. Is that satisfactory?"

Josef was shocked. "It's very generous of you. Thank you."

Jim laughed. "I'm sure before long we are both going to earn every lev. Now, as to the meetings today, have all department heads draw up their recommendations and submit it to me by Friday. You and I will select the best and follow up with requests for budget and schedule. We don't know how patient Mr. Federov will be until he sees results so we don't have much time. Now, one last question; do we have the right people running the departments? We won't fire them, just reassign them. I want you to consider reorganizing with the best person installed at each position. No one is to be shielded. Remember, both of our heads will roll if we fail."

"As a suggestion, we should put the new organization in place before we solicit their recommendations. I'll have a new chart ready for you in the morning."

"Good. I'll gather up Viktor and leave. We'll talk again tomorrow."

Once they were seated in the car and had left the plant, Viktor closed the partition between driver and passengers. "Tomas, I talked to Mr. Federov today. He asked for my opinion on how you may do." Jim looked at him with apprehension. "I told him it appears you can handle matters here and no longer need my services. I have informed him you will directly send weekly reports. He wants me back in Moscow so I leave tomorrow. Meanwhile, I have found a good companion for you. He will introduce himself soon. One last thing; I want you to wear this at all time except in the shower and perhaps even then." Viktor reached down and took off his ankle gun and handed it to Jim. "Cortex has a gun range. Practice using it continually. Understand?"

Jim accepted the gun and adjusted it on his ankle. "Thank you for everything Viktor." They shook hands.

* * *

Ivan approached Jim just before dinner. "Mr. Tomas, it is unsettling to the cook and staff when you eat dinner in the kitchen. Please avail yourself of the dining room."

Jim nodded and followed him to the dining table where a place was set at the end of the table in a formal arrangement. Two candles burned on silver candelabras on the table and the surrounding lights were dimmed. Soft music played in the background.

Jim went to the library after dinner. He sat at the desk and read the file on Cortex's products. He was more interested in its capabilities. He read a summary on the company's subcontractors. He recalled hearing KAS Engineering's subsidiary Arsenal Company manufactured the parts made from specialty material for the pistols, rifles and missile canisters Cortex manufactured under Russian licenses. He went on the Internet. He had his own ideas where additional business might reside. He deliberately ignored the standard arms markets he was so acquainted with and concentrated on the advantage of a Bulgarian-based entity His search revealed Bulgaria was concerned with keeping their aging fleet of Russian aircraft comprised of MIG-21s, MIG-29s and SU-25s operational. He noted Bulgaria had terminated their Mi-24 and Mi-17 Russian helicopters upgrade program with the Israeli company Elbit Systems, a previous client of his. Next, he pondered the status of the Russian defense industry. He knew aviation products made up half of Russia's arms exports. From his former forays in the Middle East he had heard the Russian defense industry suffered acute problems including high debt levels, old equipment and lack of qualified personnel.

It was close to midnight when Ivan knocked on the open library door. "Mr. Tomas, it is late and I understand you ordered the car for an early departure to the company. May I suggest I send a pot of tea to your room before you retire?"

Jim admired the subtlety of the reproach. He signed off and placed his notes in a briefcase he recovered from a cabinet. "Thank you. I'm on my way. By the way, Viktor leaves tomorrow. Does he have a ride to the airport?"

"I believe Captain Golarif will be taking him."

"Very well. Good night." Jim walked downstairs to his room. This was some life. He could easily understand the addictiveness of living like a prince. On the other hand, he better remember his life was on the line. Federov might have spared him once but he knew it wouldn't happen again.

Newport Beach, California

Elaine called over the office intercom. "Adam, you have a call from Chris Muncie."

Adam pressed the blinking button and smiled broadly. "Hi Chris. How's the martial arts business today? Boring I take it."

Chris chuckled over the phone. "I wouldn't have it any other way. Have you got any more information on Jim?"

Adam brought him up to date on the effort they had performed trying to find him after he landed in Paris.

"He could head anywhere in Europe by plane, train, bus or car. I'm afraid we hit a dead end."

"Do you think he'll hole up somewhere like he did here?"

"Chris, I think he's through biding his time and will go on the initiative but where and how is a big unknown. We can only wait and see if we hear something."

"Let's keep in touch. You never know."

"You got it."

Chapter Thirteen

CHANGES AT CORTEX

Wednesday, November 20
Varna, Bulgaria

Jim called Josef into his office to review the updated organizational chart. He noticed Hans retained his position. "I see you've recommended changing five of the twelve positions. Call them in and notify them and their replacements of our decision effective immediately. Reassign the former heads but let them keep their salaries conditional on their performance at their new jobs. Give raises to the replacements and let them know we expect their best. After we are through with them, post the new changes. Lastly, inform them we expect their recommendations on Friday."

They reviewed Jim's ideas for enlarging the business starting with Bulgaria's armed forces. Josef mentioned that had been considered in the past but Borichov had rejected any overture because there was little profit in it. "We didn't argue with him but we knew the Israelis weren't in it for nothing." Jim inquired about the need for the Arsenal Company citing the amount of their contracts. Josef cited their expertise and capability to create precision parts from hard alloys and polymers, an ability lacking at Cortex.

Jim considered this information. "Josef, how about checking if KAS Engineering is interested in selling the Arsenal Company. After all, I just freed up a considerable portion of Borichov's salary that added to the cash reserves. Perhaps the price may be attainable. It might be interesting to identify who their other customers are if we get that far. I'm reminded of something I encountered in the past. The Russian defense industry has a poor reputation in logistics. It was said whoever acquired Russian equipment also acquired a severe problem getting spares for repairs. This resulted in wholesale cannibalization of equipment to maintain an operational status."

"Tomas, we should have another meeting with the marketing department and run it by them. They may already have good ideas and contacts in the Bulgarian defense ministry and armed forces. We could solicit their opinions on the sales potential and find out if they have similar connections with the Russians."

"Excellent, set it up. I still have to work on a bonus system for them. Any ideas there?"

"Well we basically have each individual's sales numbers for this year and their next year's projections. Why not base the bonus on overachieving next year's figures?"

"Let's go farther. Have their department head give us the numbers from last year's performance and projection. Let's give a bonus for overachieving this past year."

"It will immediately get their attention and practically guarantee us a better year."

"Okay, when we get those numbers, we'll sit down and determine the bonus amounts."

When Josef had left the office, Jim bent over and adjusted the ankle gun holster. I should get Hans to show me the gun range. He had adjusted to having a secretary outside his office doors. "Martina, please ask Hans to come in."

Hans entered the office smiling. "Already I can do something for you."

"I understand there's a gun range on the premises. Would you show me where it is?"

"Sure. It's a good one too. We test all the firearms there."

They walked about the length of a city block and down a flight of stairs to a subterranean room. There were five slots and a counter to the side where a firearm could be loaded or unloaded. Jim reached down and pulled the gun from its holster. The range manager came up to him. "Can I see that?" Jim handed it to him. He extracted the bullets and examined their condition. "My name is Leif; I am the range manager. If you don't mind, Mr. Cassandra, I will dismantle the gun, examine the parts for wear, lubricate it and then reassemble it with fresh rounds."

After he finished, he handed the gun back to Jim. "The safety is on. Step to the nearest slot and try it." He handed Jim an ears protector and a pair of safety glasses and set the paper target range at twenty-five feet.

Jim set his feet apart and held the gun in the familiar twohand stance. He fired five rounds and stepped back holding the gun in an upward position. The paper target showed a cluster below the bull's eye. Jim looked at him for an answer. "You're used to a heavier gun. This one doesn't recoil much and it's lighter. Aim it like a flashlight." He reloaded the chamber and handed it to Jim. Jim fired another five rounds and this time they clustered in the center. Leif removed the spent cartridges and put the safety on. "Show me how you would retrieve it from its holster."

Jim replaced it in the holster and stood up. Then he reached down, raised the pants leg and pulled the gun from the holster.

The range manager put out his hand. "May I?"

Jim took off the holster and gave it to him. Leif strapped it on his ankle and stepped to one side. He dropped to the floor, left hand sliding the right pants leg up as his hand grasped and pulled the gun from the holster and the trigger was pulled five times in a fraction of a second. He got up and handed the holster and gun to Jim. "See what I mean?"

Jim nodded. "Were you in the military?" He asked.

Leif shook his head. "I was a policeman for over twenty years in some rough neighborhoods. You observed how I rapidly made myself a small target by dropping below waist level while minimizing the effort pulling and using the gun. You don't even think about not firing. Once it's out, you squeeze the trigger. You let God sort out the details after that. You should practice this move until it becomes second nature. Are you going to have a second gun?"

"Maybe."

"All right then. A box of rounds will be placed in an outside locker with your name. I'll give you a gun cleaning kit to take with you."

"Thank you for the advice, Leif. You'll see me again." Jim turned to Hans. "I can find my office, thank you."

Jim barely set foot in his office when Josef came in and announced. "Lunch time."

"Josef, we must have a company cafeteria. How about eating there today instead of the executive dining room?"

Surprised, Josef motioned for Jim to follow him.

* * *

The cafeteria was large, clean and well-lighted. He noticed two groups of card players at tables on one side of the room. It was based on the traditional style with entrées and sandwiches offered along with soda, coffee and tea. Trays were stacked at the start of the serving line. Jim picked one and moved down the line. He chose a sandwich with a Pepsi. He paid four lev to a cashier, less than $2.75. When they were seated at a table, he commented on the low food price. Josef stated the company subsidized a small part. Jim glanced around. Many of the occupants averted their eyes but clearly were surprised to see him there. After they ate, they returned to the executive suite.

Jim asked his secretary to have the company's financial officer, Abdul Shatov come to his office. When he arrived, Jim welcomed him. He remembered Abdul from the executive heads meeting. "Abdul, to save time, I'll ask a few questions on the company's economic condition. First, does the company have any long term debt?"

Abdul balanced ledgers and files on his lap but recited from memory. "None at the present. Short term debt is incurred from fronting our inventory of products and the nature of carrying contracts after the down payment in accounts receivable."

"Do we have a line of credit?"

"We maintain an LOC of ten percent of our revenues with the United Bulgarian Bank or UBB, roughly ten million USD."

"Do we have a cash reserve and how much is it?"

"We currently have a cash reserve of almost 5 million USD. However, your downward change in salary and expense account from Mr. Borichov's which we normally placed aside as an accrued liability will add to that amount by three to four million USD."

"I would like to start a personal checking account and get a credit card."

"I have your corporate credit card here for you with a limit of 100,000 USD. However, you'll have to go to the bank with your passport to open a personal account. You can fill out an application to obtain a credit card at the same time. The driver can take you there. Do you have any other questions?"

"Yes, who are the owners of Cortex?"

"Ah, we get to a delicate subject. Mr. Borichov invested his own considerable funds to purchase the company in 1984. However, he had to bring in a silent but equal partner to complete the sale because he desired a considerable portion of the land around it which in those times was cheap."

"The name of the silent partner."

"You have dealt with him. It is Mr. Federov."

"And Mr. Borichov's beneficiary?"

"It is his sister Erika who resides in Moscow and is Mrs. Federov."

"I see. Is there a Board of Directors?"

"I believe you would have to ask Mr. Federov about it."

"One last thing. I take it multiple signatures are required on large checks issued by the company. Whose signatures and what is the threshold amount?"

"Mr. Borichov was one of the co-signers. The other is myself. As for the amount, any check over five thousand USD."

"Let's change it right away. I'll replace Borichov as cosigner."

Abdul pulled out a folder and laid it on the desk. "I took the liberty of having the approval form filled out ahead of time. Please sign on the high-lighted line."

"I've run out of questions for today. Thank you for your time, Abdul."

Josef came over to Jim's office in the late afternoon to brief him on the day's events. "The new department heads are in place. There was some grumbling from the old ones but it generally pacified them when they retained their current salary with the proviso, of course. The marketing department is anxious to meet and discuss your suggestions. Do you have the time right now?"

"Let's do it."

The assembly included the marketing department head and his staff of fourteen people. The room was quiet as Jim made his way to the front and spoke to the group. "You've heard from Mr. Amorusk as to suggestions for added business. We are not relying on illegal arms sales from now on. We will fulfill our commitments and that will be that. I have nothing against being a supplier to anyone, mind you. I understand as a middle man we have to trim back the profit margin. So be it. We'll make it up in volume. We need you to find new customers and identify new product lines. We may be under-estimating the potential of the Bulgarian armed forces. We should exploit their proximity and inquire how we can assist with their requirements. Then we can challenge the engineering staff to develop solutions. This goes for our access to the Russian defense industry. Let's explore their deficiencies and see how we can fill the gap. I earlier mentioned a bonus system. I'm not thinking of a fruit basket." Jim paused to let the room have its laugh, then resumed. "The considerations to get a bonus include, for example; one, bring in regular business above your previous year's amount; two, outperform your peers; three, initiate the start of a new product; and four, sign on a new customer. Are there any questions?"

The department head stood. "Sir, will the budget be there for this increase in scope?"

"You raise a good point. Submit a revision to next year's budget and outline your requirements such as travel and new hiring if appropriate. It goes for tools such as computers and software. Conflicts in schedules and other business will be resolved by you. Thank you for your time."

The department head began to clap and was instantly joined in by the group. They filed out amid excited conversations and comments.

"Well, Josef, did they get the message?"

"I dare say they are thrilled with the prospect of showing what they can do. They have operated under the stick forever; it's a blessing to see a carrot. I really believe they will surprise us. They noticed you didn't tell them how to do their job but what was expected of them."

"We shall see. Any feedback on our query on Arsenal Company's availability from the KAS Engineering management?"

"Not yet. I can sense their dilemma. Are we proposing to buy them because we are spending too much money with them? They may think we're going to add Arsenal to Cortex at their expense. In which case, they would do well to give us a high price for the company. I'm sure we'll hear from them. There is another reason I hesitate to mention."

"Yes?"

"They think Borichov's still running Cortex and fear his connection with Mr. Federov and his organization. They may believe our offer is a first step in taking over the company. The thought of it alone will have them responding soon."

"We won't know if the price they come up with is valid. We'll need a due-diligence team if and when we get it."

"I'll have some suggestions when it happens."

"Okay, meanwhile, I'm going to conduct some private business at the bank."

Chapter Fourteen

A CONSEQUENTIAL REACTION

Thursday, November 21

It was barely past sunrise and Jim was going through exercises in the barracks building when Captain Golarif burst into the room. He threw Jim a Kevlar vest followed by a machine pistol. "Mr. Tomas. We have intruders. Two of my men are down."

Jim put on the vest and pulled the slide on the gun chambering a round. "Lead the way." They exited a side door and carefully worked their way up to the main building.

Golarif spoke into his communicator, "This is Captain Anton. Who can fill me in?" He listened. "Okay Sergeant, Mr. Tomas and I will head for the woods and come around to the front of the house. Hold your position but no firing unless you're threatened. We'll catch them in a crossfire. How many do you estimate? Shit." He turned to Jim. "There are ten of them. Stay close to me. We're going to circle around to the front. The rest of my men are alerted and will come in from the back."

They backed away and ran to the woods maintaining the house between them and the invaders. They could hear the eruption of gunfire from two directions. With the trees providing cover they ran in a crouch along the front of the estate. The rising sun highlighted men in black about one hundred feet in front firing at the guards hugging the side of the house. "Mr. Tomas, how many do you see?"

"I count seven spread out in front. If there are ten of them, we better watch our backs."

Anton spoke into his communicator. "Has anyone taken out any of them?"

"Okay, one down. We're at the front in the woods. We'll split up and start firing at them. Keep an eye out for the other two." He turned to Jim. "Stay here while I move over about fifty feet. We'll sandwich them between us and the house. If they start to withdraw by heading for the gate entrance they'll between us. Here's an extra clip."

He slipped by Jim and made his way through the woods until he was out of sight. Then Jim heard Anton start firing at the intruders. Jim used the trees for cover and fired at the closest attackers. The intruders, suddenly mindful of the assault from behind them and the possibility of an ambush, turned and backed towards the both of them. This move made them targets for the guards at the house who now advanced under a steady hail of bullets. Gunfire from the invaders shredded the tree Jim was kneeling behind. He ducked and crawled to another large tree nearer to the driveway. He looked to the side in time to see one of them coming at him. He fired a burst catching the man across the legs and into his chest. He whirled and moved away to another position as bullets flew into the space he had vacated. He shoved in the spare clip and moved again. He heard firing all around him but couldn't distinguish the sources. He knew he had moved closer to Anton. Another figure came into sight and fired at him. He dropped to his knees and fired in return. He got up and continued towards the spot where he thought Anton was stationed. Suddenly he saw him on the ground in front of him swinging his gun at him. He yelled, "Anton, it's me." The figure smiled and lowered his gun. The firing became sporadic and then stopped. Jim put the gun down and went to Anton. "Are you hit badly?"

"My arm and shoulder." Concern showed on his face. "What about you?"

"I'm okay. Did we get them all?"

Anton quizzed his men. "It's over. They have one alive." He struggled to his feet. Jim placed an arm around him and they walked into the clearing in front of the house.

His sergeant ran up to him. "We have a call to the doctor and an ambulance. We lost two men and have two wounded including you."

Anton asked. "Where is the prisoner?" They were led to a man on his knees with his hands tied behind him. "Have you learned anything yet?"

"He states they were freelance from outside Varna and claims hired to kill Mr. Borichov. We're trying to convince him to tell us who hired them. Look at their weapons." He handed the Captain an assault rifle.

Jim shrugged but Captain Anton examined it closely. "Sergeant, does this look familiar to you?"

He turned it over and opened the breech. "It's local, Captain. May I have a second with the prisoner?"

"By all means. Mr. Tomas, would you please walk me to the front?"

They heard the sing song of the ambulance's siren approaching the gate. Two of the guards went down to inspect its occupants before escorting it on to the grounds. The Sergeant returned and saluted the Captain.

"You were right, Captain."

"Thank you, Sergeant. Please see the men are taken care of. Bury the intruders' bodies in the woods beyond the barracks with a generous dosing of lye."

Jim asked. "Did you find out who hired them?"

Anton nodded. "I know who hired them but I don't know why. It was someone affiliated with a local firm, The Arsenal Company. It probably was instigated by KAS Engineering."

Jim was startled by the revelation. "What the hell?" He took in Captain Anton's discomfit. "You require attention. Let's get to the ambulance."

Anton peeled off his vest and shirt revealing a deep dark bruise on his chest where a bullet had struck the vest. He held the wound in his arm closed until the doctor applied a tourniquet. He then climbed into the ambulance and sat with his wounded men.

Jim had the last word. "Take care of yourself and rest. We'll be all right until you return." He closed the rear door. The Captain surprised him with a salute and mouthed the words. "Thank you."

Jim eyed the Sergeant. "Good work. Please thank the men for me. Where's the prisoner?"

"Sir, he died of his wounds. If you'll excuse me I'll put together a burial detail."

Jim stared at him and nodded. He was shocked by the discovery that the assault had been initiated by KAS Engineering. He thought, "Obviously, they didn't care for our interest in Arsenal. Maybe we have some leverage. I'll have to talk to Josef about it." He walked into the house to get ready for the day.

Jim went up to the library, closed the door and phoned Viktor.

"Good morning Mr. Tomas. Is there a problem?"

He related the morning's attempted assassination of Borichov and the discovery of the source behind it.

"Mr. Tomas. Please remain there while I contact Mr. Federov."

Within five minutes the phone rang. "Tomas, this is Federov. You told Viktor the story. Now please repeat it in detail to me."

Jim fully described the events of the morning and ended with the assumed reason behind the attack.

Federov listened quietly without interruption. When Jim finished, there was silence at the other end. "Tomas, I am sorry to hear the attack took the life of Mikhail Borichov. I shall fly there with his sister, my wife, to attend the funeral. Please make the necessary burial arrangements. I will have Viktor coordinate it with you." Federov hung up.

Jim puzzled with what he just heard. I didn't say Borichov was here. His phone rang again and he saw it was Viktor. "Yes?"

"Mr. Tomas. We are upset and sadden to hear of the loss of our dear friend, Mr. Borichov. Would you make sure you notify everyone immediately of the unfortunate consequence of the raid. I will fly there immediately to help with the arrangements. Mr. Federov will follow in three days. I will call when I arrive at the airport."

Jim stared at the phone. Was everybody going crazy? What was Federov up to? He began to understand Federov had an ulterior motive. Viktor would no doubt clarify it when he got here. In the meantime, he had to gather the entire staff right away and inform them of Borichov's death at the hands of the attackers.

After his announcement, everyone look sad and went back to their chores quietly. Ivan came to him and took him aside. "It is a blow to everyone here. You should wear this until after the funeral." He produced a black armband and fitted it on Jim's left upper arm over the suit jacket.

"Viktor will be coming tomorrow to assist in the funeral arrangements."

"Yes sir. I rather suspected it would be so. Will we be expecting Mr. Federov too?"

"It appears to be the case. Please have the car brought around."

Jim arrived at the plant and hurried to his office. He called Josef in right away who noticed the armband and raised his eyebrows questioningly. "Josef. Something terribly tragic occurred this morning." He related the attack upon the estate and the subsequent killing of Borichov. "Please post a notice to the employees."

"We should notify the proper authorities and the press."

"The authorities? They will ask questions and want to perform an investigation."

"I think a sizable donation to the police fund will guard against it. This will be a good opportunity to introduce you as successor. Would we expect to see Viktor?"

Jim nodded. "As soon as he can get here. He'll help with the funeral arrangements."

"I shall have the outside flag placed at half-mast and distribute armbands to the executive staff."

"Good. Close the door so we can talk. My guards determined the assault originated with KAS Engineering. You and I know the reason behind it. You were prophetic yesterday."

"I would never have thought they'd have the nerve to attempt such a bold move. I imagine they now believe our interest in acquiring Arsenal died with Borichov."

"I'm counting on it. Let's get a burial plot in the local cemetery with a headstone."

"I'm afraid there are no burial sites in the Varna municipal cemeteries. There is a crisis of space. There will have to be a decision whether to cremate him or ship the body elsewhere. Borichov was probably Eastern Orthodox. I'll line up the bishop and the city's dignitaries. Today is Thursday. I believe Monday morning would be an appropriate day. May I suggest a procession through the streets? We should consider closing the plant as well. It would be customary to have a celebration of his life. I recommend the Grand Hotel Dimyat's ballroom with food and alcohol after the ceremony."

Friday, November 22

Jim was at his desk when Viktor knocked and entered his office. Jim stood and came around to greet him. "I didn't think I would see you again so soon. I'm glad you're here."

"I noticed the flag at half-mast and the armbands. Nice touch. What else is happening?"

Jim filled him in on the preparations.

Viktor nodded approvingly. "Okay, tell me about KAS Engineering. Their upper management is located in Varna although they have large plants in and about Moscow."

"It started when I examined the books. I felt the acquisition would be a sound business move and add to our capabilities. I asked Josef to approach KAS Engineering about selling the Arsenal Company to us. The rest you know."

"Obviously, they misinterpreted and panicked. They jumped to the conclusion Borichov was going to take them over by any means and decided to conduct a preemptive strike. Mr. Federov can't take this lying down. The organization would demand revenge and retribution. This has been a busy week for you. I talked with Captain Anton on the way over. He was impressed by the way you handled yourself and the situation."

"Why did Mr. Federov have it appear Borichov was killed in the attack?"

"Sooner or later Mrs. Federov was going to be asking questions about her missing brother. Then again, there were ownership matters plus people wondering why you've taken over. This way, it's nice and clean. By the way, the Federovs will be arriving Sunday for the funeral. I recommended they stay at the house although they may want a suite at a luxury hotel."

"There is a burial problem because of the lack of space in the cemeteries. Would they want the body shipped to Moscow or settle for cremation prior to their arrival?"

"I'll ask Mr. Federov. By the way, he'll want you with him when he goes to KAS Engineering on Tuesday morning."

"Will it be safe?"

He growled. "Not for them."

"Let me see your ankle." Jim raised his right pants leg. "Good. Make sure it's a fixture. I'm going to walk around the plant. If you want me, just call."

Jim was now more at ease with the presence of Viktor. It was inconceivable they could palm off the death of Borichov to this incident but everyone was taking it at face value. Jim worried about Mrs. Federov's reaction. He glanced at the calendar. Had a week already passed? He owed Federov a weekly status report. He was going to omit Thursday's intrusion and confine his remarks to the business, He turned to the computer and typed out a one-page summary.

Saturday, November 23

Jim slept in and went down to the kitchen in mid-morning in a robe. He was not surprised to find Viktor drinking a cup of Turkish coffee and reading a newspaper. He sat down across the way and was served an omelet, juice and coffee.

Viktor notified him. "Captain Anton is back on duty."

"Already? How can it be? The arm looked pretty bad."

"He wanted to get back and see to his men. He has an arm sling. He is personally going to visit the families of the two slain men and give them a stipend. He's a good man. Oh, by the way. The guards withheld a body from the mass burial. Ivan had them put it in the meat locker. We should hear from Mr. Federov on what we do with it. I informed him a face wound made a closed casket necessary. He will relay it to Mrs. Federov and let her make the decision."

"What time does he get in tomorrow? I can drive down and picked them up if they are staying here."

"You don't have to drive. Send the company's helicopter to get them and bring them here."

"What company helicopter? I didn't know we had one. What kind is it?"

"It's a nine-passenger Ka-26 Russian civil helicopter."

"How do we access it?"

"Give your driver the information. He'll know what to do."

Jim received a call and instructions from Federov on his cell phone in late afternoon. He paged Viktor and told him of Federov's plans. They would stay at the house in the large guest suite on the second floor. They wanted Borichov cremated and the remains in an urn ready for the procession. Federov was informed the helicopter would be waiting at the airport for their arrival.

Ivan was notified of the additional guests. He assured Jim they had ample provisions of champagne, caviar and vodka. The guest room would be adequately prepared and he would add flowers. The house staff would be called in for Sunday duty. He'd arrange for a mortuary to pick up the body and have it cremated. The ashes would be delivered by nightfall. Viktor interfaced with Captain Anton with respect to the security for the estate.

Sunday, November 24

Jim nervously waited with Ivan and Captain Anton for the helicopter to arrive at the estate's front landing area. The driver had driven Viktor to the airport earlier to meet the Federovs and two bodyguards when they landed. Jim wore a suit for the occasion. Soon the sound of the approaching aircraft was heard before it was visible on the horizon. He was familiar with Russian military helicopters but was surprised to see the large commercial Russian twin three-blade rotor aircraft which appeared and settled down on the front yard. Federov disembarked first and reached in for his wife. Two servants rushed to the helicopter to retrieve their luggage. Viktor and two men followed behind. Jim was surprised to see a tall, slender woman walking gracefully beside Federov towards him. She had shoulder-long hair under a fashionable fur hat with beautiful Slavic features and wore a tasteful pants-suit and a coat with a fur collar thrown over her shoulders. Federov pointed at Jim and they came up to him. Federov made the introductions.

"Erika, this is Tomas Cassandra, the man I appointed to take Mikhail's place as president of Cortex. Tomas, meet my wife and the sister of my dearly departed brother-in-law. Have the necessary arrangements been made?"

"Everything has been done. The urn rests in the house on the mantle in the living room."

"Good. We shall have a private talk after the funeral on Monday. Meanwhile, my wife and I will freshen up. Ivan, it is nice to see you again." He nodded to Captain Anton.

The Captain bowed. "I am sorry we suffered such a terrible loss."

"Thank you. By all accounts, you and your men did well against the odds. We'll speak no more now about the matter."

The party commenced to the house as the helicopter rose in the air and climbed out of sight. Federov and his wife went to their room. She opened the closet and found their clothes had been efficiently unpacked and hung. Federov placed ice in a glass and filled it with vodka. He took out a cigarette. Erika made a face. "Dimitri, please don't smoke in here." He sighed and put it away. She looked outside the window. "Tell me about this man Tomas Cassandra."

Federov admired the fact his wife had intelligence to go with her stunning good looks. He relaxed in an arm chair. "He is a Spaniard and came highly recommended with a background in engineering. He is a military weapons and sensors expert with prior corporate experience. He was to be Mikhail's right hand man until this tragedy. I promoted him right away to ensure the company maintained continuity. He's performed admirably in a short time. Viktor told me he fought fearlessly with Captain Anton against the armed intruders. He doesn't speak Russian so we'll speak English with him. You'll have time to assess him at dinner tonight."

"You know me too well, Dimitri. My brother was a bastard but he did have a flair for business." She smiled. "Besides, if Mikhail hadn't approached you for a loan to buy the company back in 1984, I would never have met you." She spun around. "I suppose all of this is ours now. I assume you will take steps to make sure we have no more situations."

He replied sternly. "Tuesday morning. We will leave afterwards for Moscow. Monday is set aside for a day of remembrance and celebration. There is a procession with honorees and a banquet at our favorite hotel in the afternoon. I believe I'll take a nap before dinner."

Ivan had the formal dining room prepared with candles placed around the room. The dining table could accommodate twelve. The table was adorned with a lace tablecloth and matching napkins, chargers, bone china, silver and crystal glasses. A bar was outside to provide the guests with any desired refreshments. The lights were dimmed to exaggerate the candles glow. The waiters wore white shirts, black trousers and bowties, and black vests. The kitchen had prepared soup and salad choices and a combination of grilled freshly caught fish, steak and venison with various sauces.

Dimitri and Erika Federov sat on opposite ends at the head of the table. Seated in the middle on each side were Viktor, Captain Anton and Jim. Erika tapped her water glass with a knife to get their attention. "Dimitri, if you don't mind, could we alter this seating arrangement so we can all sit together in the center?"

Federov laughed at his wife's directness. "Of course, wonderful idea. This is an intimate dinner after all. Ivan, see to it while we go to the bar for drinks."

They returned and sat in the middle. Erika placed Jim at her side. Dimitri sat opposite her with Viktor and Captain Anton at his side. The conversation was light and friendly. Erika asked Jim. "Tomas, is this the first time for you in Bulgaria?"

"Yes. I haven't had a chance yet to see and appreciate Varna or the region. I plan to make time on weekends to go out and do some sightseeing."

"Where in Spain are you from?"

"Barcelona. However, my professional life has taken me away from there. I've been in the U.S., Europe, Canada and the Middle East on business."

"Are you married?"

Jim was thrown by the question. He saw Federov look his way at the question. "No, I'm not married. I'm afraid my extensive traveling makes me a rather poor candidate."

The conversation was interrupted by the serving waiters. After the dinner, Erika excused herself and returned to her room. The men went to the living room to have an after dinner drink, smoke and talk. The topics stayed away from the intruders and the plans for Tuesday morning. After an hour, Federov excused himself and left for his room. The others retired as well.

Monday, November 25

Jim, Viktor and the Federovs ate breakfast in the dining room. All were similarly dressed in black. Erika Federov wore a conservative black dress with a string of pearls around her neck. The mood was somber. They said little to one another. Ivan informed them the cars were ready for them. The Federovs rode together in one car. Jim, Captain Anton, Victor and the two bodyguards rode in an SUV. Ivan had placed the urn on the floor of the SUV.

They left for the start of the procession near the city's civic center. The armed police had erected barriers and diligently check the ID of every car entering the square. The mayor, the city council and numerous business leaders gathered by their cars. At their approach, they went over to the sedan to offer condolences to the Federovs. Then as by signal, they entered their cars and drove through the city in a procession.

They stopped at the Eastern Orthodox Church where a dais has been placed and the bishop stood and watched their arrival. Jim carried the urn with him. They assembled in front of the bishop. His amplified remarks and prayers were offered for a short interval. Then he blessed the urn and the multitude and bade them go to the hotel to celebrate the life of Mikhail Borichov. Everyone enthusiastically entered their cars for the drive to the hotel and an afternoon of eating, drinking and conversation.

Tuesday, November 26

After breakfast, Federov bid his wife goodbye. She squeezed his arm in a sign of affection and encouragement. Jim prepared to climb in the SUV but Federov stopped him. "Tomas, Viktor, please join me."

They entered the car and drove out of the driveway. Viktor talked to someone on his cell phone. He closed it and turned to Federov. "They're there."

Federov nodded. "Tomas, it is my intent to make the principal owner of KAS Engineering pay dearly for his transgression." He reached in his brief-case and handed a file folder to Jim. "I had this legal document drawn up in English for them to sign. It turns over the Arsenal Company to Cortex International. You will see there is no sale price. In addition, it is to be debt free with no accounts payable. All customers and account receivables go with the transfer as do Arsenal's bank accounts." Jim skimmed over it and returned it to Federov who replaced it in his briefcase. "You will be introduced as the new Cortex president. Viktor and his men will be our witnesses."

Jim silently wondered what the KAS management's reaction would be to this pirating of their valuable subsidiary. He didn't think they are going to be happy or agreeable.

They arrived at the KAS Engineering headquarters. It was an imposing modern multi-story building. An armed guard obviously in charge came and stopped them from entering. Viktor took the lead. "I will explain it to him." He whispered to the guard and pointed to Federov. The guard promptly stepped to one side and saluted. The four of them walked in and were escorted past armed guards to the third floor of the building and the executive offices. The title on the brass plate read, *Karlov Statsky, President.*

Federov ignored the secretary, opened the door and walked directly to the desk. A large overweight man smoking a cigar and writing looked up. His cigar dropped out of his mouth and turned pale. He leapt out of the chair and went around the desk extending his hand. Federov ignored the hand and pointed to the desk chair. "Go back and sit, Statsky. We have some business. He laid his gloves on the edge of the desk and pulled out the file folder. "Please read this over, then sign it. We will require a witness from your company, of course."

Karlov Statsky hand began to shake. "But this agreement is incomplete. Where is the compensation for Arsenal Company stated?"

Federov patiently listened. "Statsky, you are not stupid. You know who I am, what I represent and why I'm here. Call someone in here right now to witness your signature or by this evening all traces of you, your family and your relatives will cease to exist."

Statsky appealed. "I need the board's approval."

"Come, come. You are the principal stockholder and chairman of the board. I believe you are aware it is all that's required. Call your witness. Viktor, hold the paper steady for him to sign." Viktor withdrew a small caliber gun with a silencer from his coat pocket and weighted one side of the document.

A well-dressed man entered the room and looked nervously around. Statsky conceded defeat with a sinister stare at Federov and Jim. He picked up his pen and signed and dated the agreement. Federov addressed the man. "What is your name?"

"Boris Sidorov."

"Well, Sidorov, go over to the desk and witness Statsky's signature with your own and date it." The man avoided Statsky's eyes while he obeyed. Federov bent over the desk took the paper and signed his own name. "There, nice and legal. We'll leave you to change your organizational structure."

Viktor picked up the gun. Federov turned and walked out of the office followed by them. Halfway to the stairs, he turned to Viktor. "I forgot my gloves. Go back and get them for me." He continued down the stairs to the street.

Viktor returned to the office and interrupted Statsky as he started to talk on the phone. "Mr. Federov forgot these." He picked up the gloves. Statsky impatiently waved him out. Viktor reached in his pocket and withdrew the gun. In one motion he placed it against Statsky's temple and pulled the trigger. Statsky's head fell onto the desk. Viktor placed the gun in Statsky's hand and left closing the door behind him. He walked to the car and gave Federov his gloves with a nod.

Boris Sidorov watched them leave from the window. He went back to Karlov Statsky's office and realized what had happened. He closed the door and retreated to his office across the hall. He closed and locked the door. He lifted the phone and dialed a number. "Jakob. This is Boris. We just had the fallout from going after Borichov." Boris described the events including the loss of the Arsenal Company to Federov. "Cortex has a new president whom Federov has placed in charge. I don't know who he is or where he came from. We'll get more information on him. What are we going to do about it?" He listened intently and silently nodded agreement. "I understand. When the time is right we'll get our revenge. We have to wait until we can get Federov at the same time."

Federov directed the driver to go back to the house. He looked at the signed document. "I will have my lawyers file the change of ownership with the Bulgarian authorities when I get back to Moscow. When we arrive at the house, I wish to talk privately with you, Tomas." He settled back in his seat.

They went to the library and Jim closed the door. They both sunk into comfortable chairs. Federov lit a cigarette. "Tomas, you have been here slightly over a week and have increased the value of Cortex by at least $20 million, witnessed the untimely death and funeral of President Borichov, and implemented changes in strategy and company direction. I still expect to see an increase in revenues and profits. Oh, by the way, I have well-placed friends in a few of Mother Russia's defense companies. They could use help from Cortex as you have suggested. I will have them contact you for a meeting soon."

Jim was astonished at the depth of knowledge Federov possessed concerning his activities during the previous week. All he could think to say was, "Thank you." Jim noted the Federov luggage in the front hall and heard the distinctive sound of the twin turbo-engines of the helicopter as it settled to the ground. Mrs. Federov was dressed impeccably in a rust colored pants suit. She came over to Jim and kissed him on both cheeks. "I expect you will perform admirably. My husband has great faith in you. Thank you for your hospitality. Perhaps when you visit Moscow, you will allow us to return the favor." She said goodbye to Ivan and went out to join Federov who was opening the helicopter door.

Viktor passed by him and hit his arm. "Keep safe." He looked down at Jim's ankle and smiled. He and his men walked to the helicopter and entered. The door closed and soon after it rose and climbed into the clouds.

Jim checked the time. He still had the afternoon available. He paged the car and rode to the plant. He went straight to his office and found Josef waiting for him. "Tomas, did you hear the news?"

Jim thought, he couldn't know what happened. "No. What news?"

"Karlov Statsky shot himself this morning. He is or was the president of KAS Engineering. This is going to put a damper on our acquisition of Arsenal Company."

My God, that's why Viktor returned to Statsky's office; he left a message from Federov. The witness he insisted upon was used to pass it along. I guess my news about Arsenal better wait.

"Josef, that's awful. We'll have to wait and see what happens. Meanwhile, I talked to Mr. Federov and he mentioned he has contacts and friends in the Russian defense industry. I wouldn't be surprised to get a call inquiring about our capabilities. I'm going over to the gun range. I'll be back in a while."

He found Leif testing some assault rifles. "He saw Jim, instantly stopped what he was doing and came over. "More practice, Mr. Cassandra?"

"Not today Leif. I want you to order me a Glock 17 with a shoulder holster."

"Any particular reason for a Glock instead of a Beretta or H&K?"

"I'm used to it, thanks." He left and returned to his office. He called his secretary. "Martina, is there a safe in my office?"

She came in and closed the door. "Yes, sir." She went to a painting on the wall and pulled one side out. The picture was hinged and revealed a combination safe.

"Who has the combination?"

"Only myself since Mr. Borichov is deceased. She wrote it down so he could memorize it. There is a counter inside that gives the date and time the safe is open as a precautionary measure."

Jim entered the combination and opened the safe. He saw an LED readout that gave the date and time it was last opened. He wanted to go through it alone. "Thank you Martina. That's all." When she was gone he searched through and found files on a number of people including himself, Dimitri Federov, Josef Amorusk and Carlos Sengretti. He read his personnel file and was alarmed how much personal information had been collected. He took his file out and shredded it. He opened a box and found currencies of Bulgarian levs, Euros, and dollars stacked with a divider in between. There was a ledger detailing payoff amounts to names in alphabetical order going back almost ten years. "I'll keep the Glock in here during the day." He thought, closed and secured the safe, then swung the painting back against the wall.

He thought about the day's events. Federov had Statsky killed. Then there was the assault prisoner that conveniently died of wounds. What had happened to him to be able to accept these actions? He was in a Russian style wild and woolly west. Still, it was an ominous reminder to worry about his own skin if he didn't produce. There was absolutely no doubt in his mind he was expendable if he failed to measure up. On the other hand, there was a real possibility of returning home and never having to worry about a threat. He resolved to last the six months.

Jim recalled something which had slipped his mind. He wandered over to Josef's office. Jim saw a much smaller office made smaller by standing white boards and cork panels on the walls covered with notes. His desk was piled with folders. "Josef, what kind of filing system are you using?"

Josef rolled his eyes up and swept his hand about. "I know it looks disorganized but I know where everything is. The downside is I can't let the cleaning people in here for fear they'll disrupt my system. What may I do for you?"

"Tell me about the Cortex aircraft. I was exposed to one yesterday, the helicopter."

"Sorry, it slipped my mind. Sit down and let me get you the file on them."

"Them? There's more than one?"

He placed a file in front of Jim. "Let's start with this one, the Ilyushin Il-76. We use it as a commercial freighter. It's a fourengine aircraft Borichov picked up for a pittance, a victim of the Soviet Union collapse. It's been invaluable for our deliveries of product. It's capable of coping with the worst weather conditions likely to be experienced. It can carry a payload of for-ty tons over a range of two thousand seven hundred nautical miles in less than six hours and able to operate from short and unprepared airstrips. It's maintained at the Varna International Airport. The upkeep is absorbed by hiring it out to other companies on a retainer basis. The third one is the Can-adair Challenger 601-3A executive jet. It was Mr. Borichov's primary mode of transportation for trips on the continent. It's a twin-engine, wide-body aircraft capable of carrying eight to twelve passengers up to four thousand nautical miles. It has a rather handsome interior with a full complement of avionics. It's hangered at the airport too. Its excellent range attracted Borichov since Moscow is about one thousand two hundred nautical miles from Varna."

"Impressive. I'll keep them in mind."

Chapter Fifteen

NEW PRESENCES

Martina intercepted him as he returned to his office and announced in a muted voice. "Mr. Tomas, there is a sinister looking man waiting in your office. He wouldn't listen to me to wait outside. Shall I call security?"

"Let me see who it is and what he wants first. I'll keep my door open." He walked in and saw the man sitting on a chair by the desk. His broad shoulders and large head dominated the chair.

Without turning around the man remarked, "You should walk on the balls of your feet so you can retain the advantage when a person has his back to you."

"You have the advantage of me before we start. Who are you?"

The man got up and faced him. "Mr. Tomas, my name is Leonid Andreev, your bodyguard. Viktor Kharkov sent me."

"How do I know that?"

"You have his ankle gun on your right leg."

Jim smiled and held out his hand. It became lost in the grasp of the man. He radiated both strength and danger. "I never had a full time bodyguard before. I imagine I have a lot to learn."

"That makes two of us. The first lesson is to treat me as your shadow. You know it's there but you ignore its presence."

"Fine, tell me about yourself so I can gauge the length of my shadow."

"I have been in the Russian army for most of my adult life and seen action in Africa and the Middle East. I speak several languages. I was in the employ of a competitor of Mr. Federov in a similar capacity but found his brutality senseless and destructive. I contacted Viktor about employment in the organization and he referred me to you."

"I don't know I'll need you but it's a comforting thought after what I've been through this past week. Welcome to the party."

"Thank you. At first you'll be conscious of me but I assure you it will shortly pass and you will forget I am here. I need to contact your head of security and then I will be back." He left the office.

"Well, this is a new experience." He sat at his desk and lost himself in documents relating to Cortex's business capabilities and products.

In the afternoon Josef knocked on Jim's office door and walked in. He stopped suddenly sensing someone at his side. He turned and gasped at the man staring at him. He turned to Jim. "I hope he's with you and that he's friendly."

Jim laughed and introduced them. "He told me to ignore him but easier said than done. What's up?"

"As you are aware, we manufacture Russian military hardware under license. One of these is the Kalashnikov AK-47 assault rifle from the Izhmash Concern."

"I know it's reputed to be the most widespread, most copied assault rifle design in the world."

"You have no idea. It's estimated the number of AK-47s manufactured since 1947 is one for every six people in the world. It has been a mainstay for us with a unit price in excess of 800 USD. In the 1990's the weapon-cartridge complex of Kalashnikov and the Barnaul Machine-Tool Building Plant developed the unified complex of Kalashnikov AK-100 assault rifles chambered for domestic and NATO cartridges. A member of our marketing department has for years tried unsuccessful to obtain the license for it until today. They have agreed to sell us the license. That's the good news."

"There's bad news?"

"Modern machinery is needed to make the AK-100 gun barrels and parts from highly strong polymers for increased wear resistance. This is the area the Arsenal Company specializes in with their advanced tooling and processes. Now we are faced with an uncertain contracting future with KAS Engineering in the light of recent events."

Jim exerted a superhuman effort to maintain a straight face. "Let's see how it plays out. Have we received the license offer in writing?"

Josef nodded. "I have it being translated in English and Bulgarian for our lawyers."

Jim nodded agreement. "Let me have a copy when it's ready. That's excellent news. It means we can expect a wider distribution for the product. Any idea of the unit price yet?"

"Not until the engineers at Arsenal can get at it."

"Josef, I'd like to meet this persistent marketing person. Have the marketing head bring him tomorrow to join us in the executive lunchroom."

"It's a splendid idea. I'll let them know."

When Josef had left, Jim pondered calling Federov to inquire as to the status of the Arsenal acquisition but rejected the notion. *He'll let me know soon enough.* He punched a number on his cell. "Ivan, we'll have another guest staying at the house for a while. His name is Leonid Andreev. Place him in the guestroom Viktor has used. He'll be arriving with me tonight." He returned to his reading.

Boris Sidorov occupied the General Manager chair at KAS Engineering and took over as acting president to maintain the business continuity until the Board selected a successor. He presumed he had the best chance but there were significant principals in the picture. His private phone rang.

"Boris. This is Jakob. We'll meet this weekend to discuss our response to the pirating."

Sidorov hung up with a sneer. *At last we'll make sure they pay for their mitigating treachery.*

Wednesday, November 27

Jim awoke early, put on warm-ups and sneakers and crept downstairs and out the door. He started jogging to the barracks and heard a sound behind him. Leonid had on a pair of jeans and sweatshirt and ran up to join him. "Are we going to the barracks?"

Jim smiled and resumed his jog. He went to the exercise room and started working out while Leonid went to the weights and began lifts.

The guard who had spoken to him the last time entered. "Mr. Tomas, would you like to work out for a while on the mat?"

He led the way. They faced each other, mutually bowed and commenced to circle each other cautiously. The guard suddenly made a thrust at Jim's head. Jim sidestepped and delivered a spinning kick under his opponent's chin. The guard entered a defensive stance and Jim went through attack movements. Then he entered a defensive stance and his opponent went on the offensive. After twenty minutes they stopped and were applauded by guards who had heard the sounds and viewed the exhibition. They each bowed, then shook hands. Jim thanked the guard and he and Leonid went back to the house.

Jim was seated in the kitchen with Leonid eating breakfast when Ivan came into the kitchen. "I see Leonid has quickly adopted Viktor's routine."

Jim grinned and asked, "Ivan, do you know an excellent tailor in Varna? I would like to have suits fitted along with obtaining accessories."

"As a matter of fact, I do. Mr. Borichov had an excellent English-trained tailor in Varna. The driver knows the store. I'll call ahead and inform him you will require his attention. Today?"

"Yes. I prefer the afternoon."

"He'll be waiting for you."

"One more thing. I'm wondering if it's possible to find a turkey for tomorrow night's dinner."

"Are you celebrating the American Thanksgiving, sir? "I've became accustom to it."

Ivan called the cook over. "Mr. Tomas would like to have a turkey dinner tomorrow night." Ivan walked to the back of the kitchen with the cook and stood by while he made a telephone call. After a few minutes, Ivan came back to the table with a smile. "The cook informs me he can have three turkeys delivered by noon tomorrow. With your permission he will make it for the staff and the guards as well. He says he has a wonderful recipe for the stuffing."

Jim rose from the table. "Thank you both. I look forward to it." He went to his room to get ready for the day.

Jim entered his office with Leonid at his heels. He hung his coat and sat at the desk. He took out yesterday's documents and read. An hour later he was interrupted by Martina. "A call from Moscow, sir."

Jim pickedup the phone. "This is Tomas Cassandra." He listened and spoke for a few minutes. "Please send me a confirmation by fax right away." He hung up and within minutes heard the fax spilling out several sheets of papers. When it was still, he picked them up and read through them. Satisfied, he called for Josef.

Josef entered his office and sat down.

"I have some news requiring our instant attention." Josef eagerly leaned forward to listen.

"Effective immediately, Cortex International has acquired the Arsenal Company."

Josef jumped up. "Shit." He sat down slowly. "I mean what wonderful news. This is quite a coup for the company and the timing is impeccable."

"Your wording is quite apropos. What percentage of Arsenal's business is ours and what do you think is KAS?"

Josef thought it over. "My guess is we account for ten percent. KAS business, I don't know, maybe twenty percent."

"It would mean seventy percent comes from outside sources."

"Probably. What do you have in mind?"

"We need to integrate Arsenal into Cortex as soon as possible. If we had to bring them in-house it would be a lengthy and disruptive process. In addition, we would give KAS Engineering and their other customers' time to consider a replacement. I want to keep their business structure intact and establish them as a separate profit and loss center. Hopefully their pricing and interfaces can be maintained. If Arsenal can hold KAS Engineering's business, it means we'll have them by the balls. We have to get Abdul into their financials immediately. Any idea how long an audit will take?"

"If his department is authorized to work this weekend, perhaps by Monday."

"Done. I want to have their revenues, financial breakdowns, contractual obligations, sales projections, budgets and manpower. Have Arsenal deliver their records to us by tomorrow. Who would we put in charge of them?"

"I would recommend Hans Goethalz. He'll be ecstatic. He's been interfacing with them all along."

"Have Hans and Abdul report to us after you get started. Don't forget we have a lunchtime marketing guest."

"I won't. We should put out a press announcement. We have person in personnel. Should I have him do it? He'll run the copy by you first."

"Go ahead."

Martina entered his office and stated Leif had left word his order had arrived. Jim motioned to Leonid to follow him. "You'll like this part of the week."

They entered the gun range. Leif came over with a box. He inspected Leonid. "What are you carrying?"

Leonid pulled out a SIG Sauer P226. Jim noted. "I had a friend who swore by his."

Leif asked. "Cartridge?"

".357 SIG."

"I'll get a box for you in a minute." He opened the package and took out a Glock 17C and the holster. He gave it to Jim who examined it. "This is the one." He took off his suit coat, hung it up and pulled on the holster. He pulled the magazine. Leif gave him a box of 9mm cartridges. Jim loaded the rounds and inserted it into the handle. He stepped to a slot and set the paper target at twentyfive feet. He put on the ears and eye protectors and fired the entire magazine. He put the gun at his side and brought in the target. The spacing of the ten rounds was within a five-inch circle. Leif and Leonid nodded approvingly. While Jim cleaned the gun, Leonid stepped up to the slot inserted a fresh paper target and moved it out to seventy-five feet. He fired the twelve rounds and then brought in the target. The holes were within a five-inch circle. Leif, not wanting to be left out went to a cabinet and returned with a Beretta 92FS. He loaded the magazine with ten rounds and entered the slot. Another paper target was positioned, this time at the one hundred-foot marker. Leif put on the ear protector and fired rapidly. He drew in the target. The grouping was within a one-inch circle. Leonid whistled. They took the guns to the counter and cleaned them. Leif put the boxes of rounds away after Jim and Leonid had reloaded their weapons, this time with hollow point rounds.

"How are you doing with the ankle gun, Mr. Tomas?"

"Practicing the move. It's become smoother and faster now."

"Good." He stuck out his hand to Leonid. "I'm Leif, the gun range manager."

"Leonid Andreev. I'm with Mr. Tomas."

Leif understood right away. "Feel free to come and use the range anytime."

Jim glanced at his watch. "Leonid, I have a tailor appointment." He pushed the button on the cell phone and asked for the car. He left the guns in the office safe.

Jim was measured by the tailor for suits, shirts, and shoes. He picked out two hats, a robe, warm-up suit, shirts, underwear, belts, socks and ties. He bought a cashmere topcoat with scarves and gloves. He examined fabrics and color and made his preferences known. Lastly, he ordered a tuxedo, evening clothes and an evening coat. He made sure some of the shirts had French cuffs and picked out a set of gold and onyx cufflinks. "Leonid, get what you like. It's on me." The bill came to close to twenty thousand lev or about thirteen thousand seven hundred USD. Jim tipped the tailor generously. He took the accessories and gave the tailor a phone number to call when the order was completed. As Jim was driven back to the plant he was pleased at the way he had rapidly adapted to these circumstances considering the dire consequence of failure.

Chapter Sixteen

DEALING WITH AN ACQUISTION

Josef showed Hans and Abdul into Jim's office. The four sat around the conference table. The excitement of having Arsenal in the fold clearly was evident in Hans's demeanor. Jim made his position known. "In order to get Arsenal on board as soon as possible, I want to make them a separate P&L center."

Abdul responded. "We've never done it before but I can see the advantages."

"Hans, our personnel department will be obtaining their management and employees files. Go through them carefully and if you feel you want to interview them, do so. Cut loose anybody you think may be substandard or trouble. Decide on your reports. They are geographically in a different part of the city. You're going to have to make sure of your selection since you're going to head them. You've heard the good news on the Kalashnikov license. We're going to have to gear up. I want to know when we can have a production line. We have to plan to shut down the AK47 line as soon as our sales commitments are completed. I realize it will take time to get the logistics in place. Get a preliminary schedule to us so we can carve out a budget. Oh, and no purchases over five thousand USD go out of Arsenal from now on without your review and co-signature.

"Abdul, you're the second part of the management oversight. Locate their financial head and completely audit their books with him. See if there has been any tampering or improprieties. Evaluate his performance. If you determine he's competent and honest, make him your deputy. I am anxious to get their revenues and profit figures. We want to place a value on them. The agreement states we get none of their outstanding debt. Make sure of it. Change the check approval process. No checks go out over five thousand USD without your co-signature on them. I have approved weekend work for your respective departments. I want the preliminary reports from both of you by Monday and a final report by the end of next week. Are there any questions or comments?"

Abdul spoke first. "I have to calculate the accrued liability to Cortex. Besides the expense of adopting Arsenal into our company, I must know the purchase price."

Jim paused to consider his answer. "There is no charge to Cortex. The payment was made by Mr. Federov." He waited. "Nothing else? Thank you."

When they had left, he addressed Josef. "It occurs to me I forgot to include marketing. I would like to get Arsenal's marketing strategy and annual sales projections. Meet with our marketing head and have him also interface over the weekend with his Arsenal counterpart. I want his report on Monday too. I want to have a complete picture of their growth estimates before the end of next week."

He glanced at Leonid. "It's time to get out of here." He opened the safe, took his jacket off and put on the guns. He closed the safe and pressed the cell number. They left for the waiting car.

Thursday, November 28

In the morning, Jim walked down the stairs from his room and stopped short in the hallway. He couldn't believe he was seeing a large colored cutout of a turkey on the table under the chandelier. He laughed. Above the entrance into the kitchen was a sign with colored letters proclaiming Happy Thanksgiving. He walked in and called Ivan. "That was a thoughtful thing to do. Thank you. Who was the artist?"

"One of the staff went to art school."

"Tell them I appreciate their effort."

As usual, Leonid was there ahead of him. "Leonid, what is it with Viktor and you getting here before me?"

"We're hungrier."

At the office Josef greeted him with the daily Varna newspaper. He showed the Cortex article on the Arsenal acquisition to Jim. "Not bad. It made the first page of the business section. By the way, Karlov Statsky's funeral is tomorrow. Do you want anyone from here to go?"

Jim thought for a moment. "No, just send flowers. Pass the word that Arsenal stays open. Anything else going on?"

"Quiet at the moment."

Jim returned from a walk about the complex to get acquainted with their product lines. Martina informed him there was a Mr. Oleg Volkov from the Irkut Corporation on the line. The name didn't mean anything. He quickly mouthed to her to look it up. He sat in his chair and introduced himself.

The voice on the phone was gruff and talked in broken English. "Mr. Tomas Cassandra, president of Cortex International?"

"Yes, that's right. And you are?"

"Oleg Volkov, vice president of manufacturing for the Irkut Corporation."

Martina rushed in with an open folder. Jim quickly scanned it and gulped when he read Irkut was affiliated with the Sukhoi Corporation, a multi-billion dollar Russian warplane maker headquartered in Moscow.

He recovered quickly. "I am familiar with your company and honored you called. How may I help you?"

"I received the information on your company and your acquisition of the Arsenal Company from a mutual friend. He tells me Cortex is in a unique position to specialize in high-end, low volume and hard-to-build parts, and in production of low-price commodity parts. The demand for our commercial, military and private airplanes is creating a shortfall in acquiring timely aircraft parts, an unacceptable situation for the corporation. Can you meet with me and my staff next Wednesday to discuss this matter further?"

"I'll free up my calendar. Where and what time would you like to meet?"

"Here at our headquarters at ten. I will have my secretary fax the necessary contact information to you."

"Thank you. I'll be there."

He called out. "Martina, get me Josef please."

When Josef entered, Jim related the telephone conversation. "The call had to be initiated by Mr. Federov. Any thoughts on it?"

"It sounds like a wonderful business opportunity. We'll need to prepare a presentation covering our capabilities including Arsenal's. I'll get the art department on it. If Irkut knows what they want to farm out, we can request the technical specifications and a sample for every component, part or subassembly. In order to price it after we examine them, we'll need to get quantity and schedule from them. Unless they want to ship us existing tooling, we have to consider the setup costs. You should plan to arrive the day before. It'll a good opportunity to get familiar with the Challenger during the five hour flight. I'll notify the aircraft crew to plan the trip. What about a place to stay?"

"I'll contact Mr. Federov and get his recommendation. Should I bring any experts with me?"

"It doesn't sound like this meeting requires anything of the sort. It should hold until after we get our hands on the data."

"I'd like to get the Arsenal information to take with me."

Jim closed his office door and called Federov's number. He was surprised when Federov personally answered. "Hello Tomas. No problem's I hope."

"None. I called for two reasons. I received a call from Mr. Oleg Volkov of Irkut. Thank you for the referral. I have a meeting with him scheduled for next Wednesday morning in Moscow."

"Excellent. And the second reason?"

"Can you recommend a hotel in Moscow where I can get a room on short notice?

"Of course. I'll have the reservation made and send you the information. What are you doing with the new acquisition?"

"In the interest of time and efficiency, I'm making it an independent profit and loss center. It would permit a seamless integration and at the same time maintain their customers including KAS."

"Very wise. Good luck with it. Goodbye."

By late afternoon, Jim had received information from both Oleg Volkov and Federov. Volkov left the Irkut's corporate address and phone number. He requested Jim inform them where he would be staying and they would send a car for him an hour before the meeting. Federov made a reservation at the five-star Metropol Hotel and enclosed the address. He instructed Jim's flight be planned to arrive at the Moscow Airport corporate terminal no later than four on Tuesday afternoon.

Jim leaned back in his chair and took in his spacious office. I could really get used to this good life. I've got everything falling in place and the company is poised to make a good profit the way things are going. He was already looking forward to flying on the private jet to a meeting with the vice president of a billion dollar corporation. He even had a car picking him up and chauffeuring him around. He was also thinking about the special dinner being served in the evening especially for him at his mansion. He had ordered his custom-made suits just in time for the trip. Almost two weeks into this job and things couldn't be running smoother. I think I'll leave for home and enjoy a good drink before dinner.

The Thanksgiving dinner lasted until midnight. The meal was accompanied by all the trimmings with wine and after dinner drinks. Jim stumbled into bed and fell asleep before he undressed.

Friday, November 29

Jim woke up late to a throbbing head and stomach cramps. It hurt to move his eyes and his mouth tasted terrible. He found himself nauseous and barely made it to the toilet before he vomited. What in the goddamn hell got into him? He rinsed his mouth out and brushed his teeth twice. I need a bucket of coffee. He called the kitchen and asked them to send breakfast to his room. He fell back in bed. I'm not going anywhere until I get sober. I'll get on the treadmill after I eat. He called Leonid and informed him he had to get himself together before they left for the plant.

He assessed the day and night before. What was he thinking of? He had let this opulent lifestyle go to his head. He was there living on borrowed time for only one reason; to clear the slate with Federov. All of this was temporary and it hinged on a successful performance. Do your best and get rid of your illusions. He wasn't going to repeat last night's performance anytime soon if he could help it. As it was he had a full plate with the new AK-100 license, Arsenal acquisition, and the trip to Moscow.

He felt better after a half-hour run on the treadmill. He showered and dressed. He noted the breakfast dishes had been removed from his room. He scribbled a short to-do list. He needed to get a preliminary set of presentation material to review over the weekend. He called for the car.

Leonid looked at him as they rode.

Jim answered the unsaid question. "Yes, I'm fine now. Never again, I assure you."

Leonid nodded. "In this business, it can be unhealthy to relax your guard. I will accompany you to Moscow."

"I've got a schedule. Mr. Federov wants us at the Moscow Airport by four Tuesday afternoon. We have to make sure the pilots file the flight plan and let us know the departure time."

"I'll interface with them and also arrange for the helicopter to pick us up at the house in plenty of time on Tuesday morning."

* * *

Jim had settled in his office when Josef entered. "No fires this morning but it's still early."

Jim gathered his written reminders. "Josef, how good is the quality control at Cortex?"

"It is very good. Sometimes I think the department head is German."

They both laughed at the inference of extreme precision. "Why do you ask, Tomas?"

"If I was the vice president of such a large company responsible for aircraft engineering, manufacturing and production I would want solid gold assurances from my contractors. I would give the potential contractor a test case before entrusting him with the family jewels. I'd also be skeptical of their performance. I'd worry it might overload his capacity creating schedule overruns and risk degrading quality."

"All of that is reasonable. What are you considering?"

"The presentation should be preemptive. We request a single test article to demonstrate our capability and provide Irkut a means of evaluating us. But we don't want to shoot ourselves in the foot either. We'll request information on other potential parts so we can determine if they can be manufactured according to their requirements and conditions. After they have a chance to judge us on the initial item, we'll give them a cost for the rest accompanied with agreement or disagreement with the timetable."

"Tomas, it's an enticing approach. He may see it as a way of covering his ass with his corporation, appeasing Mr. Federov and getting a handle on us. It'll provide him with a win-win situation. I'll make sure our approach is spelled out in the recommendation."

"If possible, I'd like to have a rough draft to review over the weekend."

"It'll be ready."

Jim thought, I owe Federov a weekly status report. Probably nothing he hasn't discovered, he mused. He started the one-page report. Leonid walked in as he worked. "If you don't mind Mr. Tomas, I sent the driver over to the tailor to pick up your clothes. They were ready."

"Thank you, Leonid. It had slipped my mind. I can take them on the trip."

"I read your notes. Mr. Federov's car is picking us up at the airport?"

"Yes."

"I would recommend taking your new evening clothes and change in the plane when we land. You may find it timely to have them on."

He stared at Leonid. "You know something I don't?"

"Remember; never leave your guard down. See you later on."

Saturday, November 30

A downtown Varna restaurant, closed until the evening dinner hour, was the scene of a breakfast meeting. The attendees consisted of Jakob Molokan, Boris Sidorov and four other men. Jakob introduced the four men as representatives of the Russian mafia organization who arrived to protect their interests in KAS Engineering and assess retaliatory measures. They drank strong coffee and ate cakes while they talked, debated, argued and planned. They considered various options such as disrupting Cortex deliveries, assassinations, and sabotage with explosives. They agreed the primary objective was to kill Federov and eliminate the new president. The secondary objective was to turn the tables and forcibly fold Cortex into KAS. Their strategy had to ensure Federov would personally fly into Varna to handle a threat to Cortex. Therefore, they had to come up with a feint. The objective would be to lure the targets to an isolated killing ground of their choosing. In order to eliminate any hint of involvement, the involved gunmen had to be limited to at most fifteen men including the six at the table. The extra nine guns had to be from out of town. They adjourned after setting the next meeting in three weeks. Everyone was to submit a concept which had the agreed-upon elements.

Chapter Seventeen

NEW BUSINESS

Monday, December 2

It was late in the day when Josef knocked on his office door.

"I have a couple of things for you. First, here are the final copies of your presentation on paper and a CD. The art department managed to insert some of Arsenal's facility pictures into the mix. The recommendation part should get their attention."

"I'll take good care of it."

"I have Abdul's and Hans's preliminary assessments on Arsenal."

"Any surprises?"

Josef nodded with a smile. "Their revenues weren't around twenty million USD as we thought. They're closer to twenty-five million."

Jim whistled. "My God. It means Cortex will have a revenue of over one hundred and fifteen million USD on the books. How about their profit?"

Josef referred to the report. "Over six million USD. By the way, when we obtained them without debt, KAS had to eat about one hundred and fifty thousand USD on a new machine."

"What type of machine?"

"Hans has it listed here. A precision hard metal and alloy computer-controlled laser cutter from Germany capable of a hundredth of millimeter accuracy. It must have really set them back. Here's another bonus; they have a contract with the Airbus syndicate to provide high strength structural parts."

"Is it too late to include that tidbit in the presentation?"

Josef started out of the office. "Not if I can help it. I'll have a copy of these two reports and marketing's for you before you leave." He picked up the presentation copies. "I'll get these changed right away."

Tuesday, December 3

Jim and Leonid were in the kitchen at the break of dawn. Leonid reminded him to make sure he had his passport. Jim took it out and looked at it. Something was wrong. He glimpsed at the country. Damn. It was the Mexican passport not the new Spanish one. He ran up to his room and opened the safe. He retrieved the right one and breathed a sigh of relief. It would have been disastrous. He ran downstairs and found Leonid with what he construed as a grin. Jim ignored him and finished his meal. Ivan came in and let them know the helicopter was almost at the house. The suitcases were in the servants hands. The Ka-26 helicopter landed gently on the lawn and they climbed in. As soon as they had buckled in, it rose above the trees and hurled itself towards the Varna airport.

The helicopter landed by the corporate terminal where the Challenger waited with its twin GE CF34-3A engines whining. The aircraft's front entry stairway was down and a female attendant waited at the doorway. The pilots were busy going through the pre-flight checklist. A pilot saw them approach and waved. They carried their suitcases into the aircraft rather than place them in the cargo hold. Jim entered and was overwhelmed with the lavish interior. There was a four-place conference group and an aft right-hand four-place divan. There was woodwork on both sides of the entryway. The seats were covered in light brown leather on a tan wool carpet. He paused and entered the cockpit. The two pilots introduced themselves. Jim examined the array of instruments noting the digital displays and radar scope. He went to the back. The front doorway was already closed and locked. Leonid was strapped in on a rear seat. He left the large swivel seat by the conference table vacant. Jim took off his coat and settled in. The attendant chose a chair at the rear of the cabin and sat down. The pilot made an announcement. They had been cleared to enter the taxiway and reminded them to buckle their seat belts.

He relaxed and pulled paperwork from the briefcase. He slowly read the reports prepared by Abdul and Hans. Arsenal appeared to be a well-run company. The reports revealed it had been principally owned by Statsky. No wonder he had taken extreme measures to hold on to it. Jim pondered the possibility of future retaliation. He understood Federov's brutal deed was meant as an explicit warning to forestall any such intentions. He put the papers down and examined the conference table. He found access to a computer with a fold-down monitor and a satellite telephone. In addition, there was a DVD and CD player, and VCR.

Tuesday Afternoon
Moscow, Russia

Jim woke from a short nap when the pilot's voice came on. "We are going to be descending shortly. Please put your seatbelt on." The cabin clock showed almost three. He felt the descent. They landed and the aircraft taxied to the Moscow Airport Corporate Terminal.

Leonid pointed to the suitcases. Both took a change of clothes out. Jim put on evening attire, black trousers and white dinner jacket with a black bow tie. He adjusted the ankle gun. He picked up a long white silk scarf and black gloves. He put on the black cashmere top coat and placed the scarf around his neck. He thought, "If we're going to a bar, I am going to be one overdressed dude."

They drove from the airport in dense traffic and pulled up to the front of an elegant ten-story apartment building. Three men came to the car and one opened the rear door. "Mr. Tomas. Welcome to Moscow."

Jim recognized him right away. "Thank you, Viktor. Where are we?"

"This building contains Mr. Federov's home. Let me have your ankle gun. Leave your suitcases and briefcase and come with me. They will be safe." He entered a large hall with a spectacular Art Nouveau façade. They walked to a waiting elevator. "Leonid and I will leave you here. Press the tenth floor button."

Jim did as he was directed. The floor had a beautiful pair of lacquered doors directly across the way. A servant opened the door and took his coat, scarf and gloves. Jim walked across a tiled entry and entered a room with twelve-foot ceilings. Modernistic paintings hung on one side while a mural was on the opposite wall. Old and beautifully restored furniture lined the walls with arm chairs and small tables. Federov entered at the far end of the room with a dinner jacket. He inspected Jim and made an appreciative sound. "Tomas, you learn fast. Excellent. Please come with me and meet my other guests."

Jim silently thanked Leonid for his foresight. They entered an elaborate 19th century decorated living room with sixteen-foot vaulted ceilings and large windows revealing a location directly across the river from the lighted Kremlin. There were a number of guests enjoying cocktails and wine. Everyone was fashionably dressed. Their curiosity about the unfamiliar newcomer showed on their faces. Dimitri Federov led him to the bar. "Vodka martini please." One of the guests added, "Shaken not stirred." Jim joined in the laughter. Federov introduced him. "My guest is Tomas Cassandra. He is the president of Cortex International based in Varna, Bulgaria. I wish to state before they do each one of my guests can similarly boast impressive credentials." Again, warm laughter filled the room.

Jim was certain he was introduced to the president of the Russian air defense missile producer Almaz-Antey, a multi-billion dollar company. Another was a member of the Military-Industrial Commission of Russia. Federov took him to a short man in seemingly trim condition with a smooth scalp, bushy eyebrows, piercing eyes behind wire-rimmed glasses and a quiet observing air about him. "Tomas, meet an important person with an unenviable job. It is his work which keeps organizations running smoothly. Oleg, this is Tomas Cassandra."

Jim shook hands with the man. He felt the pressure of his clasp and felt the power radiate. He thought, "This is a man not taken lightly. I wonder what he does." He was distracted by Federov whispering in his ear. "Nice work getting the Kalashnikov license."

Jim thought not for the first time, "How does he know all these things? To think I considered myself a big shot running a one hundred fifteen million company; talk about your humbling moments." The women followed Erika Federov into the room to join the men. She came up to Jim and took his arm. She turned to the other women. "Mr. Cassandra is an important part of Dimitri's organization." She motioned to her husband that dinner was ready and the guests were to be steered into the dining room.

It was close to one when the dinner party broke up. Jim rode down the elevator wondering where he was going to get a taxi this time of night. When he exited on the ground floor, he was relieved to see Leonid standing at the front door. He followed him out to one of the waiting cars. "Leonid, thank you for suggesting I wear evening clothes." Leonid simply grunted and returned his ankle gun. They were dropped off at the majestic Metropol Hotel. Leonid pointed out the nearby famous Russian landmark, Red Square.

Jim went to the reception desk and was surprised to learn he was already checked in. He accepted his key and was escorted to a beautiful suite furnished with antiques. Leonid followed him into the suite and took a smaller room off the front door. Jim opened the closet in his bedroom and found his clothes hung with care. He undressed and went to bed.

Wednesday, December 4

Jim awoke to the sounds of a cart being wheeled into the front room. Breakfast was laid out on the dining table and Leonid was pouring a cup of coffee for Jim. "You get picked up in ninety minutes. Don't worry about packing. I don't have to be with you. Just call me when you finish your meeting. I'll have a car ready to take us back to the airport." They both went to the table and filled their plates.

Jim was picked up at the hotel. He saw it was another black Mercedes-Benz with tinted windows. Federov must be making a fortune with his dealership. They turned onto Leningradsky Prospekt and stopped at the entrance of an underground parking ramp. The building above it was a modern skyscraper with Irkut Corporation in large bronze letters across the top of the entrance. The driver produced identification and a visitor's log was consulted. He was waved in and drove down the ramp to a parking space by a bank of elevators. Security personnel checked Jim's passport and gave him an escorted visitor's badge.

On the ground floor, he was directed to a metal detector. The briefcase was inserted on a moving belt into the detector. Too late he realized he had his ankle gun. He bent down and undid the strap. A security guard took it and gave him a receipt. He was told in English to reclaim it on departure. It seemed to be a routine occurrence. He passed through and was met by a man in a business suit. They entered an elevator and rode to the eighteenth floor. He was escorted into a conference room containing a table easily able to accommodate thirty persons. There were eight men seated towards the front of the room. The person seated at the head of the table looked up at his arrival, stood and greeted him in a friendly manner. Jim was tongue-tied. It was Oleg whom he met at Oleg Volkov motioned for him to sit in the empty place at the table next to him.

Jim gathered from the introductions the others were in senior posts in the vast manufacturing empire. He opened his brief case and pulled out the presentation and copies he had brought.

"Mr. Volkov, I have a CD of the presentation if you have a player and screen."

Volkov glanced at the aide and he pushed a button on the wall. A panel opened at the side and a screen electronically unfurled.

Jim rose from his seat and took a laser pointer from his pocket. He spoke slowly and highlighted Cortex capabilities and products noting the ability to move raw materials to the company and large finished products out to customers with their Ilyushin Il-76. He lastly settled on the recommendation suggesting they resist taking Cortex on good faith.

"We want to earn the position as your subcontractor and seek an opportunity to prove ourselves through a demonstration of our performance. Thank you."

He sat down and listened to their discussions held in Russian. Each of the men had something to say to Volkov who listened attentively. Finally, he turned to Jim. "Mr. Cassandra, we find it refreshing to hear an offer dealing with the practicalities of our existence, namely, quality products delivered on schedule. Cost constraints are important but flexible. We are impressed with the restraint of the request in the light of your sponsorship. I am curious. Does Mr. Federov know you came to us with such a modest proposition?"

Jim had not expected such directness. "No sir."

"I see. I will direct our people to send you a test case. It will include an engineering sample, technical specifications, quantity and a delivery schedule. You shall provide an assessment of the job, an opinion of the schedule, and the cost breakdown. We shall evaluate your response and inform you our decision. Thank you for your time."

Jim understood he had been dismissed and followed the aide out of the room and down to the first floor.

At the airport Jim and Leonid, after a stop for a minor delay with Customs, boarded the Challenger. He turned to Leonid. "It was a good meeting with Irkut. I think they're going to give us a try. Unfortunately, there wasn't much of a chance to see Moscow."

The pilot's voice came over the speakers and announced they had been cleared to take off. The plane smoothly left the ground and climbed before making a turn and leveling off.

It was dusk when the plane landed at the Varna International Airport. They entered the terminal and passed through Customs before going to their car. Leonid explained. "It's too dark for the helicopter." They had a quiet drive to the house.

Thursday, December 5
Varna, Bulgaria

Jim had settled into his office when Josef knocked on the door and entered with a smile. "Here are the final reports on Arsenal. I'm anxious to hear the details on your meeting with Irkut."

Jim started with the dinner party the night before and meeting Oleg Volkov. Then he gave the account of the meeting and the outcome. Josef asked eagerly. "They didn't give any hints as to when they would be in touch?"

Jim shook his head. He picked up the reports. "Anything new?"

"Just one. Hans says because Arsenal works with composites and other exotic alloys their manufacturing has a longer time cycle. Apparently to shorten schedules and maximize profits they operate in shifts. Before Statsky committed suicide, they were debating getting a second computer-controlled laser cutter."

"Locate their analysis on it. We may have to follow through if it's as profitable as they make it."

Leonid came in during the afternoon. "How about going to the range for some practice?"

Jim felt under his left arm. Embarrassed he declared. "I forgot my gun at the house."

Leonid looked at him disapprovingly. "Never let down your guard."

Jim accepted the admonition. "It won't happen again. We'll do it tomorrow."

Friday, December 6

Jim pored over the reports outlining the financials for the two companies. Josef appeared in the doorway. "Tomas, a messenger just left this package for you. It's from Irkut."

Jim opened it and pulled out a letter. He read it, smiled and handed it to Josef who read. "This letter says they are shipping the material needed for us to manufacture the parts. More instructions will arrive with the shipment. It says parts. Does that mean multiple quantities of one part or more than one part to be made?"

Jim shrugged. "I guess it'll be a surprise. I'm just pleased they reacted so fast to our proposal. We'll pass the news on to the staff at the meeting this afternoon."

* * *

He rounded up Leonid and they went to the gun range. He practiced under shoulder draws and fired at the target. He laid the Glock down and practiced drawing his ankle gun. Then he stood at a slot and fired the ankle gun at a close-in target. When he finished, Leif came up to him with an AK-47 assault rifle. "Have you ever fired one of these?"

Jim shook his head. Leonid took the gun and pointed it at a distant paper target. He fired a burst and then brought in the target. The burst tore the target at the heart. He handed it to Jim. He replaced the target and sent it downrange. Leif gave him a lesson where the safety and fire selector were located. Jim stood and raised the gun. He fired a burst and was surprised at the mild recoil. Leif brought in the target. Jim had caught the upper left of the target. "Try it again." Jim aimed the gun carefully and fired a three-round burst. "Better. Again." Jim fired once more. The target showed the rounds were centered. "Good." Jim and Leonid cleaned their guns and put them away.

Jim held the staff meeting after lunch. After it was over, Hans approached him. "Mr. Tomas, is it possible I can introduce you to the Arsenal general manager, Yuri Sergeikov?"

Jim was mildly amused. Hans had obviously appraised the person and retained his leadership. "By all means, bring him in to my office. Josef, you too."

When they were seated, introductions were made. Jim asked Yuri Sergeikov if he felt uncomfortable with the transition. "Mr. Cassandra, it's been a delightful and painless surprise. Hans has treated me and my staff with respect and we are comfortable with the new arrangement. We have been through a tour of your facility and it is impressive."

"We understand your new machine has worked out well."

"It has exceeded our expectations on efficiency, precision and cost effectiveness. We had explored the possibility of getting another."

Jim probed for more details. "Explain."

"It is used for tough metals and alloys. Companies are moving to more expensive composites, polymers and metals to combine strength and longer wear resistance with less weight. Another machine would be useful not only to increase business but reduce time schedules and allow us to schedule fixed downtimes to perform preventive maintenance."

"We'll look into it. One other thing, tell me about KAS Engineering."

He cleared his throat. "KAS Engineering was the brain child of Karlov Statsky. As a Russian electrical engineer in the Soviet Union days, he dealt with reverse engineering electronic technology stolen from the west and replicating them. He witnessed the disintegration of these companies, obtained their equipment and personnel, and moved them to Bulgaria. He acquired loans from a mafia organization to finance his venture and paid them back with interest and a portion of ownership. KAS Engineering has extensive production facilities near Moscow. It specializes in military electronics used for surveillance, sensors and weapon systems. They perform integration and check out of the systems at their facility in the foothills of Varna where they have a large test range area emulating a battlefield."

After they left, Josef turned to Jim. "Hans seems like a different man these days. I must say he surprised me by keeping Yuri. What do you think about the second machine?"

"It's a costly piece of capital. Let's see what other capital improvements projects we'll need for next year."

In the quiet of his office, Jim wrote the weekly status report for Federov. I don't doubt he knows everything going on before he reads it. He made a note to have Josef ask production if they were running late on any contracts.

Chapter Eighteen

SURPRISING NEWS

Monday, December 9
Newport Beach, California

Adam Weatherly was in his office reviewing their current client cases when he received a phone call from Lt. Frank Malone. "Hello Adam. How's business today?"

"Less hectic. How are things up there?"

"Actually, something's turned up I found interesting which relates to you."

Adam sat up. "Really?"

"We got a hit on the name your missing man used on his Mexican passport, Tomas Cassandra."

"What?"

"Yeah, except the name is on a Spanish passport."

"It's probably not an uncommon name. Why is it interesting? Is it counterfeit?"

"No, it's legitimate. Here's the rub. The person has the identical birthday on it and it was issued after your man disappeared from here."

"Wait a minute. Are you implying it was used?"

"Yes. The U.S. has a reciprocal agreement with many countries and it was sent over as a routine notice."

"Where?"

"Moscow six days ago. Is there any reason he would have gone there? How the hell did he manage to get a passport from Spain, a country which scrutinizes applicants carefully after those terrorist train bombings? I have another question for you. Should we be treading softly? Is your guy a spook?"

He thought back to the information given by Diane Factor. "Frank, I just don't know. Let me get back to you. If anything else turns up, please call me."

Adam called Elaine and Marty into his office and told them about the conversation with Malone. They were shocked. Elaine revealed, "Adam, I'll pull his file but I seem to remember he did some work for intelligence agencies. How else could he get a foreign passport so fast? What is he doing in Russia?"

"It's crazy. Let me have his file. Lt. Malone will call if anything else comes up."

San Francisco, California

Lt. Frank Malone fingered the letter opener on his desk. This wasn't the first time he had been asked to keep track of a passport. The speed with which Factor had obtained the new one along with the area of the world he was traveling in sent up a red flag. He was going to e-mail the intelligence agency liaison and inform them of the activity. It didn't pay to step on toes in this business. If Factor was one of theirs, they might call him off.

Varna, Bulgaria

Josef called Jim. "Tomas. I'm at the loading dock. We just received a shipment from Irkut's Beriev Aircraft Company. Can you come down?"

"Be right there."

Jim entered the receiving area and spotted Josef with Hans and Yuri. "Here is a sealed, bulky envelope addressed to you. We have pallets with various materials from Beriev on that truck."

Jim opened the envelope and read the letter of introduction.

Dear Mr. Cassandra:

> *I have been instructed to provide you the following information. The enclosed technical specifications and parts are associated with the Be-103 light, multi-purpose, twin-engine amphibian aircraft. It is a full-scale program and assembled at the Irkut Aviation Plant. The aircraft has been conceived for coastal and maritime operations principally for employment in firefighting. As a serious byproduct of*

its operating environment, the aircraft is subject to corrosion, specifically, the deterioration of metals due to chemical reaction. Consequently, the critical parts and assemblies are composed of aluminum, stainless steel, titanium and silicon. Upon receipt of this letter we seek an acceptance of the effort and the attached schedule accompanied by your cost breakdown.

Respectfully,
Alexy J. Korotkov
Director, BE-200 Directorate

Jim handed the letter to Josef. "It's a case of 'be careful what you wish for'. Let's get the pallets into the store room and make copies of all the technical specifications for review. Hans, I expect this falls into your department. Let me have an initial assessment by tomorrow afternoon. The first question is, can we do it? The second, can we meet the schedule? The third of course is, how much?"

Jim walked back to his office and tried not to let his apprehension show. What have I got myself into? I thought they'd send a simple test and instead they throw the kitchen sink at us. Smart too. They kept the classified work on military aviation out of the equation. We can't afford to blow it. Well, there's nothing I can do until we review the data. Up to then, I have to keep my fingers crossed.

By and large he continued to be impressed with Federov's high level contacts. When he thought about it, he really didn't know much about him except what he had read on the Internet. He called Leonid in and asked him to close the door.

"Leonid, I'd like to learn more about Mr. Federov, the Solsnetskaya Organization and the Russian mafia. I'd like to find out what I've gotten myself into."

"I can only give you an overview. Mr. Federov is an educated man who did well for himself in the Russian Air Force. He cultivated strong connections both within the Russian military and in Moscow with Russian gangsters including members of the Vor V Zakonye, the Russian mafiya. Even before the collapse of the Soviet Union, he was on a rise to power. He assembled a group of hardened veterans from the army and using military tactics and weapons overthrew a powerful mobster and seized control of the Solsnetskaya Organization. Mr. Federov expanded the organization into broader areas. His insight led him to take over what the government ignored during its confusion. He's included key busies important to large Russian corporations. A success story is it not?"

"Impressive but Cortex is hardly a cog in anybody's machinery. Mr. Federov's organization is so large, he doesn't have to fear anybody."

"You are far from the truth. The more rackets his organization is into, the more trouble it has with other organizations working the same area. Several terrible turf wars have been fought and each time Mr. Federov has come out on top. The others continue to probe and challenge his organization. KAS Engineering is associated with one of the other stronger organizations. When they sent an assassination team to get Mr. Borichov, they crossed the line and Mr. Federov had no choice but to respond. To reemphasize his leadership position, he did it himself."

"So now I run Cortex International under the threat of Federov."

"No. You still don't understand. You run Cortex under the protection of Mr. Federov. He wants you to succeed. He believes you can make Cortex bigger than KAS Engineering with your leadership and without his interference."

"He lined us up with Irkut."

Leonid nodded. "He set up the meeting but your presentation did the rest. Irkut is so large it remains independent of the organizations except where its own good is concerned."

"I see. Thank you, Leonid."

Tuesday, December 10

Josef entered Jim's office to say Hans and Yuri were ready with their assessment of the Beriev Aircraft parts requirement. Jim anxiously waved them in. When they were seated at his conference table, Hans began the discussion.

"Mr. Tomas. Our effort began by educating ourselves with an overview of the effort in order to better understand the requirements. With your indulgence, we would like to give you the same picture." He looked inquiringly at Jim.

Jim signaled he understood and to continue.

"Very well. The Be-103 is a monoplane possessing a low-set, water-displacement wing with a root strake, all-moving horizontal tail located in the propeller blow zone The parts under consideration are associated with the tail assembly. The tail is a critical element because the aircraft does not have flaps. It skims on the wing trailing edges. There is a rumor Beriev is about to sign a contract with China for twenty Be-103s at slightly over one million USD apiece."

Jim observed. "At that price, they may have to hold the line on aircraft costs which obligates them to shop around for good, inexpensive manufacturing contractors."

Hans nodded in agreement. "Now, we get to their parts which fall in the high-end, low-volume category. There are sixteen different ones with a quantity of sixty apiece. An assembly piece can have from six to twelve sides depending on its configuration. We have been given complete technical specifications with tolerances and descriptions and locations of holes for fasteners and screws. The material on the pallets is more than enough to do the job. They generously allowed for waste and missteps on our part."

"When you put it that way, it doesn't sound like a big project."

"Let us discuss schedule and cost; they want delivery on dock in thirty days. As to the manufacturing, Cortex and the computer-controlled cutting equipment at Arsenal can meet the geometries and tolerances. The initial labor is involved with transcribing the parts data into machine language. This will be done twice by two different sets of people and their results compared for errors and verified. The appropriate material is fed to the machine and the parts are made. We perform the standard edge and burr removal and finish the piece. Our cost estimate for the nine hundred sixty-piece project with profit is 220,800 USD."

"It averages out to 230 USD each." He shrugged. "It's not a very big job. Can we meet their schedule?"

"We could do it in half the time and still use it as filler between our big projects. By the way, after we do it once and record the computer data, we can lower the price and reduce the schedule even more. The first time includes set-up costs. We should hold to the thirty-day delivery since their time increment is no doubt driven by their production pace."

"Okay. Have a proposal drawn up with contracts for me to sign and we'll fax it out. Make sure they understand it includes the one-time set-up cost. Good work on the quick turnaround. We'll find out how our bid stands against the others."

Wednesday, December 11

Josef came into Jim's office waving a piece of paper. "Our good luck vehicle is still running with four tires and a full tank. Beriev signed the parts contract and reminded us the clock is running."

"Terrific news. Give a 'well-done' to Hans. Now, our next hurdle is delivering the parts. It remains to be seen if we'll get anything more in the near future. At least we'll have something to crow about this week for Mr. Federov."

Washington, D.C.

Tom Coulter, an analyst at the Central Intelligence Agency Headquarters in Langley, Virginia, read the e-mail from the INS Office in San Francisco. He looked up James Factor in the national security data base and got a hit. Factor had been actively involved with the Air Force Foreign Technology Division a number of years back. He had an active high level security clearance presently held by Northrop Grumman. He didn't see a reason for any CIA involvement and forwarded the e-mail with his findings to the FTD headquarters at Wright-Patterson AFB, Dayton, Ohio.

Chapter Nineteen

SURPRISES CONTINUE

Wednesday Afternoon
Newport Beach, California

Elaine notified Adam, "You have a call from Lt. Frank Malone."

He snatched up the phone. "Frank. You've heard something again?"

"Adam, the passport was used again, this time leaving Moscow and entering Varna, Bulgaria. Both happened a week ago Wednesday. It may be helpful in finding the connecting commercial flight."

"Thanks, Frank. We checked our info on Factor. He worked for intelligence agencies some years back but nothing in the past ten years according to his wife."

"You know what they say about coincidences, Adam. What are you going to do?"

"With your information, we'll try piecing together a picture. Thanks again Frank."

Adam called his staff in to his office. "There's not much we can do at the moment except try to track down his movements. Marty, you found a Bulgarian connection early on in our search."

"Yes, Mikhail Borichov had a company called Cortex International in Varna."

"We'll wait until we get more information from Malone."

* * *

Adam sat back and thought aloud. "This can't be right. Why would Jim stick his head in the lion's mouth? According to Malone's information he was only in Moscow for two days. I know Borichov's dead. Why would he go to Bulgaria? He possibly be a spy. Not with his involvement in the gun battle we had."

Later, Marty came in his office. "Adam, you're not going to believe this." He handed him two pages of printouts. "I did a search of Varna's newspaper and came across these two items printed in the past ten days."

Adam read with disbelief. The first article stating Mikhail Borichov was a victim of a vicious assault by armed intruders at his house. His guards managed to kill the attackers but not before Borichov and two guards were also slain. The next one dealt with Borichov's well-attended funeral. What the hell was going on? How could Borichov die twice? He decided to call Chris and relate the discoveries.

Friday, December 13
Varna, Bulgaria

Jim conducted the staff meeting after lunch. The topics of interest discussed included the recent Irkut-holding Beriev Aircraft contract. The marketing department head brought up an idea raised by one of his people. It involved a contact with the Bulgarian Ministry of Defense regarding the upgrade of the armed forces AK-47 with the new AK-100. "The problem is most of the AK-47s are still useful. My man's suggestion is to offer to take them as tradein for the AK-100. We could refurbish them with our old line and resell them as used but with a warranty. As a side benefit we could keep our old line with the new line and make more money. If the approach is successful we could extend the exchange offer to our neighbors as well." Jim applauded the insightfulness of the concept and asked for further clarification on the trade-in price.

After the meeting was over, Jim retired to his office to get out the weekly status report to Federov. *He ought to be pleased with our progress if he actually reads this thing.*

Saturday, December 21

The six men shuffled into the back room of the restaurant. They poured themselves coffee before sitting down at the table. Each had papers in front of them. Jakob Molokan started the meeting by reviewing the outcome of the one held three weeks previously. "Okay, we have heard a review of the conditions. Now let's see if we have something we can all support. Boris?"

Boris Sidorov set his coffee down. "We have to choose something serious to get Federov out of his lair. However, we don't want him coming with troops because we couldn't match them. Therefore, we need a feint, something substantial but not serious enough he couldn't handle with a minimum of force. I'm thinking of a failed assassination attempt against his new Cortex president."

Jakob thought a moment. "I like the idea. We should consider an accompanying event to guarantee he gets riled."

One of the four men spoke up. "What about an unsuccessful attempt at bombing their beloved Il-76? It could be an aviation fuel truck remotely set off within the proximity of the aircraft. We could do it far enough before it can do any damage."

Boris grinned. "That would clinch it. Federov would be off guard figuring he could uncover the amateurs and take care of it himself. It occurs to me KAS has a natural place for our retaliation where no one would pay attention even if the racket was heard. I'm referring to the battlefield test range. We could prepare an ambush ahead of time and be undisturbed. We would need a way to draw them out there."

The other man offered. "A second assassination attempt might work. We try it openly so they give chase and follow us there. The rest of us can be waiting in the battlefield."

"Excellent. Can we count on your organization to supply the extra men when we need them?"

"Yes. Do you have a date in mind?"

"Friday, January 31."

Monday, December 23

Jim was deeply engrossed in the plans submitted by the departments for the coming year. Josef had reviewed them and annotated his comments. Jim noted Hans had included a twin computer-controlled laser cutter in the capital budget based upon the performance of Arsenal's unit especially on the complex parts configuration of the Beriev job. He had projected the second unit would be kept just as busy and would pay for itself in a year if they ran two shifts. The problem is the cost would be coming out of profit so he would have to make a case for it to Federov. Marketing had requested the addition of two more people; one a Russian to interface directly with Irkut for new business. The idea had merit.

Josef stuck his head into the office. "Tomas, any questions on the suggestions?"

Jim looked up. "No, they're clear enough. The staff did a good job of outlining their requests with the corresponding rationale. Marketing is a pleasant surprise with their constant stream of selling ideas. Their sales projections are ambitious but seem well thought out. What's new?"

"Hans just informed me the Beriev job is completed. It means it passed quality control. The parts are packaged and placed on a pallet in the storeroom to await shipment. We're closed between Christmas and New Year's. Any plans?"

"I might take a drive through Bulgaria to the surrounding areas and do some sightseeing. I haven't had any time to see the country. How about you?"

"Relatives come to visit and stay every year. We'll have a full house."

After Josef left, Jim thought about Diane celebrating Christmas this year with her family. *If I can survive for another five months, I'll be with her again. My God, wouldn't I surprise her in my present condition? My shoulder gun and ankle gun have become as natural on me as shirt and pants. Then there's my exercise regimen and gun range practice as routine as flossing my teeth. I've drastically changed from the man she knows. Is that good or bad?*

Hmm. A holiday trip is not a bad idea. On the other hand, I have access to an aircraft. Why not fly somewhere and relax? The more he thought about it, the more excited he became. *How about heading back to Spain?* After all, he had a Spanish passport and could lose himself. *He could do the Costa del Sol.* It was final. He would head there tomorrow. He better alert the pilots of his intentions and make reservations.

Wright-Patterson AFB, Ohio

Major Randy Gallas read the e-mail sent to the Foreign Technology Division (FTD) from the CIA. The James Factor reference held his attention so he requested his file from the archives. Within minutes, the confidential information was on his computer display.

It indicated the last activity was over ten years old. Gallas thought the trips to Bulgaria and Moscow were suspicious especially since they occurred under an alias. The file update noted Factor was a registered arms dealer with mostly European clients. Except for the use of an alias, his Spanish passport was the real thing. He made the notation, *Hold for Further Data*, and continued with his day.

Chapter Twenty

HOLIDAY HAPPENINGS

Tuesday, December 24
Malaga, Spain

Leonid asked. "Are you sure you'll be okay? I can travel and keep in the background."

Jim shook his head. "I'll be fine. If it'll make you feel better, I'll check in with you. I'm taking my phone so you can also contact me. I'll either be back by the 31st or right after New Year's." Jim said his goodbyes to both of them and ran to the helicopter. He settled in and buckled his seat belt. The helicopter lifted off. Jim thought, what worry warts. Then he realized if something happened to him, they would be on the receiving end of reprisals. He reassured himself nothing was going to happen.

The helicopter landed near the Varna International Airport corporate terminal. He walked to the waiting Challenger. The plane took off smoothly, turned over the Black Sea and began climbing to their cruising altitude. As it leveled off, he picked up a book to read.

Costa del Sol, Malaga, Spain

It was late afternoon when the aircraft descended through a hazy sky and landed at the Malaga Airport. Jim instructed the pilots. "Go back to Varna. I won't need you again for about a week. I'll call you when." As soon as he was on the ground, the plane turned around and headed for the runway.

Jim went through Customs, rented a car and drove to the Hotel Byblos Andaluz, located in Fuengirola and within a short drive to Marbella. His room was an oversized suite with a balcony facing lush green landscaped grounds and golf course. He unpacked and decided to stroll about the grounds. He remembered fondly the Restaurant Le Nailhac, an elegant gastronomical experience in the hotel where one could relax at a linen-set table. He would start with a martini at the Bar St. Tropez. He recalled never having enough time to enjoy the hotel or play golf due to business meetings with Middle East customers and his partner. He made up his mind to try the golf course the following day.

Thursday, December 26
Moscow, Russia

Federov relaxed in his living room wondering how Factor was spending the time off. He called Viktor, "Find out how things are going at Cortex."

"They're closed during the holiday week."

"Call Leonid and see what Tomas is doing."

After a short while Viktor came back into the room. "He's not there."

"What?"

"He told them he was taking the holidays off to rest. He took the Challenger to Malaga, Spain and sent it back to Varna. He told them he'd call and tell them when and where he was to be picked up."

He yelled, "Who told him he could go anywhere? What do you think?"

"He's a man of honor. He'll be back. You could always call his cell."

Calming down, Federov replied, "No. I'll wait. When he calls, I want to know."

Saturday, December 28
Marbella, Spain

As was his custom, Jim rose early and stopped into the pro shop at the adjacent golf course. He made a tee time for later in the morning and rented a set of clubs. It had been over six months since he last played so he looked forward to regaining some semblance of a game. He was paired with an Englishman who was also a guest at the hotel. They played eighteen holes of leisurely golf and had a drink at the bar when they finished. It seemed the man's wife was a tennis player who had made arrangements for some matches while he excised his demons on the greens. Jim found the man good company with a wry humor. He turned in the golf clubs and went back to his room. For something different in the evening, he decided to drive to the Marbella marina and eat at the nearby seafood restaurant. He made a note to call back to Varna and make arrangements for the plane to pick me up at the Malaga Airport on Monday.

Sunday, December 29
Moscow, Russia

Federov was in the study in his apartment when he received a call. "Viktor, you heard from Leonid? I see. Tomas contacted him from Malaga, Spain. It's a good place to spend the holidays. I never doubted he would call. When's the pickup? Tomorrow? Wait. Tell the pilot to file a return flight plan from Malaga to Moscow. Get him a room at the Hotel Metropol." He called to his wife. "Erika. We have another guest at our New Year's Eve party."

Monday, December 30
Malaga, Spain

Jim was surprised to hear his plane would be landing at the Malaga Airport corporate terminal before ten. Well, it still gave him ample time to check out of the hotel and return the car. The sky had a patchy cloud cover but the weather report was favorable. He watched the sleek Challenger land from the terminal's reception room, passed through Customs and was ready when it arrived by the gate. He grabbed his suitcase and smiled as he saw Jessika wave from the doorway. He climbed the entry stairs and spotted Leonid in a seat. "Did you decide to take a ride today?"

Leonid glanced up from his reading. "You know you will never, well, almost never go anywhere without me. Besides we're heading for Moscow at Mr. Federov's request."

Jim handed his suitcase to the attendant. "Really?"

Leonid nodded. "Mr. Federov expects you to attend his New Year's Eve party tomorrow night."

"He's full of surprises. Uh, oh. I didn't bring evening clothes with me." He looked at Leonid and grinned. "I get it, never let down your guard." He sat down in his seat at the conference table.

The attendant brought him a Bloody Mary and warm nuts. "I'll serve lunch later on."

It was night when the aircraft landed and proceeded to the Moscow's International Airport Corporate Terminal. They went through Customs and found the car and driver sent by Federov to take them to the Metropol Hotel.

Tuesday, December 31
Moscow, Russia

Jim dressed casually, then removed his evening clothes from the closet. He called the front desk and arranged to have them pressed and returned before the evening.

He called out, "Leonid, I'd like to see some of the Moscow sights today. Could you arrange something for me?"

"I'll get Mr. Federov's car and driver and we'll drive to a few places."

By the end of the day, Jim had driven by and seen St. Basil's Cathedral, the Kremlin Museum, the Peter the Great Monument and Red Square. They stopped at the famous Tretyakov Art Gallery and while viewing the historical pieces he paused at the gift shop to purchase a striking replica of a Russian 19th century vase. He wasn't sure but he estimated it cost over two thousand dollars. He had it giftwrapped with a card. He wrote.

Mr. and Mrs. Federov:

My gratitude for another opportunity to be a guest in your beautiful home.

Tomas C.

He was relieved to enter his hotel room and slumped in a large padded arm chair. "One would require a week and considerable energy to visit all of the sights. I think I'll take a short nap before we go to Mr. Federov's party. Please wake me in an hour." He went into his bedroom.

Jim arrived at the Federov residence and joined the guest line where the Federovs were greeting the arrivals. When he found himself in front of them, he handed the gift to Mrs. Federov and shook Dimitri Federov's hand. She turned to her husband. "Shall I open it now?" He nodded and stared at Jim.

She unwrapped the gift and held it. It drew a number of appreciative comments from the other guests. She read the card and handed it to Federov. Erika Federov leaned over and kissed Jim on the cheek. "Thank you. It's lovely."

He moved on and entered the salon where the bar was already surrounded by guests. He picked up a glass of champagne and withdrew to the side of the large room. He thought he saw Oleg Federov across the crowded room. He admired the sight of the tuxedoed men and the richly dressed women. It was if he was in the lobby of the New York Metropolitan Opera House. I would swear not a few of them are wearing Giorgio Armani. He smiled to himself; if this is going to be a habit, I better get myself one too. He was gazing at the sights outside the window when he was interrupted by a voice behind him. It was Federov. "The surprise of such an elegant gift to the hostess from a non-Russian has placed you in the unique position of being both admired and envied for your thoughtfulness. Come with me and let me get you into an appropriate group." He escorted Jim to a number of guests speaking in English and left him.

Jim found his name on a table in the dining room. He was impressed to discover a journalist for a leading Russian newspaper on one side and on the other the owner of a Moscow department store. They had a discussion in English on the world economy and the demand for Russian products including Siberian oil and diamonds. The attendance had to number over one hundred and fifty guests. Still, the efficiency of the kitchen was to be lauded because the food was served hot and plentiful. Wine decanters at each table were refilled as emptied. The orchestra continually played softly so as to not interfere with the conversations taking place. All in all, Jim rated the affair as a ten on his scale. That settles it; I'm definitely going to get an Armani.

Just before midnight, waiters passed through the guests and handed out party hats, noise makers and confetti in between afterdinner drinks and champagne. The orchestra counted down the final sixty seconds of the old year and announced the New Year with a clash of cymbals and the boom from a kettle drum. Everyone cheered and clapped with hugs and kisses for their companions. Jim thought. "I have just been through a hell of a year and it doesn't have an end in sight yet." People began filtering out and Jim figured it was a good time for him to leave unnoticed. He put on his top coat and rode the elevator to the ground floor. He saw Viktor and Leonid standing in the corner. "What in the world. They couldn't have been there all night, could they?"

As they rode to the hotel, Leonid spoke. "They liked your gift."

How in the hell did he know that? "It appeared so." He answered.

Chapter Twenty-one

SURPRISE AND THEN SOME

Thursday, January 2
Newport Beach, California

Adam was in his office when Elaine called out to him. "Adam, line one."

He picked up the receiver. "Hello."

"Adam, this is Frank Malone."

"Happy New Year to you too. What's up?" Then he realized what the call was about. "You had another hit on the passport?"

"Yep. And three guesses where."

"I don't have a clue."

"Malaga, Spain."

"Unbelievable. When was it?"

"The day before Christmas. It was an arrival and we don't know his departure location."

"It might infer he lives there."

"Maybe, maybe not. You have noticed he's one sly and careful SOB."

"Well, the destination doesn't match the passport's place of birth. He's moving around again. Let me know if anything else pops up. Thanks, Frank."

Adam waved Elaine and Marty into his office from the doorway. "You heard?"

"The guy is a piece of work. What's he doing? He can't be under duress or in danger. What do you think, Adam?"

"My gut feeling is he's planning something. He's not a guy who'll let anything rest. I'd give my vast and wondrous fortune to read his mind. I don't think he's finished with traveling or plotting."

"Are you going to inform Mrs. Factor about these developments?"

"Not yet. Let's collect more information."

Varna, Bulgaria

Jim was well rested after getting back from Moscow. Josef entered his office. "Tomas, we have received a fax from Beriev directing us to ship the parts to their factory."

"Okay. We probably won't hear anything from them unless they uncover a problem." He crossed his fingers.

"In the short term, we're planning on shipping a dozen heavyduty, four-wheel drive trucks to Central Africa in mid-January on the Il-76. Also we're working on the proposed offer to the Bulgarian Ministry of Defense to buy back the AK-47s in return for new AK-100s. We're anxious get their response to our offer. Hans will be outlining the production schedule once he completes the requirement for the new tooling."

"Have we picked up any mumblings from KAS Engineering on the Arsenal Company acquisition?"

"Nothing and you know how paranoid they were on just an inquiry into Arsenal's availability. Perhaps we've heard the last of them."

Monday, January 6
Newport Beach, California

Elaine smiled. "Adam, it's another of those phone calls." He shook his head. He knew what Elaine was referring to. He picked up the phone.

"Hi, Frank. More news?"

"Morning. Yeah, you got it. We got a hit at Moscow on Monday, December 30th. And that's not all. He used the passport on arrival at Varna on Wednesday, January 1st. This guy travels like a tourist except we both know it's like no tour we've ever been on."

"I'm still trying to piece it together too. Thanks again."

Adam addressed Elaine and Marty. "I realize we have other cases going on but we have to figure this out. We know Borichov had Cortex International in Varna. Let's do a search and get everything we can find on it. There has to be a connection between Jim Factor or Tomas Cassandra and Cortex."

Marty entered Adam's office later in the morning. "Adam, the only news I could find during the past month was a press release on the Cortex acquisition of Arsenal Company from KAS Engineering. It described Arsenal as a precision manufacturing company whose capabilities complement Cortex. There's nothing on their management, certainly no names are given."

Adam thought, there's more than one way to skin a cat. He picked up his phone and asked the overseas operator for the telephone number for Cortex International in Varna, Bulgaria. He wrote the number down and looked at the time. California was ten hours behind Bulgaria. He made a note to call Cortex from his home early the next morning.

Tuesday, January 7

Adam's alarm went off at five. He put on the light and picked up the phone number for Cortex. He dialed and waited for the connection to be made. A telephone receptionist answered "Cortex International" with an afternoon greeting. Adam asked to be connected to Mr. Tomas Cassandra. There was a pause and he was transferred. A different feminine voice inquired, "Who shall I say it is from?" Adam was so surprised he hung up. It was stupid of me not to anticipate I'd have to say something if he was there. He'd have to be careful the next time he called. What was Jim doing at Cortex? Okay, he had located him again. What now? I'm getting ahead of myself. He really had to personally verify it was Jim. How in the hell did he do that short of going over there? Whoa. He was getting ahead of himself. What if Jim was undercover for some reason? He could blunder and expose him. Damn, this was getting more complicated by the minute. I'll call Chris and see what he thinks. Right now without answers he definitely was not going to inform Mrs. Factor of these developments.

Adam called Chris's home number. After exchanging pleasantries, Adam told him of the latest news on Jim and his anxiety of stepping onto a mine field.

Chris was silent throughout Adam's discourse. Finally, when Adam reached the end, he replied. "It's remarkable. After years in a covert service, I have to agree on the sensitivity of your discovering, If we're going farther with this, we'll need some good, old fashion on-the-spot recon."

"Wait a minute. Are you suggesting what I think you are? Are you saying we should hightail it to Bulgaria and check out the situation for ourselves."

"Well, yes, I think I am. What the hell, Adam? I'm way overdue for a vacation. When's the last time you took one?" Adam laughed at the senselessness of the idea. Still, he had come this far. "I'm game if you are. My biggest concern is the possibility we may place him in harm's way if he's got something going. At least we have a way to monitor him if he takes off again. He just got back to Varna from Moscow. Let's think about the consequences before we plan the trip."

"I have an idea. Let's find out ahead of time if we pose a danger by going to Varna. Let's write a letter addressed to his identity in care of Cortex. We'll say we want to visit with him but need assurances we won't be interfering. We'll ask him to answer us by a certain date if it's okay. We cancel the trip if we don't hear from him. I'm checking the calendar. Let's plan on traveling Saturday, January twenty-fifth. It'll give our letter time to get there and Jim time to think about it."

"I like it. I'll put it together and get it mailed from here. In the meantime, we can see about reservations."

Varna, Bulgaria

Jim was working in his office when Martina informed him Mr. Oleg Volkov was on the line. Here's where we find out if Cortex made the grade. He answered, "Mr. Volkov, it's nice to hear from you. How may I help you?" He held his breath.

"Mr. Cassandra, we have inspected the parts you fabricated. They are entirely satisfactory. We are going to send another request to you. As before, it will consist of the raw material and the technical specification but no sample parts this time. By the way, did you match your manufactured part with the specific sample we sent you last month?"

"Actually, we did. I'm sorry to say the part we received did not meet the technical specification so we put it aside."

"We had to test your quality control process and intentionally gave you a non-conforming part. Congratulations on your performance and meeting the schedule. Goodbye."

Jim picked up the phone and called Josef. He described the phone call from Oleg Volkov. "Pass it on to Hans." He hung up and smiled. This was like a blind raffle. Buy a bag and hope for a big surprise within. Unlike the first time, he was looking forward to the next test.

Tuesday, January 14

Josef walked into Jim's office excited and smiling. "Tomas, guess what's at the loading dock?"

Jim jumped up and grabbed his coat. "Lead on."

When they got there, Hans was waiting with two large manila envelopes in his hand. "Mr. Tomas, this one is addressed to you." He handed it to Jim.

He took and opened the thinner package. It was a letter of introduction. He read,

Mr. Tomas Cassandra:

The Manufacturing Directorate of the Irkut Corporation has informed me of the competency of Cortex in the manufacture and on-time delivery of complex and specialized parts and assemblies. Accordingly, we wish to avail ourselves of your company's capabilities for two independent but related projects. You will examine all technical specifications and delivery schedules and prepare a proposal containing costs and statement of ability to meet the delivery dates. Our purchasing department has submitted the type and amount of material required for both projects. We desire your response within a week.

Respectfully,
Anatoly Stepanov
Director, Su-30 MKI Directorate Sukhoi Corporation

Jim passed the letter to Josef who read it and handed it to Hans. "Tomas, we have another new customer. Open the other package. I'm dying to see what we have to bid."

Jim slowly opened the second package. "This says the technical specifications are in manuals sent with the pallets. All right, here is the description of the two projects." He pulled out a drawing with a complete description. "The first project is the manufacture of the GSh-301 30mm automatic cannon. It is a single-barrel, linear-action, gas-operated cannon with a rate of fire of one thousand eight hundred rounds per minute. It is widely deployed on seven fighters and a gun pod. They want one thousand two hundred cannons in ninety days."

Hans took the drawing. "We can do this work here. What's the second one?"

Jim pulled out the second set of drawings. He whistled and grinned. "This is the big one." He showed them the drawing. He read, "The Su-30 MKI is a twin-finned aircraft. The airframe is constructed of titanium and high-strength aluminum alloys. The desired assembly description follows; the engine nacelles are fitted with trouser fairings to provide a continuous streamlined profile between the nacelles and the tail beams. The fins and horizontal tail consoles are attached to tail beams. There is an immediate need for ten of the assemblies. The rest of the fifty assemblies are to be delivered in groups of ten per month starting in ninety days." It suddenly struck him. Each assembly would be about twenty-five feet long. "How many pallets did they send?"

Hans asked the driver of the large transport truck. "He says this is just the first load and there are twelve in there. The rest will be shipped upon approval."

Josef asked. "Hans, we have to get the proposals out in a week. How's your work load?"

"The cannon proposal is independent and quickly prepared. The second proposal will require inputs from Arsenal." He looked at Jim. "We'll need to have a team working overtime and the weekend."

"You have permission. When you have all of the numbers assembled, have finance work up the costs. Then we'll review them before they go out. Josef, any idea how much we're looking at?"

Josef conversed with Hans before answering. "Our best guess per cannon is at least fifteen hundred USD. The Su-30 assembly unit may run 200,000 USD or more."

"Are you implying this contract could be worth as much as ten percent of our annual revenues?

Josef nodded. "You did a whale of a selling job. You realize Hans is going to want his second computer-controlled laser cutter?"

"If we get this job, I'll personally push it through finance and purchasing."

As Jim walked back to his office, he mused about the fates which brought him to this time and place. He knew very well the Su-30 MKI albeit by its NATO nick-name Flanker-H from his days working as an analyst under contract with the Air Force Foreign Technology Division. He knew better than anyone the avionics and weapon systems on the aircraft, where they came from and their performance. He left the aerodynamic qualities to other experts but he knew they would drool if they knew the technical drawings were in his possession. On the other side of the coin he would be a target if the Russians thought he might be a spy. It was a good thing Federov had insisted on the Spanish identity. He wondered if Federov also had a hand in this potential business from Sukhoi.

Monday, January 20

Jim was reading a draft of the Sukhoi proposal. He had inquired about the impact on current Cortex commitments if the proposal was accepted. He glanced at his in-box and saw a personal letter addressed to Tomas Cassandra postmarked from California. He picked it up with apprehension. He carefully opened it and read the letter from Adam Weatherly. He smiled after he finished it. He had never run into anybody with the persistence and intelligence of Adam. He had, without a doubt, traced him through his new passport. Apparently Adam and Chris had surmised he was up to something they might interfere with and were being extremely careful. He admired their caution and initiative. He would love to see his friends again. He wondered if he dared. They were set to travel on Saturday. Allowing for the time differential they would get into Varna Sunday evening. He read they would cancel the trip if they didn't hear from him. The fact was he longed to see them. He would think about it and make his decision the next day.

Tuesday, January 21

Jim looked over the two sets of proposals sitting on his office conference table. Each proposal had a technical and cost volume. Josef and Hans stood by to answer questions. Jim voiced his concern on the schedule. He had conceded the technical aspects were understood and achievable. "Do we place any existing projects in jeopardy with the addition of one or both programs?"

Josef deferred to Hans. "We have the necessary tooling and schedules can be overlapped if we go to a second shift. We stated in the proposal we would meet the schedule in this way."

"What are the final costs?"

"The GSh-301 cannon per unit cost came to eighteen hundred and forty USD for a total of 2.208 million USD. The Su-30 MKI assembly is roughly two hundred fifteen thousand USD totaling 10.750 million USD. Each assembly will weigh near a ton. We'd have to subcontract the wooden shipping pallets."

"Do we have any notion of how competitive our prices are?"

"I believe they are in line more or less with their other supplier without the set-up costs. Our research found the unit cost for a fully-equipped Su-30 MKI is about 40 million USD. The ability to meet the demanding schedule may be Sukhoi's major concern and is probably more important than our prices. Either way, we'll know after they receive the proposals and have had the time to evaluate them."

Jim closed his office door and placed a call to Adam using his cell phone. It would be night time there but it couldn't be helped.

Adam answered with a yawn. "Hello."

Jim replied. "You mean 'good afternoon.'" Adam sat upright in bed. "Jim, I mean Tomas."

Jim snickered. "It's Tomas and yes, you have to be careful. Are you still planning on traveling here?"

"We have a Saturday departure from LAX getting there late Sunday afternoon."

"Austrian Air?"

"Yes, a direct flight from JFK."

"I'll meet you both at the airport. Remember this and rehearse it constantly. You will be met by Tomas Cassandra. I'm looking forward to your visit. Goodbye."

Adam smiled and dialed Chris's number. "Chris. I just heard from Tomas Cassandra. We're on for Saturday."

Chapter Twenty-two

THE RETALIATION BEGINS

Thursday, January 23

At the end of the day Jim and Leonid departed the plant. As they rounded a corner, the driver suddenly braked. He shouted and pointed, "There's a car blocking the street." In spite of his size, Leonid moved fast and threw Jim down to the floor while reaching for his gun. He yelled to the driver. "Go around on the sidewalk." While the driver hurled the car over the curb, Leonid looked for the gunmen. He spotted the flash of the gun firing their way, rolled down the window and emptied his magazine at the gunman's position. The car cleared the obstruction and roared down the street. Jim picked himself up.

"What was that all about?"

"Someone set up an ambush. I didn't hear any shots hit the car. We were lucky."

"Who do you think it was?"

"My guess is your friends at KAS. It seems they still harbor a grudge. We'll have to be extra careful for a while."

Friday, January 24

Josef came into Jim's office with the head of security. "Tomas, you're going to want to hear this." The security head began. "A half hour ago, an aviation fuel truck exploded near our parked Il-76."

"Was anyone hurt? What about the aircraft? Did they catch the persons responsible?"

"No one was hurt. It was our guard at the plane who phoned me of the attempt. The aircraft is okay. It appears the explosion went off prematurely before the truck got too close. No information yet if they caught anybody. They could have been killed in the blast."

"Leonid, you heard?"

He nodded. "Someone is causing trouble. I'll call Viktor and fill him in. Whoever it is must be amateurs." He turned to the security head. "Do you have outside informants who can ask questions discreetly?"

"I do and I will also interface with the police and see what they turn up."

Later in the day, Leonid reported to Jim. "The police found the body of the fuel truck driver at the edge of the airport. There have been no other findings. The head of security will be talking this weekend with informants. He has interfaced with Arsenal's security head also to place them on alert."

"We have to be on our guard. What did Viktor say?"

"He wants to be informed the instant we isolate the source. Hopefully, it won't take long. We know who we suspect but we must be certain."

Chapter Twenty-three

A REUNION OF SORTS

Saturday. January 25

Jim sat at the desk in the library reading the impact and action reports associated with the Sukhoi work in the event it was awarded. The cannon contract could be easily assimilated. He considered the award of both programs a long shot since the set-up costs for the Su-30 MKI assembly alone were substantial. Cortex's direct labor force would increase to over four hundred employees. If the sales projections were met, the annual revenues could conceivably exceed one hundred and fifty million USD with a profit of twenty-five million.

He put the reports down and called Leonid. "I forgot to mention I have two American friends coming to visit me. They arrive tomorrow evening. Would you ask Ivan to get two of the guest rooms ready? I suspect they may be hungry as well."

Leonid made a note. "I'll make sure the SUV and driver are there ahead of time. We'll need it for all of us and their luggage."

Sunday, January 26

Adam and Chris collected their bags and exited the Varna International Airport main terminal. They heard Jim call to them and inspected his appearance. He looked vastly different; somehow straighter and more muscular. He stood next to a giant of a man with cold piercing eyes staring with a sinister air. He seemed to defer to Jim. Behind them a black SUV had a driver holding the back and rear doors open.

They warmly greeted each other with handshakes and pats on the back. Jim introduced Leonid calling him his indispensable companion. Adam noticed both Jim and Leonid carried guns. They chatted amiably as the SUV climbed the mountain road through the massive iron gates of the estate. The SUV drove up the driveway under the watchful eyes of armed guards standing in the shadows. They stared admiringly at the large house. Two attendants came out to meet them and get the luggage. Jim motioned them into the mansion.

Adam was the first to talk. "Tomas, whose place is this? It's huge."

Jim laughed. "It's mine to use while I'm working. I'll explain later. This is Ivan Covo, the master caretaker of the house. He'll show you to your rooms and you can get cleaned up. Come on down in a half hour and have something to eat."

Both Adam and Chris hastily took showers and changed into clean clothes. They walked down the sweeping staircase to the ground floor. Jim collected them and they went to the dining room where there were five place settings. Jim introduced them to a tall guest with a uniform. "This is Captain Anton Golarif. He is responsible for the security on these grounds. It's his men you saw as you drove up."

Chris asked. "I assume there are good reasons to have this kind of security besides wild animals."

Captain Anton chuckled, "It's always good to anticipate trouble."

They sat down and the food and drink was brought out. Jim talked animatedly with them. Adam noticed Jim had shed his shoulder gun although the Captain had a pistol in a holster on a webbed belt. He looked across at Leonid and saw his bulge remained. They had coffee to finish the meal and soon after Captain Anton excused himself to take care of business. Leonid wandered off as well. Jim motioned for them to follow him and they took the elevator to the third floor and entered the library. Jim closed the library door and pointed to the brandy in a decanter on the side of the room. They sat down in arm chairs close to one another.

"I owe you both a great debt of gratitude and an explanation."

Adam told how he had located Jim but was stymied by the Varna newspaper account of Borichov's death, and his trips around Europe especially because of the lack of an exit stamp at times on the passport and the absence of airline information. Jim grinned. He explained his access to the Challenger 601-3A executive jet and its utilization for his trips.

Chris noted. "So now you're committed to running Cortex. Say, how big is this company?"

"If we get the contracts in we bid on, this year it'll bring in one hundred and fifty million USD and have over four hundred employees."

Adam observed, "When I was first hired by your wife, she made it a point to tell me you were a private person who savored your independence."

Jim chortled, "Adam, you're being diplomatic. I imagine she would have said I was a loner who preferred my own company to those of others. She would have been candid and mentioned my disdain for social contact and the corporate world."

Adam sheepishly looked down. "Well, yes. There was something along those lines too. The change in your personality threw me completely off. Here you are again with a role reversal and thriving on it."

"I don't know. It just seemed as if it was a glove I put on and it was a perfect fit. The fact of the matter is, I like it. Of course I'm under pressure to perform but I never worry about it. Now, there is a serious matter to contend with. It appears there's a Russian mafia turf war brewing and I'm caught up in the middle of it. Actually, I'm probably responsible because I directed the general manager to make an offer for a local company. Dimitri Federov handled that episode as I explained. I don't doubt I'll be receiving another visit from him soon. Meanwhile, stay and enjoy the house and city. A car and driver is available to you. Please accept my thanks and let me pay the bills as a small token. I'm paid well and have an expense account. Now, you must be tired. The barracks at the rear of the grounds has an excellent exercise room. Breakfast is anytime you go down to the kitchen. Leonid and I are early birds and leave for the plant after breakfast. Ivan and your driver can locate me. Incidentally, we can't let Diane know where I am. The day may come when Federov feels he has to collect his pound of flesh. Good night."

Monday, January 27

Jim was surprised to see Adam and Chris at the breakfast table with Leonid. Chris smiled. "We're planning to do a lot of sightseeing since we've never been to Bulgaria."

Adam asked, "Is the driver armed?"

Jim answered, "He carries and has a permit. There is heavier artillery in the cars."

Leonid added, "Take the SUV for your trip. I doubt you'll have any trouble but it's armored and has bulletproof glass."

Jim looked at him in surprise. "I didn't know that. The car too?"

He nodded. "Both were bought at the Moscow MercedesBenz dealership and shipped here in the Il-76."

Chris raised an eyebrow. "You don't mean a Russian Ilyushin Il-76."

"Yes, another plane owned by Cortex."

"I hesitate to ask. What others?"

"A Russian nine-passenger Ka-26 helicopter."

"Tomas, we're going to enjoy our visit."

Jim was at the Cortex gun range with Leonid when Josef called him on the phone. "Can I see you back at the office as soon as you finish?"

"I'm finished now. I'll head back."

Josef was waiting outside of Jim's office with a fax. They entered together and sat down. "Okay, what's so demanding?"

Josef had a solemn expression. "We heard from Sukhoi."

"Oh boy. What's the bad news?"

He beamed. "They gave us both projects. Can you believe it? Here's their initial reply."

Jim read the fax signed by Anatoly Stepanov, Director, Su-30 MKI Program. "I can't believe it. No negotiations. Josef, call an executive meeting right away. This is too good not to share. Oh, oh. I told Hans he'd get the second laser cutter if we won. I better get the paperwork started."

The news spread all over the plant within an hour after the executive meeting broke up. Josef asked Jim for permission to put out a press release.

Leonid walked into his office and gave him his two guns. "Thanks. I think as soon as our notice hits the papers, we'll be in line for more trouble. Have we heard yet from the security head on his weekend hunt?"

"He confirmed the trouble originated with KAS. We have a name, Boris Sidorov. You'll recall he witnessed the agreement for Arsenal. He's currently the KAS general manager and acting president. There is a puzzling part; he's working for or with another organization representative, Jakob Molokan."

"Why is that strange?"

"Because Molokan is a professional."

Chapter Twenty-four

THE ANTE IS RAISED

Wednesday, January 29

Everyone was at breakfast when Jim entered the kitchen. Leonid looked at his watch and said. "Mr. Federov leaves Moscow within the hour. Viktor is with him."

Jim nodded. "What took him so long?"

Adam and Chris stared at Leonid. "You're talking about Dimitri Federov?"

"There's only one. Mr. Federov believes in watching over his investments."

Adam replied. "I would guess so. Cortex is a valuable company."

Leonid gave Adam a whimsical look. "I'm not talking about Cortex. I'm referring to Mr. Tomas."

Both Adam and Chris looked in wonderment at Jim.

Jim instructed Leonid. "Make sure the helicopter pilot knows his arrival time." He called Ivan. When Ivan answered, Jim told him. "We're expecting Mr. Federov this afternoon. Make sure his room is prepared. Leonid, would you mind sharing your room with Viktor?"

"It wouldn't be the first time. He might bring a couple of soldiers."

"In that case, we'll put them up in the barracks. We'll leave the plant when he lands."

Chris spoke for everyone. "It's going to be one of those days."

* * *

Leonid came into Jim's office. "Tomas, I just heard. They've landed."

Jim rose and put on his coat. He called Josef. "Mr. Federov has arrived and I'm going to meet him. I'll be gone the rest of the day. You can reach me on the cell phone if anything comes up." They left for the car.

Jim and Leonid arrived at the house shortly before they heard the sound of the helicopter coming over the woods. Adam and Chris came out the front door to watch the arrival. The helicopter settled to the ground and the door opened. Federov exited followed closely by Viktor. Federov approached Jim and shook hands.

"Trouble again?"

Jim nodded. "We might have been able to handle it and not bothered you."

Federov laughed. "Would you have me miss the fun and lose the opportunity for exercise? Besides I heard who's behind it and you do need me." He turned to look at Adam and Chris. "Tomas, please introduce me to your friends."

Jim waved Adam and Chris over. "This is Mr. Dimitri Federov and the gentleman at his side is Viktor Kharkov. Mr. Federov, this is Adam Weatherly and Chris Muncie from the States."

Federov extended his hand. "I have heard about your exploits. At first I was very angry but Tomas has helped me mellow." He laughed again and then became serious. "We will talk inside."

The six of them went to the ground floor study and sat down. Ivan asked them to call if they needed anything. Federov took the floor after he left.

"Let me see if I have this right. Tomas, you and Leonid had an encounter with a gunman who used a machine gun. This was last Thursday. He blocked the street with a car but clumsily left an opening to escape without being struck. Then, on Friday the Il-76 narrowly escaped being blown up by an airport fuel truck when it went off prematurely. Do I have it right?"

Jim answered. "Perfectly. We got lucky both times. We may not be so fortunate next time."

Federov continued, "Leonid, you found out Jakob Molokan is involved. This is the real reason why I'm here."

Leonid nodded.

Jim asked. "Who is this man? Leonid only told me he was a professional."

"He is the person who engineered the events huh, Viktor." Jim stared at him as the realization dawned. "My God. I understand. They staged the two incidents to get you here. If itlooked amateurish enough, you would come alone to deal with it. I'm an idiot not to have seen it. What's worse, you did come alone except for Viktor."

Federov shrugged. "I don't think we're as helpless as it may appear. Besides, if I would have come with support, they probably would have backed off until they had another opportunity. I think we'll be enough to turn the tables on them once and for all. Viktor, how many would you say they were going to field?"

Viktor considered. "They figure we'll be a small number and they certainly don't want it to get around, maybe twelve to fifteen."

"So we'll be outnumbered by two or three to one. That doesn't sound too bad. The question is when and where."

Jim questioned. "Who are you counting?" He looked around. "There are only six of us assuming Adam and Chris want to risk their lives."

Adam and Chris spoke together. "We're in."

Viktor replied, "I think we can count on Captain Anton Golarif."

Leonid added, "Tomas, I'm sure we can get Leif, the gun range manager."

"Very well, it makes eight very experienced men. And don't forget, we have military vehicles and weapons at Cortex. When they discover I have arrived, their plan will proceed. We can expect them to act quickly and must be prepared for it. We have to get the equipment together." He inspected Adam and Chris. "We'll have Captain Anton outfit both of you with pistols right away. Tomas, we will require a military vehicle at our disposal standing by tomorrow."

"Right. We can borrow it from a pending shipment. I'll have Leif load it with weapons and anything else we may need."

"Good. The back of the truck will also hide our number. If I was them, I'd want to spring the trap as soon as possible. Anyone for a glass of Vodka?"

Chapter Twenty-five

CONFRONTATION

Friday, January 31

Federov directed everyone take the car and SUV to the plant.

Leonid contacted Leif who took the responsibility of getting the truck out of the shipment area and loaded with weapons from the storeroom. He also placed medical provisions in the bed next to the arms. Now it was a waiting game. Federov went with Jim to his office to get a summary of the business activities.

Jim covered the two initiatives sought by the Sukhoi Corporation in association with the Su-30 MKI fighter aircraft program. Federov was surprised to hear of the solicitation and was astonished as to the scope of the effort. Jim covered the revenue, profit and employee projections for the coming year.

Federov sat back and lit a cigarette. "Tomas, I am extremely pleased with your progress with the company since you have taken control. Your decisions and leadership are excellent. After our meeting at Maxim's I felt you had something special. I will admit when you left for your holiday I had a nagging doubt I would see you again but you surprised me once more with your sense of responsibility. Your choice of friends reflects your character. After this is over, we shall talk again of your obligation."

By the end of the day, things were relatively quiet. Federov gathered the group into Jim's office. "If anything is to happen, it will occur after we leave here this evening. Tomas and I are the bait and will go out in the car. The rest of you will wait for a few minutes and follow us with the truck. We'll be in touch with our cell phones. Do not follow closely. We don't want to scare them off."

They left the plant and turned down the street towards the mountains. The driver calmly informed them that two cars had suddenly come into sight behind them. Federov had the driver continue along the route. The two cars accelerated and pulled alongside. Machine guns appeared and bullets struck the side of the car. The bulletproof glass held and the two cars raced off. Federov commanded the driver. "Follow those cars. They will lead us to their trap." He called the truck and told them what happened. The driver called out the direction of their car as he drove.

"Let's see where we're going." Jim called Josef. "Do you have your map handy? We're under assault. No, we're fine. I'm going to give you the location of where we are. See where it's leads." The driver called back their location and direction. Jim repeated it and waited. He nodded and hung up. "Mr. Federov, this is the way to the KAS battlefield test range."

Federov grabbed the phone and called the truck. Leif was familiar with the range and answered him. "He's taking you in through the front gate. I bet there's no one to stop you. They want you inside before they spring the trap. Their people are probably towards the right center where there are bunkers and trenches. To the left side are concrete buildings. We're about five minutes behind you. Slow down when you go through the gate. They'll have one or two of them block your retreat. We'll catch them by surprise when we barrel through. Don't leave the car until we get there."

They went in through the open gate. As they passed through, Jim saw two men with guns suddenly appear and start shutting the gate. They got it half way closed when the truck slammed through the gate and tossed the men like debris. Their own driver saw an opportunity to park the car by a protective mound. Within seconds the large truck pulled in beside them and the tailgate went down. They leapt out of the car and raced to the back. Captain Anton handed out AK-47s with a canister of filled magazines.

Leif came around and opened a wooden crate. He took out an RPG-7 and a special backpack containing OG-7V fragmentation antipersonnel grenades and launch charges. He explained, "Cortex manufactured these about five years ago. I wish we had NVGs."

The dark range suddenly lit up from large billboards of lights on the far sides throwing high intensity light into every recess and crevasse. They scurried behind mounds and into craters and shelters as bullets tore through the air into their position. Captain Anton split them up into three groups; Jim on the left side and one in the middle. Leif went with the center group. The outside groups were to draw fire but one at a time. Leif, in the center, would launch against the firing positions. "Remember," Anton cautioned, "it won't work more than twice. Then they'll stagger their firing."

The PG-7 coughed twice resulting in large explosions. As predicted the bursts of automatic fire came from random positions in the range. They inched their way along the ground conscious of the lights and the resulting shadows. Firing came from the rooftop of a two-story concrete building pinning the left side down. Jim yelled at Leif. "Can you get the building?' Leif loaded the RPG-7 and placed it on his shoulder exposing himself. Bullets immediately hit around him. Jim and Chris opened fire towards where the bullets were originating. They heard the grenade launch and saw the blast near the roof top. Leif cursed and settled to the ground. Jim yelled, "Leonid, check on Leif."

Bullets were now flying from both groups across the battlefield. It was getting impossible to detect from the sounds if they were coming or going from their positions. Smoke from the firings was beginning to create a low fogbank. The lights along the sides bounced off the smoke producing a blinding glare. Both sides could move up against the other without worry about being seen. Federov and Viktor were on the right side with Adam. Jim decided to keep moving forward carefully keeping the AK-47 barrel off the dirt and pointing ahead of him. He stopped to listen every time he moved. Suddenly a gunman rose ahead of him and started to aim his rifle at Jim. Jim hurled his AK-47 at the man and fell back. The gunman sidestepped to avoid the thrown gun and smirked. Jim reached down, pulled his ankle gun and fired in one swift motion. The gunman dropped with a bullet hole in his forehead. Jim rolled and retrieved his AK-47 then moved quickly away. He replaced the ankle gun and started to move silently forward. Chris shook his head at Jim's reaction and kept pace to the side.

On the other side, Federov and Viktor were slowly making their way along a concrete block house. They carefully inspected a trench before leaping over it and resumed their forward thrust. They rounded a building and dove for the ground as bullets poured into them. Federov would be exposed to the fire if it dropped any lower. Viktor made the decision to run and dive from his cover to draw the fire. He was hit in the arm and leg before Federov sliced the gunman in two with an automatic burst. "You fool." He whispered but tore Viktor's shirt sleeve off and applied tourniquets on his arm and leg. "Stay here and keep watch."

Adam came up behind Federov. He took in Viktor. "Can I help?"

"Follow me closely."

Leoniid found Leif with a bullet wound in his right shoulder.

He pushed a handkerchief into the bleeding hole, gave him his pistol and left to return to Jim's side. Leif gave a short salute to Anton who came to his side. Anton picked up the RPG-7. "I always wanted to try one of these." He carefully looked out, conscious of the bright lights in his periphery. He spotted gunfire coming from the right side about two hundred feet away from the base of one of the light towers. He front-loaded the grenade launcher. He aimed and fired ducking down after it was gone. Bullets sprayed across their position. He heard the explosion and the light tower went dark. He whispered to Leif. "Nasty toy you have here. I'll think I play with it some more." He dug into the backpack. "Hello. This one really looks mean." He inched his head up to where he could see firing coming from the left side. "Leif, what's this one?"

Leif squinted. "A run-of-the-mill anti-tank number."

Anton gave a slight smirk. "It ought to make a big bang then. Keep your head down." He loaded it into the front of the launcher and moved away from Leif until he had a dirt mound in front of him. He rested the launcher on it, aimed, held his breath and squeezed the trigger. Once it was gone, he dropped the launcher and threw himself flat against the ground. Bullets pelted his previous position unmercifully. He felt the sting in his leg as one found its mark. He heard rather than saw the return fire from Jim's position attacking the source of the bullets. He crawled to Leif. "Are you still there?" Leif patted his arm for reassurance. Anton reached down and touched the wound. "Second time in two months I've been shot." He pulled his AK-47 close to him. "I think I'll keep a lookout for a while."

Jim decided to move closer to the edge of the battlefield where the concrete light posts were located. He stood in the shelter of one of them and looked out over the range. He saw two shadows at the rear of the complex moving away. He signaled his intention to Leonid and Chris. Chris motioned for both of them to travel in that direction with a six-foot separation. Jim saw Leonid understood and would trail their movements. Jim had to crouch down to avoid creating a shadow and lost sight of the targets. He looked over to Chris who indicated a shift in their direction with his open hand. He crawled slowly through the battlefield haze aware it was stinging his eyes. Chris paused. Jim lay still on the ground trying to see through the smoke. His eyes watered and he needed to wipe them dry. He resisted the temptation and stayed motionless. He heard footsteps in front of him and saw them materialize into a pair of legs with a body attached. The man tripped over Jim's prone body and uttered a curse. Their eyes met at the same time. Before Jim could move, Chris fired upward and killed him. Jim rolled quickly in the opposite direction as another gunman appeared with a gun firing in Chris's area. Jim cut him down with a burst and all went quiet. He whispered. "Chris, are you hit?"

"Son of a bitch." Came the reply.

Jim moved over and examined him. Chris had a bloody furrow on the right side of his head. "How do you feel? Can you move?"

Chris sat up. "Yeah, but I have a splitting headache. How come it's so quiet?"

"I hope its cause we won."

"Maybe we should call out."

"You saved my life again, Chris."

"I believe you returned the favor, buddy. Let's get out of here."

Jim looked back and saw Leonid staring at them with a shake of his head. He motioned at them to follow him back the way they had come.

Anton saw the three of them. "Hey, a little help here." He patted Leif. "Hang on."

Federov heard their voices. He and Adam had Viktor in between them. They managed to get everyone back to the truck where Chris opened the medical kit. He let Jim apply a bandage to his head then assisted in putting tourniquets and bandages on the wounded. Jim pulled out his cell. "Josef, we could use a discrete doctor."

"Are you in the range? I'm still at the office. I asked our medical staff to stay late tonight in case they were needed. I'll drive them over unless you can make it here. We have excellent facilities."

Jim asked Federov. "Can we make it to the plant with everyone?"

"Yes, I believe it would be prudent." He turned to the others. "Tomas, Adam, Leonid and I will stay here and make a sweep of the range for bodies after we load the wounded and our weapons into the truck. Our driver will take you back to the plant for medical attention."

The four of them scoured the test range and found fifteen bodies including Boris Sidorov and Jakob Molokan. Under Federov's direction they arranged the bodies unceremoniously across the range from each other to give the appearance of a deadly gunfight between each group. He placed Boris in one group and Jakob in the other.

Jim looked at the bodies. "Do you think the police will buy it?"

"It's the expedient thing to do. Besides, who's going to contradict this evidence? Come, let's get out of here and see how the rest are doing."

* * *

When they arrived at the plant, they found the most serious wound belonged to Leif. The doctor decided to keep him overnight in the infirmary under observation. The rest had their wounds cleaned, stitched and bandaged. They were given antibiotic shots and pain killers. Meanwhile, the driver had located the SUV which they boarded while Leonid drove the car. They traveled in silence and disembarked at the house. Captain Anton was led back to the barracks. They all turned in, exhausted.

Chapter Twenty-six

RECOVERY AND REPARATION

Saturday, February 1

At Jim's request, Ivan made an early morning appointment with his doctor contact. The doctor brought a nurse. Between the two of them they re-examined and treated Captain Anton, Viktor and Chris. The wounds were cleansed, more antibiotics applied and rebandaged. Jim meanwhile called the plant and inquired as to Leif's condition. He would have a sling for a couple of weeks. Jim had him driven home to rest and recover.

They were in good spirits. Discussions on the previous night were delayed until later in the morning. Viktor and Captain Anton limped in with canes while Chris wore a white head bandage.

Federov assembled the group in the study. He cast his gaze over the room and nodded as if to say he was satisfied with what he had observed. He began. "I want to thank all of you for making my visit so exciting."

Laughter erupted from all of them.

Federov continued, "Outnumbered, we took on a formidable enemy on their terms. We triumphed because of your professionalism and experience. Some of us were wounded but thankfully not seriously. The two leaders were killed. I was familiar with one of them, the Russian. He belonged to a rival organization. I will have an intimate discussion with its leader about this attempt and KAS Engineering when I get back to Moscow. I would like all of you to stay here as house guests of Tomas. Get your rest and recover fully. I will not forget your efforts." With that he left the room. He motioned for Jim to follow him.

He took Jim by the arm and they walked outside about the grounds. "You and your two friends have acquitted yourselves admirably. The men have to be rewarded. I will personally take care of Viktor and Leonid. Be generous with Captain Anton, Leif, Adam and Chris. As to yourself, I am left with a quandary. I have found an excellent president who is shaping and building a formidable company and I would hate to lose him. I know you have made sacrifices and miss your family. As to your former life, it may be gone. Perhaps you have a solution?"

Jim was quiet and thoughtful. Finally he responded. "In truth, I have enjoyed the opportunity and responsibilities of overseeing your company. I don't doubt it has the makings to become very large. I'd be lying if I didn't say I would miss the challenges it presents. Perhaps I could make a suggestion."

Federov nodded.

"Josef Amorusk, the general manager, has the makings of an excellent president. He has been suppressed under Borichov for many years and has developed a veneer of caution. What he needs is a mentor who can look over his shoulder and help him to grow into the position. As you stated, I'll have an exasperating time getting my previous professional life together if at all. I could spend time with him with some salary until you feel comfortable with the transition."

"Very well, once the men can travel, you may leave. I look forward to your next assignment with Cortex. Take the Challenger for your trip home. I will leave for Moscow tomorrow and Viktor and Leonid will travel with me. Today, however, we shall relax."

Chapter Twenty-seven

FAREWELLS

Sunday, February 2

Jim, Adam and Chris watched the mid-morning departure of Federov, Viktor and Leonid as the helicopter lifted off from the front lawn. They walked inside the house and sat in the study. Jim related his conversation with Federov on his obligation.

Adam observed. "From what we've gathered, you've done a hell of a job in the short time you've been here. No wonder Federov would like to keep you even as a consultant. Were you thinking you could pick up your former professional life where you left off? It seems to me it would be difficult if not impossible."

"You're right. I left in the lurch with a lot of balls in the air. Well, I can consult here for a while."

Chris asked. "How much time do you need to get things in hand before we leave?"

"I'm thinking a week. How about sticking around and we'll take the Challenger back together."

Adam spoke for Chris and himself. "Now that's worth waiting for."

Monday, February 3

Jim rode to the plant alone. He couldn't recall when he didn't have Viktor or Leonid by his side. He thought, I bet KAS Engineering is in a bit of turmoil today. Wait a minute. What did Federov mean when he said he was going to discuss KAS with another organization? My God. He couldn't, he wouldn't. He went to his office where Josef was waiting by his secretary.

"Thanks for sticking around Friday night. How is Leif?"

"I believe he's happy to take the paid leave. His shoulder will be sore for a while."

"I have some work to do and then let's together and have an executive meeting."

He called out to Martina. "Please call finance and have Mr. Abdul Shatov come to my office."

Within five minutes, Abdul knocked on his door. Jim waved him in. "I have a few checks for you to write."

Abdul opened his notebook. "Go ahead."

"I wish to have a check written to Leif in the amount of fifteen thousand GBL. Make a check to Captain Anton Golarif for the same amount. Next, I want two checks written for one hundred thousand USD; one to Chris Muncie and the other to Adam Weatherly. The four checks will be for services rendered. One more thing, Hans Goethalz requires a computer-controlled laser cutter as soon as possible for the new Sukhoi contract. Get the necessary information from him and coordinate the immediate acquisition with the purchasing department. That will do for now. Thank you."

In the afternoon at the executive staff meeting, Jim made his intentions known. He was going on holiday at the end of the week. Josef Amorusk was to be the acting president with all vested authority until his return. He reminded everyone the large Sukhoi contracts were awarded to Cortex because of their hard work and to maintain the high standards of quality while meeting the schedule. Cortex was growing and it meant opportunities within and for new hires. He assured Josef he would be available for consultation by phone.

Friday, February 7

Jim, Adam and Chris were in the kitchen having breakfast. Captain Anton stopped by and Jim saw his limp was slightly evident. "Captain, may I see you in the study for a moment?" The two of them went into the room and Jim closed the door. "Anton, you have been a good and loyal friend. In and above the line of duty as they say. I have something for you." He withdrew an envelope and gave it to him.

Anton opened it and pulled out the check. He gasped at the amount. "This is very generous of you, Mr. Tomas."

"Actually, Anton, it was Mr. Federov who insisted upon it. Believe me, you've earned it and our lasting gratitude. Now take the day off and share it with your family."

Anton took a pace back and gave a crisp salute. He turned and went out the door with a military bearing and the start of tears in his eyes.

Later, Jim notified Ivan he and the others were leaving the next day. "I'll call the airport and have the necessary arrangements made. I plan to enjoy a holiday before I return."

Chapter Twenty-eight

GOODBYES AND HELLO

The next morning, the staff had their luggage on the front walk while they waited for the helicopter to ferry them to the airport. Soon, it appeared and settled on the ground. The bags were loaded and Adam and Chris took their seats. Ivan approached Jim and gave him a sealed envelope. "Mr. Federov asked me to give you this just before you left. He asked you wait to open it until after you left Varna. Have a good holiday, Mr. Tomas. We shall take good care of the house for you."

The helicopter landed by the Varna International Airport corporate terminal. The Challenger 601 waited with running engines. The three of them settled into the seats. Adam and Chris looked around with smiles. "No wonder you hate to leave. This is living." The attendant placed a Bloody Mary in front of Jim with warm nuts. She asked Adam and Chris for their order. "Two more of those." They pointed at Jim's table. The aircraft door closed and the jet moved towards the runway. The pilot made his announcement and shortly thereafter the plane lifted into the air.

Once in the air, Jim remembered the Federov envelope and took it out. He opened the letter and read,

Dear Jim:

You have proven yourself to be a thoughtful and honorable person. Erika and I are in agreement your friendship must be retained. She cherished your gift and felt we should reciprocate in kind. Therefore, we have initiated the legal paperwork to make you a ten percent owner in the Cortex International Corporation. Of course, we expect you will find time to ensure things run smoothly and growth continues at our com[any. Enjoy your trip. Until then, I remain,

Dimitri Federov

Jim put down the paper and stared out the window. He shook his head. Chris noted his silence. "Anything wrong?"

Jim handed them the letter to read. They laughed at his expression. "Look at it this way; you won't have to worry about a job."

"Right. Oh, I almost forgot. I have something for each of you, courtesy of Mr. Federov." He gave them each an envelope with their name on it. They looked inside and whooped. "Holy Cow!"

Chris volunteered. "You know what I'm going to do with this? I'll get a patent application filed on my harness and then I'll see about producing them."

Adam added. "I've got some equipment to buy, a couple of bonuses to hand out and maybe an increase in office space."

Sunday, February 9
California Bound

They refueled in England and spent the night in Toronto. At the San Francisco International Airport Chris exchanged warm goodbyes with Jim and Adam and left the aircraft. The plane turned and entered the departure pattern. Twenty minutes later they were heading for the John Wayne Orange County Airport in Southern California.

The plane landed and taxied to the corporate terminal. Jim thanked the crew and deplaned with Adam. He saw the aircraft await the refueling truck before he entered the terminal.

Adam shook his hand. "This has been some job for me. Don't forget to tell Mrs. Factor my part is finished. Thanks for the check. Call me some time."

Jim nodded. "You can count on it."

Jim walked to the taxi stand and entered a cab. He couldn't resist a smile. The cool air smelled fresh and clean. He was going to have to get used to his real name. Diane was going to want to hear the entire story from him even though Adam had briefed her completely before he had left. Of course, she was going to get the shortened version at first. Time enough for the rest of it.

The taxi pulled to the front of the house and Jim got out. He paused to take in his house with a fond and eager expression. "It's been way too long." He walked to the front gate and rang the doorbell. He gave a chortle when Diane's voice came through the intercom.

"Who is it?"

He replied with a grin. "A man with a package."

"Go away," was the tearful reply, "before I release the dogs."

He laughed as the gate was buzzed unlocked. The front door opened and his wife ran out. They clung to each other for a very long time. He looked over his shoulder and entered the house.

About the Author

Daniel C. Lorti is the author of the Jean Termonde Novels: *The Avignon Legacy, Knights of Honor,* and *Knights in Action*; the Jim Factor Novels: *The Missing Factor* and *The Business End,* which embody Lorti's professional background as an arms broker in outstanding suspense thrillers; *The Mulligan,* a parody on do-overs/second chances; and *The Writer's Tool Box.* Lorti is a member of Mystery Writers of America, the Historical Writers of America, and the International Thriller Writers. He currently resides in Newport Coast, California.